HOME ELSEWHERE

A Novel

Marianne Rutter

D1265077

Mimi —
Thanks for enjoying
the world of this book!
Best wishes,
Marianne

ISBN-13: 979-8-218-06468-6
ISBN-10: 8218064686

Cover design by: 100Covers
Printed in the United States of America

For my parents, Lucy and Paul, who inspired me to write this story.

For my late husband Matthew, whose love for my Sicilian-American family and whose unbridled enthusiasm for my heritage launched me on the journey to tell it.

And for my children, Lucia and Malcolm Paul, to whom the story now belongs.

A List of Characters

In America
Prisoners and Soldiers
Giampaolo Stagno, a Sicilian prisoner of war
Tommaso Mollica and Vincenzo Liguori, called 'Cenzo, his two friends and fellow prisoners

Three U.S. soldiers, all Italian Americans, from the camp:
Pasquale Tinelli, called Patsy, and Anthony Ferraro, called Tony, both from New York
Rafaele Pirone, called Rafe, from California

The Fazzio and Luna Family
Eleanor Fazzio, also called Eleanora, a Sicilian-American woman
Rosaria (Luna) Fazio, called Donna Sarina, Eleanor's mother

Carmelo Luna, Eleanor's uncle
Rosalie Luna, also called Rosalia, Eleanor's cousin
Suzanne Luna, also called Suzanna, Eleanor's cousin

Connie (Luna) Nardello, born Concetta, Eleanor's married cousin
Giovanni Nardello, called John, Connie's husband

Annie (Luna) Camastra, born Anna, also called Annina, Eleanor's married cousin
Benedetto (Buddy) Camastra, Annie's husband

Angelo Luna, Eleanor's cousin
Doris (Yoder) Luna, Angelo's wife

Veronica Luna, called Ronnie, Eleanor's cousin
Nick Raffa, Veronica's husband

The Mollica Family

Giuseppe Mollica (*Cumpari*), neighbor to the Lunas, friend of the late Carmelo Luna

Maria Grazia Mollica (*Cummari*), *Cumpari* Mollica's wife

Frannie Mollica (Francesca) and Mary Mollica (Maria), their daughters, friends to the Luna girls

Ronald Schmitt, called Ron or Ronny, Mary Mollica's fiancé

Guy Mollica (Gaetano), their son, a U.S. soldier

Louie Mollica (Luigi), their son, a U.S. soldier

In Sicily

The Stagno Family

Don Giuseppe Stagno, Giampaolo's father

Donna Concetta Stagno, Giampaolo's mother

Nonna Filomena Lombardo, Giampaolo's maternal grandmother

Salvatore Stagno, called Turuzzu, Giampaolo's oldest brother

Margherita (Battisti) Stagno, Turuzzu's wife

Giuseppe Stagno, called Peppino, Giampaolo's younger brother

Francesca Petri, called Ceccina, Giuseppe's wife

Donna Angela Petri, Ceccina's mother, a distant cousin and neighbor of the Stagno family

Patri Eugenio Stagno, born Sebastiano, called 'Bastiano, Giampaolo's youngest brother

The Palumbo Family

Zia Maria Grazia (Luna) Palumbo, called Marietta, Eleanor's aunt in Sicily, Donna Sarina's sister

Zio Antonio Palumbo, called Tonino, Eleanor's uncle, married to Maria Grazia

Pasquale Palumbo, Marietta and Tonino's youngest son

Lucietta and Emilia Palumbo, Marietta and Tonino's daughters

Part I

WARTIME

Chapter 1

Desert
When with the skin you do acknowledge drought,
The dry in the voice, the lightness of feet, the fine
Flake of the heat at every level line;
When with the hand you learn to touch without
Surprise the spine for the leaf, the prickled petal,
The stone scorched in the shine, and the wood brittle;
Then where the pipe drips and the fronds sprout
And the foot-square forest of clover blooms in sand,
You will lean and watch, but never touch with your hand.
—Josephine Miles

November, 1942, on the Tunisian/Libyan border
As sunlight broke over the Libyan desert, Giampaolo Stagno reached into his battered pack for the last sprig of rosemary from the desiccated branch he had doled out to himself for the past week. His cracked lips rebelled as he forced the sharp stinging bits of herb down his parched throat. One chew of herb. One sip of water. His self-imposed morning ration. What little he had left had to last until the end of this day, maybe longer.

No food resupply had come through to his company in weeks. None was expected for this bedraggled band of mostly Sicilian and Sardinian soldiers. In fact, it had been like this for months: days of oppressive heat that soaked his uniform with sweat, followed by nights of bone-chilling cold that inflicted full-body shivers until sleep overtook him. There was no bodily ease to be found in this cursed place.

Giampaolo and many of the men in his company were on

their second or third tour. Il Duce's grand plan for a new Roman Empire around the *Mare Nostrum* had forced reservists like him back into service along with new conscripts, as the Axis Powers escalated the war on several fronts. Giampaolo had been in Libya on his first army deployment several years before, when Hitler and Mussolini were beginning their political state-building that would ultimately culminate in a second world war.

Seasoned troops like Giampaolo were Mussolini's *richiamati*, soldiers "recalled" into service. In 1938 and 1939, during the opening salvoes of the war, more than a million and a half *richiamati* forsook jobs in fields and shops and took up arms, leaving families weeping on the doorstep. In cities and hamlets in every corner of Italy, the same sad scene played out. For Giampaolo, too: he had hardly expected to have to serve, much less struggle to survive, again. He'd kissed his mother and his *nonna* goodbye and trudged off for a second tour of duty.

He held no grudges. In this unforgiving climate, grudges were a luxury left behind. There was no energy to spare for vengeance or anger. Every ounce of effort went into surviving another day. Although some men in his company argued and debated on what slim news they had of the conflict that embroiled them, Giampaolo found that fruitless. He'd readily set aside weighty matters of global politics for just one good meal.

He'd crawl on his belly or stand sentry when and as told, although the logic of doing so just to hold a few dunes in this massive remorseless desert was lost on him. He and his mates were the occupying forces in the seesaw war between Axis and Allied forces to gain and keep a foothold in North Africa. There were rumors of German tank units that would relieve them soon. "A few days more" was always the best estimate of when relief might be in sight. None of the news was reliable, in any case. All he could do was concentrate on how to survive another day.

Stiff from sleeping on the ground, Giampaolo rose, stretched, and then rolled his dusty blanket into a tight cylinder that would fit snugly on his back when his company was inevitably ordered to move. Leaving his belongings and walking several meters from his sleeping spot, he found a cactus against which to relieve himself, and slapped his thighs to get rid of the ever-present sandy dust. Then he turned and peered into the half-light, looking for his mates. Irregular lumps all around him covered in rough blankets, the still-sleeping forms of other men in his regiment cast eerie shadows as he picked his way to where he had left his pack.

Two of his pals were awake, gathering their things together. Vincenzo Liguori and Tommaso Mollica had formed a tight trio with Giampaolo since being deployed to Tripoli. All three men hailed from southeastern Sicily. Giampaolo's birthplace was the town of Palazzolo Acrèide, a place the Greeks of old called Akrai more than two millennia earlier. Vincenzo and Tommaso both came from Florídia, a hardscrabble hamlet, half farmland, half suburb, just outside the ancient Greek city of Siracusa – marked Syracuse on the maps of the British Army. The vagaries of war had thrown these men together, and their common Sicilian heritage formed an unspoken bond that made it easy for each to have the others' backs.

"Another day in hell," Vincenzo mumbled, shading his eyes from the pinkish early-morning light now peeking over the hills of dust as he scanned the horizon.

"*Faccia du diavulu.* Face of the devil," Tommaso spat out the Sicilian curse in agreement as he tightened the straps of his bedroll.

"We freeze at night and fry during the day!" Vincenzo exclaimed wearily.

"*Dio, cuanto siti.* God, I'm so thirsty," Tommaso murmured, reaching into his pack for a rusty knife. He approached a stump of cactus growing nearby and began sawing off a slice at the top and sucking on the slice to extract the plant's scant juice.

Hunger had forced Giampaolo and his compatriots to get creative pretty quickly. Tommaso had been the first to figure out how to cut the top off a cactus and suck on the flesh to slake their constant thirst. The process took a while with army-issue knives dulled by constant use, but it was worth the effort for the momentary relief the juice provided. They munched on fronds of panic grass whenever they found it – not much flavor but, like the cactus, some welcome moisture.

All of the troops in their unit foraged constantly for rosemary bushes, whose scorched dry needles bore only a glancing resemblance to the lush herb that grew at home. A week ago, they unexpectedly happened upon a shaded valley amidst the dunes. The relative cool of oasis shadows had coaxed forth a huddle of *ficus d'India* plants with their telltale green knobs of fruit. The starved men leapt into action as one, claiming as many lumps of the unripe fruit as they could by twisting them off the branches with bare hands. The process left their roughened palms bleeding and perforated painfully with thorns. Giampaolo remembered wistfully that the same cactus pears in a much riper, rosy state made a fine finish to a belly-filling meal of pasta or a simple repast of bread and cheese on his parents' farm. He and his brothers would wrap several layers of burlap around the fruit to protect their hands while harvesting it. Here, even the rigid unripened shoots that they tore at hungrily with hands unprotected were not nearly enough to satisfy.

Vincenzo warned, "You're going to make yourself sick, sucking on that stuff."

Reaching for his own canteen, nearly empty, Giampaolo passed it to his friend. *"Megghiu biviri l'acqua.* Better drink some water. Don't you have any left at all?"

Tommaso shook his head, lifting his empty canteen from his belt and giving it a fruitless shake.

"How about the prickly pears we found? *U ficupali?*" Vincenzo queried.

"*Nenti.* None left." Tommaso pressed a hand to his abdomen. "They gave me the runs."

Vincenzo laughed sarcastically. "Well, I'm not going help you with *that!*"

Giampaolo's eyes were moist. "*Matri,* what I wouldn't give for just one of those ripe prickly pears from the garden at San Marco!" He swiped at his parched lips with the back of his hand.

Vincenzo muttered, "Only makes it worse to think about food." He pulled a dry rosemary sprig from the top of his sack and nibbled on it.

Giampaolo nodded silently and folded his blanket into his rucksack. Their unit was part of the occupation force of the legendary Italian general Giovanni Messe's newly reconstituted First Army. If it seemed to him that they were fighting over and occupying the same small patch of turf again and again, traveling in circles, he wasn't far from the truth. Several times over, the German tank commander Erwin Rommel and his Panzers carved a brazen path across the sand and claimed territory where traces of their tank tracks from a previous incursion were still visible. The Italian non-mechanized troops, infantry foot soldiers like himself and his friends, would stake a claim to that piece of desert and attempt to hold it, only to be ordered to cede it and retreat, time and again, pursued by Allied troops with better supplies and information. The Axis advance didn't seem to be moving forward at all but rather going back over old territory, two steps back for every step forward, in what seemed to amount to an agonizingly slow retreat.

Giampaolo wasn't the only soldier confused by their back-and-forth desert mission. Although their officers issued orders with a brusque indifference, even they seemed to have only the vaguest sense of which way their company would be moving, day by day or even hour by hour. On some days they would be close enough to the sea that he thought he could detect a familiar whiff of salt air. But perhaps that was just a mirage, as any perceived moisture dissipated soon enough into an ever-present blanket of dust and grit emanating from the unremitting desert at their backs.

Giampaolo's stomach rumbled, then cramped. Hunger had been the only constant he'd known almost since the day he left home again for this accursed war. His unit may move a few kilometers west, then move back a few kilometers to the east, but hunger and thirst followed him everywhere, along with the accompanying sapping of energy and cramping of muscles. A wave of dizziness overtook him as he loaded his pack onto his back and prepared to trudge forward. It was difficult to hold a thought in his head. Sometimes the hole of hunger in his stomach turned to nausea, and he would struggle not to retch up the bristly breakfast he had just consumed.

All around him the shadowy blanket-covered lumps were morphing into human form as his compatriots stirred to a waking state. Men were standing, stretching, shaking out blankets and meeting the growing daylight with the same dazed look of unsated fatigue. Most tended to their morning preparations wordlessly; a few grumbled or prodded their buddies so that they wouldn't be alone in their misery. A scuffle broke out as two men reached for the same sad handful of love grass, pulling it up by the roots and fighting over the dried blossoms for the edible seeds they contained. No matter what occupied them, all of the men wondered what futile orders they would follow today.

The three friends stood together, awaiting the rest of their company.

Tommaso reached down to shoulder his pack. "How far do you think they'll drag us today?"

"If I knew that, we'd be winning this war." Vincenzo muttered in reply.

"It's best not to complain," Giampaolo added with resignation, then held his stomach to quell the rumbling. "Just do as we are told."

Tommaso glanced around. "This looks like the same bit of road we were on yesterday."

"How would you know? This whole accursed desert looks the same," Vincenzo spat. "One dune like all the others."

Giampaolo tried to change the subject. "If we're going over the same ground, then at least keep your eyes open for *ficupali*, ripe or not."

Tommaso nodded, energized by the prospect. "Yes! Or maybe even more of that cactus we found yesterday." He inserted two fingers into the top of his boot. "Where'd I put that damn thing? I'll need that knife if we find anything edible."

"Don't worry about it yet," Vincenzo commented blandly. "Nothing around here looks too appetizing."

"Giampaolo," Tommaso began in a hopeful tone, "Do you believe those rumors about the Germans' resupply coming through?"

"What?" Giampaolo was concentrating on balancing the unwieldy pack between his shoulders.

"I'll believe it when I see it," Vincenzo stated without much conviction. *"Tudescu disgraziat'.* Those German sons of bitches wouldn't share any of their supplies with us. We're supposed to be fighting this war together and—"

"Don't say it, 'Cenzo," Tommaso cried, impatiently cutting him off. "It's no use arguing. Arguing is for the politicians."

Suddenly softening, he turned to his friend. "Look, I know. *Iu sacciu.* They treat us like we're the enemy." He shook his head. "I'll give the Germans that. They are pretty good at playing the bad guys."

Remaining silent, Giampaolo fell in step with his friends.

"Yes, I know," Vincenzo conceded. "Starving and hopeless. That's their strategy. Keep us hungry and ignorant of what's going on. Even if we're too weak to move, at least we can hold ground."

Hunger and hopelessness: what a dire combination. Rumors of reinforcements would spread, and then fade. No one was sure exactly what this meant. Perhaps there would be food rations of some kind or at least some water that they might share. Experience in this desert had shown them that the Germans weren't good at sharing. That's the way it was, they were told. Italy was responsible for resupplying its own troops, just as Germany was – a practice that on the ground bred a wary contempt among companies of men who were supposed to be cooperating. When your stomach was empty, as Giampaolo's had been for so long now, you didn't care much about military tactics, much less following orders.

Chapter 2

The U.S. camps were run in strict accordance with the terms of the 1929 Geneva Convention. All prisoners were entitled to housing, food, medical care and clothing appropriate to the climate in which they were being held. Each enlisted prisoner was granted space roughly equivalent to that enjoyed by a U.S. Army conscript – while officers enjoyed larger quarters.

—MilitaryHistoryNow.com

L ate May 1943, on the North Atlantic
The brisk salt air stung his cheeks and lungs as Giampaolo faced into the wind, inhaling deeply and training his eyes on the chalky grey horizon before him. The briny wind, chilly as it was, was a welcome relief from the stuffy enclosures from which he had just emerged. Pervasive smells of bleach and antiseptic overlaid with diesel fuel competed with the odors of last night's pork and beans dinner, his own sweat, and the inescapable muskiness of so many bodies crowded together.

Their vessel had passed Gibraltar six days ago, although it seemed like much longer. Giampaolo had notched the wall next to his bunk to keep track of their time on the water. About two days out, they had hit a rough patch. The ship plowed through steep waves that tilted its decks dangerously one way then another, tossing it about like a hapless cork in seas swollen with drenching rain. The rain gave way to frigid skies, but at least the sea had gone flat and the retching misery of seasickness had passed. The bow was finally slicing through calmer waters once again, making decent time westward.

The scuttlebutt among the prisoners was that they would soon be steaming into New York Harbor. Some of the Italians could piece together some English phrases and a few could charm bits of news from the mostly uncommunicative American MPs who guarded them. But by and large, the 'Mericani on board regarded their charges with suspicion. They referred to the Italians as "dirty" and "lazy," and it was difficult to miss the undisguised loathing directed at them as their Yankee stewards corralled the prisoners from bunk to mess hall or from shower stall to cot.

On deck or below it, Giampaolo found the chilly gale a respite. He had had enough of the desert to last a lifetime. Dust. Sand. Thirst. Hunger. He had raised his arms in nervous relief when his company, trapped in those accursed rocky outcroppings near the Matmata Hills, was finally rounded up by khaki-clad teams of British troops. In all, he and more than a quarter-million others, Germans and Italians, had been captured as that Tunisian campaign ended, prisoners taken in a war in which many of them had been reluctant participants in the first place.

Capture proved worse than fighting, at first. A squad of Free French troops herded Giampaolo's company like animals into rough overcrowded pens topped with barbed wire, where they stood or squatted for hours on end, uncertainty about their fate swirling around them like gun smoke. They had no shelter from searing desert heat during the day and numbing cold at night. Desert insects tormented them, leaving welts everywhere on bodies already badly sunburned. Food and water were scarce, hygiene non-existent. Some of their captors had helped themselves to the prisoners' personal belongings, taunting them and showing no remorse for the inhumane conditions. For several weeks Giampaolo and his compatriots had been moved from one makeshift enclosure into another, and finally to Bizerte, to an enormous sandy field stubbled with dry weeds and straw, where they had been counted, tagged and given scant fare to eat, really nothing more than crackers and water.

Then had come the long ride westward. The captured soldiers were packed into cramped cattle cars, shoulder to shoulder, for transport toward Oran. When the rattletrap doors of the railcars finally opened, large tents stood ready to receive them. To the eyes of the Italian prisoners, emaciated and famished, weak from exhaustion, and many ailing from infection and dehydration, these austere habitats seemed a comparative paradise. The weaker among them had to be helped or lifted down from the railcars, this time by American GIs. Under the sheltering tents, they were at last given more substantial sustenance: boiled eggs and milk, bread and butter. They received two rations of water a day while their American and British guards awaited orders.

One morning, the prisoners were brought to wait at dockside alongside rows of massive vessels moored there. Steamships with strange names like Agwileon and Borinquen, commercial liners hastily converted for troop transport and appropriated by the U.S. War Department, cast long shadows on the pier. Other vessels, known as Liberty Ships, had dropped anchor farther out at sea, beyond the harbor's immediate reach. A prisoner in their group who understood some English explained in Italian what little he could make out from the rapid-fire patter of the military police guarding them. The irony did not escape Giampaolo: he might soon be a prisoner in, of all things, a "Liberty Ship." British Navy vessels were also approaching from beyond the harbor's mouth. All were being readied to take on their captive passengers.

Eventually, the Italians had been marshaled into two rough queues on the staging quays, one bound for England and the other for America. That small bit of intelligence was all Giampaolo needed to know. Some others in his company didn't seem to care, but Giampaolo and his two Sicilian friends crowded into the line bound for the American transports. Enticed by rumors that one would eat better there, Giampaolo wanted to make sure his head was counted among the prisoners being sent to the United States. If the meager rations of questionable origin and aroma that they'd been issued since being taken prisoner were any indication, the American devil you didn't know might just be better than the British one you did.

The endless waiting on the hot docks finally came to an end. Once aboard ship, Giampaolo had gratefully embraced the moist comfort of being close to the Mediterranean Sea, a balm at once strange and familiar. Their vessel was one in a sizable convoy of Allied ships taking the young soldier and his companions away from the merciless desert. For Giampaolo, that change could not come soon enough.

* * *

Now approaching land, he rested his forearms on the railing, letting the welcome cold of the metal seep in and dangling his folded hands in the wind. Shaking off the last of his desert nightmares, Giampaolo concentrated on the tiny shapes bobbing in the water. These gradually grew into the more distinct profiles of ships and boats of all sizes and types, and the vague silhouette of an enormous city took shape on the horizon. The deck grew crowded with men straining to catch what would be for most of them a first glimpse of this Land of Milk and Honey, a place with streets paved of gold, whose fabled wonders they enumerated in luminous detail. These may be the shores of their sworn enemy, but to most of the men on this ship, America also represented adventure and, possibly, opportunity. Perhaps their Liberty Ship would portend good things for them, after all.

"Stagno!" Giampaolo heard his name echo over the heads of the prisoners around him.

He glanced over his shoulder and raised his hand in greeting.

"Over here!"

Vincenzo and Tommaso inched toward him, elbowing their way through the throng for a place beside him at the railing. The prisoners hadn't yet been issued specific orders, so the scene on deck was a melee of bedraggled men with rucksacks and packs slung over shoulders and backs. Tattered Italian army uniforms hung off their gaunt, scrawny bodies, ill-fitting, reeking, and dirty, a consequence of many days marching and poor sanitation before they had boarded ship, conditions not improved by close quarters at sea.

Finding two beefy American MPs eyeing him and his friends suspiciously, Giampaolo recognized the overt disdain he had grown used to seeing on the countenances of the guards. He said nothing. Survival in this new environment was still uppermost on his mind, and as a prisoner of war he was at the mercy of these men. Now he steeled himself. So be it that these Americans thought the Italian prisoners were all "dirty" and "lazy." No matter that their bodily filth and physical frailty had begun with their own army's months-long ordeal, as the soldiers were left to fend for themselves in the desert. Never mind that things had gotten worse for them as prisoners, starving and living in conditions unsuitable even for animals. At least they were bound for America, with some food in their bellies.

Tommaso muttered under his breath, jutting his chin toward the guards. "Watch out for those two. They don't seem to like any of us much."

Vincenzo spat on the deck indignantly. "What? We're just waiting here like everybody else."

Giampaolo ducked his head but remained silent. Perceiving his friend's indignation about to boil over, Giampaolo implored in a tense whisper, "For God's sake, 'Cenzo, don't say anything."

Vincenzo gave the MPs an angry look and whispered back,

"They look at us like we're causing trouble!"

Tommaso remarked evenly, "They're just doing their jobs."

Unable to leave it alone, Vincenzo persisted. "Well, they're a little too enthusiastic about keeping us in line, if you ask me."

When one of the American guards suddenly gave a couple of prisoners a rough shove, Tommaso gestured toward the encounter with a lift of his chin. "See what I mean?"

But Giampaolo had turned away from his friends, distracted by a commotion among the other prisoners. "Look!" He shouted and pointed into the misty air toward the opposite shore.

And there it was: a mammoth statue of a woman in long flowing robes the greenish patina of weathered copper. She wore a star-pointed halo, and one arm was thrust confidently skyward holding aloft a torch that seemed to glimmer faintly in the mist. An eerie silence befell the men on deck as they steamed past the monument, a wave of awe rising like an unspoken prayer from the deck. As if Lady Liberty were an honored saint carried on the shoulders of a procession in some remembered *festa* from their home towns across the sea, some of the men crossed themselves, knelt on the deck, and lowered their heads.

Silently they steamed past the lady in the harbor.

Soon the cacophony of ship's bells, escalating whistles, and grinding winches signaled the ship's approach alongside a bustling pier. Each prisoner clung tightly to his meager possessions as they were marched in single file down a narrow gangplank and onto solid ground. Giampaolo felt unseen waves buffet his lower body as he tried to get his bearings. "Sea legs," he thought, and sighed, realizing it would take a few hours, or days, until he got acclimated to dry land – this time as a prisoner of war in earnest, for who knew how long.

Although it had been a cold passage by sea, the weather was warm on land. On the busy pier, the prisoners were ordered to sit with packs at their side on the sweltering pier. Though it was only late May, the sun soon left their tattered uniforms soaked with another layer of sweat. To pass the time, the three friends shared cigarettes as they huddled dockside. Before too long, a line of sturdy trucks, with olive-green canvass roofs stretched over metal frames, pulled alongside the pier. The throng of prisoners rose and shuffled toward the trucks. When it was their turn, Giampaolo and his friends clambered aboard and sat on the hard benches to either side. As the vehicle started to move, fresh air wafted into the truck from an open ventilation flap on the roof.

Vincenzo wiped his brow and reached into his breast pocket for another cigarette from a pack the Americans had given them that morning. "What now?" he murmured as he lit two and passed one to Tommaso.

"God only knows," Tommaso whispered back, desperation in his tone. He crossed himself quickly.

In spite of himself, Giampaolo chuckled. "All of a sudden, you're praying to the saints." He raised his eyes to heaven and put his hands together in a mock-prayerful gesture. "But I think it's too late for help from them."

The truck rumbled to a stop. Tommaso stood up and parted a seam of the thick canvas curtain that covered the back of the truck to glimpse outside. "Trains," he said. "They're putting us on trains."

Vincenzo swore. *"Diu miu,* no. Just like Bizerte!" He shuddered at the memory. "Those cattle-cars were like ovens."

One truck at a time, the prisoners were ordered down from the transports and across a broad platform to a waiting train. In front of each train car stood a table, equipped with neat stacks of paper, a large stamp-pad and an array of stamps. MPs stood guard at each table, and a couple of burly rifle-wielding soldiers hustled the prisoners into a single file in front of each table. Each prisoner was given a form onto which he was told to print and sign his name. After he did so, a guard at the table briskly pounded a date stamp on the bottom of the form, and another copied the prisoner's name in neat block letters on the front and flyleaf of a small booklet before handing it to the prisoner.

"These are your temporary PW identification papers!" one MP bellowed from the front car of the train. "Don't lose 'em or you will face disciplinary action!" There was quiet murmuring among the Italians until one of the American MPs saw their confusion. He translated the officer's edict into Italian and added instructions on what to do with the forms. American guards at some of the other tables began to do the same thing.

Vincenzo squinted. *"Chi dissi?* What's he saying?"

Tommaso hushed his friend. "Quiet! I think there's another one over there repeating the orders in Italian." He turned an ear toward the MP shouting in American-accented Italian, then addressed his companions. "He's saying we need to write our names and sign the paper."

Giampaolo nodded. "Some of these Americans here know Italian."

Vincenzo nodded in agreement. "At least that's better than on the ship. There, they only knew one language." He held up a fist.

"C'mon, Vincenzo, it wasn't so bad." Giampaolo remonstrated.

Tommaso added with a shudder, "Yeah. We could have been sent to Russia." He lifted a callused palm and bit the side of his index finger for emphasis.

Vincenzo's eyes took on a haunted look. "But when we hit that storm at sea, I thought we were all going down. And I don't swim."

Giampaolo laughed. "How is it possible that you have lived your whole life on an island, in a port city, near beaches and the sea, and you never learned to swim?"

Vincenzo angered quickly. "Oh sure, a day at the beach. A goddam day at the fucking beach!" Then he turned serious. "I can hold my own. But not in thousands of meters of water in the cold Atlantic!"

Tommaso urged his friends towards the table. "Come on, it's our turn."

New identification booklets in hand, the prisoners ambled toward the waiting passenger cars. Giampaolo scampered up the train's iron stairs, eager for a look inside. The door to the Pullman car was propped open. Inside, row upon neat row of seats faced forward, ready to take their cargo.

Vincenzo emitted a low whistle of appreciation, then exclaimed, "Look! We're in first class! *Primu classi!*"

The men expressed approval and disbelief as they found places on the well-cushioned benches. The door to their car closed with a loud snap as they looked around.

"I wonder if it's a mistake?" Tommaso ventured, disbelieving the luxury around him as he patted the velvet-covered seat.

"Well, let's enjoy the 'mistake' while it lasts!" Vincenzo exclaimed. He reached over to pull down the window, admitting air into the stuffy car. Grinning, he took his seat, put folded hands behind his head, leaned back, and stretched his legs in front of him.

Sitting at the window, Giampaolo inserted his identification booklet into the torn breast pocket of his shirt and patted it, as if to reassure its safekeeping. Then he turned toward the window to watch as the last of the prisoners boarded the train. Soon their car lurched forward and the train began moving slowly through a maze of tracks. They passed through a succession of tunnels and as the dark partitions of the train depot receded, streets crowded with tall brick buildings whizzed by. Before long, gritty cityscapes gave way to verdant views of trees and neatly plowed fields.

An American soldier entered the car and addressed the men formally in Italian. *"Attenzione: benvenuti agli Stati Uniti d'America.* Attention: welcome to the United States of America. As prisoners of war you are in the custody of the United States government. Blankets and provisions will be provided for your trip." With that, he turned and left the car. From the same door, three American soldiers entered, arms piled high with blankets. Behind them, another soldier wheeled a cart with water, soft drinks and packets of food wrapped in waxed paper.

Vincenzo gestured toward the blanket that was held out to him. *"Madonna!* It's summer!" He exclaimed. "Do they think we'll get cold? *Matri, chi cauddu!"*

"Use it as a pillow." Tommaso put words to action by wadding up the blanket and placing it behind his head.

Giampaolo was distracted from the lush landscape outside the train window as the concession cart approached. The prisoners were helping themselves, so he took two tall glasses of water from the shelf. A glass in each hand, he thirstily chugged both without stopping for breath. Vincenzo tossed a waxed paper packet to him.

"You missed the food!" he exclaimed. The three friends unwrapped the packages to find two thin slices of soft, snowy white bread with even slices of pink ham and pale-colored cheese between them. Tommaso sniffed the food suspiciously.

"Eh, mància, stunat'! Eat, you fool! It's not bad," Vincenzo exclaimed, finishing his own sandwich in three enormous bites. He jumped up and ran after the cart, returning in a moment with three more packets which he distributed among them. Giampaolo bit tentatively into the bread. As the taste of soft fresh bread met his tongue for the first time in months, he bit again hungrily, then devoured the rest and quickly unwrapped the second sandwich.

A prisoner behind him was holding aloft a piece of the pink

meat from his sandwich. "*Ecco: prosciutto 'bollito'!* Look here: 'boiled' ham." He laughed as he waved the slice of ham in the air. "One of those American fellows is 'Bruzzese. He told me."

Overhearing the comment and wiping his mouth with the crumpled wax paper, Vincenzo exclaimed, with a sideways glance at Tommaso. "I'm not complaining. They could call it shoe leather, and it could *taste* like shoe leather, and I would still eat it. You should, too." Tommaso silently finished his sandwich without comment, but Giampaolo grunted in agreement. Hunger had been their constant companion during those long dry months in the desert. Maybe the rumors he heard were true: you *did* eat better in America.

* * *

The train gently braked to a stop, lulling Giampaolo from a deep dreamless sleep. He opened his eyes, momentarily confused as to his whereabouts. Then it broke over his consciousness: America. He was in America.

He sat up, rubbing his eyes. Bright sun streamed into the train car, lighting up motes of dust floating in the air. Outside the summer morning was already hot and still. Vivid green weeds poked up spindly arms between the train tracks, beyond which a broad wooden platform stretched, with tables in tidy rows. Some of the tables appeared to have food and drink ready for the disembarking prisoners. Others seemed to be dedicated to paperwork, staffed by American soldiers waiting expectantly, each with a thin black binder of lined paper and a stack of pencils. At the front of the tables, an American soldier with three stripes on his sleeve barked orders loudly over the din of the train. He seemed to have the attention of everyone within earshot.

At the end of each car, a military policeman was stationed, firearm over his shoulder. The prisoners regarded the MPs as a kind of gauntlet to be walked before they could exit the train. As when they had disembarked the ship, canvas-roofed troop trucks were lined along the platform waiting for the train to disgorge its cargo. The MPs chatted easily with the guard-soldiers ready to receive the prisoners on the platform. They laughed and eyed the prisoners with bored condescension.

Since boarding the train in New York, the prisoners had been traveling for a few days. En route, the train had sped dizzily through uncompromising cityscapes grey with grime. As they headed west, the urban landscape had given way to small towns with neat clapboard houses and, in turn, into fields green with lettuce and cabbage. Now it seemed they had arrived at yet another train platform where they would form lines and produce their identification papers, one more disembarkation point where there would be trays of sandwiches or donuts and cups of the weak American coffee they'd grown used to.

Vincenzo shrugged his pack onto his shoulder. "This place is called 'Kokomo'," he commented, chuckling, to no one in particular. "Ko KO mo," he repeated, accenting the second syllable. "I saw the sign as we went through the station. Like Lago Como? *Forsi ci sugnu 'Taliani qui?* Maybe there are Italians here, from the north?"

At his comment, Tommaso thrust out his chin and shrugged. "*Cui canusciu?* Who knows?"

The three friends shouldered their rucksacks and clambered off the train car together with hundreds of other prisoners. In what had by now become routine, they lined up in single file, ID booklets in hand, behind tables staffed with American GIs who would stamp their papers with another arrival point and date. Then they would follow orders barked at them in American English they didn't understand.

While they waited, Tommaso muttered in disgust, "Here we go again. *Chisti 'Mericani* and their forms."

Giampaolo shrugged and let out a half-hearted chuckle. "What else do we have to do right now?"

21

Vincenzo squinted at another sign above the train platform. "Indiana. EEN dee AH nah. Sounds like an Italian word, too." He pondered the possibility, then carefully enunciated the words as if they'd been written in Italian. "Ko KO mo, EEN dee AH nah. Maybe there *are* Italians here!" He gave Tommaso an optimistic look.

Paperwork completed, the three men boarded trucks idling by the chain-link fence to depart to another destination still unknown. After several hours of jostling and bouncing shoulder-to-shoulder with other prisoners, they disembarked still deeper in this strange part of Middle America called Indiana.

Aside from the imposing but brief glimpse of the port of New York with its swarm of American Navy vessels and carriers, Camp Atterbury, Indiana, was the prisoners' first real exposure to the organizational might of the United States Army. Before them stood a massive military metropolis. The camp spread as far as the men could see on the flat Midwestern plain.

Right in front of them, behind a high chain-link fence, the scene bustled with soldiers – to the left side of the camp's entrance, row upon row of American recruits could be seen marching in parade or undergoing training exercises. To these wizened veterans, they looked so green, but still they emitted an unfamiliar air of confidence and determination, as if they could take on and conquer whatever faced them in battle. To the right side, arriving prisoners – both Italians and Germans, still scruffy and unkempt in battle-tattered uniforms – stood in separate lines to be photographed and have fingerprints taken. Behind them, a line of prisoners was being dispatched to the latrines, where they would be disinfected, showered, and issued new uniforms. Farther on, still other prisoners in new khaki clothing, their hair shorn and their faces clean-shaven, were organized in work details and stood awaiting assignment to "non-military labor" in factories and farms that the war had emptied of able-bodied American workers.

As he waited with the other prisoners, Giampaolo took in the enormity of the place. Dozens of barracks lined the perimeter of the camp inside the chain-link enclosure. Near the barracks stood an array of taller rectangular buildings with stenciled signs advertising every imaginable service a soldier could want or need – a post office, a movie theater, a barber shop, a library, a bakery, a laundry. An immense structure dominated the middle of the camp's landscape, a hospital built to serve the myriad medical demands of GIs and prisoners alike. The entire place teemed with energy. On the left, the American side of the camp, every movement of every soldier seemed an expression of American military precision and order. On the right, where the prisoners were being processed, an air of resignation and uncertainty tainted their slow progress from one line to the next.

After delousing and fingerprinting, Giampaolo and the other prisoners were issued plain khaki uniforms with the letters "PW" stamped on it. Then each man was assigned quarters in one of the low rectangular barracks outfitted with rows of neat cots, each one made up with clean white bedsheets, pillows, and green or brown blankets.

At first Giampaolo and his friends could scarcely believe their luck. No more sleeping on the ground in makeshift bedrolls. No more waiting in fenced-off desert pens or huddling together in train cars meant for cargo. Here in America, every prisoner had his own bed and his own small space in the dormitory with other prisoners. The appointments at the camp may have seemed spartan to American eyes, but to these prisoners the place seemed luxurious. Everything was scrupulously clean and well-tended; every prisoner's needs were anticipated.

The next morning began early with a clanging reveille, dispelling dreams from even the soundest sleeper. The prisoners hastily dressed in their new duds and hurried to the mess hall, where a filling breakfast of coffee, eggs, toasted white bread, and unfamiliar meats like thin strips of fat-streaked bacon and tiny bland sausages awaited them. Every day! For the first several days of this princely treatment, Giampaolo pinched himself for reassurance that he hadn't died and gone to heaven.

Well-fed and wide awake, Giampaolo and his friends boarded a troop transport for the hour's drive to fields where acres of early corn stood, already tall and ready to harvest. They were given bushel baskets and were dispatched among the rows to pick the corn, twisting and snapping the ripest ears. Stripping to his undershirt in the hot Indiana sun, Giampaolo worked in the lush green fields cheerfully, marveling at the sturdy stalks with large ears of buttery yellow corn so different from the diminutive cobs they picked for animal feed at home. He gaped at the large flat expanses of farmland that seemed to go on forever, endless rows of green reaching to the horizon. He planted his feet with wonder on rich black loam so unlike the rock-strewn hills of his family's farm back home, where he and his brothers had to coax every spindly shoot of winter wheat from the ground.

After several weeks, the prisoners were moved to another smaller camp in Austin, Indiana, with accommodations nearly identical to Camp Atterbury's. Clean sheets and comfortable cots. Clean uniforms and new boots. And food, plenty of it, readied with regularity and dispensed without fanfare. "Three squares a day," the American guards called it.

From Fort Austin the morning transport took them not to fields and farms but to the front gates of Morgan Packing Company, a hulking, many-windowed canning facility, where the prisoners took their places for 8- to 10-hour workdays on food processing and canning lines. Convoys of large trucks rattled toward the plant each day, bringing tomatoes and pumpkins and myriad other vegetables freshly harvested from nearby fields in Scott County. The produce was offloaded into massive piles many times taller than Giampaolo, soon to be shuttled on conveyor belts into the building to be cleaned, sorted, and cooked. Giampaolo marveled at the precise efficiency of the whole operation. He learned how to peel cabbage, removing the core and the head with a drill, and separating the leaves. He minded the baffling machinery that performed a host of tasks, turning a constantly changing array of vegetables into rows of shiny tin cans. The labels on some of the cans showed foods he recognized, like bright green peas and white potatoes, but others contained strange concoctions like baked beans and sauerkraut.

Just as Giampaolo was becoming accustomed to the routine of factory and camp, his company was on the move again, in September. They travelled again in passenger cars reconfigured for troop transport, heading east. This time the train chugged into a busy military base from which the prisoners could smell the sea and salt air. They presented their identification booklets to the GI clerks for assignment to a new camp at Port Johnson, New Jersey. Showered, fed and wearing clean uniforms, Giampaolo and his friends found themselves once again close to where their American prisoner-of-war adventure had begun: the harbor of New York City was clearly visible just across the waterfront.

Before leaving Indiana, the Italians had learned with the rest of the world of Mussolini's ignominious undoing and of Italy's agreement to collaborate with the Allies. As the news broke, they had no idea what immediate ramifications this dire news would have for them. The events that shattered their homeland and unbalanced the Axis seemed worlds away from their straightforward, predictable, and comparatively comfortable existence as prisoners of war.

At the new camp, the prisoners' work rotation brought them to piers crammed with American troops and ships departing almost daily for the war in Europe. One day blended into another in the routine of prison-camp life, but at least the work at Port Johnson was more varied than in Indiana. On any given day, Giampaolo might be pressed into service as a makeshift stevedore, stowing supplies in the hold of one of the hulking cargo ships that lined the waterfront. On another day, he would be handed a bucket and mop and ordered to swab a grimy dock where supplies had just been unloaded. Giampaolo welcomed the brace of fresh air on deck and the briny smell of the sea overlain with the pervasive scent of diesel.

On other days, there were duties in the camp itself – train or truck cargo to be moved, or duties in the always-busy kitchens behind the mess hall – what the Americans sneeringly called "KP." On being assigned to kitchen patrol, some of his fellow prisoners picked up on the GIs' disdain for the job and started resenting it too, but Giampaolo never minded. Being in the kitchen meant that at mealtime he could maneuver a place at the front of the mess line and claim a generous helping of everything while it was still hot. He'd proudly earn the epithet of "chow hound." Those memories of hunger and thirst in the desert were still too fresh in his mind.

* * *

As the calendar turned to 1944, the months of January and February passed without much fanfare, and by March, warmer days chased away the windy chill of winter on the waterfront. One morning, as their truck rumbled its way to the docks, Giampaolo noticed delicate white snowdrop blooms and the first green shoots of daffodils poking through the crusty winter ground at the camp's entrance gates. The air felt softer too, as if the whole earth was coming alive again.

That evening a meeting was called for the prisoners in his brigade. They filed into the mess hall where they had eaten a few hours earlier. Two American officers stood at the front of the room, along with an Italian officer from his company. One of the Americans addressed the group in clear Italian. Something called Italian Service Units were being formed here at the camp among the Italian prisoners who wanted to volunteer. This service concept recognized Italy's new status as collaborator with the Allies and gave the prisoners a chance to cooperate more fully with the war effort. Those who volunteered for the ISUs, as they were called, would undergo screening by U.S. military intelligence officers and be subject to U.S. military law and regulations. They would sign a declaration, a pledge of fealty to the Allied cause and a promise to help in whatever ways might be required. In exchange for their cooperation, they would be given wartime pay just like American soldiers. They would be allowed off the base in supervised circumstances, and would get weekend leave as well. Although joining the ISU was optional, it was encouraged.

The alternative was to refuse to collaborate and to remain a prisoner of war indefinitely. Some of the officers argued that it would be disloyal to Italy to accept the new proposal. Under these new service units, and by virtue of pledging to help the Allies, they would likely be pressed to reveal Italian military secrets or other sensitive information. Although such intelligence had likely outworn its value by the time it reached them in the camp, divulging it would nonetheless make cooperating officers feel like turncoats.

For Giampaolo and enlisted men like him, the choice was more pragmatic, betting an unknown against a certainty. It was impossible to predict how long the war would go on. Since that was the case, why not live out their time as prisoners as comfortably as possible? He and his friends knew nothing of the war's higher strategies; as foot soldiers, they had no military secrets to share. Nor were they likely to be pressed for information of that sort; if asked, of course, they could honestly say they had nothing to report. Why give up a good thing right in front of them with the war's outcome looming but still uncertain?

These options were the ones Giampaolo weighed as the meeting ended. As soon as the American officer finished speaking, the room broke out in a cacophony of voices as the prisoners started talking all at once. Giampaolo turned to his friends.

"*Chi pensi tu?* What do you think?"

Always impulsive, Vincenzo burst out, "Of course, I'll sign! Give me the paper!"

Tommaso just stroked his mustache pensively and said nothing.

"Not so fast, 'Cenzo," Giampaolo held up an index finger, wanting to hear first what Tommaso was thinking. But Vincenzo was not to be dissuaded.

"What's there to think about, Giampaolo?" He tapped his friend's shoulder with the back of his fingertips. "Italy's finished in this war. We're on the side of the United States now." He began ticking off his arguments on his fingers, one by one. "We've been here, what, almost a year now?· We've had good food and plenty of it, every day, a clean bed to sleep in, clean clothes, new socks and dry boots. And the officers leave us alone." Vincenzo paused meaningfully and lowered his voice. "Do you remember where we were not so long ago? Remember Libya? The desert?" He paused for effect and shuddered. "Remember Bizerte?"

Giampaolo nodded. He knew Vincenzo was right. Even at home, before the war, things weren't so good. He glanced at Tommaso, who still seemed uncertain and confused.

Tommaso reluctantly broke his silence. "I suppose you are right. But what about what the officers are saying?"

"Sure, sure, maybe the big shots have to think twice about this." Vincenzo was defiant. "But we don't. For once, I'm glad not to be the boss!"

Lines were forming at tables to one side of the mess hall. A handful of the prisoners were already walking away with sheaves of papers in their hands, sharing the forms among themselves. Some were rushing to the table and signing the declaration on the spot. The three friends joined the crowd surging forward and waited their turn.

Chapter 3

"Fort Benning, Ga., Sept. 12 (AP)---A special Te Deum mass was celebrated here today for 800 Italian prisoners of war to mark the capitulation of their native land to the United Nations and to express their appreciation for kind treatment during their internment. The mass was celebrated and the Holy Sacrament administered by Rev. Father Roderick MacEachen, who was assigned to the Vatican in 1918 and now serves the prisoners of war as chaplain."

—The *New York Times*

June 1944, on a train in New Jersey

The train wheels click-clacked a rhythmic lullaby in the warm passenger car. A sunny cloudless day illuminated the landscape speeding by as Eleanor's eyelids drooped. Aimlessly she glanced down at her ivory silk blouse, trimmed in lace and caught in a short-sleeved cuff with pearl buttons. Why had she donned her summer Sunday best for this trip? Well, after all, it *was* Sunday and they were eventually going to Mass. She looked askance at the open window above her head, second-guessing her decision to pull down the metal sash at the beginning of their journey. The narrow gap did seem to keep the sultry air moving a little bit. She had thus far avoided getting spattered with the soot from the locomotive's smokestack that drifted in periodically through every open pane or crack the entire length of the train. She reached across the bench for the pink sweater she'd brought with her, and wrapped it loosely around her shoulders. It wouldn't provide much cover, but it was something.

Eleanor glanced around her. Each of her five fellow passengers was passing the time in her own way. Her friend Mary Mollica was gazing out the window as a patchwork of farmland whizzed by. Her cousins Rosalie and Suzanne – the "Luna girls" – leaned upon one another, napping, heads nodding gently in time with the train's rocking cadence. Mary's sister Frannie studiously read her book, absorbed and unconcerned.

A flutter of nerves unsettled Eleanor for a moment: if they couldn't find Mary and Frannie's cousin when they got to the parish hall, this whole trip would have been for nothing. Tommaso Mollica had written them when he arrived in the States. He was their age – early thirties – and yet he'd probably lived two lifetimes in the complicated realities of the war. The Mollica family had learned from his letters that Tommaso had been captured as a prisoner of war and shipped to America, and was interned in a military camp in New Jersey.

Eleanor knew plenty of men who'd gone to fight the war – brothers and cousins, fathers and friends of people she knew who were serving from Europe to the Pacific. Servicemen in uniform were commonplace on the streets of her hometown these days. But the men they would see and meet today were different. They were enemy combatants. They were Italians who had been fighting with the Axis Powers and caught in the crossfire of the North Africa campaign. They were prisoners of war.

On weekends when she went to the cinema with her cousins, she had seen the newsreels about the war. It was the way most Americans learned what was going on, over there. The names of some of the key players in the conflict, Rommel, Montgomery, Patton: these had become as familiar to Americans as the Hollywood stars who featured in the films that followed the news of the war. To Americans who picked up the morning paper or turned on the radio, once-exotic names like El Alamein and Tobruk had grown nearly as recognizable as the names of homegrown places like Kokomo,

31

Indiana or Jamesport, Pennsylvania.

Common as these reports of the faraway war had become, the mission on which she and her cousins and friends were embarked that morning still felt strange, with a slight edge of excitement and, yes, danger. Who knew what these prisoners would be like? They had actually been to those mysterious places, had walked and slept and raised arms and fought in circumstances out of the ordinary for people like herself. She wondered if what little she knew of the war, from the scratchy movie-house newsreels or, third-hand, from American GIs' letters home, would change that day. She would actually meet people for whom those far-off dots on a map had been grim reality for weeks and months, even years on end. They had lived in those places and done things about which the wartime bulletins could not do justice. Perhaps they had even killed other men, in defense of an idea – or merely so as not to be killed themselves. She shuddered and pulled her sweater more tightly around her shoulders.

After Pearl Harbor there had been a great rush, the patriotic urge to defend home and hearth stirring in many who enlisted on the spot. Some of the young men she knew from the Italian-American families who constituted her world in Jamesport had signed up as soon as Uncle Sam put out the call – like her cousin Angelo's gang of friends from the ballpark. In those heady days, it seemed like all the young men were marching off to war. Frannie's husband Joe Vespico had enlisted immediately, so Frannie had moved home with her parents. Mary's sometime beau Donny Schmidt had signed up, too – to the immense relief of *Cumpari* Mollica and *Cummari* Angelina, who hoped that perhaps time and distance may nip the budding romance with the shy young man. After all, he wasn't Italian. It was difficult to imagine that so many fellows she knew – neighbors, cousins, friends -- were fighting against men like the ones they were about to meet.

Thinking about these things too deeply made her head ache.

She knew that to Frannie and Mary's parents, this unfamiliar nephew Tommaso was *family*, first and foremost. They had received letters from him soon after he arrived in America; prisoners weren't discouraged from writing to family and friends, much like most American GI's did. *Cumpari* Mollica and *Cummari* Angelina sent their daughters on this journey with their blessing, eager to learn anything they could about their family in Sicily through this young man, to see how the relatives over there were bearing up through the horror of this long war. She suspected the Mollicas would have gone to greater lengths than this to make contact.

As for her own family, her mother sent letters and packages with regularity to Eleanor's aunt and uncle and their family in Sicily. None of their immediate relatives, here or there, were involved in the fighting, Eleanor's male cousins being too young still for military service. Nonetheless, Donna Sarina believed in taking some action, of the sort that was practical, readily available, and possible. She was doing what she could, in her own way, to help her family in Sicily survive these terrible times.

Eleanor put these thoughts aside. This trip was a diversion, an unexpected respite from the monotonous routine of work in the factory. She was venturing just a bit into the unknown, taking a few baby steps to the edge of the wartime experience; that alone made this sojourn feel like an adventure. Besides, for every cinema newsreel that carried reports of bloody battles and gruesome injuries, there was another alongside it showing the smiling faces of so many handsome young men, cheerfully doing their duty in far-away places. The world may be breathing the deadly fumes of war, but romance was also in the air.

Eleanor let herself drift, giving in to a pleasant drowsiness induced by the train's rhythmic rocking. It brought her back to another time and place. In her memory-dream, she was a young child in another train car, this one crowded with exhausted newcomers like themselves, carrying Eleanor Fazzio and her mother away from the chaotic terror, noise, and confusion of their arrival in a new land.

Chapter 4

"Give me your tired, your poor,

Your huddled masses yearning to breathe free,

The wretched refuse of your teeming shore;

Send these, the homeless, tempest-tost to me,

I lift my lamp beside the golden door!"

—Emma Lazarus

January 1920, Ellis Island

They had been a week at sea in the freezing North Atlantic. The crossing had been so unlike the perpetual balmy comfort of sun-kissed Sicily, the only home Eleanor had known. Halfway through the voyage, severe sea sickness had overtaken her mother. The usually spunky 28-year-old Rosaria Fazzio, Donna Sarina to all who knew her, was so overtaken by dehydration and weakness that she had been remanded to the ship's infirmary, leaving her frightened little girl to seek hollow comfort in the arms of other *paesane* women on the ship. Fortunately for Eleanor, her mother had befriended others in the group of twenty Sicilian souls from their town who embarked together in Messina. They were crammed together into overcrowded berths in the swarming "third-class" bunk-space in steerage, filling the belly of the great ship. The women took pity on the terrified little girl, taking turns bestowing comforting hugs and sharing with her portions of the meager provisions they had set by for the crossing.

After what seemed an eternity to six-year-old Eleanor, the

journey was over. Her mother, pale and still sickly, emerged from the infirmary, gathered their belongings, and took Eleanor's hand as the steamship approached the dock. But before she was reunited with her mother, as the ship made its way into New York harbor, the little girl was nearly swallowed in the crush of passengers all around her. As they spilled onto the congested decks, an unstoppable horde shoved and elbowed one another for a first glimpse, however brief, of the fabled Statue of Liberty. Here at last was the lady in the harbor who, it was said, was a blessing and a good omen for all who saw her as they passed by.

Tearfully reunited with Donna Sarina on the deck, Eleanor felt a sharp slice of terror as she walked down the rickety gangplank to dry land. One little fist clutched desperately to her mother's larger one, and the other hand gripped the handle of a little wicker basket that held her prized china tea-set, the only memento of home she had brought with her. Somehow she had managed to safeguard the basket throughout the long journey. Another long wait on the docks, the wind off the water whipping at their thin garments, as palpable hunger overtook her, made worse by the incapacitating fear of what might happen next. What came back to Eleanor most keenly in her memory-dreams were the smells. The brisk harbor breeze with its tinge of brine blew away the stench of steerage, the reek of sweat and urine and damp wool that had clung to the back of her throat for the long days at sea. Then a ferry arrived, spewing a new set of smells: diesel fuel, rotting fish, and acrid smoke belching from its chimney-stacks.

Eleanor clung fiercely to her mother's skirts as they shuffled aboard the smaller steamer for the short trip to Ellis Island. Once on land again, she and her mother huddled together, trying to discern the meaning of the orders barked at them in a strange tongue. She gazed up as they passed through the large doorway of a forbidding brick façade. They entered a cavernous low-ceilinged entrance-hall. The passengers' luggage was being dragged onto tables for customs inspection, then repacked haphazardly for them to reclaim. All manner of luggage lay strewn about: trunks and boxes and trussed-up bed linens, some disgorging a lifetime of possessions, piled together in no discernible order. Reluctantly, mother and daughter relinquished their meager baggage, except for the precious basket to which she still clung. They were herded up a wide set of stairs and into an enormous hall lined entirely with white tiles vaulting to an arched ceiling high above them. The din was deafening. Eleanor looked up. The place was so packed with overwhelming chaos and noise that her singular memory afterward was of the ceiling of the big white room.

Exhausted, the pair slumped down on one of the long wooden benches lined up in rows that filled the white echo chamber. More interminable waiting, more orders barked in strange English, as mother and daughter were steered for inspection through a series of smaller rooms, to wait and wonder at the humiliating rituals to which they were subjected. In one of these overcrowded spaces, Eleanor held her little body stiff with fear as a doctor poked and prodded, painfully inverting her eyelids and peering into her eyes with a bright light. Farther on, an official seized the lapel of Eleanor's coat and pinned a paper tag to it, showing the little girl a chilling toothy grin and then pushing her back into her mother's skirts. In another crowded room, they were hauled before a tall desk from behind which a trio of immigration officials and a translator sat, trying to extract information from her mother and making notes on cards. Soon they were shunted on to yet another small chamber to await approval being stamped on their travel papers.

Some of the workers were kind. The ones who spoke a rudimentary Italian seemed to show a sad sympathy. Some bestowed a distant smile or patted Eleanor's cheek off-handedly. She and her mother were just two more immigrants among the hundreds of thousands processed through these doors each week. In another room a large table was set on a high platform, and a mustachioed man peered down at them with disdain. As another official approached them, Eleanor huddled closer to her mother, terror written on her face. The official fingered and turned over the paper tags pinned to their lapels before inscribing them with new markings. These odd hieroglyphics of letters and numbers that they didn't comprehend would spell their fate in and out of this inhospitable place.

For a few panicked moments while they waited once again in the big white room, Eleanor lost grip of her mother's hand. She set the miniature woven basket momentarily on the bench next to her as she groped for her mother's comforting grasp. Reclaiming her mother's hand, she turned again to retrieve her favorite toy, but it was gone. She had lavished love on that little basket during the journey, and it had brought comfort and familiarity to her at the lowest moments. She had fondled its delicate bone handle, opened its miniature clasp with care and withdrew each tiny cup and saucer in turn. When she was reassured that all was well with the tea-set, she had rewrapped each piece fondly and nestled it back in place. Now the one prized familiar object from home that had sustained her through this ordeal had been taken from her, never to be recovered. Distraught, Eleanor gave in to an explosive fit of frightened tears that promptly drew a terse reprimand from her mother. She succumbed to a few long minutes of muffled sobs and hiccups before letting a numb silence mask the dread she felt about this awful new place, a terror so acute she could recall its metallic taste like blood on her tongue.

Travel documents and train tickets were shoved into her mother's hands, and after another ferry-ride, mother and daughter entered another cavernous building – this time the railroad station in Jersey City, New Jersey. Eleanor caught a whiff of divergent strange aromas, coffee and onions and melted butter emanating from a substantial food stall nearby that was doing a brisk business selling provisions to immigrant travelers. A large white sign hanging above the counter advertised their wares in four languages. Eleanor's mouth watered and her stomach grumbled. It had been days since they had eaten real food. Another immigrant, a man dressed neatly in threadbare clothing, was standing at the counter and turned to look at her fondly.

"*Scusami, Signora,*" he addressed Eleanor's mother in a kindly tone. "*A picciuridda avi fami?* Is the little girl hungry?"

Relieved to hear a familiar Sicilian dialect, Donna Sarina smiled wanly at her fellow traveler. "*Sí, Signor,* she is. We haven't eaten since we were on the ship, but –"

"*Lasciami fari, signora,* let me do it," the man stroked Eleanor's head. "*Iu mi máncio puro,* I am eating something myself." He pointed at the half-eaten sandwich on the counter.

Before she could remonstrate further, the man drew a paper-wrapped package from his satchel and pressed it into Sarina's hands. Looking at Eleanor, he said softly, "*Te' ccà, bubbidda.* Here you go, my little doll."

Sarina's eyes filled with tears as she unwrapped the sandwich and tore off a hunk for Eleanor, who bit into it eagerly. Her voice broke as she whispered, "*Grazî,* thank you." She rewrapped the bread and added, "*Diu sabbinirìca.* May God bless you." She gathered their meager belongings and took Eleanor's hand.

Showing their tickets wordlessly to several conductors, the pair was directed to a platform below the station's main waiting room. From there, they had climbed a few sturdy metal steps into the waiting train, whose cars were already packed. Energized by the kindness of a stranger, Sarina had found her footing. With unwonted feistiness, she firmly elbowed others aside and hustled her daughter toward a couple of hard benches onto which she settled them for this last leg of their journey. Calmer now after her meager sustenance, Eleanor turned a tear-stained face toward her mother. Sarina's strong hand grasping her daughter's shoulder was the little girl's fragile but welcome reassurance that they were safe now. The train's rocking motion lulled her, exhausted, to sleep, curled against the warmth of her mother.

* * *

Eleanor awoke with a start, allowed her eyes to focus, and looked around. Frannie was still reading her book, and Mary was absently folding and unfolding her sweater. Her cousins were awake now, too, and were looking out the window, captivated by the urban landscape whizzing by. The train finally pulled to a stop, and the five young women navigated their way through the bustling train station at Newark. On the curb outside the depot, Frannie commandeered a taxicab and they climbed into it, cramming into the back seat. After a cramped but blessedly short ride, they unfolded themselves in front of a grand edifice. Our Lady of Mount Carmel Church stood in dignified elegance, the rosy golden brick of its ersatz Renaissance façade at once imposing and peaceful. The main entrance, now crowded with worshipers, was fronted by a swath of pavement that led to the church steps. The bells in the tower just behind the church pealed welcome.

"You sure this is the right place?" Rosalie asked in low tones as she emerged from the cab after her sister, so the cab driver wouldn't hear.

"That's what the letter says," Suzanne whispered back, consulting a piece of blue airmail paper with handwriting on it that she unfolded from her purse.

The girls assembled in a semicircle on the curb, patting their hair and smoothing wrinkles from their clothing as the taxi drove away. The parish was hosting a special Mass of welcome for a group of Italian prisoners of war from the camp at Port Johnson. It was to be followed by Sunday dinner in the church hall. The event was hosted by the Sodality of Our Lady of

Mt. Carmel. Eleanor frowned fleetingly. If it hadn't been for her mother's long-standing loyal membership in the sodality's local chapter at home, she suspected she never would have been allowed on this trip unchaperoned. The frown gave way to a self-satisfied smirk as she indulged the feeling that she'd gotten away with something. Well, she wasn't alone. Eleanor, her cousins, and their friends were good traveling companions. The same little group had made trips together to Atlantic City a few times. The distraction of boardwalk, sand, and surf satisfied them until the next rare excursion away from home that they might afford. In the end, this wasn't so very different. After all, it was just for a day; they would return home by the evening train and report to work at the factory at seven o'clock tomorrow morning, all without skipping a beat.

For weeks before the trip, there had been vigorous debate among the young women about what to wear. With little else to occupy their paltry leisure, these young ladies invested an inordinate amount of time and attention on the subject. Eleanor had firmly advocated skirts and blouses – at once smart, and also comfortable for boarding and changing trains. A plain summer dress simply would not lend the air of worldliness she wanted to effect. A cotton frock was all right for wearing to church or going out in Jamesport, but just not dressy enough for the wider world. Her cousins Suzanne and Rosalie and the Mollica girls all followed her lead, and so the entire troupe was attired in a manner very much in vogue at the moment (at least according to the magazines Rosalie brought home): short-sleeved blouses of linen and silk with touches of lace or piping on the bodice, and dark skirts of lightweight summer cotton.

Considerations of what to wear had evolved from a practical consideration to something of a hobby and an entertainment for the Luna girls. When they were little, Rosalie and Suzanne always wore nearly identical dresses, sewn for them in successive sizes by their Zia Sarina. Eleanor's mother would cleverly refashion the same frock that she crafted for her older nieces in a slightly smaller size for her daughter, and a still smaller size for her youngest niece Veronica. There was nothing that Rosaria Fazzio couldn't create from a scrap of fabric.

Donna Sarina, as everyone but her nieces called her, had been well trained: she was already an experienced tailor of men's suits and coats when she emigrated. She'd soon discovered, however, that there was more demand for her skills making women's clothing than menswear. Fortunately, women's apparel was much less complicated to sew, so she parlayed her skills into a steady paying job. Of course, as a practical matter, she also sewed all of the clothing for the entire family. Not only was it cheaper to make clothes for her brood: they also fit better, and with so many girls to outfit, if the dress or blouse was still in good shape when it was outgrown by one girl, it could easily be refitted for a younger one. So the Luna girls (Eleanor Fazzio was always lumped together with her cousins) always had something acceptable to wear. They were always neat and well turned out.

There was always some project, more likely two or three, that Donna Sarina worked on at her sewing table in the basement of the Luna home. She had shrewdly purchased one of the old Singer machines when the plant where she worked was upgrading to newer models. Once home, it was rarely idle.

Sewing had become the family profession, of sorts. All the girls eventually followed Donna Sarina as workers in the textile businesses that dominated the factories and mills of Jamesport. Their Zia Sarina had taught them what she could, but each girl had intuitively adapted and honed Sarina's instruction into a unique talent or skill that helped her stand out from the crowd – an important attribute if you wanted to keep a factory job. Rosalie's tiny neat stitches quickly drew the forelady's notice, and she was assigned to the finishing work on the "best in class" samples that the bosses would use to display the newest styles. Those sample garments were shipped to New York City for the buyers to use in pitching the garments to the retail outlets. Suzanne's attention to detail made her well suited for the examining table: she scrutinized each piece of finished merchandise— seams, stitches, and hems—snipping off any stray threads and shaking it loose of wrinkles. Having passed muster, her pile of examined garments would be sent downstairs to the shipping department, where they would be folded neatly, wrapped in tissue paper and packed for shipment.

Despite all this sartorial talent around her, Eleanor never had much aptitude for needlework. Or if she did, she was never confident enough to indulge it. Oh, she could sew a button or mend a rip well enough, but when it came to anything more complex, she felt as if she grasped the needle with five thumbs. But because she was Donna Sarina's daughter, the forelady had taken her on anyway, assigning her as a "bundle girl" on the factory floor. For this tedious task, Eleanor didn't earn as much per hour as her cousins. But she took pride in her work and performed her duties fastidiously – a practice which burnished her mother's already solid reputation with the factory bosses.

The plant where the Luna girls worked was a brick hulk occupying an entire city block in the heart of Jamesport. It sat among many similar brick buildings that went on, block after block, in that section of the city, harboring businesses that employed a goodly portion of Jamesport's population. A pair of heavy wooden doors admitted the workers into a stairwell – like the whole building, drafty in winter, sweltering in summer – whose steep metal steps climbed up five floors. The front half of the first floor, with windows facing the street, was reserved for the bosses and office girls, while behind it sprawled the noisy shipping department, separated by a thick brick partition from the offices. At the back, large doors that could roll up and down faced the alleyway behind the building, where trucks slid into the waiting bays to unpack fabric and other raw materials, and then to load the empty trucks with cartons of finished garments.

Each upper floor of the factory was defined by a different function of the garment manufacturing process, or by the different types of garments it produced. The process began at the top: garments made their way around the fifth floor, where the basters and seamers worked, applying the first stitches to the raw fabric fresh from the cutting machines. On the fourth floor, pockets and linings would be set into each frock. On the third floor, zippers were sewn in place, buttons applied, and buttonholes stitched and snipped. There was also a large cutting table, at which the forelady or a trusted worker could cut out single samples of a garment, if needed. At the same table, lace trim, piping, and other smaller segments of fabric would be measured and cut to specification by entry-level workers as a first test of their skill and workmanship. The second floor was where all the finishing work was done – hemming, labeling, and other handwork – and the garments were examined for irregularities. Those that weren't "perfects" were set aside as "seconds," to be sold to employees at cut-rate prices in the factory's outlet store. From that point, the finished pieces of clothing went to the shipping department and eventually, out into the world of fashion commerce.

Eleanor's job was identified as "unskilled labor" – she couldn't operate the seaming machines that triple-sewed the seam and trimmed the fabric's raw edge in one go, nor was she trained on the one-footed zipper machine, nor to run the button press. But her job nonetheless required considerable hustle and keen powers of observation. When she arrived for work each Monday, the forelady would tell her on which floor she would be working for the week. Then, from the time she punched her card at the clock every morning until punching out at the end of the day, Eleanor would make her way in a circuit around the assigned floor, trundling a bulky cart loaded with bundles of cut fabric pieces, enough for two dozen garments each. She stopped at each station to offload the next batch of fabric and make sure the operators were always well supplied.

"Piece workers," these skilled seamstresses were called, because they were paid by the piece – the faster they worked, the more money they earned. Each bundle was tied with a scrap of fabric that had a perforated paper ticket with the bundle's number on it. As she dropped a new bundle on a piece worker's table, Eleanor tore off a ticket stub, jotted down the worker's number, and tossed it into a small bin on her cart. The stubs enabled the forelady to keep track of the whereabouts of each bundle of garments-in-progress at any given point in time. Most important for the piece workers, the stubs were the basis for getting paid for work completed. As she passed each worker's station, Eleanor took note of how much of the worker's bundle remained and mentally calculated how soon the worker was likely to be ready for the next bundle. She kept track of which workers worked quickly. She didn't ever want to incur the wrath of an especially speedy operator by not having the next bundle available for her to start immediately upon completing the previous one. If Eleanor was slow to supply a piece worker with more garments to sew, she would invariably hear a terse shout, "Bundle!" She worked hard to avoid hearing that shout echo through the shop floor.

As a bundle girl walking the entirety of each floor and working on every level of the building, Eleanor should have been able to make friends with co-workers all over the plant. But that possibility was undercut by her position as a lowly "bundle girl." If the factory had a caste system, she was an "untouchable," at the very bottom of the heap. So she kept her counsel and wordlessly observed the traits that seemed to characterize each group of operators.

The women who set the zippers were an especially

clubby group, and that job seemed to attract the coarsest personalities. The machines they operated were deemed to take the greatest amount of skill, so their piece rate was higher than that of other operators performing simpler tasks like seaming or hemming. They formed an elite tacitly acknowledged by the other workers, and they held themselves apart, cackling with laughter at the bawdy jokes they tossed at each other above the din and whirr of their machines. The zipper setters ripped through a bundle of garments in no time, their apparatus set to work at maximum efficiency. The machine's "foot" would grasp the end of the zipper while nimble hands fed the fabric past flying needles. The setters would move rapidly from one garment to the next without stopping to snip the thread between them. This would make for more work for trimmers like Eleanor's cousin Suzanne at the end of the line, but the setters didn't care. It saved precious time on each bundle and put more money in their pocketbooks at the end of each week. The zipper setters never looked up when Eleanor made the rounds; they just grunted or nodded curtly when she left a new bundle for them.

In another section of the floor, the seamers were a quieter bunch. It took concentration to match two pieces of fabric together precisely before stitching an even seam. Yet the extra time and particular attention to each garment they sewed didn't earn them more money: the seamers' piece-rate compensation was less than the zipper setters were paid. Eleanor bristled a bit at the injustice of it. The procedure that took more time and effort should garner higher pay. Yet that wasn't the case. The seamers and hemmers were invariably the nicest people, she noted; they often looked up as she wheeled by, pausing to smile or say hello.

In the lunchroom or at coffee breaks, too, the women usually congregated with their own teams. The zipper setters would start in first, tossing teasing barbs in her direction, lipstick-stained cigarettes dangling from their lips. Or they would made nasty asides deliberately intended to exclude the single girls – dirty jokes that only the married women would "get," that would raise the color in Eleanor's cheeks. They seemed always to be laughing at her expense.

So it was no wonder that Eleanor didn't cultivate friendships with the women who worked the same long hours at the factory as she did. For one thing, most of them weren't Italian, but German or Irish or Polish. They would return to different neighborhoods and social circles at the end of each long day. When the whistle above the plant's main entrance screeched to end the work day, the insistent drone of the machines would fall silent in an instant, all at once, a momentary peace broken almost immediately by the shuffling of chairs and slamming of drawers. The low buzz of human conversation replaced the machines' din as the workers packed up for the day, hurrying to the front of the line for the first buses to leave the employee parking lot.

Some lucky ones drove their own cars to work. These women didn't seem ever to be in a rush to leave, buttoning their coats carefully and taking a few extra moments to tidy up their workspaces. These were often the same women whose husbands were away in the war, so they had the luxury of driving the family car to work – cars that would have been driven by the men of the house, now absent. These were the women who worked to fill the void of empty days and lonely nights, who went home to babies tended by grandmothers, or to children who were welcomed home from school by neighbors. Some of them had vertical flags with white stars hanging on their front windows, each star signifying a loved one – husband, son, brother – who was fighting in some distant land. These women kept their hands busy and prayed against the terrible day when a military van would park at their door, the doorbell would ring, and a telegram would arrive.

Work in the textile mill paid the bills, but it wasn't Eleanor's or her cousins' only aspiration. Eleanor's cousin Rosalie had recently completed a course in hairdressing at a local trade school. As she would proudly tell anyone listening, she was now a "licensed beautician." Rosalie was far too shy to practice her new craft on anyone other than immediate family, however, the upshot (not to say "benefit," since some of her attempts were still at the trial-and-error stage) being that the Luna girls now regularly sported the newest bob haircuts (or close to them), or had hair treated with the latest Marcel Waves.

Working with hair had given Rosalie a heightened interest in fashion generally. And there was much to entice a girl's fancy in the newest styles for women coming out of New York. She was forever bringing home a page torn from a fashion magazine read in the doctor's waiting room, or a newspaper clipping someone had saved for her, extolling the virtues of some new fashion trend. Between Zia Sarina's skill at the sewing machine and Rosalie's knack for fine needlework, the Luna girls never wanted for chic embellishments to their wardrobe, albeit less expensive handmade versions. They experimented with silk flowers worn as corsages or colorful scarves fashioned jauntily around a neckline. Their simple but well-fitting frocks, enhanced with the latest stylish touches, produced the lucky effect that all three young women usually put their best fashion foot forward.

Chapter 5

An Ironbound parish since 1889, Our Lady of Mount Carmel Roman Catholic parish is the third oldest Italian-Catholic Church in New Jersey. Parish members have included Mother Cabrini and future Bishops of Brooklyn and Paterson.

—from the parish Facebook page

June 1944, Newark, New Jersey
Chicly attired: on this sunny June Sunday, that was the impression the group of five young ladies made on casual observers in front of Our Lady of Mount Carmel church as they emerged from the taxi. They huddled momentarily in front of the church, brushing wrinkles from their clothes and patting their hair. Rosalie reached toward her sister. "Here, let me fix that curl," she offered as she set one stray ringlet at just the right angle on Suzanne's forehead.

Eleanor glanced down at her blouse and skirt, absentmindedly brushing and patting, pinching and straightening, setting herself to rights after the cramped cab ride. Her clothes would do. She withdrew a mirror and a small compact of face powder from her purse. Deftly flicking the lock on the mirror, she took in her reflection. Large wide-set brown eyes framed with dark lashes gazed back at her. Frowning, she turned first one way then the other, self-consciously studying her too-large nose with the prominent bump on its bridge: wasn't she supposed to have a "good side"? She never could find one. Eleanor ignored her best features – her eyes – and sighed instead at the sight of her worst, that all the fretting in the world would not change. At least, her pale ivory skin was clear and smooth.

Turning to and fro again, she dabbed powder on her nose and cheeks. Her rouge was sufficient; her cheeks seemed rosy enough. She squinted at the sky to gauge how strong the sun might be as the day wore on. She was certain to pink up with sunburn if she spent even fifteen minutes out of doors. With her index finger she smoothed full eyebrows that no amount of plucking seemed to tame. She outlined the edge of her lips with her fingernail, neatening the edges of the new dark red color she'd applied in the train. Another quick frown as she patted her springy brown curls, drawn up on top and falling to cover the nape of her neck in back. The style had looked so smart in Rosalie's fashion magazine, but the end result hadn't lived up to expectations. Why was her hair always so unruly just when she needed it to behave? She took one last resigned look in the mirror before snapping the compact closed and returning her things to her purse.

Eleanor turned and asked, "Fran, do you know where we are supposed to go, to try to find your cousin?"

"I have the letter right here--" Suzanne offered Mary the folded square of blue paper from her pocketbook.

Frannie nodded reassuringly to her companions and instructed, "After Mass, just follow me." With that, she snatched the letter from Suzanne's outstretched hand and quickly slid it into her purse. "Let's not be late for Mass. It's nearly eleven o'clock."

The five women ascended the few wide church steps in a tight group, joining worshippers from the parish and other visitors like themselves. Many of these people had brought their hopes to church that morning, lured by the prospect of meeting young men recently arrived from the old country. Never mind that these were prisoners of war: the parishioners pinned their faith on finding amongst them a neighbor, a *paesano* from villages in Calabria or Abruzzi that they still thought of as home, someone who could possibly bring them news of relatives whose fate was obscured by the fog of war.

Inching forward in the crowd, the women found their way to one of the few still-empty pews in the massive church. As she genuflected, Eleanor drew in a breath. The herbal aroma of carnations mixed with the saccharine trace of roses at the back of her throat, reviving memories of funeral parlors and death and sadness. The dominant spice of incense soon overtook it – not the overpowering waves of benediction after *novena*, while the priest held the monstrance high overhead, but the lingering peppery notes that always clung to the pews and the altar in the aftermath. She drew her sweater around her shoulders in the tomblike cool of the church's large apse, kneeling to say a prayer. To her left and somewhere behind her, a baby's wail arose, and she turned toward the sound. The embarrassed parents tried quietly hushing their child into silence, but the cries continued unabated. The mother rose hastily and left the pew as the little one's sobbing turned into loud hiccups. Eleanor suppressed a smile as the mother's echoing footsteps receded, and the infant's whimpers were finally swallowed into silence behind the heavy wooden doors of the crying room at the back of the church.

As the church bells sounded the hour for Mass, muffled footsteps could be heard at the rear of the church. The double doors swung wide and a procession of khaki-clad men walked solemnly up the center aisle toward the altar, and filed into the first few empty pews reserved with ribbons. The men were mostly dark-haired and swarthy; some were clean-shaven, but others sported well-trimmed mustaches. As they filed past her pew, Eleanor noticed an oval patch of dark green on their sleeves just below the left shoulder, with the word "Italy" embroidered on it in white. In their hands the men carried the same familiar pleated cloth caps she'd seen on American enlisted men. Leading the procession were two men who seemed to be in charge, wearing Army uniforms, hats in hand. They turned to face the prisoners when they reached the altar rail and watched while their charges sidled into the reserved pews and stood in place. Two more American soldiers brought up the rear of the column and waited in the aisle until all the prisoners were in place. The Americans faced each other and executed crisp salutes, then turned and found places in the pews with the prisoners. Then, on cue, with a muffled rustle of many feet moving in unison, the entire uniformed group then sat down together.

A hushed silence had fallen over the congregation as the prisoners marched into the church. Eleanor was struck by how ordinary these men seemed – they didn't look like The Enemy. In fact, they seemed very much like the young men she knew from her neighborhood at home. Were it not for the differentiating patch on their sleeves and a vague impression of foreign-ness, she thought she would not have been able to distinguish them from American soldiers.

Presently, a bell tinkled near the altar, signifying that the Mass was about to begin. The congregants rose to their feet when the priest entered from a side door behind the altar, with three altar boys attending. The priest's gold vestments shimmered in the rays of sunlight slanting down from stained glass windows behind the altar. The acolytes' red cassocks, mostly covered by snowy white surplices they wore on top, were bright spots on the altar steps. The priest began the Mass by signing himself with the cross, the worshipers reverently mimicking his actions. Then with his back to his flock, he took his place in front of the ornate altar and intoned the opening invocation. His singsong Latin chant formed the basso to the altar boys' muted responses in treble range, as the words of the Confiteor echoed through the church, its rhythm familiar and hypnotic.

The parishioners took their seats to hear the Word of God from the Old and New Testaments, then rose for the Gospel, and sat again for the sermon. Eleanor's mind drifted. Her eyes alighted on an old woman dressed in black several pews in front of her, mouthing the words of the rosary as she moved the beads through gnarled fingers. An old man in a threadbare suit knelt beside her, head bent in prayer. They, too, seemed familiar, a humble pair much like many others in her parish church at home, prayerfully oblivious to the celebrant's words.

Soon, the melodious chiming of the altar bells signaled the Consecration. Kneeling worshippers redoubled their pious poses, heads down and hands folded, as the priest held aloft first the sacred host and then the chalice of wine, his quiet Latin murmurs imperceptible from a distance. From a small table nearby the altar boys took in hand the gold patens – the signal the congregation had waited for. One pew at a time, communicants sashayed into the center aisle and shuffled forward to kneel at the altar rail for the Eucharist. After the priest laid the host on their tongues, many made a pious sign of the cross or paused for a reverential moment before rising to their feet and returning to their pews. One wave of prayerful communicants was replaced by another along the length of the altar rail, until everyone in the church had received the sacrament. An occasional cough, a throat cleared or a nose blown, were the only sounds as the Communion ritual proceeded. The soft rustle of fabric whispering past Eleanor's pew married with the quiet footfalls of many shoes on the marble floors as people filed down the aisle, then awkwardly clambered over the kneelers to regain their original seats.

Ablutions briskly concluded and sacred vessels set on the altar once more, the priest knew better than to prolong the final prayers: his flock's patience would be at an end. Parishioners were eager both for the bright sunshine outside and the bountiful Sunday dinner that awaited them in the church hall below. Intoning a quick prayer of thanksgiving, he turned, one hand outstretched, to administer the final blessing. Another soft peal of bells signaled that the Mass was at an end, and the celebrant left the altar with the acolytes by the doors through which he had entered, receding into the quiet confines of the sacristy.

Even before the sacristy doors closed, the congregation was on its feet, moving *en masse* from the cavernous church downstairs to the lower level. The sounds of conversation in Italian and English echoed through the church and on the stairways leading to the parish hall. Eleanor found herself swallowed by a swirl of color: bright summer dresses on the little girls, and their mothers and aunts, stood out against the men in somber jackets and starched white shirts. Friends called greetings to one another across the aisle, some stopping to hold conversations in the pews. One annoyed mother cuffed her overeager young son as he tried to push his way through the crowd. As the church slowly emptied, Eleanor strained for a better view of the front pews where the prisoners had been seated. The beribboned pews stood empty now: they must have passed downstairs to the church hall by a different staircase. Eleanor and her cousins found their exit blocked by a trio of middle-aged women talking animatedly, unaware of those waiting behind them. Frannie turned impatiently and whispered, to her sister Mary rather than to the offending women, "Mass is over! Let's get going!" The five young women turned and exited in the opposite direction, where the pew beside them stood empty.

Descending the stairs to the church hall, they were met by tempting aromas of roasted chicken and tomato sauce. Entering the vestibule of the lower hall, they found a table set up, staffed by a group of smiling women from the parish who served as a kind of welcoming committee. True to her earlier promise, Frannie seemed to know exactly what to do and stepped up to the table, immediately peppering one of the women with questions. Eleanor, her cousins, and their friend Mary hung back and waited, looking beyond the foyer into the expansive hall, where a sea of tables draped in white tablecloths were gaily decorated with flowerpot centerpieces of pink and yellow begonias with miniature American and

Italian flags perched among them. Folding chairs were tucked neatly under each table.

Soon Frannie approached her entourage with a white index card in hand and pulled them inside the hall.

"They had the Italian fellas register by last name. They're all over there." Frannie gestured toward one long wall where clusters of prisoners milled about expectantly. Large placards were taped to the walls above their heads: A—E, F—J. As Eleanor and her friends approached the soldiers, she could see they wore name tags. Flamminia, Pasquale. Giuliano, Carlo. Luciano, Calogero.

"You speak Italian better than any of us," Frannie urged Eleanor forward. "See if you can find him."

Squinting to make out the names on the prisoners' breast pockets, Eleanor made her way through the milling crowd, repeating her question as she searched among them. "Mollica, Tommaso? Mollica, Tommaso?"

Hearing her voice, one prisoner broke away from his group and approached them. Stagno, Giampaolo. Eleanor squinted at the name tag affixed to his shirt, and then took in his face. A pair of friendly hazel eyes gazed intently at her. A neatly trimmed mustache framed his upper lip, upturned in a half-smile. He looked at her and gestured questioningly with his cloth hat, echoing her query, "Mollica, Tommaso?"

Eleanor responded, *"Sì, sì!"* and pointed to her group who had pressed in closely behind her. Enunciating carefully, she asked, *"Lo conosci?* Do you know him?"

"Sì, sì!" Giampaolo echoed her words and broke into a broad grin. In a lilting Italian, he replied, "Yes, I know him. He's over there. I'll take you to him, *Signorina.*"

Giampaolo nodded and smiled at the rest of Eleanor's party, then he turned a broad back to them. *"Scusate,"* he intoned, making a path for them through the throngs of uniformed prisoners. He raised a hand in greeting to two other Italian soldiers standing a few feet away. As they approached, Eleanor read their name tags. Liguori, Vincenzo. Mollica, Tommaso.

Giampaolo nodded to his friends and launched into rapid-fire Italian, of which Eleanor caught only the tail end, in which he was explaining to Tommaso that "the pretty one was asking for you by name." Another lively exchange among the soldiers ensued, accompanied by a few quick laughs and nods before Giampaolo turned to her again with a smile. "Mollica, Tommaso!" he gestured grandly toward his compatriot with a flourish.

Eleanor stepped forward, peering at the soldier he had identified. *"Quelle sono le vostre cugine.* Those are your cousins," she explained, pointing toward Frannie and Mary huddled together not far away. She was suddenly self-conscious of her halting Italian, heavily overlaid with an American accent. Hearing the men speaking familiar Sicilian dialect, she relaxed and answered them similarly. "They are my friends and they came today to find you." The women had made their way to them and crowded behind her. Frannie pressed the blue air-mail letter into her hand.

Recognition flitted through Tommaso's eyes when he heard Eleanor speaking the dialect from home. Then he looked at the letter. *"Ah, sí, sí!"* he exclaimed, proffering his hand to his cousin. Frannie grasped it with an awkward pause, then laughed and embraced the soldier. She pointed to herself and enunciated, "Francesca," then, pointing to her sister, said, "Maria." The soldier nodded and embraced his other cousin.

An awkward silence befell the small group. Suzanne and Rosalie had been hanging back a bit, shyly observing the scene, until Eleanor drew them forward. She turned to Tommaso and took over the introductions. Pointing in turn, she introduced her cousins to him, using the Italian forms of their names. *"Suzanna e Rosalia Luna. Mie cucine,"* she explained, then added, "but we are like sisters." They smiled and shook Tommaso's hand in turn.

The awkward silence returned. Eventually Giampaolo nudged Tommaso with a sharp elbow, so the soldier turned to the women and said in Italian, looking toward Eleanor to translate, "Excuse me. My friends want me to introduce them." Grinning broadly, Vincenzo stepped forward eagerly and shook each woman's hand, enunciating his name with each handshake. Then Giampaolo made the rounds in turn, saving Eleanor for last. "*Stagno Giampaolo. Piaceri,*" he said, grasping her hand firmly and looking at her. "It is my pleasure." As Eleanor absorbed the kind curiosity with which he was gazing at her face, her heart skipped nervously. Giampaolo elongated the handshake for a beat longer until his pals jostled him and let loose more rapid-fire dialect that she didn't quite catch. More laughter.

With a start, Eleanor realized that her unofficial role as translator had everyone turning to her, waiting for what came next. She turned to the men and said, "*Assitamo nzemi?* Shall we sit together?" All three nodded enthusiastically. Then to her cousins, "We should find some seats." Frannie had already stepped briskly toward an empty table, her sister Mary at her side, and placed her sweater on one chair, her pocketbook on another.

The three soldiers crowded Eleanor as they made their way to the table Frannie had commandeered. They surmised that she was the only one who spoke the dialect more or less fluently. Although all of the girls had grown up hearing Italian spoken among the adults in their lives, they weren't expected to use it so they had embraced the language unevenly. In the mill where Rosalie worked among many Italian women from different parts of Italy, she had picked up quite a bit and would occasionally venture a dialect word or two. Frannie, the only married one among them, had inherited in-laws who spoke only Italian. Her Joe was serving with American troops somewhere in Europe, and while he had been away, of necessity her Italian vocabulary had grown. But her American-accented pronunciation was even more conspicuous than Eleanor's, with the result that her words frequently were garbled, frustrating her attempts to be understood. From the soldiers' banter all of the women could pick up a word here or there, but mostly they deferred to Eleanor.

Eleanor found herself seated between Giampaolo and Vincenzo, while Tommaso, the sought-after Italian relative, sat between his cousins Frannie and Mary. Suzanne and Rosalie took the seats on the other side of Giampaolo. But they may as well have been across the room, or in another place entirely. The handsome soldier seemed intent on devoting his attention entirely to Eleanor.

From the kitchen a parade of savory dishes emerged, carried by volunteers from the women's sodality. Before long, the clink of glasses and cutlery overtook the din of voices echoing through the space, as the guests took heaping quantities of roast chicken, ricotta-stuffed manicotti, and salad, and then fell ravenously on their food. Between bites of chicken, Eleanor tried making small talk in Italian with the two prisoners seated next to her. Turning from side to side, she tried not to favor either one, making conversation with each in turn. Eventually Vincenzo turned to Frannie, on his opposite side, who was making valiant attempts to engage him with her halting Italian. Vincenzo scooted his chair closer to her in an effort to decipher what she was saying. It apparently took all of his concentration as he leaned toward her, his brow wrinkling and his ear inclined to catch every syllable. On the other side of Giampaolo, Suzanne and Rosalie were looking about the room, wordlessly taking in the scene – and blissfully ignorant, apparently, of how hard Eleanor had been working to stave off the strained silence that had fallen between herself and Giampaolo. Exasperated, she addressed them pointedly in English.

"Anything to add to the conversation?" she whispered, at once desperate and sarcastic.

Suzanne glanced up in surprise. Rosalie, apparently oblivious to the remark, was engaged with one of the sodality ladies over her shoulder as she was offered seconds of manicotti from a large platter.

"I can't think of anything to say," Suzanne stammered. "You know I don't speak Italian well," she added defensively, lowering her gaze to the table and staring as she chased a last bite of salad around her plate with her fork.

Sensing the undercurrent of tension between the young women, Giampaolo gave her a kind look and said softly, "*Chi suces'?* What's happening?"

Eleanor lifted her chin to find him gazing directly into her eyes. They were hazel, she decided; or were they grey with brown flecks? Was that the same thing? The corners of his eyes crinkled now in a smile as she realized he'd caught her staring at him. Heat rose to her cheeks as she turned away, then glanced back quickly with a rueful smile.

"*Nenti.* It's nothing," she replied quickly, realizing that she sounded breathless.

"*Iu capisciu,* I understand," he supplied with a nod. "Your cousins do not speak Italian, and they are concerned about offending us."

"*Sí,*" Eleanor exhaled a relieved laugh. "Something like that." She let the subject drop rather than attempt anything more by way of explanation, and the moment passed.

"Tell me about your mother," he asked, and when she looked at him again, his eyes were lit with genuine interest. In the earlier back-and-forth, Eleanor had mentioned her mother several times. Now she sketched out the basic outlines of her biography for him – how her father had died still a young man and then her baby sister soon after, and her disconsolate mother began to imagine a kind of salvation in emigrating to America. Here, Eleanor's Zio Carmelo, had also been widowed when his wife died in childbirth after their youngest daughter was born. Eleanor filled in the details, explaining how her mother and her uncle joined forces to raise his brood of six children, living in the house across the street from Zio Carmelo's good friends, the Mollicas. When she mentioned that she was born in Florídia, the hometown of his two prisoner friends, Giampaolo's eyes sparked with recognition. But he let her continue with her story, uninterrupted, watching how she used her hands to gesture casually or to underscore a detail, never looking directly at him. When she realized she had gone on for probably too long, she stopped abruptly, placed her hands in her lap and looked at him apologetically.

There it was again: that crinkly-eyed half smile that drew up one side of his mouth unevenly, giving her the impression that he was amused but not laughing at her expense, or that he was thinking about a joke he wasn't willing to share yet. For reasons she couldn't fathom, Giampaolo's smile put her at ease. The tension dissipated and now, when the conversation ceased, the silence between them was no longer strained but companionable and comfortable.

So absorbed had they been in their conversation that Eleanor and Giampaolo failed to notice that the ladies of the Mount Carmel sodality had cleared and cleaned the tables efficiently all around them. They were still talking quietly, heads inclined together, when the scrape of chairs being stacked around them stopped their conversation abruptly. Eleanor rose and looked around to see her cousins headed toward the door. Giampaolo rose as well, and walked with her toward the stairs that led to the church's main entrance, but he touched her arm lightly before they joined the others.

"Eleanora," he began, "I enjoyed talking with you very much."

"*Piaceri,*" she intoned softly, echoing his lilting Sicilian pronunciation. "The pleasure was mine."

He paused, as if there was more he wanted to say, but Eleanor didn't give him the chance, hastening up the stairs to catch up with the rest of her party.

That evening, on the train, Eleanor's little group sat quietly as the wheels clacked rhythmically, bearing them toward home. The steady low hum of tracks clicking beneath them lulled her into a peaceful state, neither asleep nor fully awake. Her mind was back in the church hall, conversing with Giampaolo in low tones. The recollection felt more like a dream than a recent memory of a pleasant afternoon, as if she'd been watching herself sit and talk, eat and move through space. She tried to recall what they had talked about, and she couldn't bring to mind any specific thing. The only clear recollection in her mind were Giampaolo's hazel eyes attentively watching her and his lips breaking into that crooked grin.

Frannie broke into her reverie. "Tommaso said he could ask for a pass to visit us at home in two weeks."

Eleanor started abruptly at this piece of news. "Really?" she said after a pause, holding her breath.

"Yeah. The Italian prisoners in the Service Units can get weekend passes just like American GIs."

"Wow. I didn't know that." Eleanor's voice squeaked and she prayed she didn't betray too much excitement. "That'd be really nice for your mom and dad. To meet Tommaso, I mean."

When Frannie offered no additional explanation or comment, Eleanor continued.

 "Would he travel alone all that way?"

"Oh, no," Frannie replied. "All three Italian fellas would come."

Eleanor's heart skipped a beat as her friend continued.

"They have to apply for weekend leave, and an American soldier would have to accompany them."

"Can they do that?"

"Yes, but I guess sometimes that's the real hang-up," Frannie added. "Tommaso said sometimes they have to give the Americans a little 'encouragement' to come along," she nodded knowingly. "If you know what I mean."

"You mean, a bribe?" Eleanor's eyes went wide with surprise.

"Well, let's just say American soldiers don't take kindly to 'babysitting' duty in their free time unless they have an incentive."

"I see."

Then Frannie smiled, a satisfied look on her face. "But if they manage it, I can tell you, my parents will be very pleased."

"Oh?"

"Yes. In fact, my mother expressly told me to invite him for a visit." She shrugged. "She is so naïve. I didn't think there was really a possibility, Tommaso being a prisoner of war and all. I figured they'd all be kept behind locked gates all the time. So I didn't promise anything."

Rosalie, who'd been listening to the exchange intently, joined in. "One of the sodality ladies told me that these Service Units changed everything."

"Really?" Eleanor's intent expression encouraged her cousin to continue.

"Yes. She said that since Italy is now officially collaborating with the Allies, the U.S. government is giving these guys a break. If they signed up for a Service Unit, they get the same privileges as American GIs."

"Are the three of them all in a Service unit?" Eleanor wondered aloud.

"Must be," Frannie supplied. "Otherwise they wouldn't have been allowed off base today."

"What else did Tommaso say?"

"Well, he couldn't believe how great things were in the camps. Even before the Service Units started up."

At that, Rosalie shook her head. "For him to think that, they must have had it pretty rough in North Africa," she mused. "Or back home."

Eleanor realized that none of the men with whom they'd spent the day had elaborated on how they got here or what their experience had been like before they arrived. With a flush of embarrassment, she realized that she hadn't even asked. The conversation at the table had been somewhat constrained by the language difference, but when they spoke it was all small talk. Neither Giampaolo nor the others had volunteered anything about their war experience or the recent past. His polite inquiries had adhered to the present, or he had asked about her family and her life. It was pretty one-sided, she realized ruefully.

Maybe she would get a chance to change that if he came with Tommaso on the proposed visit.

"When will Tommaso let you know if he is able to come?" she probed Frannie for more.

"I'm not sure. But he did say he would ask about it as soon as they got back to camp." Guessing the real reason for Eleanor's curiosity, Frannie eyed her shrewdly. Eleanor blushed, realizing she couldn't put anything over on her friend. "Don't worry," she added with a knowing wink. "I'll let you know as soon as I know something."

Chapter 6

The late Olga and John Bianchi entertained small groups of Italian POWs in their home on Baltimore Avenue in Dundalk, Maryland. "They appreciated being invited into our homes," said Mike Pirisino, brother of John Bianchi.

—Susanna Rosa Molino, *Baltimore's Little Italy: History and Heritage of The Neighborhood*, chapter 3.

July 1944, Jamesport, Pennsylvania
For Eleanor, the next two weeks crept by. Several letters had passed back and forth between Tommaso and his American cousins, and Frannie generously shared all of the details. A date had been set for a weekend visit. The Italian soldiers would arrive on Saturday, accompanied by an American army private, and would stay until Sunday. With their son away at war and Mary and Frannie temporarily bunking together, the Mollica home had room to put the soldiers up in bedrooms going unused at the moment.

Saturday finally arrived, the day "the Italian fellas" were coming to visit. Today would be a day for a nice summer dress, Eleanor thought as she placed her bare feet on the still cool hardwood floor. Something light, cotton or seersucker. The gentle early-morning breeze stirring the curtains was already warm.

The entire Luna clan was invited across the street for a meal in the Mollicas' home when the soldiers were expected to arrive in early afternoon. With her mother and the older generation of Italian-speaking Mollicas on hand -- *Cummari* Angelina and *Cumpari* Giuseppe spoke Italian to one another at home –

Eleanor's translating skills probably wouldn't be in as much demand as two weeks earlier. And she was glad of it. She didn't relish being in the spotlight. Maybe today she could just be one of the crowd. She smiled to herself. She was looking forward to seeing Giampaolo Stagno again.

Just after noon, Eleanor and her cousins stood at the Mollicas' front door and rang the bell. Her mother would follow in due course. All had hands full of dishes and cloth bags with tempting things to add to *Cummari* Angelina's already laden table. The preparations had been going on for days now, and the Mollica household was a hive of activity since early that morning.

As she took the front steps, Eleanor admired the neat symmetry of green and white striped awning that overhung the porch, its fringed edges flapping lazily in the light breeze. *Cumpari* Mollica installed that awning painstakingly every spring, unfolding and tightening the metal frame and unraveling the canvas from its burlap cover. Just as carefully each autumn, he took it down, reverently rolling the canvas panels and collapsing the frame under the eaves of the porch where it would weather the winter.

The awning's shade would be welcome today. The calendar was two weeks into July and the day was a scorcher. From within the house, the enticing aroma of peppers roasting on the backyard grill drifted toward them as Mary opened the door. As soon as the weather turned warm, *Cumpari* Mollica would remove the heavy plastic tarp, brush away any remains of last summer's charcoal and scrub the grillwork in readiness for a new season. When the small stand of parsley he planted in one corner of the garden grew fragrant leaves on sturdy stems, he would trim a generous handful, securing the stems with a rubber band. *Cummari* Angelina would use the parsley nosegay like a brush, dousing every grill-bound item generously with a piquant mixture of olive oil, dried oregano, and lemon juice. Her husband would tend everything as it cooked to mouthwatering perfection – generous beef steaks and plump chicken breasts, thick slabs of eggplant, zucchini and portobello mushrooms halved lengthwise, onions quartered with root ends intact, and green and red bell peppers roasted whole.

The Luna girls made their way to the back of the house, where Mary and Frannie relieved them of their wares. Every surface in the bright steamy kitchen was covered with plates, cutting boards and produce of every imaginable sort. IEleanor marveled at how *Cummari* Angelina managed a kitchen that was very busy yet orderly and neat. This family matriarch was clearly used to preparing large meals for a horde of hungry mouths around her table. The girls embraced their hostess in turn and gave her a respectful kiss on each cheek. While her daughters returned to their cutting and chopping chores, *Cummari* Angelina deftly shooed the girls out of the kitchen to await their guests in the cooler confines of the living room.

Eleanor, Suzanne, and Rosalie had just settled comfortably on the sofa when a blue Ford station wagon with wood-paneled doors pulled up at the curb outside. Five men in military uniform piled out, laughing and boisterous, and ambled up the steps leading up to the Mollicas' front porch. The soldiers' tan shirts were neatly pressed: there were crisp pleats in the trousers and they wore beige neckties. Three of the soldiers had the "Italy" patch on their sleeves; a fourth bore a red keystone insignia and the last had one chevron stripe. They unfolded their pleated garrison caps and put them on as they approached the door. The three Italians hung back while their American chaperones stepped forward. Showing himself to be the leader of the troop, the soldier with the chevron rang the bell.

Eleanor had heard the commotion in the street when the men arrived, and from her seat on the couch, she craned her neck through the doorway to catch a first glimpse of the visitors.

"Hullo, ma'am, I'm Private Second Class Pasquale Tinelli." The soldier's voice carried clearly into the house as *Cummari* Angelina hastened to open the door, a bit flummoxed to hear the soldier's polite greeting in English when she was expecting Italian soldiers. Private Tinelli shook her hand. "This here is Private Anthony Ferraro," he said, pointing to the other American GI. "But you can just call me Patsy and him Tony." He grinned affably, removed his hat and, at her welcoming gesture, sidled past his hostess into the living room. "Something smells terrific!"

The three Italians shuffled in behind the Americans nervously, removing their caps as they entered the house.

When Tommaso saw his uncle peering from behind *Cummari* Angelina, he recognized him immediately from family photographs. There was no mistaking the striking family resemblance. For *Cumpari* Mollica, it was like looking at a younger, healthier version of himself. Years of hauling and placing heavy stones as a master mason and bricklayer had taken its toll on the older man.

Tommaso shouted impetuously, *"Zio!"* and went to embrace his uncle. They clung to one another for a moment, and when they parted, Eleanor glimpsed tears misting the eyes of both men. Then Tommaso turned to his aunt and greeted her warmly. *"Zi' Angelina!"* he cried and enfolded her in a hearty embrace.

The emotion of the moment was contagious. The Luna girls had stood up when the men entered, and now they hung back by the staircase as Mary and Frannie greeted their cousin. Recovering himself after the poignant greeting, *Cumpari* Mollica turned his customary charm on the two American chaperones and shook hands heartily.

Eleanor's eyes searched the room until she lighted on Giampaolo. He was the last to enter the room, and she found him staring at her. Then a bright smile lit his face. Amidst

67

the general melee of greeting and embracing, he waited a few moments, then stepped across the room and stood right in front of her. "A pleasure to see you again, Eleanora." He extended a hand. Eleanor felt a catch in her throat as she took it in her own. Giampaolo's hazel eyes captured hers, and she exhaled, realizing that she had been holding her breath. When he broke their grasp and she was seated on the sofa once again, Eleanor looked down to find her hands trembling. Giampaolo confidently took the place next to her.

Introductions complete, a jumble of English and Italian conversation swirled about them. The American soldiers chatted amiably with her cousins. *Cummari* Angelina was already deep in discussion with Vincenzo. Frannie and Mary had whisked themselves away to the kitchen to secure cold beverages. And *Cumpari* Mollica was already leading the whole group toward the back door for a tour of his pride and joy: his kitchen garden, replete with lush plants of basil, tomatoes ripening on the vines, and roses in glorious bloom nodding on a carefully tended trellis.

That left Eleanor and Giampaolo alone together on the sofa.

Through the lightweight screen door the substantial outline of an older woman could be seen ascending the front steps. Her simple gray cotton dress was well-made, conforming well to her squarish frame. Her steel-gray hair was meticulously combed and tightly pulled back in a neat bun at the nape of her neck. As Donna Sarina had crossed the street, a basket of ripe peaches in her outstretched arms, she glanced sideways and greeted a neighbor on a nearby porch with a wordless nod. Then she turned and rang the doorbell.

Eleanor jumped to her feet, ready to help her mother, but Frannie materialized from the kitchen and beat her to the door. "Donna Sarina!" she called out warmly as she swung open the screen and relieved the older woman of the fruit basket.

"Mr. Cianci brought his truck around this morning." Speaking in her lilting Italian, Donna Sarina gestured to the fruit. "So I bought some for you. *Talé,* here you go." She gazed about the room and smiled when she saw her daughter. "Ah. You're here."

Behind her, Giampaolo had already scrambled to his feet and waited, hat in hand, to be introduced.

"Mamá, this is Giampaolo Stagno." Eleanor enunciated clearly in English to her mother, then stepped away as he extended his hand. The soldier nodded deferentially and addressed Eleanor's mother in Italian as he took her hand. *"Piaceri.* Signora Fazzio, it is my great pleasure to meet you."

Relief flickered in Donna Sarina's eyes on hearing the soldier address her in Italian. She knew English well enough to make her way at work in the factory, on the bus, at the bank, or in the local shops. At home she and Eleanor usually communicated in their native Sicilian dialect, but of late her daughter had started encouraging her mother to become more comfortable speaking English. The war had redoubled Eleanor's fears that as Italians they would be suspect among their neighbors. And that could lead to trouble. Eleanor didn't want any trouble.

The Italian-language newspaper *Unione,* to which the family subscribed, had recently reported frightening headlines from the west coast that were the stuff of Eleanor's worst nightmares. Italians living in America, whether they were citizens or not, were now classified as "enemy aliens" by the U.S. government. Some had been imprisoned; others were being ejected from their homes and sequestered in certain parts of the cities where they lived and worked. In coastal California cities like Monterrey and Eureka had become home to them, they had established modest businesses and had built new lives. Then war had come, changing the calculus of their American neighbors' regard of immigrants from Axis Power nations from diffidence to suspicion to outright hatred. In the west, families like the Mollicas, with sons fighting the war as American enlisted men, were forced to observe stringent curfews and to abandon their livelihoods. Italian fishermen were barred from their boats, afloat but standing idle now in the very piers and ports where the men had plied their trade. Although California seemed very far away, such things could happen here. Speaking English to each other, Eleanor reasoned, was one small insurance policy against the possibility that her family's loyalties would be questioned. They were American citizens, after all.

"The pleasure is mine," responded Donna Sarina to Giampaolo in Italian with a small smile. Eleanor glanced at her mother's face. The older woman examined the young soldier keenly, her countenance a mask of politeness as she took him in from the buttons of his well-pressed shirt to the tips of his well-shined shoes. Dim approval seemed to register there, Eleanor realized with some relief.

Cummari Angelina emerged from the kitchen, smiling and perspiring. She wiped her hands on her apron and embraced her friend, kissing her soundly on both cheeks. The conversation continued in Italian. "Sarina, such beautiful fruit you brought! You shouldn't have."

"Just something small, for after the meal."

"Won't you sit? Francesca, get Donna Sarina some of that good almond milk from the icebox."

"No, no," Donna Sarina remonstrated, remaining on her feet. "I can't stay. I have sewing to do. I'll return later, for dinner." With that, Eleanor's mother turned and walked briskly through the screen door onto the porch. *Cummari* Angelina called after her, pressing her to stay, but Donna Sarina was already down the steps and crossing the street.

Frannie sidled up to Eleanor and whispered conspiratorially so that only she could hear. "Sure. She came just to bring the fruit." Eleanor didn't miss the smirk on Frannie's face as she blushed and took her seat again on the sofa. Frannie slid back toward the kitchen without another word.

Unaware of the exchange but still reeling a bit from Donna Sarina's stern inspection, Giampaolo sat down again, giving her a sheepish smile. They were alone again. He broke the silence.

"The weather's been very hot, hasn't it?" he asked her in Italian.

"Yes," she responded, "But it's always like this in July. It'll get cooler in late August, and then it'll get hot again. Just when the children must go back to school." She smiled at the memories of donning a dark serge uniform and a long-sleeved blouse on those hot days of early September.

Giampaolo seemed to relax a bit. He's nervous too, Eleanor realized with a smile and changed the subject. "What would you be doing back at the camp, if you weren't here visiting with us today?"

He lifted his shoulders in a noncommittal shrug. "On Saturdays and Sundays we can do what we like." When Eleanor's face registered surprise, he continued. "On weekdays, they take us by bus down to the docks. We sweep the decks, we unload the boats. We put the boxes in trucks. We do whatever work they give us." He paused, then added proudly, "And we get paid for it."

Eleanor's eyes widened again. "Really?"

"Yes. Eight American dollars each month. They used to give us only coupons for the camp store, but now we get American dollars too, that we can spend anywhere, even if we leave the camp. I usually use mine on food and cigarettes."

Suddenly mindful of her manners, Eleanor jumped to her feet. "Oh my goodness!" she exclaimed in English, then switched back to Italian. "Are you hungry? I am so sorry I forgot to ask when you arrived."

Giampaolo laughed, "No, no," but Eleanor was not dissuaded.

"*Scusami,*" she said, touching his hand lightly and dashing off to the kitchen, returning soon with a bowl bearing two of the peaches her mother had just brought and a small plate of *biscotta*. "Frannie will bring beverages."

Her friend followed, carrying a tray of glasses with ice and bottles of beer and soft drinks. "Here we go," Frannie said as she settled the tray on the coffee table in front of the pair. At that moment the rest of the group burst through the door, their garden tour complete. Like pigeons homing to their mark, the soldiers had followed the snacks and drinks into the living room.

"I'll get some more glasses," Frannie said, scurrying back to the kitchen.

Vincenzo, his eyes gleaming, pointed to the familiar silhouette of the soda bottles lining the tray. "Coca Cola!" he shouted with glee, showing off his best American accent.

From that point, the afternoon and evening had passed too quickly. Her mother reappeared for the meal, seating herself at one end of the table between her hosts. The trio of the elder generation conversed in low tones, muffled almost entirely by the boisterous mixture of English and Italian from the soldiers and young women, seasoned by frequent peals of laughter. Eleanor wished she could read her mother's mind as she sat impassively at the far end of the room. Only an occasional glance from Donna Sarina in Giampaolo's direction, just to Eleanor's left, gave her to understand that her mother was taking her measure of the man.

After the meal, the young people retired to the cool shade of the backyard. In deference to the Italian soldiers, *Cumpari* Mollica had set up a game of bocce on the soft grass. The soldiers formed into teams designed to let the Italians show off their skills. Only when the long summer evening's light had begun to fade did Eleanor realize that she couldn't recall the specifics or pleasantries of the day. She only remembered

Giampaolo's simple kindnesses. Whenever he looked at her, his hazel eyes twinkled warmly and her heart skipped a beat.

On Sunday morning, with already warm sunlight streaming in the window, Eleanor opened her eyes and a rush of excitement flooded over her. She washed and dressed and joined her cousins in the kitchen, where Rosalie was pouring chilled coffee into tall glasses.

"Too hot to eat this morning," her cousin said, gesturing to the drinks. "This should be enough. Want milk in yours?" She passed glasses to Eleanor and Suzanne. Eleanor opened the refrigerator and added a splash of cold milk from the bottle before lifting the cool liquid to her lips.

The caffeine soon enlivened her. The girls made quick work of their drinks, leaving empty glasses in the sink just as her mother appeared in the doorway. "Ready?" she inquired, gloves and purse in hand. Donna Sarina Fazzio never stepped out the front door of her spotless home without being completely and well put together: dress, stockings, hat, and gloves in fine weather, an expertly-tailored coat in cooler seasons. They walked in single file toward the door, and with passing glances and last-minute pats to hair and makeup as each passed the large mirror over the living-room sofa, the four women stepped onto the front porch.

The soldiers and the Mollica girls waited on the sidewalk across the street, a cluster of beige uniforms brightened by Frannie's and Mary's flowered cotton dresses. The Luna girls and Donna Sarina crossed the street and the group set off toward the church.

The sidewalk on their street was wide enough for only two to walk abreast. Before she could turn around, Eleanor found that Giampaolo had sidled up to her, a friendly smile on his handsome face. *"Bon giornu, signorina Eleanora,"* he greeted her formally, touching two fingers to his cap. Eleanor noticed a small circle of green fabric adorned his hat, matching the one on his sleeve, with "Italy" embroidered in white letters. She returned the smile and fell in step beside him.

After a few short blocks, the pavement grew more crowded with churchgoers as they approached Holy Family church. Ascending three wide steps leading to the carved archway of the entrance, Eleanor paused as Giampaolo reached in front of her to hold open the door. Inside, the cool marble columns of the church soared above her. The familiar scent of incense rose to her nostrils, mixed with the aroma of wax from candles melting on the side altar. She reached for the holy water font, dipped two fingers in, and made the sign of the cross. The group filed into the pews together, and Eleanor found herself kneeling next to Giampaolo. It would be difficult to concentrate on the Mass with him so close by. She glanced over her shoulder and saw her mother installed in the pew behind them. A tiny frown – her mother's patented look of disapproval – crinkled the older woman's brow. Eleanor turned back to face the altar just as the bells sounded to signify the beginning of the Mass.

Today, the customary intonation of the Latin prayers hadn't lulled her into the habitual stillness that Eleanor equated with prayer. Today, she was only keenly aware of the man at her side. Giampaolo was silent throughout the service. The sermon was given in Italian at this Mass, in deference to elder parishioners, but it benefitted their guests and another small group of Italian prisoners who were visiting this morning. Only once had she chanced a fleeting look at him: he was smiling to hear Italian spoken from the pulpit. Through the communion to the last "Amen" and the final chiming of the bells as the priest left the sanctuary, she had scarcely been oblivious to the familiar ritual. Her entire being had been alert to Giampaolo Stagno sitting, standing, kneeling beside her.

After Mass, a veritable river of parishioners flowed down the narrow stairs, coming to rest at long communal tables where the Communion breakfast had been set. The rasp of wooden folding chairs scraping the linoleum floor muffled voices as people jostled for places at the tables. As the church bulletin boards proudly announced, the mothers' club of Holy Family Parochial School was hosting this morning's Communion breakfast. A dozen or so women lined one side of the church hall, smiling in welcome, wearing aprons over their Sunday dresses and waiting expectantly to serve the hungry communicants.

The group descended on an empty table. Giampaolo subtly steered Eleanor to·the seat next to his. They all helped themselves to hot coffee from carafes, and bowls of sugar and pitchers of cream made their way from hand to hand around the table. While they were awaiting their breakfast, Giampaolo rose from his chair and made his way to the other side of the table. Bowing deferentially to Donna Sarina, he spoke in low tones in her mother's ear. Eleanor watched as two spots of color rose in her mother's cheeks. She seemed to hesitate briefly, then turned toward the young soldier with a tight smile and a small nod of her head. Giampaolo rose to his full height, his face happy and his cheeks flushed, and hastened back to his seat next to Eleanor. Wordlessly, he sat down again, a triumphant grin turning up one side of his mustache.

A bespectacled young mother in a yellow apron smiled at the soldiers as she set a platter of scrambled eggs and another of bacon and toast on their table. Everyone tucked into the food hungrily. Eleanor helped herself to some eggs, intrigued and disconcerted equally by the exchange between Giampaolo and her mother. She gave him a sidelong glance. He looked around the table, waiting until everyone else was absorbed by the food or by conversation, and then he leaned toward her.

"Your mother has given her permission that I might write to you," he whispered in her ear.

Eleanor's eyebrows lifted in surprise, and she turned toward him. Giampaolo was smiling, his sunny hazel eyes warm, waiting for her reaction. Even as her heart turned over, Eleanor schooled her face to cover her excitement. But she couldn't stop the heat that suffused her cheeks and caused her to quake inside. Realizing he was waiting for her to say something, she whispered, "All right. Yes. I would like that."

As they walked back to the house, Giampaolo slowed his pace to let them lag a few paces behind the rest of the group. Sensing his intent, Eleanor's heart beat faster as she slackened her steps to match his. His hand found hers, and he threaded their fingers together.

"We will be leaving now, Eleanora," he spoke softly.

"I know."

"I will write to you."

"I will write back."

"Perhaps you can visit me at the camp? The other Italians have visitors on the weekends."

"Perhaps."

Noticing his face fall as he read indecision in her answer, Eleanor leaned in and added with emphasis, "Yes, I will come to see you. I would like that very much."

Giampaolo's face broke into a sunny smile. *"Ti vuliu ben' assai, Eleanora.* I like you very much."

"Magari iu," she answered, this time with a tremulous smile of her own. "Me too."

Chapter 7

Military personnel felt the most connected to home through reading about it in letters. Civilians were encouraged to write their service men and women about even the most basic activities. Daily routines, family news, and local gossip kept the armed forces linked to their communities.

–"Letter Writing in World War II," in *Victory Mail* exhibit of National Postal Museum, The Smithsonian

July 1944, first letters
A few days later, a letter arrived for Eleanor. She unfolded a single sheet of stationery, taking in Giampaolo's spidery handwriting in blue ink, and began reading.

16 luglio, 1944

Carissima Eleanora,

I am pleased to write this letter to you since seeing you again last weekend. I was also glad to have the chance to meet your esteemed mother. I am very sorry, I can write only in Italian. But you speak Italian so well, I feel sure you will be able to understand my letter.

I hope you are all well. I felt so happy and welcome at the home of the Mollicas, and so did my friends. We all had a wonderful time, but most of all I speak for myself. I was very glad to see you again.

Life here at the camp is nothing special. On most days we board the bus in the morning and they take us to the waterfront to do whatever jobs they have that day. Loading and unloading the ships, sweeping the decks, running small errands, simple things. Our working hours are very regular, we are at the docks until about 5 or 6 o'clock, with a break to eat in the middle of the day. We get a couple of rest times twice a day – I think you call them coffee breaks? Coffee and American donuts!

The food in America is very good, although it is different from home. We have a big breakfast every day – eggs, ham, toasted bread. That's something I'm not used to. In cold weather there is hot cereal, sort of like the cuccía we have for Santa Lucia, only smoother and made of oats. You eat oats here! At our farm in San Marco, we feed oats to the animals. The same with corn. Imagine how surprised I was, when I got to America, and saw whole ears of boiled corn on the table at suppertime! In Indiana we ate a lot of corn. The only thing I don't like is the American bread. It's too soft!

We always have a lot of food. In the mess hall, we take a tray and go up to the window. We can have as much as we like! A few of the fellows from my company were cooks back home in Sicily, and they got permission to take over the kitchen one or two days a week. The American officers always come into the mess hall on those days! They really love their spaghetti and sauce. So we have pasta sometimes too.

There's going to be another chicken dinner in two weeks at the church in Newark, not next Sunday but the one after that. I hope you will have the time to travel and see us again? It will be just like last time. There will be Holy Mass first and then dinner. Please write soon and let me know if you will come.

With my best regards to your cousins and especially your mother,

Affectionately,

Giampaolo Stagno

19 luglio, 1944

Dear Giampaolo,

Your letter arrived yesterday and I was glad to hear your news. I am happy to respond in Italian.

It must be interesting going off to work at the port each day. Do you see lots of Navy ships? I would guess the harbor would be full of them. It must also be nice to smell the salt air every day. We don't get to the seaside much, although my cousins Suzanne and Rosalie and I went to Atlantic City in southern New Jersey last summer. There's a wooden trail built over the sand – we call it a "boardwalk" – where you can stroll and ride bikes. There are lots of little shops selling different things, food and trinkets. We always bring salt-water taffy home with us. Have you ever had it? It's sort of like torrone, *a soft chewy candy, and it comes in lots of different flavors.*

The weather continues to be hot here. At least it's good for ripening the tomatoes. We always put up a lot of tomatoes and sauce in August. Also peaches, and if my mother can get them, fresh quinces, to make jelly.

I was glad to hear that you get more free time on the weekends. I heard that some of the churches and sodalities like Our Lady of Mount Carmel are taking groups of the Italian soldiers into New York City for shows and concerts. Have you been to New York City yet?

My friends the Mollicas are planning to come to see their cousin Tommaso again at the church in Newark next time. They have asked me to come with them. My mother will also come. I am looking forward to seeing you again in less than two weeks.

Sincerely,

Eleanora Fazzio

Chapter 8

Approximately five million Italian Americans lived in the United States in 1940, and this demographic meant that many ISU members had relatives and friends that could come to visit them. Saturday evenings and Sundays were the two days of the week when most visits took place.

—Conti and Perry, *World War II Italian Prisoners of War in Chambersburg*, p. 61.

A ugust 1944, Newark, New Jersey
Those summer days passed at a snail's pace. One day followed another in the airless brick factory buildings with no let-up from either the stifling heat or the stultifying routine. At least there was some relief at night. At sunset, her cousin Angelo might walk a few blocks to the local ballfield to watch a baseball game. The girls might pull up chairs in the darkened garden, sitting and sipping iced tea, watching fireflies flit among the foliage. In the kitchen, Donna Sarina might slice up cold juicy wedges of watermelon to slake their summer thirst. Then Angelo would return with a big smile on his face and animatedly describe each inning, each foul ball, each exciting strike-out. Angelo's tales of athletic prowess fell mostly on deaf ears of his family full of women, except for his quiet sister Suzanne, whose eyes would shine as she drank in every last detail of the great American pastime.

This year, on the all-too-brief weekends that punctuated each long work week, Eleanor kept her hands busy with household chore. But her mind often strayed to Giampaolo. She couldn't suppress the small thrill of anticipation that coursed through her every time she thought of seeing him again.

On the day of their outing to Newark, Eleanor rose early and dressed with care, dabbing a bit of cologne behind both her ears and on her wrists. The cool liquid felt good on her warm skin. She lifted a wrist to her nose and smiled at the delicate jasmine scent. She was going to see Giampaolo again.

The train chugged to a stop in Newark as the conductors called for passengers to disembark. She caught a faint wisp of the jasmine scent as she jumped down from the steps and turned to help her mother. Only Frannie and Mary had joined the two of them this time, and they had gone ahead in search of a taxi.

"What a long trip!" Donna Sarina exclaimed, brushing the wrinkles off her dress and reaching up to re-insert the pearl-tipped hatpin holding the simple woven straw pillbox in place. Her graying hair was neatly tucked up in its usual bun at her neck, and she patted it to make sure every strand was in place.

"Oh, *mamá*, it's not that bad," Eleanor responded in Italian to her mother, allowing her exasperation to show. She brushed the front of her blue linen dress, regarding with pleasure the neat pin-tucks that defined the shape of the bodice from neckline to waist. She smoothed the skirt and then enfolded her arm in the crook of her mother's elbow to hasten her along.

The pair climbed the stairs and crossed the cavernous waiting room of Newark Penn Station to the wide doors that led to the street. The Mollica girls were waiting at the curb with a taxi driver, his cab doors wide open to receive them. He tipped his hat politely to Eleanor's mother as they approached. The women climbed in and settled for the short ride to the church. In a few minutes, Donna Sarina made the sign of the cross as the church's rosy yellow brick facade came into view. Eleanor climbed out of the cab first to assist her mother, while Frannie paid the driver. The four of them formed a small circle on the sidewalk, securing bobby-pins, straightening skirts, brushing blouses. Churchgoers were milling about and climbing the steps to claim a spot for Mass in the church's cooler interior.

Eleanor consulted her watch. "We have about ten minutes before the Mass will begin," she noted, and then glanced up to the arched entrance. To one side of the open door she spotted Giampaolo and Tommaso. He saw them at the same instant and motioned to his friend. The pair of soldiers dashed down the steps to join them on the sidewalk.

"Bon giornu, Donna Fazzio." Giampaolo respectfully greeted her mother first, then cast a long gaze at Eleanor, taking her in from head to toe. *"Bon giornu, Eleanora,"* he said softly.

Eleanor felt a blush rise from her shoulders to the roots of her hair. *"Bon giornu, Giampaolo,"* she managed to stammer.

In a few moments the two Italians arranged themselves between the women in pairs, Tommaso with his cousins on either arm and Giampaolo taking charge of Eleanor and her mother. He advanced slowly, giving Eleanor's mother ample time to negotiate the stairs. Soon they were inside the church, which was filling rapidly. The pews were a kaleidoscope of color: Italian prisoners in drab khaki interspersed with the bright summer dresses and sober sport coats of their American relatives and friends. The little party made their way down the center aisle and were soon being guided into two pews. As she followed Giampaolo's lead, Eleanor realized that a couple of buddies were already saving places for them in the front of the church. She nodded and smiled gratefully to Giampaolo as they took their seats.

As was her habit befo re Mass, Donna Sarina knelt down and reached inside her purse for a small pouch of soft leather from which she withdrew her rosary beads. Even if she didn't have enough time to complete the entire rosary before the mass began, she'd always counseled Eleanor to begin, at least, and finish the prayers after Holy Communion. To Eleanor's surprise, Giampaolo drew a set of black rosary beads from his pocket and commenced to pray, his lips moving silently in the prayers as his fingers slipped over the beads, one at a time. Eleanor followed suit, rifling in her pocketbook for her rosary; but her prayers were distracted by the scene all around her. A lot of people-watching could be accomplished before the bells rang and the priest made his way to the altar.

Eleanor recalled nothing of the hour-long service except the momentary thrill of Giampaolo's arm on hers when they rose to receive the Eucharist, and his hand a gentle touch at her back guiding her back into the pew.

After mass, a wave of awkward silence fell between the couple as they made their way into the church hall that had been set once again for Sunday dinner.

"*Comu stai?* How have you been?" Giampaolo began in Italian, then he chuckled softly. "I should have asked before…"

"*Staiu bonu, grazî e tu?*" Eleanor responded, grateful that he'd broken the ice. "I'm well, thanks, and you?"

"As well as a prisoner of war can be, I suppose," he grinned, and then turned to face her. "You look beautiful in that dress. That color of blue becomes you. *È beddu.*"

Eleanor's cheek flushed. "Thank you," she murmured, then caught a stern look in her mother's eye.

Donna Sarina was a woman used to making her own way in the world. She glanced briefly at the tables that were already starting to fill with Italian prisoners and their American visitors.

"Donna Sarina," Giampaolo interrupted, as if reading her mind. "My friends have reserved a table for us. I hope that will be all right." He turned and lifted a hand to several of his compatriots who were waving them over to an empty table they had secured.

The older woman's stern expression softened just a bit as they made their way to the seats being held for them. As they approached the table, Eleanor recognized the other Sicilian prisoner, Vincenzo, as well as Patsy Tinelli and Tony Ferraro, the two American soldiers who had accompanied the Italians to Jamesport a few weeks before. They had tipped up the chairs at the table where they were seated, to hold places for the group.

Patsy greeted them jovially. "Hiya! Welcome to Newa'k!" he practically shouted over the steadily rising din at the tables around them. "Tony and me, we volunteered to accompany these guys because we know the grub will be swell – much better than the mess hall back at camp," he remarked with a knowing shove of his elbow into Tony's ribs. Tony grinned widely and nodded.

Everyone angled for a chair. Giampaolo held one out for Donna Sarina, then installed Eleanor in another one and himself next to her. Mouth-watering aromas enveloped the hungry diners from the large kitchen at one corner of the room. Generous bowls of pasta with tomato sauce were the first to emerge, followed by trays laden with meatballs and sausage cooked in the same sauce. Baskets of crusty bread and bowls of freshly grated cheese already stood on each table. After the tasty feast was consumed and plates were cleared, large bowls of tossed salad greens were passed. Then the diners began helping themselves from the array of glistening fresh fruit arranged in decorative baskets that doubled as centerpieces on every table. Small paring knives set on each table made quick work of apple cores and peach pits. While Eleanor looked on, Giampaolo neatly scored a fresh pear, peeled it, and divested it of its core, arranging the cut-up fruit in neat slices next to Eleanor's napkin. "*Máncia*, eat," he urged her gently with a smile, pointing to the napkin. She took a piece and smiled, mouth closed, as the pear's sandy flesh left a sweet burst of flavor on her tongue.

After the fruit course, large plates mounded with cookies, fragrant with scents of lemon and almond, were served. Coffee was poured, and the sweets disappeared quickly, with only a few telltale crumbs left behind.

As the guests rose from the tables to stretch their legs, the large doors to one side of the hall were thrown open, revealing beyond them the lush greenery of the rectory garden encased in a tall wrought iron fence. Really a small enclosed private park on the parish grounds, the garden was awash in color and sunshine. Roses abounded in neatly tended beds and climbed the trellises strategically placed along carefully tended pebble footpaths. Shiny wooden benches peeked between the greenery, offering pleasant shaded nooks in which to rest. Standing by the open doors, the pastor stretched out his arms in welcome and invited everyone to stroll the garden at their leisure.

Giampaolo sprang to his feet. *"Caminamu n po'?* Shall we take a little walk?" he inquired hopefully, looking first at Donna Sarina and then casting a glance at Eleanor to include her in the invitation. As it was midday and the hottest part of the afternoon, Eleanor feared that her mother would say no, so she quickly added, in English, *"Mamá,* maybe you'd like to sit for a while in the shade on one of those nice benches and get some fresh air?" Concern clouded Giampaolo's expression until the older woman acquiesced. "But not for too long," Donna Sarina remarked with a curt nod.

As they proceeded to the garden, Eleanor leaned over and whispered to Giampaolo to find a bench for her mother. The couple installed the older woman in a secluded spot, whereupon she fished a black lace fan out of her handbag, splayed it open and began fanning herself vigorously. Her expression was impassive as her daughter took the soldier's arm. They walked away slowly, meandering along the well-tended paths that snaked through the garden.

"Eleanora," Giampaolo began in Italian, his tone serious, "I have to tell you something that you might not believe." He paused before continuing. "I really like being in America."

Surprised, she laughed at first, then turned to him, catching the drift of his meaning. "You mean because you're a prisoner? I might not believe you?"

"Yes, I am a prisoner of war," he replied in a somber tone. "But this is not the worst thing that could happen to me. As a prisoner here in America I am treated better than I was as a soldier at war, in the Italian Army, or even as a prisoner in Africa, in a French prison. America is a big, strong, powerful country," he continued. "I see that every day at the port. I saw it from the trains when I came from Indiana to this place. Then he added with a touch of melancholy, "The war is not being fought here. There is only destruction wherever the war is. Italy is in ruins now. Especially Sicilia."

"Do you miss home?" she asked.

"Of course. I miss my family. I miss the farm where I worked the land with my father and my brothers. I love my homeland, too," he finished wistfully.

A silence fell between them. Eleanor tried to change the subject.

"I know America has made a big impression on you, but it's not always wonderful here."

"What do you mean?"

"We had to struggle when my mother and I first came." Eleanor tightened her hold on Giampaolo's arm as she began to tell the story of a little girl and the strange new place in which she had landed, a place that didn't feel at all like home.

Chapter 9

Certain occupations were targeted by Italian immigrants who provided the expertise and training to allow new workers to enter the workforce. These were barbers, masons and garment workers. At the turn of the 20th century in cities such as New York, Newark, NJ and Philadelphia, PA, one in five barbers were Italian immigrants. In the case of masons and stone workers, the number was about 1 in 10. Garment workers numbered about 1 in 20. These percentages increased significantly from 1900 through 1930.

—ItalianTribune.com, in "Italian Americans and Organized Labor"

January 1920, Jamesport, Pennsylvania

It was a bitterly frigid January day when her Zio Carmelo had met Eleanor and her mother on the platform of the Jamesport train station. This small American city with German roots and tidy brick row houses was strange and overwhelming. And it was so cold. Her uncle lifted her bodily from the train steps and enveloped her in a crushing hug, affectionately dubbing her with the pet name that would stick with her until he died: "Noriedda! Noriedda!"

Carmelo Luna was a tall, solid man, his broad shoulders honestly earned in his trade as a stonemason. He had a brush of a graying mustache and long sideburns that skirted the lines of his long face. She could still recall the rough brush of his whiskers on her cheek and the scent of pipe tobacco that clung to the lapel of his coat. Setting Eleanor on the pavement next to him, he had then embraced his sister, rocking her back and forth in his arms for several minutes. When the pair separated, she saw the glistening tracks of tears on both of their faces.

Picking up their meager belongings on his strong shoulders, he led the anxious newcomers through the melee of the station and outside to a bustling street. The day was bright and the air clear as crystal, but her lightweight cloth coat was poor protection against the North American midwinter cold. A glaze of frozen snow blanketed everything and crunched underfoot, piling up against the corners of buildings and doorways. She shivered as she regarded the frozen white ground with wonder and fear. Horse-drawn cabs idled along the curb, the horses restlessly pawing the cobblestones, the drivers patting their charges' haunches comfortingly as men and beasts waited for arriving passengers to engage their coaches.

Before they stepped into the street, her uncle pointed to the piles of grey-brown manure that lay in the gutter, bits of hay sticking out every which way. He grinned and murmured in a gruff basso voice, "*Sta 'ttento!* Be careful!" He chucked Eleanor under her chin playfully; his teasing gesture was meant to draw a smile on her serious face, but it was in vain. As they reached the intersection, a couple of noisy motorcars rattled past, one heaving a raucous "Ah-OO-kuh!" at them that sent the little girl skittering back to the sidewalk and into her mother's skirts. Terrified tears filled her eyes and her lip shuddered. Without speaking a word, her uncle stopped right there on the curb and hoisted her up again. She was enveloped in the comforting circle of strong arms once more, as he stroked her hair and whispered soft syllables in the clipped Sicilian accent that soothed her immediately.

Hand in hand and arm in arm, the trio proceeded on their way, walking a few short blocks from the station before turning onto a narrow thoroughfare, nearly deserted at this midday hour, with rows of brick houses lining both sides of the street.

Her uncle paused before one in the middle of the block and gestured grandly, "*Stammu a casa.* We are home."

Eleanor tilted her head back to take in the tall three-storied structure of whitewashed brick that would become her new home. It went up and up. The only buildings of that size in the hometown she had left in Sicily were churches or government buildings made of limestone or the new stuccoed cinema that had thrown open its doors with great fanfare just before they departed. All this brick was something new entirely.

There was a sudden rustle of the curtains at the large picture window on the first floor of the house. Eleanor caught sight of a pair of large dark eyes and the round face of a small boy about her own age. By the time she looked again the face was gone, but the curtains still stirred slightly. In a trice, Zio Carmelo scaled the five wooden steps up to the front porch and parked their baggage beside the front door. With a wide, welcoming smile, he beckoned his sister and niece inside.

In the living room, lined up was a row of five children, all girls but one, their eyes all pinned on her. They stood silently as her uncle introduced his children one by one. Donna Sarina stepped forward and bestowed a warm hug on each of her nieces in turn: Annina, the oldest and already a young woman, her long hair pinned back in a neat bun and a thoughtful, bemused expression on her face; and Concetta, next in line, also on the brink of womanhood but more solidly built and serious than her older sister. Then came two girls on the brink of adolescence: Suzanna, small, slight, and calm, with a shy smile; and hanging back behind her, Rosalia, the youngest girl but already as tall as her older sisters. Finally, Sarina took the small hand offered by Angelo, the smallest of the troop, as she drew him toward her for a caress. His was the face Eleanor had glimpsed at the window, his curly dark hair punctuated by a stubborn cowlick that stood up on the crown of his head. With his chin tipped brazenly over Eleanor's mother's shoulder, Angelo peered at her unabashedly. Zio Carmelo was explaining to her mother that the baby, Veronica, was still too small for the orphanage that had taken in his other children when their mother died. She was still under the care of the good Sisters of Saint Joseph in Philadelphia, and would remain there another few days until the newcomers were settled in. Now that his sister had arrived, Carmelo would no longer need to pack his younger children off to an orphanage while he worked each day or when he left Jamesport for a week at a time to put his expert mason's skills to practical use.

Eleanor had left behind in Sicily a tight-knit household of adults who spoke to her familiarly and lovingly, where she had been doted upon, the only child and grandchild, the center of her small universe. She was now thrust into a new home full of cousins, some older than she and some younger, speaking a strange language. Here, she was another middle child in a large family in which she would have to learn to stand up for herself. For these reasons and others, what her Zio Carmelo had described as "settling in" would not be easy nor would it be quick.

Those early days in her new homeland had been anything but comfortable. Enduring the taunts from the other children in the first school she attended because she didn't speak any English. Feeling the isolation of growing up within an alien community of mostly Italians, on the poorer side of town. Gradually becoming aware that there was an entirely different world, another reality beyond their street where English was always spoken and creature comforts were taken for granted. Beyond the confines of their sheltered community, the world of *"gli 'Mericani"* was a place populated with another race of people, fair-skinned, round-faced and confident, conversing easily in English. Theirs was a world set apart, where comfort and privilege seemed to lie ever beyond their reach. It was an environment full of apprehensions, where glances mildly curious to openly hostile were aimed her way as Eleanor and her cousins walked the streets together in a tight group. Sometimes she observed the outsiders (who really were the insiders here) pointing at them and whispering conspiratorially. When that happened, she would hang back behind her cousins or draw closer to her mother and her uncle for the protective shelter their presence offered. Unlike Alice through the looking-glass in one of those books that had begun to fascinate her, with pretty pictures and strange English words, Eleanor did not long to leap into that other world so much as to keep it at arm's length, fearful but curious what it must be like to live and move about there.

Not long after they had arrived, when the nagging cough she'd had since the Atlantic crossing just wouldn't subside, a kindly *paesana* neighbor recommended a physician. Memories of the rough impersonal physical examinations they had endured at Ellis Island made her mother reluctant to submit Eleanor to that experience again. After countless reassurances from well-meaning neighbors, and hoping to come away with some medicine in a bottle to help her daughter, Donna Sarina finally sought an appointment. The kindly man of medicine had seen the disease in recent immigrants many times, and for this sick little girl in particular the prescription was worse than the hacking coughs that racked her body. The doctor had informed her mother as gently as he could that Eleanor had tuberculosis, and because of its contagious virulence he would need to report her case immediately, and she would need to be quarantined for treatment in a specialized sanatorium immediately. After the wrenching and tearful goodbyes that set a new standard for terror in her young heart, she had been admitted the very next day to a facility some fifty miles away, to cure her malady while shielding her family and their neighbors from it.

Eleanor had spent nearly eight agonizing months in that sterile cold place with its alien implacable walls of white tile. During her first weeks she was relegated for constant bed rest to a tiny cot with iron slats, redoubling her dread that this was a prison and her sentence would never end, despite reassurances from a few kindly attendants. Soon and for a number of weeks she was wheeled each day to an adjacent open-air porch where the best medical thinking of the time held that exposure to fresh air and sunshine would rid her frail body of infection. Eventually she was allowed out of bed under the strict supervision of medical staff. If there were other children at the hospital, she didn't cross paths with them. She couldn't have visitors, either, so she was completely cut off from the new American family to which she was just beginning to adjust. Isolation was the proscription for tubercular patients, a lonely and frightening existence for a little girl.

The day finally came when Eleanor was deemed cured of her tuberculosis and allowed to go home. "Home" had been an elusive concept when she had first arrived in America, but now it meant something supremely significant. During the months in the hospital, her vague memories of the three-story brick row house had transformed into an ideal of outsize importance in Eleanor's mind. It was the last place she remembered feeling safe, a harbor for which she now yearned desperately. Her new home took on significance in her absence from it even as childish memories of Sicily faded, supplanted now with roots sprouting in the still-unfamiliar American soil.

At the sanatorium, she had observed orderlies scrub the austere tile surroundings mercilessly several times each day, to subdue the contagion of the disease. The caustic odor of antiseptic at first stung her tender nostrils and made her eyes water, but she taught herself to accept it and embrace it as a necessary discomfort of that time and place. Once at home again and young as she was, Eleanor began mimicking the hospital attendants' behavior, scouring and purging the rooms of the Luna house with manic energy. These rituals brought her an odd comfort. The act of scrubbing and banishing every bit of dirt and dust seemed to help her re-claim her stake in a visceral way. She was making the house her home.

Her mother welcomed the zeal of Eleanor's cleansing rituals as a sign that being cured of her illness had matured her daughter in useful ways. Under Donna Sarina's guiding hand, the Luna household was already orderly and well-organized, a practical necessity with so many underfoot all the time; now it became a temple of cleanliness. Her cousins fed off her energy, and soon their labors were divided into neatly compartmentalized specialties. Suzanne loved to sweep and care for the rugs, so that was her domain. Rosalie polished the wood furniture to a high gloss, and carefully brushed down the upholstery of every chair and sofa. Eleanor herself took charge of the bathrooms, keeping the porcelain of the claw-footed tub blindingly white and sterile. But these frequent practices not only benefitted their crowded living environment. At least here, in their own domain, for any non-Italian strangers who happened to cross their threshold, the Luna family was doing its level best to counter the stereotype of "dirty Italians" they heard so often, whether spoken plainly or whispered behind-hand.

Just when the routine of hard work and very occasional leisure had settled into a contented pace, the Lunas were swallowed by unexpected tragedy. Carmelo Luna, head of the household and its chief breadwinner, suffered a heart attack and died. Sarina had uprooted herself and her daughter to help her widowed brother in middle age establish a home in which to raise his children. Now here she was, a widow but still young herself, thrust in the role of single parent and sole provider. By this time the two eldest Luna girls had married. Annina, the firstborn, had married a serious and earnest young man, Benedetto Camastra, also an immigrant Sicilian, and they had two little girls of their own. The second daughter, Concetta, had wed Giovanni Nardello, an older man with a fledgling grocery business on the first floor of a substantial house with a comfortable second-floor apartment for their growing family. That still left Sarina with three nieces, a nephew and her own daughter to feed, clothe, and care for.

The untimely catastrophe thrust some difficult changes on Eleanor and her cousins. School, however rudimentary, suddenly became a luxury they could ill afford. In order to survive, all hands were needed on deck. Thus it was that, still in their salad days, the Luna girls and their brother exchanged schoolbooks and chalk dust for the hum and rattle of the textile mills, punching a clock early each morning and toiling until the finishing buzzer announced the workday's end.

On the factory floor, Eleanor and her cousins rubbed elbows daily with the world of *"gli 'Mericani"* – blue-collar and working poor women who like themselves worked to pay rent and put bread on the table. Some of these women were from farm families for whom the uncertainty of the Great Depression meant augmenting their household income at the hands of industry, or forsaking entirely their agrarian legacy. These women and girls were German and Scotch-Irish, mostly from families who'd lived for generations in Oxford County. Even though by economic measures they were no better off than the Lunas, to Eleanor they seemed to have advantages she and her cousins did not. Some of them trekked to the factory each day from the outskirts of the city, where they lived on farms made smaller by hard times, where the men of the family still eked out an existence coaxing a handful of crops from the ground, or feeding a small flock of animals whose milk, meat, or cheese fattened the family purse even as it stocked their cupboards. In Eleanor's mind, this parallel existence invested these workmates' domestic circumstances with an air of permanence and stability that the Lunas and other Italian-immigrant families could only imagine.

Eleanor and her cousins applied themselves to factory work alongside her mother, turning over to a common household fund their meager earnings at week's end. After a frugal ten years of relying on the steady modest income of five wage-earners besides herself, by dint of rigorously saving every extra penny, Donna Sarina Fazzio was finally in a position to look for a bigger house. The Luna family moved from the "old neighborhood" on Jamesport's south side, where they had been surrounded by other new arrivals, Italians, Jews, and Poles, to more spacious quarters in a sturdy, well-built brick row house on the city's north side. Except that the houses on their block each sported a rectangle of grass framing a generous porch facing the street and a small fenced-in garden at the back, their new neighborhood did not look so very different from the old one, but somehow it seemed more cheerful and felt less crowded than their old street. Except for the Mollicas, who had moved in across the street, their new neighbors, like their factory coworkers, were Irish and German. Everyone spoke English here. In their new space, they would not hear Mrs. Marchese shouting the latest gossip in her raspy Calabrian dialect as she pinned sheets and towels to the clotheslines. The priests in the local parish church hailed from towns with names like Wicklow and Wexford. Their mostly Irish congregation celebrated St. Patrick's Day with gusto. The German Lutherans made the deep-fried doughnuts they called fasnachts as a last blast of pre-Lenten largesse. No front lawns boasted colorful statues of St. Anthony of Padua or alabaster ones of the Virgin Mary cocooned in a scalloped half-orb that her cousin Angelo disdainfully called the "Madonna on the Half Shell." What Eleanor wouldn't give for the familiar sight of a few of those statues in her new neighborhood! At Christmas, or on hot June days of the *feste*, there would be no elaborate multicolored lights festooned across alleyways. In summer, they would hear the wail of bagpipes from their Scots-Irish neighbors' living room, and in winter a dignified evergreen wreath hung on every door and discreet white candles glowed in the windows.

Eleanor paused. A heavy sigh brought her back into the present, and she was mortified to realize that she'd been talking non-stop. She looked at Giampolo apologetically. What she saw in his eyes was sadness and sympathy, but also something else – an unfamiliar, distant longing.

"And now you are American, *tu si 'Mericana,*" he began. "It is a wonderful thing, to be a part of this great country, to be able to earn a living and to live as you like." His voice was wistful.

Eleanor's heart swelled with pride. She *was* proud to be an American, a sentiment that had only grown stronger as the war deepened. She had *earned* her place in this country. She had worked hard for it.

"When this war is over, I don't know what I'll find when I go home." Giampaolo continued, a faraway look in his eyes.

"But your family is still there...?"

"Oh yes," he continued. "But it will never be the same. My parents are getting older. My father cannot work the farm himself for much longer, if he still does. I don't know how my older brother will have managed on the land, pretty much by himself, or even if the farm is intact. I've been gone for a long time. My two younger brothers are priests – well, the youngest is studying to become one. They're probably safe enough. The Church takes care of its own. But no one has heard from my brother Giuseppe since we both went off to this war."

"Did he go off to serve with you?"

"We left home at the same time. But he was in a different division of the army when he served, so they put him back in his old company. I don't know where he was sent, or even if he is still alive." Giampaolo covered his eyes briefly with his hand. "The Italian army is ruined. Italy is ruined. Even when I left, several years ago, it was already in bad shape. Once Peppino and I had gone our separate ways," his voice caught as he murmured his brother's familiar nickname, "there was no way to communicate with him, or even with other army companies serving near us in Africa. We just went where we were ordered to go, and hoped for the best."

Eleanor sensed that this subject was a difficult one for Giampaolo, but she was touched that he entrusted her with these deeply felt memories. She reached for his hand and grasped it. They walked for a while in silence, lost in their separate thoughts.

* * *

8 agosto, 1944

Dear Giampaolo,

It was wonderful to see you last weekend. I enjoyed every part of the trip – the train ride to Newark, attending Holy Mass, sharing the nice dinner the sodality ladies prepared, and most of all our walk and talk in the garden. The only bad part was having to say goodbye.

Nothing much is new here. It is stifling to work in the factory during the summer. Since it's been so hot for more than a week now, the forelady had the janitors bring in a few fans to keep the air circulating, but it doesn't help much – it just pushes the hot air around. I try to keep moving to stay cool. It's my job, anyway, to pass out the bundles to each piece worker, so it's better to be able to walk around than sitting still in one place for hours.

We are planning a picnic at French Creek State Park next Sunday. There's a pretty lake there that has a little beach where we can swim and cool off.

Perhaps we can make plans for another outing soon. Let me know when will be the next time you can get time away from the camp on a weekend. The Mollicas would like to have their cousin come to visit again, and I'm sure you would be welcome to come along, too.

Sincerely,

Eleanora

12 agosto, 1944

Dearest Eleanora,

It gave me such joy to receive your letter! I too enjoyed seeing you and your mother and your friends in Newark. What a feast the church women prepared! The food in camp is pretty good but not like what I remember from home. That's what the wonderful meal brought to mind. It was as if I was sitting in the kitchen, eating nonna's pasta.

Today is Saturday, so I have some time on my hands. It's not my turn for weekend leave, so I'm just spending time here in camp – and I have time to write to you. When we have spare time now that we are in the service units, the American soldiers and our camp wardens let us entertain ourselves pretty much however we like. If we can't get a pass to go off the base, some of the fellows will get up a game of calcio, or gather to play their musical instruments, like a little band. They're pretty good! Some of the Americans organize day trips for us prisoners, to New York City and Coney Island. I haven't been on one of those trips yet, but I would really like to see Times Square. The fellows who've been there say that Broadway is lit up so brightly at night that it seems like daytime! I can't imagine it.

The weather has been very hot here, too. During working hours I'm usually shipped off with most of our group to work on the docks. At least there's usually a breeze near the water, but the American navy ships we work on are so huge, and there are so many of them in the harbor, that you really can't see too much of the sea. They load us up on buses from the camp in the morning and bring us back at night. The work makes the days go faster, so I don't mind.

Tommaso is working out plans with Patsy and Tony, the American soldiers who came with us, to visit his cousins again for the holiday you have in September – it's called Labor Day? They say that will mean an extra day off. I have asked him to include me in the plans because I would love to see you again.

Until soon, I hope,

Yours, with affection,

Giampaolo

A few days later, Eleanor's mother wrote to her sister in Sicily.

15 agosto, 1944

Carissima Maria Grazia,

How are you getting on, gioia mia? I think of you every day and wonder how you are managing with this awful war tearing the world apart.

I hope this letter reaches you. Did you get the packages I sent in June? I know the mail service is very slow with the war on, but I live in hopes that the few things I sent you may be of use. In case they haven't reached your door yet, I sent one box with fabrics, a lovely polished cotton and some seersucker which is very popular here for all kinds of clothes in the very warm weather. I hope you can make something for yourself, and still have fabric left to make dresses for Lucietta and Emilia, or maybe an apron or two. I tucked some money into the folds of the fabric – are you getting the money I send in each package? The smaller box had some nylon stockings that Suzanna got at the factory at a good price. We can't get silk stockings just now, because of the war, but we try to buy the nylon ones when we find them. I also sent some American dress patterns which maybe you can adapt for your use, some buttons and nice thread in a few different colors, needles, pins, and bias tape for finishing seams and hems. There are also packages of soap (with money tucked in), some cologne for you and razor blades for Tonino, and some trinkets for the girls.

As the weather gets colder here, the shops will start carrying woolens and heavier fabrics. I'll try to send some of those to you, but I know you won't need anything like the heavy winter coats we wear here. I know it must be very difficult to get everyday items, with the war on. The stories we hear about the condition of things over there are very sad. Let me know what else you need, no matter how small it may seem to you – especially anything for your boys, as I haven't sent them anything in the last few packages – and I'll try to send it.

We had firsthand news of how bad Sicily was hit by the war – first the Germans overrunning everything, then the Allied troops storming in right behind them. We hear the American soldiers give out chocolate bars and cigarettes, but that won't help you clothe your family. We got the news from some Sicilian soldiers who are being held as prisoners of war over here. Can you believe it, there are camps full of Italian soldiers over here! Some of the local churches have started hosting dinners for them. Cummari Angelina's nephew is a prisoner in one of the camps, and he came to visit with some other fellows from his troop and a couple of American soldiers from Italian families over here, who are in the army too, working as guards and wardens in the prisoner camps. A lucky assignment for those fellows, if you ask me, not to get shipped out to where the fighting is!

I must close this letter to get it to the post office. Dearest sister, you are in my thoughts constantly and in my prayers always. May God bless you and keep you safe through these terrible times. Write back soon if you can and let me know about the packages.

Kisses and hugs from your sister, who loves you and wishes you well always,

Sarina.

Chapter 10

The family (*la famiglia*) is the most important aspect of an Italian's life. It provides emotional and economic support to the individual and often forms the basis of their social circles...It is not unusual for the immediate family and extended family to live together and be deeply involved in each other's daily lives.

—https://culturalatlas.sbs.com.au/

L ate summer 1944, Jamesport, Pennsylvania
The incessant summer heat finally broke as August ended. Mornings were crisper, the sky bluer. Fall always brought Eleanor the feeling of being on the edge of something new, perhaps because it put her in mind of the new school year when she was a child. Even though she had gone only as far as the ninth grade, Eleanor had enjoyed every minute of school. The excitement of knowing the answer when the teacher asked a question, the adrenaline rush of being the first to raise her hand, and the pride when she was called on and got it right – these things evoked in Eleanor a deep love of the classroom, and an abiding respect for what went on there. Homework had given her an excuse to indulge her love of reading, something she could still do when she could find time. Although she never questioned the necessity, she had hated having to give up school for the monotony of the factory.

As September of 1944 approached, however, the anticipation in the air was keener because Eleanor had a new set of daydreams. She found her thoughts drifting often to a certain handsome Italian prisoner. In fact, now that she and Giampaolo were exchanging letters regularly, it was getting more difficult to displace him from her thinking entirely. And she didn't want to: daydreams about him were now her constant companion, and they made life sweeter.

The Labor Day holiday approached, and with it the next visit of the Italians and their American companions. Whenever she thought of the approaching weekend, a trill of excitement coursed through her. The visitors would arrive on Saturday and stay at the Mollica home for three days, until the evening of the Monday holiday. Donna Sarina would make the meal at the Lunas' home when the group arrived. They planned a picnic on Sunday afternoon at a local park if the weather was fair. Monday would be given over to the parade and other public events at City Park, where there would be musical entertainment at the bandshell. Once again and all too soon the weekend would be over and Giampaolo would be gone; but in the meanwhile, Eleanor resolved to live in the moment when it arrived.

She rushed home from work on Friday, eager to complete her weekly house-cleaning chores. Donna Sarina ran a tight ship; just because this weekend promised to be busier than usual didn't mean that she would tolerate any deviation from the usual household routine of scrubbing and cleansing, dusting and setting the house to rights. In truth, the Luna home was always in order: clean as a whistle and neat as a pin. The intrusion of guests wouldn't warrant much more than was already the exacting daily standard for Donna Sarina. Nonetheless, Rosalie paid special care as she dusted the living room where they would entertain their visitors. The room brimmed with the waxy smell of furniture polish, and every surface of just-buffed wood shimmered with a burnished glow. She cranked up the Victrola with a record of Italian opera music and tackled her job with gusto.

Meanwhile, Suzanne made sure the household linens, air-fresh from drying in the backyard sunshine, were folded with precision and stored in the linen closet. She took down the clothesline, rolling the rope in large loops over one arm and hanging it on the designated peg in the cellar stairway. She put the clothespins in the cloth bag her aunt had cleverly fashioned over an old wooden hanger for that express purpose, and hung it next to the clothesline.

Eleanor swept the floors and passed the vacuum cleaner carefully over the rugs. They'd soon tackle the autumn house-cleaning, when the summer-weight rugs were rolled up and cleaned for storage, and carpets with a thicker pile were laid in place for the winter. Later in the fall, her cousin Angelo would roll up and tie off the striped awning that shaded the front porch during the warm weather. They would pop window screens from their frames, brush them free of summer dust, and store them in the attic. They would pull down and secure the storm windows against the colder months to come. They would exchange the sheer airy curtains that fluttered in the summer heat for more substantial drapes to shield windows from wintry drafts. They would repeat the process in reverse every spring.

That was the litany of seasonal tasks the Luna family tackled with unfailing regularity, but the controversy this routine always seemed to engender was ever new. Every family member second-guessed the quality of everyone else's work, or the best way to accomplish the job: Was the awning tied securely enough to withstand snowstorms? Were mothballs really needed to protect the summer curtains? Did the winter drapes hang straight? Eleanor never minded the work but always dreaded the arguments.

All of that would be for later. Eleanor determined to enjoy the last bit of summer sliding into fall, when days were still balmy but nights had a refreshing edge to them, when summer's warmth still showed up every day and winter's cold was just a chilly threat. Finishing her sweeping, she stored the broom and dustpan in a corner of the kitchen. Her mother was stirring ground meat browning in a large pot on the stove.

"What else?" Eleanor inquired, knowing that Donna Sarina had a mile-long mental checklist of things still to be done.

"The houseplants need to be watered," her mother supplied. "And don't forget to wipe up any water that spills – it will stain the floor."

"Sí, *Mamá*," Eleanor replied, with a touch of pique. She had been doing these same tasks for years, but her mother didn't seem to realize she didn't need to be reminded about leaving standing water on the hardwood planks. She ignored the comment and nodded toward the pot. "Is that for supper?"

"On a Friday?" Her mother asked incredulously. "Of course not. I'm making *frittata* for supper. You know we always have eggs on Friday. This is for Saturday dinner. I thought I'd get a head start on the sauce." She turned back to her pot as it emitted an aromatic sizzle and said, her back to her daughter, "You could set the table."

Without a word, Eleanor reached for the pile of cloth napkins. Even with these, there was a strict, practical code of use. Each linen square had a family member's initial penciled onto one corner so that they could be reused for weeknight suppers until washday, when the everyday linens, including the tablecloth that was shaken out after each night's use and stored in a drawer, would all be laundered together and hung out to dry. Mindlessly she sorted forks and knives from the flatware drawer and turned to the kitchen table, everything in hand.

As she spread the tablecloth over the well-worn wooden table, she looked over her shoulder and asked, "What else are you making for tomorrow?"

"We'll have a *primu* and a *sicundu*," Donna Sarina replied, not answering her question.

Taken aback, Eleanor nearly screeched, "What?" Donna Sarina never used such formalities to describe what would essentially be a family dinner. She slid a napkin and a fork into place in front of each chair, waiting for a reply.

"It's only proper." Donna Sarina gave the sauce a vigorous swish with her wooden spoon. "We'll have the pasta first. It's too hot for soup. And then meat afterward, with salad. I sent Suzanna for the groceries. I've asked Gi'vanni to trim the round steak carefully. I hope he remembers," she mused with a worried voice. "Of course, I'll go to market tomorrow."

Eleanor sighed. Nothing, not even an out-of-the-ordinary visit from a group of Italian men that included her daughter's prospective beau, would interrupt the normal weekend routine of the Luna household as capably managed by Donna Sarina Fazzio. Was her mother's brusque tone a way of signaling disapproval? Perhaps it was only an unaccustomed bout of the nerves.

The weekend had begun in its customary fashion. Saturday morning may be reserved for her mother's weekly pilgrimage to the local farmer's market for fresh produce. But on Friday afternoons after work, groceries were procured, and not just from any supermarket. No, the business of purchasing the weekly stores of food was kept all in the family as much as possible. Cousin Connie, Suzanne and Rosalie's older sister, had "married well." Her husband John Nardello had his own thriving little neighborhood market across town. Any family running its own business usually managed more easily than families whose wage-earners depended for livelihood on the vagaries of bosses in textile factories, coal mines, or steel mills. This was the good fortune that Connie and John Nardello enjoyed, along with their large family – a daughter and six sons born in rapid succession, the youngest two a pair of twins. As a result, Eleanor rarely saw her older cousin, who always seemed exhausted and distracted by her boisterous flock. When Eleanor did see her cousin, Connie was the epitome of practicality, never given to sentiment of any kind. Life was too busy for that. So the Friday afternoon excursions were a chance for Connie to have a social moment with her aunt as well as for the Lunas to patronize the family grocery enterprise.

When Donna Sarina arrived each Friday, John would already have packaged canned goods and other weekly staples in a carton. She'd greet him as "Gi'vanni" – as much an old-world term of endearment as a thin noose of criticism that she could tighten if he failed to trim to her exacting standards the meats she selected. So, John would always wait for his in-law before wrapping up the meat. He would always have saved a nice fat *iaddina* – chicken – for their Sunday dinner, which would then become Monday night's chicken soup with *pastina*. He would pound the beef cutlets just the way she required them. He would slice extra fat from the cuts of beef and pork under her watchful eye, carefully wrapping up the trimmings in a separate paper package if she wanted to use them instead of oil for frying a bit of onion for sauce.

Conveniently, too, the Nardellos' establishment was just across the street from the home of the other married Luna girl, the mild-mannered eldest sister Anna (Annina, to her Zia Sarina, but simply Annie to the rest of the family). So the weekly grocery run inevitably became even more of a social occasion, too, with time set aside to drop in and visit Annie, who was one of Donna Sarina's favorites. She and her husband Benedetto Camastra (whom everyone called Buddy) were raising their own brood of children, all dark-eyed and serious like their father, in a tidy row home. Buddy lovingly tended their backyard patch of well-trimmed grass and lush plants and flowers with his legendary green thumb. Temperamentally, Buddy was grim-faced and stern – he was as sober as his wife was sunny. Although his somber countenance concealed a kind and generous heart, only the rarest smile broke over his craggy features: when it did, it was like sun breaking through clouds. The pair were well-matched opposites because Annie's genial demeanor and her near-perpetual smile gave the impression that she'd just heard a good joke and could not contain her amusement.

Unlike her sister Connie, having a large family seemed scarcely to faze Annie. In sharp contrast to the Nardello's noisy nest of chaos across the street, the Camastra household was orderly and quiet, in part because Buddy Camastra would have it no other way. Nor did it matter that this late-afternoon hour was a most inconvenient time for a visit, just as Annie was trying to get supper for her husband and five hungry kids on the table. She calmly greeted last-minute drop-ins to her home with equanimity. The visitors, whoever they were, simply pulled chairs up to the table as Annie served pieces of flaky white fish with a flourish of lemon juice or plunked some fried potatoes on small plates for everyone to taste. Whenever Eleanor came on one of these visits, she silently prayed that there was another miracle of loaves and fishes in the wings in Annie's kitchen, because her cousin was blithely serving everyone her own family's dinner.

The Friday night grocery-expedition-cum-family-visit to the Nardellos and Camastras was firmly entrenched in practice among the Lunas. But for fresh produce, Eleanor's exacting mother went elsewhere. Every Saturday the farmer's market attracted dozens of vendors who plied their fresh wares from farms across two counties.

Eleanor's cousin Suzanne usually accompanied her Zia Sarina to the market. As they stepped inside the large stone doorway into the cool of the massive market, the place echoed with a pleasing cacophony: the singsong of vendors peddling their wares, the metallic squeak of wheelbarrows hauling goods to-and-fro, the harsh klaxon of truck horns signaling that more fresh merchandise had just arrived outside. The sweet floral aromas of ripe strawberries and bananas intermingled with the grassy pungency of fresh cut stalks of rosemary and basil.

Dewy heads of lettuce perched next to bunches of bright green broccoli and ruddy beets. Farther on, the coarse tang of freshly cut slabs of meat met the earthy odor of entire carcasses of pigs and whole legs of lamb hanging at the butcher's stalls. Donna Sarina and Suzanne picked their way carefully over uneven cement floors wet from just-rinsed produce at the greengrocers' stands or melting ice draining from the fishmonger's tables.

In her well-proscribed circuit of the colorful stalls, Donna Sarina always preferred to patronize the Italian farmers first, well known as fellow members of Holy Family parish. It was a logical extension of patronizing the Nardellos' grocery business. She and her niece made a beeline to the Cianci stall for fresh produce. Mr. Cianci always had the freshest salad greens and the best-looking cauliflower and eggplants. The glistening fresh wares he purveyed were his life's work, cultivated at the farm that he and his wife owned on the outskirts of town. Once (but only once!) in August every year, the Lunas would pile into Angelo's car and make the trip to the Cianci farm for bushel baskets of fresh tomatoes, fragrant peaches, crisp apples, and tiny golden quinces. Donna Sarina turned that ripe bounty into gleaming jars of tomato sauce, peach halves, and apple and quince jelly that stood gem-like in rows on the shelves of the family's cold cellar. She had to make enough to last all winter and into the spring, until fresh produce became plentiful once again.

At the farmer's market, Mr. Cianci's fresh fruit was always choice, too, except for the bananas; for them, Donna Sarina went down the aisle a few steps farther to Mr. Sedoti's stand, where she would also purchase root vegetables, mushrooms and potatoes. Nearby were booths selling cheeses and delicatessen items, fresh breads, and baked goods from local purveyors. While she made her selections at the vegetable stands, Donna Sarina would dispatch Suzanne to Albertini's bakery stall for several loaves of crusty bread, and then to

Calabrese's *salumeria* booth for cold cuts for lunch sandwiches – always salami and provolone cheese, plus several other choices left up to Suzanne from Donna Sarina's short list of "approved" items she had committed to memory. These cold cuts would have to stretch for a week's worth of bag lunches, yet not make too big a dent in the household budget. Once a month, Suzanne augmented the deli order with a container of black olives in brine or a one-pound block of "grating cheese" – Romano or Parmesan, whichever was cheaper by the pound. With the shopping completed, if Donna Sarina was feeling magnanimous, she sometimes sprang for sticky buns or almond bear-claw pastries from the Amish bake shop, which she would save for Sunday breakfast after church.

On this Friday evening, unusually, Suzanne had been sent to Nardello's to collect the weekly groceries on her own. She walked in the Fazzios' kitchen door now, burdened with paper sacks. "There's more in the car," she nodded to Eleanor as a terse request for help. Glad for a respite from sweeping, Eleanor sprang out the door while her mother began unloading the bags.

Bright sun spilling onto the window sill roused Eleanor on Saturday morning. A quick glance at the clock on her bedside table told her she'd forgot to wind it last night. She'd fallen into bed exhausted more by the many petty disagreements with her mother than by the household tasks she'd taken up after supper. Her cousin Suzanne's voice carried upstairs through the screened kitchen window below.

"But, Zia, two loaves of bread will surely be enough!" An edge of temper laced her cousin's voice. Eleanor surmised that Suzanne was being asked to backtrack to the Italian bakery for more provisions.

"No!" Her mother's strident negative rang out. Donna Sarina would brook no opposition today. "We don't want to appear stingy, and we don't want to run out! Lots of men to feed today. We're not used to that."

Hurriedly, Eleanor threw on the work clothes that she had doffed onto the footboard of her bed last night. She brushed her teeth with more haste than care and splashed water on her face, then dashed downstairs to insert herself into the quarrel.

"Ah, good. Eleanora." Donna Sarina greeted her daughter tersely without turning from the sink. "There's still a cup of coffee left for you." She gestured with her paring knife toward the percolator in the corner. An enormous bowl at her elbow held tight circlets of romaine lettuce that she was rinsing in the sink. Two glossy cucumbers and two green peppers awaited their fate under Donna Sarina's knife.

"Is there room for all that salad in the refrigerator?" Eleanor couldn't resist interrogating her mother's intensive preparations. The dish wouldn't be required on the table for hours yet, and the late morning sun was already hot.

"*Sí, certu!*" Donna Sarina cast an annoyed glance in Eleanor's direction. "You can wash that fruit and put it in the basket." She inclined her head toward the kitchen table, where her cousin was unloading a bounty of peaches, plums, apples, grapes, and pears. There were even two pint-baskets of silky purple figs, a rare treat, nestled among the fruit tumbling from damp paper sacks onto the table. Suzanne must've bought all the wares in Mr. Besuzzi's farm truck this morning.

A harbinger of coming fall bounty, the tinkle of a bicycle bell heralded the approach of Albino Besuzzi, a neighbor who would park his ancient rig laden with fruits and vegetables from his Victory garden on summer Saturdays at the curb in their neighborhood until his wares were all claimed. Donna Sarina turned away from the sink and cast an assessing glance at the table, zeroing in on the figs. A beneficent smile lit her face. "*Matri, chi bedda frutta!*" She nodded approvingly at her niece as she pinched the figs and fingered the grapes.

Two enormous trays of lasagna stood on the stovetop, ready to be heaved into a hot oven. A pot of sauce simmered on the back burner, emitting the enticing aroma of simmering tomatoes and basil. Her mother must have been toiling for hours already this morning, Eleanor surmised.

"Our guests are expected at two o'clock?" The upward lilt in Donna Sarina's voice signaled uncertainty. Eleanor took this to mean she should call the Mollicas for confirmation. Her mother finally turned toward Eleanor and eyed her critically. "You're not wearing that, are you?"

"Of course not!" her daughter shot back, then calmed herself. "I just thought you might need some help with the cooking. I'll change later."

"Lèviti 'I ccà! Get out of here!" her mother exclaimed, more harshly than she intended. Then, more softly: "Go on, I don't need help here." She turned, intent once more on her task at the sink. Nonplussed, Eleanor shrugged and took the almost empty percolator in hand. She poured herself some coffee and as she took a big gulp, looked at Suzanne and rolled her eyes. Her cousin's mouth twitched, upturned on one side as she repressed a laugh.

Eleanor drifted into the dining room where Rosalie was counting neatly pressed napkins that matched the snowy white linen tablecloth already in place on the massive table that dwarfed the room. She pointed and asked her cousin, "How many leaves did you put in?"

"Every last one." Rosalie glanced toward the kitchen doorway. "Express orders. Fifteen, sixteen, seventeen – there!" She patted the neat pile of linens triumphantly.

"There will be *seventeen* of us?" Eleanor queried incredulously.

"Why, yes," her cousin answered. "Angelo and Doris will be here, and Veronica doesn't go anywhere without Nick these days." As if to explain the large number, Rosalie ticked off her fingers to count her brother and his wife and her younger sister and her beau.

"Nick Raffa!" Eleanor exclaimed, her tone judgmental. "Let's make sure he doesn't turn the conversation towards prize fighting."

"Oh, he's not so bad, Eleanor," Rosalie chided her cousin. "Ronnie worships the ground he walks on."

"Have you met his family?" Still piqued from the disparaging exchange with her mother, Eleanor chose this particular nit to pick and continued. "And that awful dark house." She shuddered when she thought of the Raffa family home, a tiny damp structure in a meager settlement on the county line. It always looked ready to sink right into the roiling waters of the Schuylkill River, just a few yards from its front porch.

"Well, I like him," Rosalie stated firmly. "So what if he likes the fights? Afterward he always brings us that homemade pizza and those fava beans from the Victor Emmanuel Club." Rosalie licked her lips. "Besides, they're getting married soon and then you'll see the guy every day." After the wedding, Nick and Veronica were moving into the third-floor apartment of the Luna house until they could save money for a home of their own.

Eleanor grunted as she began moving chairs into place at the table, while Rosalie distributed the napkins. "What?" Rosalie asked, her gaze askance. "It's not like that apartment upstairs hasn't been used before."

* * * * *

As with other struggling immigrant families, the times had not always been kind to the Lunas. The extra space upstairs had been a godsend, an upper-story haven for extended family as, one by one, the Great Depression had dashed their American dreams.

Early in 1931, as the waves of the Great Depression started

swamping America's working class, Buddy Camastra lost his job and very soon afterward realized that he could no longer make the payments on the tiny house where he and Annie were raising their family. When they lost the house, Donna Sarina immediately suggested that they take over the three-room space on the top floor of the Luna house.

Buddy was a proud man, and it had never sat well with him to have to accept charity, however temporary, from his in-laws. His own parents had stayed behind in Sicily when he set off for America, so he had no older relations to fall back on. But he needed to put a roof over the heads of his growing family, so he grudgingly agreed, "just until we get on our feet." Buddy repeated this mantra often, embarrassed and ashamed that this turn of events had forced him to accept the charity of his wife's relatives. Finally landing some work, for four years he toiled at two jobs, redoubling his efforts to get out from under the financial burden that oppressed them. Before reporting to his regular shift in the maintenance shed at the railroad yard, he arose at three in the morning and delivered milk for a few hours. Exhausted and at wits' end, he finally succeeded in saving enough to put down a deposit on a home. So it was that Buddy and Annie came to live in the tidy little row house on a hilly street just a few steps from Connie and John Nardello's corner grocery store.

Soon enough, a similar fate befell Eleanor's cousin Angelo Luna and his bride, Doris, not long after they married. They had one baby and another on the way. Doris's large family had no room for them, so once again, Donna Sarina supplied a key to the Luna house and access to the third-floor apartment. Fortunately, Angelo's luck improved quickly as the wartime economy took off. He landed a good job with the railroad, and he and Doris had moved to a tiny home of their own last year.

Now in their early thirties, Suzanne and Rosalie were still unmarried, with no active prospects. Only Veronica, the youngest Luna girl, had a fellow courting her. Her shy ways and petite form had caught the eye of the irascible Nick Raffa – the subject of Eleanor's petulant disapproval.

Eleanor reached for the stack of china plates on the sideboard. She loved her mother's best china with its delicate pastel flowers and gold borders, pulled out only for Easter, Thanksgiving, and Christmas. This morning, she took it as a token of the significance her mother must be placing on this dinner. She and Rosalie quickly finished setting the table and stood back to admire their work. A china plate gleamed at each place, neatly bordered by a carefully folded linen napkin and silverware placed with precision on either side of the plate. Down the center of the table, wine glasses stood like so many sparkling sentinels standing guard until they would be pressed into service.

"I think I'll cut some roses from the bushes out back," Rosalie exclaimed. "They're in full bloom just now, and they'll make a nice centerpiece!"

Several hours later, everything stood in readiness. Eleanor felt refreshed from her bath as she donned a light cotton dress in a dark green paisley pattern that set off her pale skin. Descending to the living room, she paced anxiously in front of the big picture window, fixing her eyes on the Mollicas' home across the street for signs of the soldiers' arrival. Soon, a large olive-green station wagon with U.S. Army lettering on the side pulled up and five men in khaki uniforms piled out. She found herself counting heads until her gaze lighted upon the trim figure she sought: Giampaolo Stagno had arrived. The others scarcely mattered.

Unable to mask her excitement any longer, Eleanor chirped nervously, "They're here!" and bounded toward the front door.

Cumpari Mollica was waiting on the sidewalk, pumping the hands of each soldier in turn and welcoming them. *Cummari* Angelina emerged under the striped awning of the front porch, smiling broadly as her daughters Mary and Frannie crowded her from behind.

It looked as though this was the same contingent who had made the trip last time, all of them spiffy in neatly pressed khaki uniforms. Tommaso Mollica reached out to hug his uncle, while Vincenzo Liguori hung back, watching. The two boisterous Italian Americans, Patsy Tinelli and Tony Ferraro, were there as well, Patsy climbing out of the driver's seat and Tony securing the passenger doors. Giampaolo stood on the sidewalk, looking toward the Luna house, when he spied Eleanor striding down the front steps and making ready to cross the street.

She closed the distance between them quickly, taking both of Giampaolo's hands. He enfolded her in a quick embrace, then kissed her on both cheeks in the continental way. Eleanor gazed at him momentarily before she realized that they were the focus of the entire group's attention. Her cheeks flushed pink as she turned to greet the other men.

Rosalie and Suzanne had crossed the street after Eleanor and were now part of the commotion on the Mollica's front steps. Eleanor finally had the presence of mind to gesture toward their house and invite everybody in. She looked toward the front porch and there stood her mother, wearing a prim smile.

They made their way across the street, young and old arm in arm, up the Lunas' front steps and into the living room. Giampaolo sought out Donna Sarina and greeted her respectfully. Her mother's expression broadened to a smile, for which Eleanor was surprised and grateful. The other Lunas, Angelo and Doris, were already in the living room, and Veronica stood alongside Nick. Patsy Tinelli was playing impresario, confidently handling introductions to all and for all. Eleanor was glad he took the reins to help the guests overcome the initial awkwardness of so many first-time meetings.

At Donna Sarina's insistent invitation, *"A tàvula! A tàvula, tutti,"* everyone drifted into the dining room and found seats at the table. Her mother's spot was always at the head of the table closest to the doorway, more easily to enable the inevitable frequent trips to and from the kitchen. Eleanor left that chair vacant for her mother and took the one right next to it. Giampaolo quickly commandeered the chair on her other side.

Eleanor found herself glancing about uneasily as she sat, the only woman at a table full of men. Her cousins, Angelo's wife Doris, and the Mollica women all had evaporated into the kitchen to offer their help serving the meal. Uncharacteristically, before their guests had arrived, Donna Sarina had issued Eleanor a stern edict not to leave her seat to help serve the meal but instead to remain at the table, as makeshift hostess in Donna Sarina's place. Eleanor realized that she was the only one of the younger women with enough facility in Italian to make things comfortable for the guests who spoke no English; Doris wasn't even Italian. She wasn't sure this had occurred to her mother, but perhaps it had. In any event, the men were settling into easy conversation without her help – except for Giampaolo, who had fixed his gaze on her as if waiting for her to say something.

"Comu si, Giampaolo? How have things been with you?"

"Beni, tutto beni, Eleanora. Everything's fine. And you?"

She smiled at him as she smoothed her napkin on her lap. He smiled back and followed suit.

Meanwhile in the kitchen, Donna Sarina assumed command, directing what needed to be done and in what order. *Cummari* Angelina slid into her accustomed place as first lieutenant, with the younger women serving as attentive foot soldiers ready to be deployed. Platters of steaming food soon emerged from the kitchen in a steady stream. Frannie, Mary, then Rosalie and Suzanne in turn delivered their delicious-looking cargo and took their places at the table. Doris and Veronica followed with still more plates. *Cummari* Angelina materialized from the kitchen and sat down, and finally Donna Sarina slid into her chair. *"Pregu, pi favuri, manciámu, tutti!"*

Everyone fell on the food. Squares of the delectable lasagne were heaped on plates, the stringy hot mozzarella stretching in impossibly long strands until eager fingers finally ended the contest. The first course made its way around the table and silence reigned. After a few bites, the young men murmured syllables of approval between mouthfuls, still chewing and shoveling in the next bite. Finally taking a forkful of steaming lasagna herself, Donna Sarina nodded toward no one in particular, a bemused half-smile expressing contentment as her guests enjoyed their food.

When the pasta had been consumed, Frannie and Rosalie whisked the lasagna trays into the kitchen and replaced them with large shallow bowls containing fragrant meatballs and two kinds of Italian sausage, sweet and hot. Donna Sarina was in her element, pressing more food on the young men, making sure that there was extra sauce and grated cheese to everyone's liking, and passing around baskets of Italian bread, its snowy crumb and crunchy crust impossible to resist. *Cumpari* Mollica made sure to refill the soldiers' wine glasses without prompting, and quietly inquired if the ladies wanted more.

The women cleared plates once more, and Suzanne placed two piles of small bowls at the other end of the table, in front of *Cummari* Angelina. Doris and Ronnie emerged from the kitchen with two enormous bowls of glistening salad greens, already tossed with Donna Sarina's simple blend of vinegar and olive oil with a sprinkle of dried oregano. While the hostess finished her last few bites of sausage, *Cummari* Angelina served and passed bowls of salad, heaping the fresh cool greens into each bowl and passing more bread. Serving and clearing, serving and clearing: with so many female hands to tend to things, the entire operation proceeded like clockwork.

The Mollica girls removed the salad bowls to make room for yet another round of clean plates and generous baskets of fresh fruit, dewy and cool from the icebox. From the sideboard, Suzanne placed onto the table a tall glass in which stood a bouquet of mismatched paring knives. The Italian soldiers took eagerly to the fruit, eating it in the style of the old country as Giampaolo had done at the church supper a few months earlier – the ripe juicy cheeks of a pear or apple firmly grasped in one hand and paring knife in the other, first peeling away rind all in one piece, then coring and removing the pips, and finally spearing the fruit with the tip of the knife to pop it into their mouths.

Giampaolo eventually pushed away from the table and patted his stomach. *"Basta!"* he muttered with a satisfied grin. A rumble of agreement arose from the soldiers. They all leaned back in their chairs, as if to accommodate stomachs full from the familiar, satisfying meal. Then, on cue, they reached into their breast pockets for packets of cigarettes and offered them to each other. Rosalie slipped ashtrays onto the table in front of the men as they lit up, plumes of smoke encircling the dining room chandelier. The burbling percolator soon filled the air with the enticing aroma of coffee. Pointing to the sideboard, Donna Sarina instructed her nieces to distribute cups, saucers, and small plates for sweets. *Cummari* Angelina ducked into the kitchen, as familiar as her own, and emerged with the coffee pot, her daughter Frannie on her heels with a stout sugar bowl, a pitcher of milk, and teaspoons.

"Dorci?" Donna Sarina queried the table rhetorically as Suzanne pulled the plastic wrap from a platter of cookies decoratively arranged with Jordan almonds peeking from between, and placed it at the center of the table. The coffee and sweets were soon consumed with appreciative murmurs, as quickly as the rest of the meal.

"What a feast!" Patsy's jubilant compliment pierced the air of contentment in the room. That one is never at a loss for words, thought Eleanor, quietly pleased that the meal had come off so well. Her mother beamed at the American GI.

As the women began clearing the rest of the dishes from the table, *Cumpari* Mollica herded the men toward the kitchen and out the back door, to the patch of lawn where he had laid out his old set of bocce balls. Eleanor knew she would have to do her bit with the after-dinner clean-up before she could join Giampaolo outdoors. She scurried to join the circle of women at the kitchen table, scraping plates. Rosalie immersed a large pile of dishes deep into a steaming tub of suds in the kitchen sink as Suzanne stood by, a clean dish towel poised to tackle plates and silverware from the drying rack. With so many hands doing the work, it was soon finished and the kitchen arranged in Donna Sarina's usual precise order.

Eleanor dried her hands and peered out the kitchen window. Down on the lawn, the men were engaged in a lively game of bocce, smoking and laughing. Not wanting to disturb the scene, she slipped outside and onto the painted wooden bench on the back porch. Hearing the screen door close, Giampaolo glanced up and saw her. He left the game, took the half-dozen steps two at a time from the yard to the porch and sat down next to her.

"Your *mamá* went to a lot of trouble to feed us," he began, referring to her mother in the way that Eleanor would.

"It was no trouble. We usually have a crowd for supper at least once a week," she responded amiably. "It's actually easier to cook a big meal on a weekend, because we don't have to go to work."

"Everything was so good." Giampaolo paused, then in a voice suddenly thick with emotion, he continued. "It reminded me of home."

Stunned, Eleanor realized that it had never occurred to her before that he might be homesick. These soldiers had already been through so much, she thought. Even though they were grown men, they could miss what was familiar, what was remembered with affection.

"How long has it been since you were home?" she asked softly.

"I left home on June 29, 1940."

Eleanor did a quick mental calculation. "You've not been home in more than four years?"

Giampaolo nodded, his eyes looking off sadly toward the middle distance. "It was the feast of Saints Peter and Paul."

Eleanor's heart warmed at his simple piety. Many Italian Americans still measured their year by the ecclesiastical calendar. Her own mother did so. It was a throwback to a time when most could not read nor write. The feast days of the church calendar gave farmers and tradespeople in the old country a temporal yardstick, of sorts. They could keep track of the long hard days of working in fields or toiling at their trades more easily if they knew how soon they would be rewarded with the respite of a single day's rest. Half of each holiday would be spent in church, but there would also be feasting and time with family and friends – the peasant's only real notion of leisure.

"I remember the date because my youngest brother was going to Rome." Giampaolo's comment stirred her out of her musings. "'Bastiano. He's in the seminary."

"Really?"

"He was hoping to be in Rome for the *festa*, but he stayed home because I was leaving."

Her attentive silence encouraged him to continue.

"I left school when I was twelve," he said, recalling working the land with his brothers as barely a teenager. "Turuzzu is the oldest. He was already working on the farm, and Peppino was going to follow right after me. My *papá* needed us to plant the crops and tend the animals. You don't need much schooling to do that."

Giampaolo then recounted his personal history of growing up on a rocky outcropping in southeastern Sicily. He was the second of three boys; there had been four, but the youngest had died as a toddler, drowned when he slipped and fell face down in the stream that coursed through the family farmlands. His mother's piercing screams of anguish still echoed in his ears when she found his brother's little body, stiff and lifeless, in the water. Tragedy like that was the stuff of life everywhere, but especially on a farm: death follows life as inexorably as time passes and the seasons change. God sent these travails, but their lives went on and so did the work of coaxing crops from the rocky soil. After his brother's death a pall had settled over the Stagno household for some time. Only the birth of another son several years later seemed to rebalance life for the family. Once again, Giampaolo's *nonna*, Donna Filomena Lombardo, was a fixture at their sturdy three-story home on the corner of a small street that led onto the main concourse of the town of Palazzolo. There she lived and cared for her youngest grandson just as she had done for the others when they were small.

From adolescence, the elder Stagno brothers would return to their home in town only on Sundays, bicycling the twenty kilometers from the farmhouse in San Marco to Palazzolo on rutted, rocky roads. The rest of the week they spent at the farm with their parents, sleeping on straw-stuffed mattresses on the floor of the rustic two-room farmhouse and rising with the sun to tend the myriad chores of life on the land. On the farm, the brothers took turns caring for a small menagerie of animals – some cows and goats, a donkey, two dogs, and a collection of ever-reproducing cats. His mother milked the cows and made fresh *ricotta* every morning, and that, with some hard bread and a few olives, became their rustic lunchtime fare.

With three sturdy sons nearly grown into adulthood and

helping him run the farm, Giampaolo's father had become prosperous – a relative term, to be sure, in the hand-to-mouth daily life of eastern Sicily in the early years of the twentieth century. But with the breathing room of a little money saved up, the proud Don Giuseppe Stagno was insistent that, unlike the older three, his youngest son, Sebastiano, should continue his education past the rudimentary elementary grades. The paterfamilias had visions of having perhaps a doctor or a lawyer in the family, so once his youngest child had completed grammar school, he remanded Sebastiano to the good priests in Siracusa, members of the order of Servants of Mary. There he would continue his studies and perhaps, one day, qualify to study at the university in Catania.

Sebastiano, however, soon dreamed other dreams.

At a young age, Sebastiano had exhibited a keen intelligence and a lively curiosity about the world beyond his years. He had learned lessons of simple piety at the knee of his devout *nonna,* who taught him his prayers and repeated humble Gospel stories in her quiet voice. Older now, and at school among men of faith who imbued these familiar fables with nuance and subtlety, he craved to learn more. His inclination for scholarship broadened the boy's horizons. He saw his teachers as role models, and came to understand that his education was opening up to him new avenues of pursuit. He was venturing beyond the confines of the simple life he had always known, and there would be no going back. He began to look at his education as a blessing and a sign that he should use his talents – his intellect and his ambition – to serve the Church's interests as well as his own.

And so Don Giuseppe's treasured dream of his youngest son returning home to Palazzolo, an educated man in an honorable profession who could become a pillar of their community, evaporated the day Sebastiano told his parents that he would become a priest.

Sebastiano entered the order of the Servants of Mary, the same one whose priests had given him his formal schooling. Besides obligating them to take vows, the order also required its members to adopt a new name in religious life, signifying a new spiritual identity in the priesthood. Each new priest would forsake his baptismal name and choose a ministerial one with some familial or ecclesiastical significance, by which he would become known from the day of his ordination going forward. When Italy declared war on the Allies in June of 1940, Sebastiano had just begun his religious studies and had been chosen to continue them at a seminary in Rome. In another few years, he hoped to be ordained as Patri Eugenio Stagno, a tribute to the baptismal name of one Eugenio Pacelli, known to Catholics around the world as Pope Pius XII.

As Giampaolo recounted his story in a quiet American backyard half a world away from his home, he had no idea that Sebastiano's plans to study in Rome had been delayed and possibly derailed entirely by the war. He didn't know that his brother Peppino, who had been conscripted into the Italian Army along with him, was absent without leave from his infantry company. During the hard months Giampaolo had spent in North Africa, Peppino had wandered the countryside in northern Italy, hiding in barns and relying on the kindness of strangers for sustenance. There were others like Peppino, soldiers separated from their regiments who had to rely now on a shared antipathy of Italy's unpopular leader among his countrymen. Soldiers like Peppino prayed that the farmers and townspeople they chanced upon hated Mussolini enough to resist turning them over to the Italian authorities as deserters.

Giampaolo had received no word at all from home during his time as a soldier and now as a prisoner. His brother Salvatore was too busy running the family farm to write letters. It wasn't in Turuzzu's nature to sit down and write letters to his brother away in the war. Their parents and grandmother, being virtually illiterate, placed the onus on the youngest member of the family to serve as correspondent. Even in the early years of the war, the handful of letters Sebastiano had sent to his brothers never reached them, lost in the vagaries of frequent troop movement and poor communication among the Italian divisions in North Africa. Sebastiano had no way of knowing that his brother Peppino, in hiding on the mainland, was virtually unreachable. When Giampaolo arrived in the United States, with improved mail delivery prioritized for combatants and prisoners alike, he still never received news of any personal nature, only the most general information about the fortunes of his island at war – how the British field marshal Montgomery and the American general Patton had crisscrossed Sicily, each in a rush to claim it for the Allies, laying waste to the landscape and leaving the island tank-rutted and impoverished. He wondered how his parents and grandmother were surviving the horrors of war – if, indeed, they were still alive.

The banging of the screen door interrupted their conversation. Rosalie emerged from the kitchen with a large tray laden with a pitcher of iced tea and cold bottles of beer. She descended the stairs and set the tray carefully on the picnic table in the backyard. The men snatched up the beers with gusto. Eleanor went down to the table and poured a glass of tea for herself. Snagging a beer for Giampaolo, she went back up to the porch and sat down again on the bench where they had been talking.

"Is all of your family from Palazzolo?"

He nodded. "My mother has some cousins in Ragusa, but otherwise that's it."

"I was born in Florídia, near Siracusa. Do you know it?"

"Yes, of course!" Giampaolo pointed to his two friends, intent on their bocce game. "That's where Vincenzo and Tommaso are from. It's only about thirty kilometers from Palazzolo."

"I don't remember much of my birthplace," Eleanor admitted with regret. "We left when I was just five years old. My father had died two years earlier, and then my only sister died when she was just a baby. At least that's what my mother has told me. *Mamá* was very sad. Nothing could console her."

She paused, remembering the melancholy into which her mother had sunk, dealing with so much loss as a young woman not yet twenty-five years old. A puzzled look crossed Giampaolo's brow. "You had only one sister? But I thought – " He gestured toward the house.

A smile of understanding crossed Eleanor's lips. "Ah, *sí*. Suzanna and Rosalia are actually my cousins. Their father, my Zio Carmelo, was already here in America with his family. His wife, my Zia Antonietta, died when my youngest cousin was born. Veronica? You know, Veronica and Nick, from dinner?" He nodded.

"We learned that Zia 'Tonina had died giving birth to Veronica. It was just after my baby sister died. *Mamá* took it as a sign, since Zia 'Tonina had died that same month. That's when she started talking about coming to America." Eleanor sipped her iced tea. "*Mamá* felt she had no future there any more, but here, she could help my uncle raise his family."

Giampaolo's eyes cleared in understanding. "*Giá capisciu.* Now I understand. You and your cousins were raised like sisters."

"*Sí, giustu,*" she nodded. "My father's family in Florídia was not too happy about Mamá's decision to leave. I was their only grandchild. They felt that by taking me to America, they would lose me, too, just as they had lost their son and their other granddaughter. They tried to persuade Mamá not to go. But she can be stubborn when she makes up her mind." Eleanor pursed her lips and paused pensively. "No, emigrating to America was certainly not a popular plan with the Fazzios."

"Do you still have family in Sicily?"

"Oh yes. My mother's sister lives in Florídia still," she continued. "Zia Marietta has a big family too, four sons and three daughters. The youngest, two of the girls and one of the boys, are all younger than me and were born after *Mamá* and I had moved here." She looked at him steadily. She spoke of her aunt and her cousins, but she knew Giampaolo was still thinking of home and his own parents. She added, "My aunt and uncle have been having difficulty managing since before the troops came to Sicily. Not much has improved since the liberation."

He sighed. Worry lines creased his forehead. "I've heard that things are very bad at home."

"We've heard that too."

Eleanor pondered the grim reality. By this point in time, Giampaolo's home could have been reduced to a pile of rubble. For her, home was here, safe and sound and far away from the devastation of war. She couldn't imagine what it would be like to have gone for entire years without any news of loved ones and beloved places.

Then she thought of the things sitting on her sewing table upstairs, items awaiting a cardboard box to send to Zia Marietta in Sicily. Everyday items she took for granted. At least twice a month without fail since the war began, her mother put together packages for her sister's large family. Donna Sarina would box up practical things like fabric for making clothes (like Eleanor's mother, her aunt was a skilled seamstress); incidentals like threads and needles, socks and shoes, soap for washing and bathing, and always an envelope of American dollars. Once she had sent a line of rope and clothespins and some cans of condensed milk from their meager family allotment. Another time Eleanor's mother sent her to the hardware store for a new dustpan and brush, which had promptly gone into a package along with spools of twine. Sarina wrote her sister weekly, imploring Marietta to send her a list of what they needed that she could perhaps procure and send in the next package.

Of course, there was wartime scarcity in America, too. That scarcity expressed itself in the Luna household through simple things, as well. The carefully rewound lengths of used string stored for reuse in a kitchen drawer. Tin cans systematically opened at both ends when the contents were gone, and flattened with a stomp of a foot on the kitchen rug, then tossed in a carton kept for periodic recycling to support the war effort. The book of food ration stamps stowed for safekeeping in a cubbyhole in the desk, next to her savings account book and the brown bank envelopes for paying the weekly mortgage. Still, even amid rationing and paltry supplies of household goods on store shelves, Sarina Fazzio saw her adopted American home as a land of virtual plenty compared to the privations her sister's family must have been experiencing in Sicily, and so she sought to share whatever she could.

Letters from Sicily were few and far between. Eleanor and her mother had come to expect this. The war in Italy was causing havoc everywhere in that country, not least disruption of conventional government services like the mail. Things seemed to be the worst in Sicily. On the bloodiest battlefields so far in the European theater, Sicily's military lines of communication – let alone its civilian ones – were frayed badly. For all Donna Sarina knew, her letters and packages never reached their intended destination. Newspapers reported that Italy's failure to resupply its troops during the Africa campaign had been a critical factor in the eventual Allied triumph there. Those very same Axis defeats had brought Giampaolo to the United States as a war prisoner.

American newsreels at the movie houses had recently begun to paint a more cheerful picture for the American and Allied troops. Even as her American pride was boosted by these bits of news from the front, Eleanor's heart told her that things would not get better for families in Sicily as the war progressed. Perhaps the outright fighting in the streets had slowed or stopped, but a longer Allied occupation had begun. Eleanor and her mother resisted contemplating this larger picture for long. As if the war had changed nothing, Sarina stubbornly wrote her weekly letters to her sister and sent them into the void. Eleanor dutifully posted the packages her mother prepared, never sure they were being received but unwilling to dwell on the horrific conditions that would prevent the packages from being delivered.

Now, as Eleanor watched Giampaolo's worried face, she understood his apprehension about his family's fate. Putting on an outward confidence she didn't feel, she reached out and patted his hand.

"I'll pray for them."

Giampaolo shifted slightly in his seat, but the look of worry remained. Eleanor descended the few stairs to the lawn and took another bottle of beer from the tray. Before opening it, she gestured to him. "*Àutru*? Would you like another?"

He nodded. When she reached the porch, he took the bottle from her, slick with condensation and now no longer cold.

A cheer erupted from the clot of soldiers on the lawn. Vincenzo finished *Cumpari* Mollica's bocce game with a victorious flourish. Patsy pounded him on the back.

"You know what the Brits would say, Vincenzo? 'Jolly good, old sport!'" Patsy feigned a British accent and tipped his fingers in salute.

Tony snorted. "Give this guy six months in a barracks in Britain, and he thinks he's the King of England."

Patsy ignored his American buddy as he laughed and slapped Vincenzo's shoulder.

The shadows were lengthening in the garden before the last round of bocce was abandoned and the party returned to the house. Giampaolo and Eleanor lingered on the back porch.

"Tomorrow we will have a picnic. And Monday is Labor Day," she began. "Will you be coming to the parade?"

Giampaolo shook his head slowly.

"We must return to camp tomorrow."

Eleanor was crestfallen. "Oh, no...we thought you'd be coming with us."

"I am very sorry. Honestly, I would like to see what an American Labor Day parade is like. But I don't think we Italian soldiers are welcome."

"What do you mean?"

"Sometimes, when we go out in town, people see the Italy patch on our uniforms, and they frown or scowl at us. Some shout 'Go home!' and call us names. Our wardens don't forbid us to go out in public, but they do tell us to go as a group and ignore those who shout at us."

"Giampaolo, I didn't know..." Eleanor was momentarily dumbfounded, but soon she recalled the days immediately after war was declared. Angry citizens of her hometown drove past the Italian Catholic church just as Mass let out, taunting the Italians spitefully. It was an ugly scene. Eleanor had been shocked – she and her family were all American citizens, after all – but soon she realized there was no point reacting to that prejudice. Her mother had instructed them all to keep a low profile when they went out in public – don't provoke, don't engage. Eleanor's approach was complete withdrawal. She would put her head down and walk quickly past strangers, lest they be among those who harbored ill will toward Italians, or toward Germans for that matter. There were lots of Germans in Oxford County, but many had been here for generations. The Italians were relative newcomers, and because many of them had swarthy skin and dark hair, they were easier to pinpoint and ridicule.

"What can one do." Giampaolo shrugged, his comment a statement more than a question, and he jutted his chin forward as if to underscore it. She touched his arm sympathetically. Then he surprised her by placing a hand on her waist and giving her a gentle sideways hug.

"Maybe someday I'll see an American holiday parade." He smiled wanly.

* * *

For the rest of the weekend, Eleanor had gone through the motions of picnicking and watching the Labor Day festivities. The days after the soldiers and prisoners returned to their base seemed dull and colorless without their spirited conversation and a next visit to look forward to. Now that a connection had been established, an invitation to visit again could just as easily come from her as from the Mollicas. What if they were to host the group for a real American Thanksgiving? Eleanor decided to enlist the cooperation of her Mollica neighbors.

One early October day on their lunch break at the factory, she and Frannie were enjoying the glorious fall weather as they took a turn around the parking lot. Eleanor casually turned the chatter toward the coming holiday.

"John put a sign in the market window last week reminding his customers to order their turkeys. Can you believe it? Thanksgiving will be here before we know it."

Frannie sniffed in agreement and commented drolly, "Time flies when you're having fun."

"Any relatives coming to visit?"

"No, not that I know of. Unless we invite Tommaso."

Eleanor let the sentence hang in the air for a moment. "Any chance of that?

"Now that you mention it, that's a good idea," Frannie responded.

"*I* didn't mention it, you did!" Eleanor exclaimed.

"Well, whatever."

The circuit of their walk complete, the two women returned to the plant entrance. Frannie worked in the same building as Eleanor, on one of the upper floors.

"You'd love that, wouldn't you?" Frannie teased her friend with a sly grin. The Labor Day outing and its aftermath had left no one in doubt of Eleanor's affection for Giampaolo.

"Well, I certainly wouldn't mind if Tommaso were to come and bring Giampaolo along."

They pulled open the heavy door and climbed the stairs. Eleanor focused her attention on each metal tread as she climbed, letting the conversation idle.

"I'll mention it tonight," Frannie responded as she continued up the stairs. Eleanor held the door ajar on the third-floor landing for a moment. She hoped her joy hadn't been too transparent. With a happy smile on her face, she went back to work.

24 ottobre 1944

Carissimo Giampaolo,

How are you? I hope you are well. We are all well here, working as usual. Not much changes here.

How are things in the camp? I hope that you are being treated well and not forced to work more than usual. I also hope you are also getting a chance to enjoy your free time on the weekends.

As you may know from the American soldiers, a big American holiday is coming up in November: Thanksgiving. Were you here for it last year? On Thanksgiving, we stop and give thanks for all of our blessings. The holiday commemorates the day when the first English settlers in America made peace with the Indians who lived nearby. They held a big feast in thanks for having made it through the hard first winter in their new land. To honor this tradition, American families roast a big turkey and make a lot of other foods customary for the season to go along with it. We always have potato filling, dried corn, and cranberry sauce.

Am I making you hungry? I hope so, because I'd like to invite you to come to our house for Thanksgiving.

Frannie is writing Tommaso to invite him and Vincenzo, too, so perhaps you could come with them if it's allowed? Your American friends Patsy and Tony will probably go home to be with their families for the holiday, but they are certainly welcome to celebrate with us, too. The holiday is on a Thursday, and I don't have to work on Friday, so perhaps you could stay through the weekend?

Let me know as soon as you can if you can get permission to leave the camp, and if you will come.

With affection,

Eleanora

30 ottobre, 1944

Carissima Eleanora,

What joy to get your letter! I was glad to hear you are well and happy, and so very glad you took time to write me.

I am very well and keeping busy. We are still working on the docks every day and we come home each night very tired. There is less light in the evenings now, and the weather is cold. Our American guards have issued us winter coats and hats and the thickest rubber boots you ever saw!

I have spoken to Tommaso, who got a letter from Francesca as you said he would. We will be coming for the holiday. He is eager to see his cousins again, and Vincenzo will come along, too. We have requested permission to travel from Thursday morning, November 23, and return to camp on Sunday, November 26. Patsy and Tony have got leave to visit their families, so the commanding officer will assign a different military chaperone to accompany us. We cannot travel alone, and we will probably travel by train this time. The car Patsy used for our trip in the summer was his brother's, who'll be home for the holiday too and wanting it back. And the staff car we drove last time won't be available to us again – it was lucky we got to borrow it then. Once our chaperone is assigned, we three will give him money to purchase our train tickets. Then our plans will be complete.

I'm looking forward very much to seeing you again. I think of you often and hope you think of me.

With affection,

Giampaolo

Chapter 11

Thanksgiving involves a huge meal shared at home with family and friends. Turkey is the main course, along with stuffing, vegetables, potatoes and gravy, cranberry sauce, bread, and pies, almost always pumpkin. Many Italian-American families, however, celebrate this day with the traditional turkey dinner, while also adding some recipes from their Italian ancestors. My own family maintained the American traditions without any added pasta dishes or Italian touches.

—*Italian Talks* (Baglioni Hotels Guidebooks)

Thanksgiving Day 1944, Port Johnson, Bayonne, New Jersey

It was still dark when Giampaolo awoke and stole carefully from the warmth of his blankets, so as not to disturb his sleeping bunkmates. He dressed as quickly and quietly as he could in the clothes he had placed near his bed the night before.

"Tommaso!" His hoarse whisper echoed in the still-dark sleeping quarters. He could just make out his friend at his cot down the row, stuffing things into his rucksack. He and Tommaso were billeted in the same barracks; Vincenzo was in another dormitory nearby.

"Give me a minute. I'll meet you outside," came back the muted response.

He heard the rumble of a Jeep just beyond the barracks door. "He's here!" Giampaolo whispered again, more urgently. He grabbed his pack and threw on his coat. Gently opening the door, he winced as the hinges squeaked.

"Iu veniu, I'm coming!" Tommaso called quietly and crept outside on tiptoe, the door lock clicking softly behind him.

Outside, the military vehicle idled, with two American GIs in the front seat. Plumes of cigarette smoke escaped the windows on both sides.

"Here they come," one said to the other.

Emerging from another barracks some dozen yards away, Vincenzo scuttled stealthily across the hard-packed dirt of the compound towards them, dragging his knapsack and coat behind him.

"You guys get some chow?" the driver asked Giampaolo. At his quizzical expression, the soldier put his fingers together and lifted an imaginary spoon to his mouth.

Giampaolo shook his head. *"No. Treno."* Then he added in stilted English, "Eat later."

"Ciao," the American soldier in the passenger seat called out in greeting, waving them toward the back seat of the vehicle. *"Ammunin'!"* Relieved to hear familiar dialect, the three Italians grinned, clambering aboard and hoisting their packs onto their laps for the ride to the train depot.

The soldier next to the driver twisted around to face the three prisoners shoe-horned into the back of the vehicle. *"Piaceri,"* he held out a hand in greeting. *"Mi chiamo Raffaele. Raffaele Pirone."* Then mixing Italian with English, he added, "Everyone just calls me Rafe."

Giampaolo grasped his hand. *"Piaceri.* Giampaolo Stagno." His friends took their turns greeting the American. When Tommaso said his name, Rafe asked, "Mollica? So you're the guy with the cousins."

"Sí, sí!" Tommaso chuckled, continuing in Italian. "We're going to my cousins' house. They live in Pennsylvania."

Rafe turned back to face the driver and translated. "We're visiting that guy's family." He gestured toward Tommaso with his thumb. "Nice of them to invite them for Thanksgiving. Me, too!"

The driver replied with a shrug. "I don't get leave until Christmas. So I'll just be eating chow today in the mess hall. But it should be better than usual. One of the guys who pulled KP told me there'll be roast turkey. And the pumpkin pie should be swell."

Light was just breaking over the horizon as they stopped at the camp's gate to show passes to the guards. Once through the checkpoint, the Jeep turned its back to the port and made its way along country lanes that quickly gave way to urban neighborhoods lined with modest houses. Dawn grew to full daylight while Giampaolo took in the gritty streets of Jersey City as they gave way to industrial zones on the city's edge. More trim neighborhoods flew by, and soon the soldiers were in the midst of tall buildings, broad storefronts, and small gated squares that comprised the heart of Newark's commercial district. Street signs with strange American names zoomed past: Orange Street, Fulton Avenue, Broad Street, Market Street. Along one thoroughfare a row of taxi cabs awaited their fares; on another wide avenue, buses were taking on and disgorging passengers even at this early hour of a holiday morning. Giampaolo strained to see the higher reaches of buildings towering overhead. Some had names painted onto their brick facades; others bore lights that named the establishments: "Adams Theater," "Allen & Bros. Pianos," "Boscobel Hotel."

Negotiating the city traffic with ease, the driver swung the Jeep efficiently into a parking spot in front of Penn Station.

"Siamo arrivati! We're here, let's go," shouted Rafe as the travelers scrambled onto the sidewalk and shouldered their packs.

Rafe hollered out to the driver of the Jeep. "Thanks a lot, pal, I owe you one," he said, waving farewell and tapping the vehicle's hood twice as it began to pull away from the curb.

The American reached into his breast pocket and pulled out four tickets. "We made good time. Let's grab some coffee." Seeing their puzzled looks at his English, Rafe asked simply, "*Caffè?*"

At that, the Italians nodded in unison and they headed into the station.

The cavernous waiting room with its vaulted stone ceiling was lined with sturdy benches of polished dark wood, giving the place an air of quiet grandeur. Rafe consulted the train timetables overhead. "We'll leave from Platform 3. *Binario numero tre*," he repeated to the three Italians, holding up three fingers. "*Abbiamo mezz' ora.* We have a half-hour till we board the train."

Rafe pointed toward a luncheonette on one side of the waiting room, its neon "Open" sign blinking a bright welcome. The four entered and found seats at the spotless Formica and stainless-steel counter. A perky waitress in a red gingham uniform, her blonde hair piled under a matching cap, approached immediately.

"What can I get you fellas?" she asked, winking at Giampaolo.

Rafe took over and ordered for them. "Got any good Danish this morning, sweetie?" He smiled at her, letting the uniform work its khaki charm. In Rafe's experience, well-pressed military garb never failed to impress a young lady far better than civvies would do. Military dress was a constant reminder that it was wartime, even far away from the front. Soldiers were everywhere. Khaki and brown uniforms and sailors' whites were visible in almost every corner of America these days, but especially in transit, at bus stations, train depots, and piers.

She cracked her chewing gum twice as she turned to peer down the counter. "Looks like you're in luck, soldier – we have cherry and cheese Danish this morning."

"How about two of each, then, and four coffees?" Rafe's cheeks dimpled in a cocky smile designed to take her breath away.

"Sure, soldier, coming right up!" She grinned as she stuck her pencil behind her ear and headed for the tall glass dome that arched over two layers of baked goods – assorted slices of homemade pie and mouth-watering pastry.

While awaiting their breakfast, Rafe turned to the three prisoners and spoke to them in Italian. "My parents are from a town called Isola delle Femmine. It's near Palermo. I was born there but came over here when I was three."

The Italians nodded in unison. Tommaso said, "We're all from Sicily too. Your Italian is quite good."

"I grew up hearing it at home," Rafe offered with a shrug, as if it was nothing. "Most of the families in our neighborhood speak Italian." Then he added for good measure, "My father has a fishing boat near San Francisco."

The waitress returned with arms laden with small plates, each with a flaky pastry on it. She doled them out, one in front of each man, then reached under the counter for cups and saucers, and poured four cups of coffee.

The foursome dug into the flaky pastry hungrily and made quick work of their breakfast. Since the counter was idle but for them, their server leaned back on the wall to observe the young men, her arms crossed, her face open with friendly curiosity.

"What's the patch on your sleeve for?" She asked, pointing a painted red fingernail at the "Italy" patch on Vincenzo's arm.

Knowing what she was asking, he looked at her sheepishly, then mumbled, *"Prigionieri."*

When she looked confused, Rafe took his cue. "These guys are here temporarily," he explained. "They fought in North Africa and were captured as prisoners of war. The patch designates their home country."

Her eyes widened. "Italy? Ain't they the enemy?"

"Technically, yeah, although not really anymore," Rafe continued, then paused to gauge her reaction. "As you can see, they are just guys like us."

The young woman's smile faded as she refreshed their coffee. She turned to Rafe and asked curtly. "Anything else?"

Discerning the sudden chill in her tone, he said simply, "Nah, that's it. We got a train to catch. Just the bad news, please."

She pulled a slip from her pocket and scribbled on it hastily. As she set the bill in front of Rafe, her face crumpled in an unbecoming sneer. "Don't you have any *American* buddies to hang out with?" she hissed. "It's Thanksgiving, for Chrissake."

Rafe looked her straight in the eye, as if daring her to say more. Then he nodded, plunked some money on the counter and told his three companions in a low voice, *"Andiamo.* Let's go."

The four slid from their benches. Giampaolo turned to find the waitress staring at them, so he winked and turned his head slightly, in farewell. With a pronounced sway to her shoulders, she turned dismissively and strode to the other end of the counter.

Once outside the restaurant, Rafe turned to the three men. In Italian, he said, *"Mi dispiace molto.* I'm sorry about that." He added balefully, "I get that attitude from people sometimes too. Even from some of the guys. Once they hear I was born in Italy, or if they overhear me speaking Italian on the telephone when I call home, they think I'm not to be trusted."

"We know," Giampaolo said quietly.

The group fell silent. Then Rafe put on his cap and checked

the schedule again. "Let's go find our train." The Italians shouldered their belongings and followed the American GI across the waiting room to a series of numbered doorways, each leading to a stairway down to the tracks one level below. When they got to Platform 3, they found the train already there, with conductors at each door to check passengers' tickets. Rafe handed over four tickets. The conductor glanced at the men briefly, taking note of their uniforms, and waved them inside.

Once inside the train, Vincenzo found a group of four seats, two facing two with a table in between. The soldiers stowed bags and coats on the racks above their seats and got comfortable.

Rafe's mind was still on the incident in the café. "Makes me very angry," he said. "After Pearl Harbor, my family got a lot of guff from the officials in my town back home." He folded his hands on the table, then added by way of explanation, "Bad blood."

The Pirones' house was a tiny frame structure in an unassuming neighborhood not far from the ocean in the seaside town of Monterey, California. It was home, the only one Rafe remembered, the only one his younger brothers and sisters had ever known. Most of the other houses on their block were owned by Italian immigrants like his parents, most of them fishermen from Sicily, Naples, or Genoa.

In January of 1942, shortly after Rafe had enlisted, the Pirones and most of their neighbors were informed by city officials that Italians were now forbidden in the zone of the city where their homes were located. Like many of their neighbors, the Pirone family was forced to move. Rafe's father found a cramped dark apartment a few miles east of the waterfront where he kept his fishing boat, and they moved in. He would now have a long walk to reach his boat each morning, and would have to do the same each night after a strenuous day at sea and on the docks.

Rafe's mother was distraught at having to leave their home. She knew no one in their new neighborhood. The space was far too small for the family. They were crowded on top of each other in the airless flat. After several tearful sessions with his father explaining that they had no choice, she made the best of their straitened circumstances. Tears still rose to her eyes nearly every day as she longed for the sunshine in their tiny backyard and the smell of salt air.

The rent they now had to pay for the apartment gouged the Pirones' already stretched household budget. Rafe's father reluctantly put a "For Rent" sign on the family house they still owned near the waterfront. If he could find a tenant, it might help cover both the mortgage on the house and the rent on the apartment where they now lived. But it seemed no one wanted to rent from Italians. In June of that year, the situation got worse. Curfews were imposed on Italians, many of whom had already earned their U.S. citizenship. Some had sons like Rafe who had volunteered for the armed forces right after Pearl Harbor, and were away fighting in the war.

The curfew put further strains on Rafe's father, as he was now forced to conduct his fishing business only during daylight hours. It meant fewer hours at sea and fewer fish to sell. If he were caught after curfew in a restricted part of town – like the waterfront – he would be subject to arrest. There had been some close calls.

But not everything was bleak. Alfredo Pirone was a familiar figure on the waterfront, and some of his American neighbors and fellow fisherman sympathized with the family's plight. One acquaintance, a man whose fishing boat was moored near Pirone's vessel, would touch his cap when he saw the Italian on the waterfront past curfew, hurriedly cleaning the deck or wrapping the lines. Neighbors who lived on the block where the Pirones' home stood empty dropped by the pier, leaving packages for Alfredo to take to his family, rationed items that they knew would be difficult to get except in areas of the city now off-limits to him. All the while Rafe's father had stoically endured, carefully maintaining his boat and keeping a low profile to avoid trouble. As the summer turned to fall, Rafe heard rumors that sympathetic Californians all over the state were petitioning the governor to ease up on these restrictions. The situation was even worse for Japanese residents: they had been uprooted from their homes and neighborhoods and installed in camps, some several hundred miles away. No one seemed to be pleading their case to the authorities. And so, nothing changed. As the war dragged on in distant corners of the world, life continued drearily and without sign of improvement for the Pirones of Monterey.

The Italians now understood the sneer and snide remarks of the waitress a bit better. The significant distance Rafe would have had to travel would have eaten up most of his holiday leave, but that wasn't the only thing that kept their chaperone from being at home with his family on this holiday.

"I miss my family," Rafe admitted, concluding his story in Italian. "A lot has happened since I left. Not that I could do much to help their situation if I were there."

Tommaso brightened and said, "Never mind. My cousins will make you feel very welcome in their home during our visit."

"Yes, it's nice to get out of camp for a while. Kind of makes you feel normal again, like there's not a war going on." The passenger car lurched and they were underway.

As the cement smokestacks of Newark faded to a gray smudge on the horizon, the train carried them through fields with low brown stubble where tall stalks of green corn had stood two months earlier. The low hum of conversation in Italian between his friends gradually lulled Giampaolo to sleep. When he opened his eyes, the countryside had given way to a cityscape once more: street after street of tidy brick row houses signaled their arrival in Philadelphia.

"We change trains here," Rafe motioned to the city speeding by. "This city is called Philadelphia. We board another train very soon after we arrive."

The conductor called out for Broad Street station, then a few minutes later for 30th Street, where the four men were to get off and transfer to the train for Jamesport. With only a few minutes to spare for their connection, Rafe hustled them off the Pullman car, up one set of stairs and down another onto a smaller platform where the train for Jamesport soon chugged into the station in a cloud of steam.

It was fully one o'clock before the Mollicas' car pulled up to their home. Frannie had met the four men at the station alone, because it would make a tight squeeze fitting them all into the family car. Giampaolo's face fell when he did not find Eleanor on the depot platform awaiting him, but it made him all the more eager to see in person the young woman he'd been seeing in his dreams for weeks now.

The wait hadn't been easy for Eleanor, either. She had hoped to be part of the welcoming committee when the Italians got off the train, but practicalities had foiled that plan. As soon as she saw their neighbors' automobile park across the street, she shot out of the front door without thought of putting on a coat, despite the frosty air.

Giampaolo was just getting out of the car when he looked up. There she was, smiling shyly, waiting for him on the sidewalk. He held her shoulders and leaned in to place a kiss on each cheek. She smelled like gardenias.

"*Binvinutu, Giampaolo.* Welcome," she stammered.

The other men were shaking hands with *Cumpari* Mollica. Tommaso introduced Rafe to his uncle and provided a brief biography. "He's from California. His family is Sicilian!" Rafe grinned and grasped the older man's hands.

Time stood still for the pair still on the sidewalk. Eleanor looked him over, then rubbed his arms briskly. Giampaolo hadn't bothered with a coat either. She finally broke the silence.

"You must be cold."

He laughed. "We were packed so tightly in the car that I didn't mind."

The rest of the group was making their way up the stairs to the porch where *Cummari* Angelina waited, a bulky sweater over her apron and a contented smile on her pale face. She opened her arms to embrace her nephew. Frannie turned around and noticed Eleanor and Giampaolo leaning together on the curb.

"Come on, you two!" she called to them.

Giampaolo grasped Eleanor's hand eagerly and led her up the stairs.

Everyone took seats in the living room. Mary had mixed up a batch of whiskey sours in her mother's prized crystal pitcher. She served them promptly in ice-filled lowball glasses, and the whiskey soon loosened tongues as everyone relaxed. As it wasn't the Italian custom, the Mollicas weren't given to serving appetizers or even cocktails, except on rare occasions, and then prompted largely by the younger generation who were embracing American ways. This was one of those occasions. Frannie came into the living room with a bowl of olives (the plump black ones preserved in brine, imported from Sicily) and a bowl of *lupine,* large white lupin beans with a nut-like flavor that had been soaked and softened in salted water and that for Eleanor always signaled the coming of the holidays.

Soon they were beckoned to the table for a first course of soup, Donna Sarina's homemade *vrodu* with tiny meatballs and fine pasta. The soup dishes were cleared with dispatch to make way for an array of *virduri,* side dishes the likes of which Giampaolo and his Italian comrades had never seen: a mashed-potato casserole rich with butter and fragrant with celery, onions, and lots of parsley; a darkish yellow mash of dried corn, surprisingly sweet and hearty; a platter of mixed roasted vegetables in which he recognized chunks of eggplant and potato, three colors of peppers, tangy slow-roasted tomatoes, small sweet *cipuddi,* onions, and soft cubes of *cuccuzza,* a yellow squash familiar to Giampaolo. An oval dish containing a dark red jelly went around the table: Eleanor called this American dish cranberry sauce, but it did not resemble any sauce he had ever tasted – very sweet and slippery on the tongue but with a bitter bite to it.

The turkey, of course, was the showstopper, its huge domed breast a mouthwatering mahogany hue from hours of basting in the oven. *Cumpari* Mollica sliced it expertly, first twisting off the enormous drumsticks whose succulent chunks of meat practically fell off the bone, then cutting precisely into the breast and shearing off generous slices of white meat. The gravy that was passed after everyone had been served some turkey was also unlike anything Giampaolo had ever eaten – thick with the pan drippings and tangy with fresh herbs. The gravy's decided aftertaste of rosemary drew him back momentarily to those terrible starving days in the African desert. He shook off the thought and dug into the vegetables, determined to eat enough to erase the memory of hunger pangs. Today he was faced with happier choices and the prospect of a belly full of delicious food.

"What, no *maccherone*?" Rafe joked to the two older women at the table who were the architects of the feast.

Cummari Angelina clucked quietly and whispered audibly behind her hand. "Sarina, I told you they would want some!" To spare the pasta on this occasion apparently had been a decision reached only after much argument between the two matriarchs.

Donna Sarina set down her fork with ceremony and looked sternly at the young man. "This is an American holiday, *miu figghiu*," she intoned in the Sicilian dialect. "You should know that. In our homes," she undertook to speak for herself and the Mollicas both, "we cook American food on American holidays." She resumed eating, the indignity addressed.

Suitably chastened, Rafe then apologized. "I was just ribbing you, Mrs. Fazzio," the soldier appealed contritely, then added, "Everything is just delicious. *Daveru bono.*" For emphasis, he dimpled his cheek with his index finger.

Cumpari Mollica was quick to pour more wine. He reached over and grasped two bottles by the neck, arose, and proceeded around the table to refill glasses, beginning with the Italian guests. His wife threw him a guarded look, silently urging moderate pours, lest the young men sink into a drunken haze before coffee was served.

Throughout the meal Eleanor smiled and laughed at everything that Giampaolo said to her. He spoke softly, leaning over and whispering so that only she could hear. She returned the favor by making sure his plate wanted for nothing and his wine glass was full. A few times their hands touched as they passed the food around the table. She blushed at each touch, then willed it to happen again soon.

"Is this anything like the food you'd be having at home in California?" Frannie directed her question to Rafe with a twinkle in her eye.

"Well, yes, it is, although instead of soup we would often start with fish of some kind – clams or scallops, or the catch of the day." Rafe laughed, then shrugged. "Occupational hazard, I guess, since Dad's a fisherman."

"I hope you are leaving room for dessert," Eleanor's cousin Suzanne piped up. She'd been sitting quietly throughout the meal.

That was Eleanor's cue to praise both of her cousins for their contributions to the meal. She looked at Giampaolo as she spoke. "My cousin Rosalie always makes the meatballs for the soup." Rosalie beamed and cast her eyes down. "But Suzanne bakes the best pies. She made three for today!" Eleanor held up three fingers, and now it was Suzanne's turn to blush and smile.

"*Tri dorci!* It's too much," groaned Tommaso, placing a hand on his stomach. Vincenzo joined the chorus as the women cleared the plates and savory leftovers.

"Don't forget, *mi amuri,*" *Cumpari* Mollica chimed in as his wife removed the turkey platter from the table. "Tomorrow, hot turkey *zang-weech!*"

Cummari Angelina shook her head merrily. "That's my Pippo for you. Not even finished one meal and he's planning the next one." As she turned to go into the kitchen, her husband patted her derriere affectionately.

The welcoming aroma of freshly brewed coffee made its way from the kitchen, as Suzanne proudly set the first pie on the table. Rosalie arrived with a large knife, a serving spoon, and a big bowl mounded with vanilla ice cream. Mary came in with a second pie, and Suzanne carried the third herself: in all, pumpkin, mincemeat, and shoofly.

Seeing Giampaolo's quizzical smile prompted Eleanor to explain the differences. Using a mixture of English and Italian, she began.

"That's pumpkin," she pointed to the orange-gold confection in the middle of the table. "*Cuccuzza,*" she summoned the dialect word.

"*Sí?*" he questioned. The pumpkins and squash he had eaten at home were always cooked as a vegetable in savory fashion, or sometimes used in filled pasta like ravioli.

"*Chiddu,* that one," she said, gesturing to a pie with a mounded dome of crumbs on top, is called 'shoo-fly.' Because," she explained, "it's so sweet that when you set it on the window-sill to cool, you have to constantly 'shoo' the flies away from it." Her fingers performed the outward brushing motion in the air. "*'A Musca disgraziata, vattine!*"

"*E chistu ccá?* And this one?" Giampaolo pointed to the last pie with a custard-like dark brown filling.

"It's called 'mincemeat,'" she replied. "It's, well...it's unique. Fruits like raisins and apples, and spices like cloves and nutmeg. And a little something else. *C'e carni dentro.*" She thought of the hunk of suet hanging on the bird feeder in *Cumpari* Mollica's garden, and she giggled as Giampaolo's eyes grew round.

"*Quinni non è dorci?* So it's not sweet?"

"*No, è abunnanza dorci,* it's plenty sweet all right." The spices and the rum in which the mincemeat was soaked made the whole concoction taste nothing whatsoever like meat. She searched for the right descriptor.

"*I sivu fa la torta vagnátu, ma non sali,* the meat fat just makes the pie juicy, but not salty," *Cummari* Angelina explained with a smile.

The three Italians bobbed their heads in understanding.

Suzanne finally chimed it. "Yes but, for the last few years, I've had to make it without suet. Because of meat being rationed, I couldn't get any." She shook her head regretfully. "I hope it's not dry."

"I don't care what's in it or *not* in it, it looks delicious," Rafe exclaimed. "I'll take a slice of each!"

As the dinner wound down, everyone made their way into the living room in search of comfortable seating and a place to talk. Sitting next to Giampaolo on the sofa, Eleanor wanted to make sure she would see more of him during the weekend that stretched before them.

"*Chi fai dumani?* What are you doing tomorrow?" she asked.

He looked toward his friends and Rafe, who responded for the group. "We don't really have anything planned."

"There's a Christmas bazaar in the church hall on Saturday. *Na festa.* The ladies' sodality sells arts and crafts, and there's food to eat. Would you like to go?" She addressed the center of the room but looked directly at Giampaolo.

"*Sí, sí!*" he responded with enthusiasm.

"That sounds like fun," echoed Rafe. The other two Italians nodded, and then turned to *Cumpari* Mollica, who had unwrapped a box of cigars and was passing them around.

"Okay, then," she responded, "we can meet at noon and walk over together."

"*E dumani?* What about tomorrow?" Giampaolo searched her face eagerly.

"*Cosa da fari in casa,* I have things to do in the house. I always like to begin decorating for Christmas – *pe' Natale* – on the Thanksgiving weekend. There's so much to do..."

"Oh, you," Frannie broke in with just a touch of impatience. "You're as bad as my dad and his next meal. We're not even done with one holiday and you are on to the next!" She laughed teasingly.

Eleanor grew defensive. "Well, it's just that there is so much to do. I love the smell of evergreen boughs in the house." She paused and added in low tones, "With the war on, I think we need as much Christmas cheer as we can get."

A momentary silence descended on the table.

Giampaolo asked in a soft voice, "*Bisognu aiutari?* Do you need help?"

"Well, sure..."

"*Sugniu prontu pe ti,* I am ready to help you however I can."

"*Grazî*, Giampaolo," Eleanor replied. "Perhaps we could even shop for a Christmas tree."

Frannie interposed again. "It's way too early to put up the tree!"

"Well, ok, but we could buy one and bring it home," Eleanor countered. "We can put it in the stand outside and bring it into the living room later." She knew that Donna Sarina would insist on a thorough house-cleaning before the Luna household got too deeply into holiday décor. Rooms had to be aired out. Cobwebs had to be dusted from every corner. The Luna girls had already made headway on some of these chores over the past few weekends, but the annual drape-hanging melodrama was yet to be endured. She certainly didn't need Giampaolo to witness that.

"Anyway, we can buy some greens for the mantel," Eleanor ended the discussion with finality and a sharp look at Frannie. "It's supposed to be a nice day for a walk tomorrow."

"*Alluda, amuninn'!* Then let's go," Giampaolo added amiably and smiled at her.

Chapter 12

To obtain the family Christmas tree during WWII there was no need to drive out of town (most families did not have a car) as Christmas trees were sold right on Somerset Street in Raritan. You paid your three dollars and carried your tree home. It was common for families to purchase their tree just a day or two before Christmas.

—from "Christmas in Raritan [NJ] during World War II," www.raritan-online.com

The day after Thanksgiving 1944, Jamesport, Pennsylvania

Arising the next day to bright sunshine streaming through her bedroom window, Eleanor lifted the sash and took a deep breath. The air outside was positively spring-like, making it hard to believe that December was just around the corner. It would be a fine day for a walk.

By the time Eleanor made her way to the kitchen, Suzanne was already hauling out the ladder and Rosalie had set up the ironing board in the living room.

Suzanne gave her cousin a long look. "Ro and I can put up the drapes this year."

"I can help too," Eleanor insisted. "Just let me have a cup of coffee."

Rosalie joined in. "No, it's OK. We know you want to be with that fella of yours."

"He's hardly my 'fella'!" Eleanor fairly shrieked in response.

"Hush now," Suzanne remonstrated, "or Zia will be up in arms."

151

"So you two planned this?"

"Well, yes, if you must know," Rosalie replied. "There's always so much to do on housecleaning days, but we got ahead of things already. We can handle the last of it. Besides, you always hate hanging the drapes."

Eleanor took in her cousins' faces and thought she detected a forlorn expression in their eyes. It struck her: perhaps each was wishing she had an Italian fellow of her own. She kept these thoughts to herself and added in a near-whisper, "Anyway, I'm not sure *Mamá* will let me see him on my own." She glanced toward the kitchen where the crash of pots and pans could be heard.

"Oh, for heaven's sake!" Rosalie exclaimed.

"Does she have to know?" Suzanne asked. "She didn't hear your conversation yesterday. Anyway, we can keep her busy with us while you go out."

"And if you two come back with a tree, she'll be grateful that that job's been handled for another year." Rosalie added with a triumphant nod.

"Wow, you two did really think this through!"

"Yes, we did," Suzanne said firmly, brooking no opposition, "so get yourself ready and scoot over to Mollicas' before we change our minds."

Surprising them, Eleanor hugged each of her cousins in turn and planted affectionate kisses on their cheeks before scooting back up the stairs.

In less than fifteen minutes, she was across the street on the Mollicas' porch, ringing the doorbell.

Mary came to the door, then with a sly smile she turned and called over her shoulder, "Giampaolo! It's Eleanor here for you."

Eleanor hardly had time to roll her eyes when Giampaolo

appeared at Mary's elbow.

"Bon giornu!" he greeted her brightly.

"Bon giornu," she replied. *"Tuttu beni?* Ready to go?"

He already had his coat in hand. He put it on and they walked down the stairs together. As he fell in step with her on the sidewalk, he took her gloved hand in his.

In a few short blocks they reached a busy street corner dominated by the cheery visage of Klein's Drugstore, a local favorite, its red plaid curtains flapping a welcome every time the door opened. Despite its name, Klein's was much more than a drugstore. Its large picture windows facing the street at right angles were lined with an odd assortment of merchandise: silk lampshades and boxes of Twenty Mule Team Borax stood side by side with bottles of rubbing alcohol, hatpins, suspenders, and bars of Fels-Naptha soap. On the top shelf, gleaming apothecary jars filled with jewel-toned liquids and powders reminded patrons of the healing vocation of the store's proprietor. Inside, behind a window set into the wood-paneled wall that separated the pharmacy from the rest of the shop, portly Mr. Klein would dispense both prescription medicines that the doctor ordered and home-grown remedies to help ease a neighbor's toothache or a new mother's worries. Dominating the center of the shop was a U-shaped soda fountain of black slate with polished swivel stools, and metal taps and spigots ready to delight customers, young and old, with sweet and fizzy treats.

Every year at Christmas, Mr. Klein and his son roped off a large square of pavement in front of the store. It set the boundaries for a seasonal outdoor market where Christmas trees and holiday greenery were sold. A wooden sandwich board on the corner advertised the types, sizes, and prices of the trees and wreaths. Some of the sturdy firs stood erect, their boughs lacing together to form a lush bower within the rope borders, enfolding the little holiday shop with the heady scent of fresh pine. Other trees lay aslant in a large pile to one side, still wrapped tightly with burlap and string. Tags on each tree fluttered in the breeze, beckoning holiday shoppers to take a closer look. Toward the back of the space, a pair of wooden sawhorses supported a plank of rough plywood, a makeshift table for swags of pine and fir, boxwood and yew. Alongside the table rose a column of evergreen wreaths in graduated sizes, and bunches of holly boughs tied together hung from pegs on a plank of splintery wood. Underneath the table, like an afterthought, was a mound of fragrant loose boughs with tiny pinecones still on them.

In a patched plaid jacket and heavy work gloves, his wool cap jammed down on his forehead, a middle-aged man with a slight paunch and a day's growth of beard held up a tree for close inspection by a father and his two children.

"I like it!" exclaimed the pigtailed girl.

"Nah, not big enough," replied her brother. "And too fat around the bottom. Just like you!" He tugged his sister's hair and she chased him around and among the stands of trees.

Ignoring the commentary, their father negotiated the price of the tree he liked with the merchant.

Eleanor took in a deep whiff of the clean piney scent as they stepped closer. "Mmm, I love the smell of evergreens," she exclaimed, exhaling slowly.

Giampaolo smiled and looked around. The aroma of evergreen was at once sharp and mellow at the back of his throat, evoking the high meadows in the hills at home when he and his brothers went hunting in winter for rabbits or foraging for wild mushrooms.

They walked over to the table of greens.

"*Beddu, beddu,* that's very pretty holly," she exclaimed. "Look at all those berries. But we don't need to buy any: we have a big holly bush that my Zio planted in the backyard several years ago. *Cumpari* Mollica always trims it for us, this time of year."

"*Fazzu iu?* Perhaps I can do that for you when we return," he offered.

Already on to the next task, Eleanor hummed absently as she sorted through the loose fir boughs for a few large ones with the fullest needles.

"*Vui accatari n' àrvulu?* Do you want to look at the trees, too?" He gestured toward the family, their purchase complete, the father now preparing to shoulder their purchase for the walk home. The merchant had wrapped the tree in burlap and was giving change to the man.

"Let's walk around and see them all first. *Fa beni cusí?*" she asked. He nodded, and when she had set aside the fir boughs she wanted, he reached for her hand again. Together they strolled at a leisurely pace around the stall. She regarded each tree critically and then turned so they could retrace their steps.

"Can I help you good folks?" the man in the cap addressed them.

"Just looking, right now," Eleanor replied. "But I will take those two pine boughs on the ground."

He ambled over to the table and picked them up.

Eleanor walked back to a tree in the corner of the enclosure and pointed. "*Chistu?* What about this one?" She looked at Giampaolo for a reaction.

The merchant hustled back to them, reached into the middle branches to grab the tree by its trunk, and pounded it firmly on the ground a couple of times to shake off loose needles.

Eleanor regarded it uncertainly. "No...I don't think so," she paused and strolled away without actually addressing the shopkeeper.

"What about..." Eleanor spied two trees in the middle of the row, squinting and inclining her head slightly as she compared them. "This one?... No, this one." She pointed first to one tree, then selected its neighbor.

The attendant was at her elbow in a flash, giving her new choice the same treatment as before.

"No..." she hesitated again, looking back to the corner. "*Chi pensi tu?* What do you think?" she queried Giampaolo in Italian.

"*Uguali,* they seem the same to me," he murmured. With a grin for the merchant, Giampaolo shrugged, rolled his eyes and followed her.

She paused for a long moment, then moved farther down the row. Stepping back, she inclined her head, eying another tree critically. "Let's see this one."

The merchant silently did her bidding. Giampaolo gave him a sympathetic look as she pulled down a few branches. "This one's brown inside. No." She turned on her heel and returned to the corner of the enclosure.

"I'll take this one," Eleanor pointed emphatically to the first tree she'd examined.

Huffing in exasperation, the merchant followed her down the row and asked, "You sure now, lady?"

Eleanor firmed her chin and nodded briskly. "I'm sure."

Giampaolo looked relieved as she paid the merchant. "I'm taking those two boughs, too. No need to wrap the tree. We're only going a few blocks." He looked at her uncertainly, then shrugged and tipped the top of the tree toward her.

"*Giampaolo, purtiamo nzemi?* Can we carry it together?" She gestured toward the bottom of the tree and reached toward the top. Inserting a gloved hand, she grasped the narrow upper trunk firmly. The merchant returned with the greenery. Eleanor took it from him with her spare hand.

"Okay," Giampaolo said to her in English. "Okay, okay!" he

repeated with emphasis, winking at the tree seller.

They returned to the Luna house the same way they'd come, Giampaolo wincing slightly once or twice when the rough bark of the fir tree jammed against his palm. To relieve the twinges, he switched hands a few times. Soon they were at the back gate. Eleanor swung it open and gestured for him to follow her. Just below the back porch, she raised up her end of the Christmas tree and motioned for him to set it down in that spot.

"*Méttiri nell'acqua,* put the bottom in water." She gestured to a bucket she'd filled for the purpose and left sitting on the step. She moved the bucket next to the tree. Giampaolo reached in to grasp the trunk, wincing again as the bark and needles dug into his fingers.

Seeing him cringe, Eleanor took his offended hand once the tree was upright.

"*Ma com'é,* Giampaolo? You're bleeding!" she exclaimed, dismayed, seeing the scratches on his right palm.

"*Nenti,* it's nothing," he replied, rubbing his palm briskly against his coat.

"Let me see the other one," she demanded, and he sheepishly turned over his left hand for inspection. A few scratches had swollen the skin, but there was no bleeding.

"*Macari, nun cusí pegghiu,*" he murmured. "It's not so bad."

Taking him by the arm, she led him quickly up the steps to the back porch and opened the kitchen door. They passed inside.

In the kitchen, her mother looked up, startled.

"*Chi suces', figghia mia?* What's going on?" Glancing first at the pine needles clinging to their coats and then at Giampaolo's bleeding hand, Donna Sarina quickly figured it out for herself. With a disgusted snort, she left the room, returning in a few moments with a small white porcelain bowl, some pieces of soft cotton gauze and a tiny vial of mercurochrome. She placed them on the table, gave Eleanor an angry squint, turned on her heel and left the room.

"*Assetta ccá,* sit down here," Eleanor ordered curtly as she drew a chair from the table for Giampaolo.

When he was seated, she turned his wounded hand over gently. Sticky smudges of pine resin adhered to his palm and fingers, and the scratches that had perforated the skin were bleeding. She filled the bowl with warm water, then reached into a kitchen drawer for a clean dish cloth which she immersed in the bowl and wrung out carefully.

"*Dimmi si ti fazzo duluri.* Let me know if I'm hurting you," she said softly as she began to apply the soft cloth to clean the scrapes and dried blood. She glanced into his eyes, and the warmth she saw there startled her. A blush crept into her cheeks even as she tried to ignore his gaze, and bent to her work.

After a few moments, satisfied that she'd expelled any lingering germs, she opened the vial and squeezed a few drops of the orange medicinal liquid onto a piece of gauze.

"*Mi dispiaci,* I'm sorry, this will sting a bit," she said softly as she patted the abrasions with the antibiotic. Dabs of bright orange dotted his palm where he had been bleeding before. He laughed.

"*Porca miseria!*" Giampaolo exclaimed, seeing the bright stain on his palm. "Now I really look wounded!" He stared at his hand with astonishment. Glimpsing the distress on her face as she looked away, he quickly consoled her. "*Nmporta.* Never mind, it doesn't matter." Then, with his index finger, he lifted her chin to look once more into her eyes. "Eleanora."

She was unprepared for the softness of his lips and the bristle of his mustache as he pressed a kiss to hers. It was the briefest of kisses, but enough for them both to feel a charge of emotion spark between them. Abruptly, she took up his other hand and turned it over, preparing to treat it as if nothing had passed between them. As she began the task anew, he placed his cared-for hand on her arm while she worked.

"*Te' ccà,* there we go," she exclaimed, as if to punctuate the intimate moment. Not really wanting to move away from him, still she did so, and a swell of awkwardness came over her, pinking her cheeks again. She pursed her lips in a prim expression that to those who knew her was a telltale sign of Eleanor's embarrassment.

She averted her eyes as she put things away. Giampaolo just sat there, smiling at her. She touched his shoulder and said softly, "*Amuninni,* let's go." Although they had stepped apart, her voice was gentle, affectionate. Satisfied for the moment, he stood and followed her out the back door.

That evening, Eleanor stepped back from the living room mantelpiece and evaluated her work.

Fresh Douglas fir boughs now adorned its entire length, with sprigs of holly in full berry brightening the whole. She'd unearthed two red candles in the dining room hutch, and found small star-shaped glass holders to nestle them among the greens. The simple design was quite festive, differentiating the space just enough that all who entered knew the Luna family was welcoming the coming Christmas season. After he insisted on pruning the holly bush, Giampaolo had handed her a dishcloth sling full of the shiniest leaves with the reddest berries and then rejoined his compatriots at the Mollica house across the street. Eleanor had incorporated the beautiful holly into the holiday greenery, bedecking the mantel as well as a wreath of greens lying flat on the dining room table to form a simple Advent centerpiece that the family would light each December evening: one rose candle and three purple ones signified the four weeks of the ecclesiastical season. She had also filled vases with extra greens and holly, and set some aside to use as a swag on the front door.

The spicy scent of fresh pine filled the air, and she inhaled a satisfied whiff.

Her mother stole in behind her and placed a hand on Eleanor's waist. *"Bedda,"* she murmured softly.

She turned and hugged her mother, a silent contrition for having overstepped any unspoken bounds earlier that day. Donna Sarina clung to her daughter a bit longer than was her custom. Softly she asked in Italian, "So you really like him, do you?"

"Sí, Mamá."

"Well, then I suppose I must write to your Zia Maria Grazia."

Horrified, Eleanor's eyes sprang wide open. "No! No!" her cheeks went hot as a stream of panic overtook her.

Surprised at her daughter's reaction, Donna Sarina asked simply, *"Ma picchí no?* Why not?"

"It's too soon."

"Too soon to find out about this man's family?"

Alarm swirled in her stomach at the prospect of her mother's interference, involving family and asking favors from their faraway relatives about a circumstance of which she herself was still quite unsure. She was attracted to Giampaolo, that was clear, and he seemed to return the affection. But just how serious was he?

Eleanor was completely unable to frame words. No reason came to mind that was good enough to stop her mother's inquiries. Anyway, it was probably futile: Donna Sarina had gotten an idea in her head, and she would likely go ahead with it. This strong-willed woman had resolutely made her way in her adopted homeland for years now, charging toward challenges that would have daunted a lesser being. Finding out all she could about a stranger who was interested in her daughter, by any means at her disposal, was Donna Sarina's way of protecting her family. It hardly seemed a challenge, and to her mother's way of thinking, Eleanor knew, it was absolutely the right and proper next step to take.

"Mamá..." Eleanor remonstrated plaintively.

"Cosa pinsari? What can you be thinking?" Her mother's tone was soft but firm. "We know nothing about him!"

Reluctantly, Eleanor sighed and let the subject drop. Her mother was right, on some level. Turning it over in her head, Eleanor also realized that this gesture signaled a turning-point. This was Donna Sarina's way of accepting the inevitable. Truth be told, it was actually quite a big step.

Still, the idea of her distant aunt back in their Sicilian hometown making inquiries about Giampaolo's family filled her with dread. It seemed intrusive in the extreme. His family likely had no idea of their son's whereabouts, much less if he was even alive. Surely it would be better for the Stagnos to have some news first from Giampaolo himself? She knew only that he hadn't had any letters or news from his family since he left for the army; she didn't know if he had attempted to reach them. Or, for that matter, if he had, had any news reached his family? Eleanor pouted, her cheeks still burning.

The tense moment between mother and daughter ended abruptly as her cousin Rosalie bounded into the room. "Zia, do you want to bring the eggplant casserole to Mollicas'? It's time to go across the street."

Donna Sarina brusquely resumed her head-of-household formality. *"Certu!* Of course," she told her niece, and hurried off toward the kitchen, relieved to drop the subject, too, for now, and leaving Eleanor standing in the middle of the living room with a decided frown on her face.

"What's wrong?" Rosalie demanded.

"Nothing!" she replied sharply, and took off up the stairs.

* * *

The lamps in the front window of the Mollicas' living room cast a golden glow into the still evening air, beckoning the four women as they approached their neighbors' front door. Before the doorbell had chimed, the door swung open.

"Come in!" Frannie beckoned as they stepped into the vestibule. Bellows of masculine laughter escaped from the living room just beyond.

The soldiers all stood as the Luna girls and Donna Sarina entered, greeting them with shouts of *"Bona sira!"* and "How are you?" The spirit of the room seemed jovial, and Eleanor observed the half-empty pitcher of whiskey sours on the coffee table. Drinks had been consumed. They'd have some catching up to do.

Rosalie marched directly toward the kitchen, carefully holding with wadded-up dish towels the still-warm earthenware dish of *milinciana,* eggplant in sauce, herbs and *ricotta.* Suzanne followed on her heels. A fragrant mélange of tomato and basil wafted through the room as they passed. That left Donna Sarina and Eleanor to the attentions of the jolly men lounging in the Mollicas' living room.

The room went quiet and all eyes were on Giampaolo as he stepped forward and formally grasped Sarina's palm. "Donna Sarina," he said as he shook her hand in a manner just a bit too formal for the circumstance. His cheeks were pink with merriment. He turned to Eleanor. *"Bona sira, Eleanora,"* he spoke the words gently near her ear. At that, Vincenzo nudged Tommaso exaggeratedly and the two men exchanged glances, a move not lost on Eleanor's mother.

Donna Sarina eyed the two Italians sharply, issued a curt *"Bona sira"* in their direction, and moved on to the kitchen too.

Eleanor found herself standing in front of an empty spot

on the sofa where Giampaolo had been seated. He gestured gallantly to the seat. *"Vui assitari ccá?* Would you like to sit here?"* Tommaso and Vincenzo exchanged knowing looks as she sat, Giampaolo next to her.

Rafe was the first to speak up. "We heard you got a Christmas tree today."

"That's right," she acquiesced, then inclined a nod toward her seat-mate. "With Giampaolo's help. We got it home and everything."

He grinned, then clapped and rubbed his palms together. When he turned his mercurochrome-stained hands outward for all to see, the men broke out in raucous laughter.

Eleanor blushed. Clearly the Christmas tree expedition had already been the subject of some conversation among the men.

Giampaolo noticed her discomfiture and immediately turned serious. As the others joked and laughed, alternating conversation between Italian and English, he wrapped an arm lightly about her and squeezed her waist. *"Mi dispiaci,* I'm sorry, *Eleanora,"* he whispered.

She said nothing, merely reached for his hand at her waist and gave it a reassuring squeeze.

The conversation at the supper table was easy and jovial, at least in part owing to the generous refills of red wine that *Cumpari* Mollica kept pouring. The patriarch of the family was in his element. Having all these young men around his table made him miss his son Luigi keenly; he was used to the company of young men, Louie's companions, who were always hanging around the house. Now they were away at war, a generation of young men scattered around the world fighting for lofty ideals far removed from the personal sacrifice. *Cumpari* Mollica didn't traffic much with principles or politics; when the war hit home, robbing him of his only son, then he minded. Having soldiers visit for a weekend was bittersweet.

On one hand it was a reminder of the privations Louie was likely enduring, at that very moment. But it gave Giuseppe Mollica an excuse to play the generous host, a role he enjoyed but seldom got the chance to play in these grim days.

At the other end of the table, Frannie kept the conversational ball rolling, making it easier for her sister and friends to pick up threads here and there. *Cummari* Angelina and Donna Sarina sat shoulder to shoulder, preoccupied with making sure the food on the table was up to their standards – delicious and plentiful. Every so often her mother graced Eleanor with a tight, inscrutable smile, more an outward show of amiability toward the strangers at the table than any hint of what she was really thinking.

Although she felt a bit out of her element, Eleanor enjoyed herself. Giampaolo seemed to be doing so, too, seated next to her, his leg occasionally brushing hers under the table, their fingers touching as they passed platters of food. So this was what it was like, being wooed by a man who liked her, who found her attractive. She'd heard the women at work talk about flirting. She didn't know how to flirt, really didn't even know what it meant. But this affectionate exchange between them felt natural. She warmed to his attention, a feeling both peculiar and thrilling, and felt a magnetic pull course through her when eyes met or hands touched. The wonder of what would happen next felt both exhilarating and precarious.

Chapter 13

League of St. Andrews Readies for Christmas Bazaar

"Mrs. Paul Gillett of E. Stadium Blvd., chairman of the League of St. Andrew's Christmas bazaar, is show above (left), exhibiting to Mrs. E. T. Vincent of Melrose Ave., one of the many dolls to be displayed at the bazaar Dec. 6 in Page hall of St. Andrew's church."

—*Ann Arbor News,* November 24, 1944

Novrember 25, 1944, Jamesport, Pennsylvania
The tumult of noise and energy in the church hall easily absorbed the cold blast of air that propelled Giampaolo and his friends into the warmth inside. He was to meet Eleanor here. She had come about an hour earlier, bringing Donna Sarina's beautiful crochet-work and Rosalie's lovingly fashioned doll clothes as items for sale. He glanced around the auditorium crowded with tables selling all sorts of wares, all the more creatively imagined and crafted given wartime shortages of many basic materials. The group disintegrated quickly: hardly inside the door, Rafe found an attractive young lady to flirt with, and was already walking arm in arm with her from booth to booth. (The uniform did seem to work wonders for the charm index with pretty girls.) Vincenzo and Tommaso were beating a direct path to one of the food stalls, where, underneath a sign advertising "Funnel Cakes," a couple of young women were serving up large golden rounds of fried batter, airy and lacy as doilies, on paper plates, showering each with generous dustings of confectioners sugar. The pungent scent of hot oil mingling with sugary

sweetness tickled Giampaolo's nose and brought with it a pang of nostalgia, putting him in mind of the fried dough delicacies called *crispeddi* his mother made on Christmas Eve.

Giampaolo gazed around the room until finally he saw her standing behind a craft table. Eleanor looked up, smiled and waved, then bid a quick goodbye to the other women staffing the table. He snaked his way through the crowd until they were side by side. "*Ciao, amuri,* hello, sweetheart," he greeted her with unmistakeable affection and crooked his elbow. Eleanor smiled even more brightly as they began making a turn around the room from table to table, arms linked. She had never been in public on the arm of a man she cared for; another first for the weekend, she thought with a thrill. Every so often she stopped and introduced Giampaolo to friends and neighbors. He filled out his military garb very pleasingly, she thought. Was it her imagination that she was the envy of more than one young woman as they strolled around the hall?

Giampaolo was surprised and gratified that he was accepted so warmly. Here among the Italian-American community of a Catholic parish, the Italy patch on his sleeve seemed to be a talisman of welcome, not a cause for contempt. The cacophony of conversation, shouts, and laughter was interrupted by occasional announcements over a scratchy public-address system. Wisps of conversation in Italian reached his ears and faded quickly as he turned to see who was speaking. A few times, Eleanor searched his face to calculate how her young man was finding this chaotic American scene with a heavy Italian accent. Finding bewilderment and uncertainty there, she suggested they get a bite to eat. Food always broke the ice, bridged differences, smoothed the rough edges. Food was the great comforter.

Someone passed by with a paper plate that left in its wake the delectable aromes of fresh bread, cheese, and salami.

"*Vui tastari 'n badagghiu,* would you like a sandwich?" Eleanor pointed to a stand where they were being made. It looked to him as though individual loaves of Italian bread, dripping with generous douses of olive oil and sprinkled with oregano, were being stuffed with all manner of *salumi,* cold cuts and cheese, tomatoes and lettuce."*E tu?* What about you?"

"I'll try a bite of yours."

"Okay, okay!" Giampaolo laughed as he trotted out one of the few English expressions he knew that had worked so well with the tree merchant the day before.

She made her way to the front of the stand and placed an order while he waited to one side, trying to avoid the jostle of the crowd. He watched the commotion swirling around him: friends greeting, children shouting, parents scolding. It was a glorious melee fueled by the added anticipation that Christmas uniquely brings. It reminded him of the crowds at the summer *feste* at home, holy days that were celebrated in the streets of every town in Italy. A statue of the virgin Mary or the town's patron saint was placed on a raised plinth and borne on the shoulders of a half-dozen young men. Local musicians would materialize and form an impromptu band to serenade the saint, and the procession would wind its way through the streets of town, pausing every so often as a youngster was lofted up to totter momentarily on the statue's platform and throw coins into an alms bowl or pin money on the saint's fabric cloak. Games and day-long feasting were capped off after dark by bombastic fireworks displays that lit the skies and echoed loudly in the lanes and byways of each town.

In a few moments, Eleanor was back at his side with a mouthwatering hunk of stuffed bread. She had asked the server at the stand to cut off the end of the roll with some of the sandwich ingredients inside, and she proceeded to claim this small piece. "*Chistu è pe mi,* this bit is for me," she took an enthusiastic bite. "I like the heel of the bread."

Giampaolo looked at her quizzically and tried to frame the

English word " 'Eel'?"

She crossed her foot over one knee and pointed to the heel of her shoe. *"Caccagnu,"* she intoned the dialect term. "We use the same word for this part of the shoe and the end of the bread loaf. Huh, huh, huh." She aspirated the initial letter a few times for emphasis, and repeated the word. "H-eel."

Understanding dawned on his face and he chuckled. "Sí. 'Okay'. 'Eel'." Switching to Italian, he said, "Now I've learned two American words!"

Eleanor swallowed the chuckle that arose in her throat at his eagerness with English. She lifted her portion of sandwich to her mouth and bit. Juice from the tomato and olive oil dribbled down her chin. She swabbed the mess with a paper napkin.

"Mància!" Her mouth full, she lifted the plate toward him.

He hungrily took a bite. Although it was neatly cut, the sandwich was stuffed wide with so many things that he found it difficult to get his mouth around it completely. He bit, then chewed, separate familiar flavors melding into one new combination on his tongue. *"Bono!* It's good," he mumbled between bites.

Eleanor carried the plate and stepped off to one side of the busy hall to get out of the festival traffic. Giampaolo followed her, sandwich in one hand, napkins in the other. They stopped to eat, turning toward each other wordlessly. The thick bread took a lot of work. She chewed, looking at him. With another big bite, he did the same. A rivulet of olive oil dropped onto his chin. She grabbed a napkin and swiped it clean before it dripped onto his uniform collar. He smiled and took her hand, repeating her motion on her own face. Unaware that her chin needed attention, she smiled and nodded thanks, her mouth still full, and kept eating. She watched him lift the sandwich to his mouth for another bite, and then stared, transfixed, as he chewed, the mustache on his upper lip moving in apposition to his jaw. Crumbs of bread and cheese clung to his mustache.

No longer in possession of the napkins, she lifted an index finger to his lip and brushed them off with her nail. His mouth stopped in mid-bite at her touch, and their eyes met, completing the momentary intimate exchange. She looked away quickly, dropping her gaze to the floor while he polished off the sandwich.

Rafe and the young lady he was squiring around the hall emerged from the crowd. "Hey there!" he called out companionably. He introduced his friend to her as Angela Salvucci. Eleanor recognize her name. She greeted Angela and turned to do the honors for Giampaolo.

"How about a beer? *Na birra?*" Rafe said, clapping him on the shoulder. "They're selling them over there." He pointed to one corner of the hall where a line of men waited to be served.

The four young people moved toward the beer stall and Rafe stepped up to order for them all. "None for me, thanks," Eleanor called after him as he took a position in the line. *"Nun mi piaci 'a birra*, I don't care for beer," she explained.

Rafe returned momentarily, balancing three beers on a small tray. Giampaolo and Angela each took one. After just one sip, the foam clung to his mustache and upper lip. Eleanor swiped at it with her thumb, wiping it clear.

Rafe took in the gesture and smiled. "So." He addressed Eleanor in English, his words clearly meant for her. "You two, huh? Getting along pretty well."

She said nothing, just lowered her head and fixed her eyes on the tips of her shoes. Then she glanced up, jutted her chin out and looked directly at Rafe to mask her insecurity. "Yes. Why? Does that seem strange to you?"

Rafe lifted his empty palm in surrender. "Nope, not at all." He grinned. "Not strange at all!" He raised his beer and drank most of it in a few large gulps, leaving a mustache of white foam on his own upper lip.

Sensing that some hidden meaning had been exchanged between the two, Giampaolo looked at her with curiosity. *"C'é prublema?* Is something wrong?" He glanced from Eleanor's face to Rafe's and back again.

"Nenti, it's nothing," she responded quickly, and the moment passed.

Empty beer glass in hand, Rafe turned to his date and crooked an arm in her direction. "Shall we walk?" Angela nodded, flipped a hand in farewell to Eleanor, and the two were soon swallowed up in the milling crowd.

Eleanor faced Giampaolo, who was draining his beer glass. She was suddenly at a loss for words. Rather than speak, he just reached over and tucked a stray curl behind her ear. She sucked in a quick breath.

Giampaolo's gentleness was unexpected. His tender attentions surprised and delighted her. She wasn't used to the company of men, and what she did know seemed all bluster and bother, shoving and pounding and pushing. The men she knew – her cousin Angelo, *Cumpari* Mollica, the brothers and fathers of her friends -- seemed to inhabit a violent, volatile world that frightened her. It seemed a place apart from her world, one mostly full of women, the only world she knew. But Giampaolo was different. He was thoughtful and uncomplaining, and his deference felt affectionate. She reminded herself that he must live in that other world too – after all, he was a soldier, and had experienced war. But when he was with her, he was attentive and gentle.

He reached for her hand, which still held the crumpled napkin. He took it, placed it in the now empty beer glass and carried it to a nearby table. *"Amuninn'?"* He looked at her with a small smile, his steady gaze an affectionate promise that he would follow where she led.

Giampaolo simply took her breath away.

Chapter 14

"They stand in front of the gates leading to the trains, deep in each other's arms, not caring who sees or what they think. Each goodbye is a drama complete in itself, which Eisenstaedt's pictures movingly tell. Sometimes the girl stands with arms around the boys' waist, hands tightly clasped behind. Another fits her head into the curve of his cheek while tears fall onto his coat. Now and then the boy will take her face between his hands and speak reassuringly. Or if the wait is long they may just stand quietly, not saying anything. The common denominator of all these goodbyes is sadness and tenderness, and complete oblivion for the moment to anything but their own individual heartaches."

—*Life Magazine*, Valentine's Day edition, 1944

Late November 1944, Jamesport, Pennsylvania
When the taxi departed from the Mollicas' home on Sunday afternoon with the four men, an unsettled feeling crept into Eleanor's soul as she stood on the sidewalk with her cousins and friends. Her eyes had misted as they got into the cab, the three Italians in the back seat and Rafe in the front, to give instructions to the driver. There had been no occasion for a more intimate farewell. Giampaolo had hugged her and kissed her on both cheeks, the same way he had bade goodbye to all the women. She felt cheated of the chance for another warm memory. Yet she was certain they had grown closer in just a few days. Sharing childhood stories and family anecdotes, they had come to know each other better. Eleanor was certain her affection was returned. Still, she wondered ruefully whether or when they would meet again. No words or

plans had been put forward for another visit. The last memory emblazoned on her mind was his wistful smiling face in the taxi window, waving goodbye to her.

"Well, that's that," Frannie said with a tone of finality as the cab pulled away. Eleanor looked daggers at her: Frannie 's words seemed to signal the end of a nice but trivial episode. But for Eleanor, this wasn't trivial, and she hoped fervently that it wasn't over. She resolved to write Giampaolo at the first opportunity and promptly answer any correspondence from him. Even if she was never to see him again, they could exchange letters.

3 dicembre 1944

Caro Giampaolo,

It was so lovely to have you share our Thanksgiving holiday. I hope your trip back to camp was smooth and uneventful.

I need to thank you, too, for your help with buying the Christmas tree. Getting it home and fitting it into the stand is always the worst chore, but you made it easy this year. (Have your hands healed, by the way?) And also thanks for helping me decorate the fireplace. We lit the candles for a little while last night. The mantel looks so pretty and has given me the Christmas spirit earlier than usual this year. Next weekend, we'll put the tree in one corner of the living room and decorate it with lights and ornaments.

Are there Christmas decorations at the camp?

There is always so much more to do before Christmas that I have tasks every night when I come home from work, and on the weekends too. My mother always wants to mail a package to my Zia Marietta early in December so that it will reach her before Natale. I did that earlier this week, and bought our Christmas cards and stamps. Each of us (Suzanna, Rosalia, and myself) will address some of the cards, but Mamá likes to sign them all. Each of us also has friends to whom we send our own Christmas greetings.

I guess that's an American tradition, or does your family send cards at Christmastime, too?

Then we have cookies to bake. Mamá makes a couple of kinds you'd probably like and would recognize, but I like to make several varieties that are from American recipes: chocolate chip, sugar cookies in Christmas shapes (decorated with red and green sugar!), gingerbread cookies and almond crescents. Mamá always makes a big batch of giuggiulena to have on hand when friends drop by.

In the middle of the month, of course, is the festa di Santa Lucia. We always make cuccía in honor of the day. Mamá puts some in jars for the rest of the family who don't live with us. My cousins Connie and Annie and their children all love cuccía too and look forward to eating some each year on December 13.

There are also presents to buy and wrap. Mamá used to do it all by herself but now Rosalia has taken over that task. Annie's and Connie's children each get a little something each year from their Zia. This year there will be one more, for Angelo and Doris' little boy. That's twelve gifts to buy! She picks one present for the girls – a scarf or a pair of gloves – and one for the boys, usually a tie or a shirt. Then Rosalia buys them in as many different colors as she can find. Ro loves to wrap each gift herself – she's so good at it that we all let her handle the job. She writes cards for each of the kids and piles them into two large bags, one for each household.

Well, I guess that's enough for now. Write me and tell me the news in the camp.

Affectionately,

Eleanora

10 dicembre 1944

Carrisima Eleanora,

I was so happy to get your letter. It seems a long time already since we were together. I hope you will remember the good times we had on my last visit. They are happy memories for me already.

I hope your mother is well, and your cousins too. It sounds as if you are very busy at Christmas.

I am well and keeping busy, as usual, here at camp. Most of us are still working on the docks during the week. We load and unload things from the ships, and sometimes clean the decks. But everyone is in a good mood these days. I guess it is because Christmas is coming. As we are driving back to camp after dark each night, we pass by houses that have lights strung on them or on the bushes and trees in front. They look very bright and pretty – like the streets at home during the feste in the summertime.

Things are a lot different here than last Christmas. Last year, we had better food than usual in the mess hall on the holiday, but we were still under guard and we felt very much like prisoners. We couldn't feel glad in our hearts or be festive. I thought a lot about my parents and my nonna then. Now, since we have been in the Italian Service Units, the situation is much better. Of course, we have more freedom to come and go, even to take time away from camp with a chaperone, as we did last month when I visited you. There is a Christmas tree in the mess hall, too – a great big one with lights and other decorations. I am glad we didn't have to carry such a big one home to your house! A few of the fellows have got a small band together, with the help of the Americans who found musical instruments for them to play. They are practicing for a Christmas concert. They sound pretty good already! Hearing them practicing the familiar songs reminds me of home.

A few of the fellows are talking about going into New York City on December 23. That's the Saturday right before the holiday. An Italian American club in Jersey City, the Società di San Gennaro, is sponsoring the trip. They'll take a group of us by bus from camp into the city. We'll see Broadway and all the lights, have lunch at an American diner and maybe even see a show. They'll bring us back to camp by suppertime. They say the city is beautiful at Christmas. All the shops are decorated and lit up with lights. Maybe I will go, too. On Christmas Day, there's going to be a special Mass here in the camp for all of us prisoners. I guess some fellows are getting leave, but I'm not sure yet what we'll be allowed to do.

Well, I must go. I want to mail this letter so it goes out tomorrow. Write again soon.

Yours with affection,

Giampaolo

14 dicembre 1944

Dearest Giampaolo,

It was wonderful to get your letter. Since we had made no plans to visit again, I wasn't sure if you would remember to write.

It's as busy as ever here right now, getting ready for Christmas. I made two kinds of cookies over the weekend. The gingerbread men came out really well. I decorated them with raisins for the eyes and for buttons down the front. I also helped Mamá decorate her Christmas wreath cookies. They look so pretty with white icing that looks like snow and tiny multicolored cunfetti that look like Christmas lights. It was Suzanne's turn last night to entertain her friends for their weekly card game, so I arranged some cookies on a plate for them to snack on. Everyone said the plate looked really pretty. Mamá was pleased, too.

On Christmas Eve we'll go to Mass as usual and come home for a late supper afterwards. Mamá and Cummari Angelina always get together to make the fried smelts. They take turns doing this task in one kitchen – last year was our turn, so this year they'll be doing the work across the street, at Mollicas'. Mamá always says that it is silly to have <u>two</u> kitchens smelling like fried fish on Christmas Eve. Veronica will be glad to have the run of the kitchen, as she always waits until the very last to make a pile of pizzelle. Nick gave her a pizzelle iron, which she treasures ever since he carved their initials into a heart in the very middle of the waffle iron's design. We all thought that was very romantic of him to do. Now every cookie she makes says "V&N" on it.

What are your plans for Christmas? Did you decide to go on the trip to New York City?

Write again soon and let me know,

Affectionately,

Eleanora

18 dicembre 1944

Carissima Eleanora,

I guess it's not too early to wish you Buon Natale, a very happy Christmas, as you'll probably be reading this letter close to the holiday.

I wanted to write you soon after getting your latest letter to ask a favor. It seems our American friend Patsy Tinelli will be back in camp for New Year's, but he would just as soon spend it somewhere else. I saw him in the mess hall yesterday just after he got his weekend orders. He hinted to me that he'd love to visit the Mollicas again. He told me that since New Year's Day is on a Monday this year, he can get leave for the whole weekend until Tuesday. He thought we could, too. So I am writing to see if we might impose on your hospitality and that of your wonderful friends the Mollicas once more. Tommaso will be writing his cousins a letter, too, and sending it off the same time as mine.

Hoping to see you again very soon,

Your affectionate

Giampaolo

21 dicembre, 1944

Buon Natale, Giampaolo!

Writing this letter in haste so that you will perhaps receive it before the holiday weekend.

176

With your last letter, I got the best Christmas present yet – the news that you'll be able to visit for New Year's! I am so happy. I don't care if there is nothing else under the tree for me this year. Your presence is all I really wanted for Christmas.

YES, PLEASE COME. Plan to come for the entire weekend – from Friday through Tuesday if you can. The Mollicas will be happy to see you and the other fellows. (However, not as happy as I will be...) Bring the whole gang, as we say in America. Let me know your arrival date.

With love,

Eleanora

Donna Sarina's Christmas letter to her sister:

21 dicembre 1944

Carissima Maria Grazia,

A very happy Christmas to you, my dear sister. I think of you every day and wonder how you are doing. Perhaps this awful war will pause and give you a few moments of peace.

I hope this letter reaches you. Did you get the packages I sent earlier this month?

Dearest sister, I have a favor to ask of you and Tonino. I have not spoken of this in my letters to you before, but now it seems there is reason to ask.

My Eleanora has met an Italian man, and it looks like she has her heart set on him. His name is Giampaolo Stagno and he hails from Palazzolo Acréide. You know the town, it's in Provincia Siracusa, not far from Florídia. He is a soldier in the Italian Army and was captured in the fighting in North Africa. He and his company were shipped here to a prisoner's camp near the city of New York. Our good friends, the Mollicas, have a nephew in the same regiment as Giampaolo, who was captured at the same time. When the Mollicas' two daughters went to visit their cousin in the camp,

Eleanora, Suzanna, and Rosalia went along. And that's when Eleanora met this fellow. I've met him, too, several times. The Mollicas' nephew has come to visit and brought Giampaolo along when he came. They were here for our Thanksgiving holiday, the big festa we celebrate in November.

Marietta, could you make some discreet inquiry about this man's family? Tonino probably knows people from his town, or nearby. All that I know about the Stagno family is that they are farmers – they work a piece of land somewhere near Palazzolo. I know that he has a brother who's in the seminary in Rome. I believe he has other brothers and sisters, but he hasn't told me much about them.

Even now it may be too late to stop the inevitable. You know how stubborn my Eleanora can be. But if they plan to marry, I would like to know more about this fellow. Even though you are still there, it is my dearest hope that Eleanora will not return to Sicily to be with him. She is an American now and I pray she will stay here. But those thoughts are for another time.

My dear sister, I hope that I have not asked too much with this favor, but it will ease my mind to know more from you about Giampaolo Stagno. I will be grateful for whatever you can find out.

Know that you are in my thoughts and prayers always. God bless you and keep you safely through this war. Write back soon and let me know about the packages.

Big kisses and hugs from your sister, who loves you and wishes you well always,

Sarina.

Chapter 15

La Festa di San Silvestro is celebrated December 31 on New Year's Eve. As with most Italian festivals, food plays a major role, and families and friends get together for huge feasts. Tradition calls for lentils to be served on New Year's Eve because they symbolize money and good fortune for the coming year... In ancient Rome, to ring in the New Year, people gifted each other honey and figs, to represent a sweet new year, and a bay branch for good fortune. A similar tradition continues in Naples, where figs are wrapped in laurel leaves.

—*Toscanaslc.com*

After Christmas 1944, Jamesport, Pennsylvania

Eleanor glanced at the calendar on the kitchen wall: Friday, December 29. She looked out the window into the yard. A fresh coating of snow glistened on the grass and the pavement. It clung to the eerie shapes her mother's prize rose bushes made, now carefully wrapped in burlap against the winter's cold. She folded her arms and hugged herself, as if to ward away the cold. She hoped the weather wouldn't delay their arrival.

She paced impatiently from the kitchen to the living room. Taking up a post at the big picture window, she glanced up and down the street, hoping to see Patsy Tinelli's car drive up and park in front of the Mollicas' home. No one was about, at this early hour: it was barely eight o'clock. But she was fully dressed and full of anticipation, too. To occupy herself while she waited, she reached for the Christmas cards piled up on the table. She took a seat in one of the two armchairs facing each other on opposite walls in front of the window, giving the best view of the street. Mindlessly she thumbed through the cards, opening a few and rereading the handwritten greetings. Most were simply signed, and were from people she saw nearly every day: her neighbors, cousins, friends from church. Several were to her mother, from members of Donna Sarina's sodality, the Mount Carmel Society. Even that reminded her of Giampaolo: she recalled the day they'd met, after Mass at the church in Newark. As she thought of him, her heart thumped nervously. She glanced out the window again. Still nothing.

Her cousin Rosalie came into the living room and took the chair opposite.

"You're up early."

Eleanor gave her cousin a sideways smile.

"Oh," Rosalie said dully, "I forgot." She eyed Eleanor's neatly pressed collar beneath a soft dark blue sweater, and the carefully arranged gold chain and cross placed over the blouse's tiny pleats. "You look nice."

Eleanor nodded and regarded her cousin wordlessly, knowing her anticipation was betrayed by how carefully she'd dressed and how anxiously she sat by the window.

"What time will they get here?" Rosalie asked.

"I don't know exactly."

"The trip takes a couple of hours, anyway."

"Yes, I know."

"So it won't be until noon—"

"Yes, I know!" Eleanor burst out impatiently.

Her cousin looked wounded. "You don't have to jump down my throat."

"Sorry, Ro. It's just that...I'm just...I don't know." Eleanor let her words hang in the air.

Rosalie rose from the chair.

"I haven't had breakfast yet. Want some coffee?"

"No, thanks, I've already had two cups. But there's plenty left in the percolator."

Alone again by the window, Eleanor's thoughts drifted. She wondered idly what Christmas would have been like for Giampaolo and the other Italian prisoners in the camp. Not able to stretch her imagination too far in that direction in her current state, she tucked the thought away to ask Giampaolo about it when he arrived.

Christmas in the Luna household, this year as ever, was cheerily predictable. On Christmas morning they had each exchanged a gift -- something simple and inexpensive – a pair of gloves, a scarf, or perhaps a pen and some note-cards. As a group they had attended the second morning Mass – early enough to avoid families with hordes of little children, late enough to sleep an extra half-hour as a holiday luxury. The church was bedecked in Yuletide glory: an abundance of poinsettias on the high altar and all around the tabernacle, a feast for the eyes after the quiet solemnity of the four weeks of Advent.

For the Lunas and their Italian neighbors, the Christmas holidays were marked by the presence of traditional beverages. There was anisette for their coffee on Christmas morning: Donna Sarina poured a thimbleful in her cup, and kept some in a bottle on the kitchen counter to sprinkle on *biscotta*. Throughout the season a bottle of the clear licorice-flavored liqueur stood on the server in the Lunas' dining room to offer in their best crystal sherry glasses when friends came to call. Some families chose Christmastime as the appropriate season to uncork homemade wines and *limoncello,* carefully preserved on shelves and in kitchen pantries for just this occasion. *Cumpari* Mollica always showed off his handiwork proudly at this time of year, swiping the bowls of each wine glass with

181

a soft cloth before decanting the garnet-colored liquid and serving it to family and friends with a satisfied grin.

There was, as in every Italian household during the holidays, an abundance of food. Christmas Eve was marked with a meal of fish and seafood, to observe the abstinence from meat that the Church required of all observant Catholics. Italians did the tradition one better by concocting special seafood dishes just for that occasion. And Sicilians, in particular, were masters at that.

On Christmas Eve, Donna Sarina always made her stew of *baccalá.* The markets that catered to Italian holiday tastes would put out the dried salted codfish, pale and stiff as whitewashed planks of wood, standing in baskets near the deli counters. The sweet-and-sour stew was a labor of love: the dried codfish needed soaking and rinsing and constant attention over several days to soften it and ready it for incorporation into the stew with root vegetables, tomatoes, potatoes, and the final incongruous and purely Sicilian addition of prunes and raisins. Special cookies, candies, and sweets were stored in tins on nearly every surface of the kitchen, and these were brought out after every meal and for the enjoyment of acquaintances who dropped in, making the customary rounds of Christmas calls to everyone they knew. Everything culminated in a profusion of food on Christmas Day itself, starting with the festive yet comforting *minestredda* of *pastina* and vegetables. To keep things simple and easily expandable for more at the table, Donna Sarina reprised the Thanksgiving meal of roast turkey if she could get one, chicken if she could not. Cranberry sauce would always appear, as well as dried or creamed corn and a potato casserole. In the days that followed, the Luna table swelled with family members and friends at all hours of day and night. Getting together with family inevitably meant eating with family.

The car pulled up to the curb in front of the Mollica home,

the houses on both sides of the street now a familiar sight to Giampaolo. The sedan's windows had steamed up during the road trip, and Giampaolo used the cuff of his shirt now to wipe the window clear. He peered across the street to the porch of the Luna house. Was that his Eleanora sitting by the window?

Tommaso and Vincenzo had unfolded themselves from the cramped quarters of the back seat and were stretching on the sidewalk as Giampaolo clambered out. Patsy's closing the driver's-side door muffled Eleanor's voice.

"Giampaolo!" He looked up to see Eleanor crossing the street in quick strides toward him. He grasped her outstretched hand firmly, then pulled her into the circle of his arms, kissing her soundly on both rosy cheeks.

"But, Eleanor, my treasure, you have no coat!" he exclaimed.

"I'm not cold," she said with a sunny smile.

The other three men stood in a semi-circle, watching the pair greet each other. Then they broke into laughter. Patsy was the first to speak.

"Okay, you lovebirds," he smirked, "Let's get inside." He shepherded them toward the house.

Cumpari Mollica had flung the front door wide open, despite the chilly air, and was making his way down the steps to grasp his nephew by the shoulders in an affectionate bear hug.

Giampaolo kept Eleanor tucked close to his side as they walked up the steps and into the warmth of the Mollicas' living room.

From the picture window across the street, Donna Sarina stood silently observing the scene on the pavement outside. When the soldiers and her daughter had gone inside and the door closed, she turned to see her nieces huddled close behind her, doing the same thing.

"Léviti dduóco! Move away from here!" Frowning at having been caught spying on the activity across the street, she raised

her arms, shooing them from the window as she strode away herself, but not before she noticed the knowing smiles on the faces of her nieces.

New Year's Eve arrived: the weekend had sped by, what with local excursions to entertain the guests. In the evenings, raucous rounds of lotto, Parcheesi, and card games enlivened the Lunas' big dining room table. At the Mollicas' house, the merrymakers loaded paper rolls of music into the spool box of the old player piano, and pumped the pedals till the music advanced and the piano played, as if by magic. The piano tunes inevitably brought on impromptu song-fests: Vincenzo, it turned out, had a lovely clear tenor voice, so he indulged his friends and hosts by singing Italian folk songs that brought a mist to Sarina's eyes.

The young people had made the requisite pilgrimage to ogle and admire the big Christmas tree in the traffic circle that marked the center of Jamesport's small downtown. Replete with ropes of tinsel garland and large red Christmas balls, it twinkled as if to cast a holiday spell. It was magical when the tree's lights shone through a sheen of fresh snow at dusk.

They had driven up Mount Neversink to the town's curiosity, a Chinese pagoda nestled in the trees on the downslope of the mountain. The views on a clear day were quietly majestic. From one side of the building's wraparound porches, you could see for twenty or thirty miles east across the valley, and from another side, the vista caught the hillsides stretching toward the southeast. Even if the landscape was mainly just the neat but unremarkable patchwork of streets that comprised her hometown, Eleanor loved the view. As she always did when she stood there on top of the mountain, she vowed to return more often. She loved gazing down at the place she called home.

Much as Eleanor had enjoyed the many things that the family

and friends had done together as a group, it was the unplanned time in between that she had coveted the most, because it gave her moments with Giampaolo. The couple had gone on long walks, mostly to escape the house and have some solitude together. He had been especially deferential to Donna Sarina, and several times had broadly hinted that he wanted to speak to her mother before he left on New Year's Day. Eleanor was already dreading saying goodbye to Giampaolo again the next day. Donna Sarina had begun cooking the mid-afternoon holiday meal, and the soldiers' motorcade would have to leave immediately afterward, while there was still daylight, allowing time to make the two-hour trip and check in before the camp's curfew.

Of course, throughout the weekend, there had been food – food aplenty, with many dishes that bore the shimmer of holiday treats, made only once a year. They had feasted on her mother's prize recipe of *stimbaradu,* "melting chicken," a stew made with chicken thighs that most closely resembled the consistency of the wild rabbits of the original dish: a succulent concoction of chicken layered with chunks of fennel and onion, green olives and capers and mint, smothered in a broth of red wine brightened with a splash of vinegar. Donna Sarina started the dish in a large Dutch-oven casserole on the stove top and then simmered it slowly for hours in a low oven until the whole house was redolent of the aroma of simmering wine and olives. She had procured another large chicken that she roasted and served hot, with plenty of leftovers for sandwiches served up with American mayonnaise on thick slices of bread carved from the Italian loaves always found on the Luna sideboard. She thriftily stored the chicken carcass wrapped in paper in the refrigerator. It would make a generous soup for a weeknight supper when they all returned to their workday schedule the following week.

By noon, Donna Sarina was lavishing attention on the centerpiece of her holiday menu: a pork roast, a rare find in these days of wartime shortage, that Gi'vanni had managed to procure and for which she had forsaken a ransom of red points from her monthly rations. It would be a meatless start to 1945 in their house, she thought ruefully. The traditional side dishes included broccoli florets steamed and dressed while still hot in olive oil, vinegar, and a single minced garlic clove. There would be potatoes boiled in their skins, skinned immediately and cut into chunks, doused with olive oil and a splash of vinegar, then salted and peppered well and finished with plenty of chopped parsley. Naturally, there would be *lenticchie* – lentils – too; no self-respecting Italian New Year's feast would be complete without them in some form, for the good luck they would bestow on the household in the coming year. But there was also a small baking pan with stuffed shells, standing temptingly ready on the kitchen sideboard. Eleanor had learned that fresh ricotta with pasta was one of Giampaolo's favorites – he told her that it brought back memories of his childhood at the farm in San Marco – so she had asked her mother to indulge the young man's preference. Some minor grumbling from Donna Sarina concealed that she didn't mind the extra bit of work and was secretly pleased that she could provide this savory surprise for the Italians.

Giampaolo had been distracted for much of the day, Eleanor had noticed, and finally she took him aside.

"Cosa sbagghiada? Is there something wrong?"

"No, no," he reassured her, then said gravely, "Before I go, I would like to sit with you and your mother. Alone."

Catching his meaning, Eleanor's heart climbed into her throat. "I see." She went to the kitchen and drew her mother aside to speak softly to her. Donna Sarina nodded and sighed ever so slightly as she wiped her damp hands on her apron. She followed her daughter to the young man's side, and they made themselves comfortable on the living room sofa, mother and daughter side by side, their backs straight and their expressions open. Standing, Giampaolo faced them, nervously fingering his uniform, cap in hand. Rosalie and Suzanne had withdrawn to the kitchen.

"Donna Sarina," he began, "it can come as no surprise to you that I have interest in Eleanora." He glanced at her but remained unsmiling. Eleanor's lips turned up in a small smile of encouragement as she looked back at him.

Saying nothing, her mother merely shifted in her seat. After a moment which to Eleanor seemed an eternity, he continued.

"I love her and would like to ask you for her hand in marriage."

Still mute, Donna Sarina looked into the eyes of the earnest soldier. Finally she spoke.

"My son, I am not surprised to hear you say that you care for my daughter. I have seen it with my own eyes." She paused, then continued. "But first, before I give permission, I have to ask, where would you live?"

"Well, it's true I don't have much to offer, and I don't know what I'll find when I return home after the war. We have the farm in San Marco—"

"No!" Donna Sarina's single syllable rang out. There was an undercurrent of anger in her voice. "It's impossible. My daughter will never return to Sicily!" With that, she stood and strode to the back of the house, toward the kitchen.

"Giampaolo," Eleanor began, a touch of sadness overlaying her surprise at her mother's reaction. "I don't know what to say."

He nodded regretfully and took a seat beside her. "I expected this," he sighed as he took up her hand.

"You want me to live in Sicily?" she asked incredulously.

"I was hoping that you would consider it," he implored, hope fading from his expression.

"I'm afraid I'm not ready to do that," she answered firmly, but her eyes filled with tears. "We never talked about this."

"I see. I understand." Giampaolo still held her hand as they sat in silence. There seemed nothing more to say.

After several minutes, Eleanor found her voice.

"I love you, Giampaolo," she said, her voice breaking.

"And I love you too, Eleanora," he replied, giving her hand an earnest squeeze.

"Is there no other way for us?" she implored.

"I don't know," he replied.

Giampaolo knew of other Italian prisoners in the camp who had formed attachments with American women in much the same way as he had with Eleanor. He had not heard of any who had married, but he did not believe that would be permissible, even under the more relaxed regulations that members of the Italian Service Units enjoyed. He had neglected to ask. Now he wished that he had more answers.

"When I return to the camp, I will see if there is another way," he told her. But the sadness in his eyes expressed more than his words.

Because of this turn of events, the Lunas' New Year's Eve was blunted by a pall over the couple that infected the rest of the household. Eleanor moved around in a fog of sadness, hardly eating and avoiding her cousins' sympathetic glances.

When it came time for her to say goodbye to Giampaolo and the others the next day, she was half-hearted and sullen. From the driver's seat, Patsy Tinelli, ever the jovial center of the group, tried in vain to lighten the mood as they climbed into the car for the return trip to the camp. But soon silence fell over the group as they proceeded on their way.

Vincenzo finally broke in. *"Bo,"* he said, dismissively scraping his fingernails under his chin in an outward gesture of indifference. "Giampaolo, this is not the end of the world. You have a broken heart. She has a broken heart. Time will mend the sadness."

Giampaolo's face was despondent, but he voiced resignation nonetheless. "I know."

They continued in silence for a few miles, then Giampaolo turned to Patsy and asked, "Do you know of other Italians who have married American women?"

"I can't say that I do, Giampaolo."

"Is it permitted?"

"I don't know."

"How do I go about finding out?"

Patsy thought a moment. "This would be a question for the camp commander."

Giampaolo's mournful mood persisted, but there was a tone of resolution in his voice, "Then I must find out. I must try."

Chapter 16

It was illegal for a POW to marry in the U.S., but after the war Washington enabled the fiancées of former POWs to set sail for Italy on surplus troop transports with a chaperone (often an aunt or mother). Each carried the documents required for a legal marriage in Italy and two trunks of personal luggage. By marrying in Italy, the women could then legally bring their new husbands back to America to live.

—from *American Prisoner of War Camps in Idaho and Utah* by Kathleen Kirkpatrick.

J anuary and February 1945, letters
3 gennaio 1945

Carissima Eleanora,

I am writing to let you know that I have petitioned the camp commander to see whether it is permissible for me to marry you here in the United States, given my current circumstances. There are other fellows here who have American sweethearts, but none have been married. I don't know what will result from my inquiry. I only know that I need to find out. That still leaves the question of where we would live. But let us take one step at a time.

Life here hasn't changed much from times before. It is extremely cold working on the docks these days, so one of the Americans told us to buy the warmer underwear that they sell at the general store here at the camp. I did so right away. It's made of tightly woven cotton and covers every bit of my arms and legs. Then I put my uniform on over it. The weather is still bitterly cold and the wind cuts through, but now I don't seem to mind it as much.

I hope you are well, my treasure, and not dwelling too much on our predicament. We will find a way. I hope that your mother is not angry with me. I will write to you again soon, my love, and I hope you will write back to me.

With my love,

Giampaolo

10 gennaio 1945

Carissimo Giampaolo,

It was wonderful to get your letter. I am much better now than on New Year's Day.

I am sorry that I couldn't be more pleasant before you left, but our "predicament," as you called it, is all I can think about. All around me and for years now, girls have been marrying soldiers without any complications. It doesn't seem fair that it has to be so much more difficult for us.

Giampaolo, two weeks ago I could never imagine myself considering leaving home to marry you and live in Sicily. Now, though, I have tried to imagine what that would be like. I try to let my imagination picture what it would be like living as your wife in Sicily. There is so much that I don't know about your home and your family that it's almost impossible to form a clear picture in my head.

However, my mother has not changed her mind. She can be very stubborn, but honestly, I understand how she feels. She came here with nothing but me, and she built a new life here. Our life is good – better, I think, than life must be now in Sicily, from what little we have heard from my Zia Marietta. Mamá does not want to lose me to the country she left behind. I don't blame her because, to be honest, I feel the same way.

Write soon and let me know what the camp commander advises. I am not sure how we would make it work to marry here, with your status uncertain and the war going on. But that would seem the only way we could proceed.

Yours,

Eleanora

As Eleanor sealed the envelope, a swell of hopelessness washed over her. Maybe it would just be better to forget Giampaolo entirely. Her heart told her that wasn't going to be easy, because she was in love with him already. She had turned thirty-one on New Year's Day. By most social calculations, she was already a spinster. She had never been besieged by suitors, much less marriage proposals. She didn't have many chances to meet young men at the factory since most of the workers were women, and the fellows who did work there just weren't her cup of tea. None were from Italian families, for starters, and most seemed coarse and uninteresting. Those guys honestly scared her.

She had known a few nice-looking fellows at church. That was the most likely place to meet someone with husband potential. But nothing ever seemed to develop: they would be friendly to her, but romance just didn't seem to be on the minds of these young men, where she was concerned. She supposed she wasn't attractive enough – too short, an unenviable figure with a straight, short-waisted torso and too-thick ankles. She often felt outright frumpy in this Betty Grable pinup era of pronounced feminine curves. Anyway, since the Luna clan had moved to the northwest section of the city, away from the Italian neighborhood, Eleanor ran into those fellows only at church, and even then, not very often. For the past few years, it seemed all the young men were away fighting the war. Until Giampaolo came along, Eleanor had pretty much resigned herself to living as she did, surrounded by her mother and unmarried cousins. Not that she was ungrateful – it was a good life, a much better life here (her mother frequently reminded her) than they would have had in Sicily. Listening to those remonstrations from her mother had made the idea of living anywhere but America seem completely out of the realm of possibility.

Until Giampaolo.

He was kind and solicitous from the moment she'd met him. He was handsome – dashing, even, in his khakis, with that mustache on his upper lip and hazel eyes that seemed to see right through her. He seemed sincere when he said he loved her.

The whole situation seemed hopeless, yet Eleanor clung to a vague hope that things might resolve themselves favorably. Giampaolo promised to make official inquiries about marrying her here. But how would that work? He would have to be in the camp for the foreseeable future. They didn't have living quarters for married couples there, not that she'd ever noticed or heard of. Could they have a Nuptial Mass? Would she have to travel to the camp, or could they marry here, near her home? These questions went unanswered and seemed only to engender more questions in her mind, or to point to impracticalities and impossibilities that would never be surmountable. Long ago, she resigned herself to always being unlucky in love. Even now, it seemed her luck would not change.

22 gennaio 1945

Mia carissima Eleanora,

I am writing with the news that I got just today from the commandant of Italian prisoners in the camp. It is as we suspected – marriage between a prisoner of war and an American citizen will not be permitted.

I am sorry to have to give you more bad news yet again, as it puts another roadblock in our plans. I don't want us to stop exchanging letters, because I still have great hope that some chance will come our way in the future. For now, I will continue to write to you, and I hope you will reply.

Eleanor dropped the letter in her lap as her eyes flooded with tears. She was alone in the living room, so she covered her face with her hands and sobbed softly. After a few moments, fearing she wouldn't be alone much longer, she composed herself, dried her eyes and resumed reading.

There is not much else to report. Word from the war front is sounding worse for the Germans and better for the Allies every day. One of our officers, a prisoner here with us, told us that Mussolini is in hiding and it is only a matter of time before Germany falls, too. We don't get much news directly because even though we Italians are no longer technically enemy combatants, there is still a sense of distrust. Things are not so bad among those of us in the ISU's, especially the enlisted men. We are just workers on loan to America for now. But hearing this news, it makes me wonder how long this war will go on.

Please write me when you receive this letter and tell me, my love, that we can continue our correspondence for now.

Affectionately,

Giampaolo

1 febbraio 1945

Carissimo Giampaolo,

We heard that in the spring, the church in Newark where we first met is starting up the Sunday dinners for Italian prisoners once more, and will sponsor them every two weeks. The first will be on March 4. I'll come to as many of them as I can if you tell me you can join me there. I'll be coming with my mother and the Mollicas, who want to see Tommaso.

At least we can spend some time together and talk.

I'm writing this in haste to put this in the mail so you get it very soon. Please reply and let me know if you can go to Newark on March 4. I'll write a longer letter soon.

Sending my love,

Eleanora

4 febbraio 1945

Carissima Eleanora,

What joy it will be to see you again! I am only sorry that it won't be sooner. The news about the kindness from the ladies' sodality in Newark has reached us, too. I am sure that I can get leave to go to Newark for Sunday Mass and dinner. There will likely be a large group of us going – the Americans are saying they may just as well charter a bus as send us all on the train.

There has been talk in the camp of what will happen to us after the war ends. There is now no doubt that the Allies will win the war; it is just a matter of time. And no one – not the Americans, anyway – will tell us prisoners exactly what to expect. The Italian officer who has often been a good source of news on these matters is talking about repatriation – which means we will all be transported back to Italy at some point. Of course, the war would have to end officially before any of this happens.

Looking forward to our visit in Newark,

With my love,

Giampaolo

Chapter 17

Sunday [was] the day of the week when the highest numbers of Italian Americans came to visit the PoWs...on the back of the photo was written 'dolci prigionie americane' (sweet American captivity).

—Photo caption, page 70, in Conti & Perry, *World War II Italian Prisoners of War in Chambersburg*

March 4, 1945, Newark, New Jersey

The trip by train to Newark, and then by taxi to Our Lady of Mount Carmel church, had by now become almost routine. Fighting the rain this morning made their journey less pleasant than in the past. As she and her mother stood at the curb, waiting with Mary and Frannie Mollica to board a cab from Penn Station to the church, Eleanor struggled with her wet umbrella, trying to keep it from dripping on the well-wrapped package of goodies she was bringing to Giampaolo to take back with him to the camp. He had mentioned at Christmas that he really liked a local sweet treat, Tastykakes, that were made in Philadelphia. So when Eleanor went to Nardello's store to do the weekly food shopping, cousin John had packed up a couple of boxes without charging her a dime for them. "For your young man," he whispered and winked as he handed her the paper bag.

The four women piled into the cab and gave the driver their destination.

"Must be some big doings at the church today," he remarked.

"Oh?" Eleanor queried. She'd taken the front seat next to the cabbie.

"Yeah, there's a couple buses down there already. Place is lousy with guys in uniforms. What's going on?"

"Chicken dinner for the troops!" she replied with a smile. "And a special Mass, of course."

"Of course." The cabbie tipped his cap as they pulled up to the church, where two buses were just pulling away, having deposited what looked like hundreds of soldiers at the steps leading up to the church entrance.

"There's Giampaolo!" Eleanor cried, opening the taxi door and climbing out.

"Don't worry, I got the fare," Frannie called after her.

Eleanor was already scrambling up the church steps, calling after him. Giampaolo turned, hearing his name, and stopped to wait for her, a big grin on his face. He kissed her on both cheeks and then asked, "*Unn' é a mamá?* Where's your mother?" He glanced over her shoulder, then descended the stairs quickly to help the rest of Eleanor's party navigate the wet pavement.

A bit out of breath, Donna Sarina reached her daughter's side at the wide landing of the church's front door, leaning on Giampaolo's arm. The Mollica sisters followed close behind. "Get inside!" her mother ordered. "Let's get out of this rain!"

In the church vestibule, Tommaso waited for his cousins, Vincenzo at his side. *"Bon giornu!"* The men exchanged embraces and kisses with the new arrivals before joining the stream of congregants entering the church. The group found space in two empty adjoining pews, genuflecting and crossing themselves as they took their places, then turning toward the altar emblazoned with candles and flowers at the front of the church.

When the Mass had ended with the priest's final *"Ite, missa est,"* the entire congregation seemed to rise and move as one toward the doors. Vincenzo had departed after Communion to the church hall, on a mission to secure ample seating for their party.

"We can take our time," Giampaolo whispered to Eleanor and her mother. "Vincenzo is getting us a table."

"A good thing, too," exclaimed Donna Sarina, a bewildered look on her face at the milling crowd which, with a good deal of genial shoving, all seemed to be headed for the single large door at the entrance to the church.

Tommaso pointed to a door on the side aisle. "Let's go that way," he said to his cousins with a wink. The door led to a quiet narrow staircase which led them downstairs to the backstage area at the front of the church hall. The enticing aroma of roasting chicken greeted them as they made their way down the stage platform. Standing to one side of the cavernous room, Vincenzo spied them right away. Waving wildly in their direction, he called, "*Ccà ci siamu,* here we are, over here!"

"Clever fellows," Frannie murmured to her cousin. "Tommaso, between you and Vincenzo, we didn't have to fight the crowds, either on the stairs or down here, among the tables."

"The least I can do for my dear cousins," Tommaso replied in Italian with a smile as he held out chairs for each of his cousins to sit. "We learned a few things about getting by in the army!"

Giampaolo helped Donna Sarina to a seat, then he did the same for Eleanor and took the chair beside her for himself. Presently, one of the sodality ladies, her Sunday dress obscured by an oversize white linen apron, materialized from the kitchen with baskets of bread for their table. Two others similarly attired followed with pitchers of beer and lemonade.

The din of many voices rose to a dull roar as the dinner proceeded and conversation ensued. By the time coffee and cookies were passed around to all of the tables, the rain had stopped and the sun emerged. Strong shafts of sunlight speared through the transom windows of the church hall. Chairs scraped as diners rose to move into the garden.

The sunshine outside lit a glistening sheen on the damp shrubs and trees. Crocuses and snow drops peeked through the dirt beneath still-bare branches. Giampaolo gestured to allow Eleanor to step onto the garden path before him, then he took her arm.

"It's still too wet to sit on the benches, but we can take a walk."

She nodded as they headed toward a trellis overarched with wisteria branches heavy with buds. In another month this bower would be heady with the floral perfume of cascading purple blossoms.

"Eleanora, there is something I want to tell you."

"What is it?"

"In the mess hall the other night, I overheard some fellows at the next table. One of them was talking about a situation like ours."

Eleanor glanced sidewise at him and said nothing, but kept to the path.

"This guy was talking about how he wanted to marry his American girlfriend."

"And?"

"Like me, he must have asked the commandant about this and learned that it was not allowed. At least not here, not while the war is going on."

She turned to face him so she could observe his expression as he spoke. He continued animatedly.

"This fellow said we are all going to be repatriated after the war ends, but then his *zita* was going to come to Italy and they would be married there."

Disappointed, Eleanor only murmured, "I see."

"Eleanora, don't you see? We could do that too!"

"Yes, I suppose..." she began. "But that isn't the issue, Giampaolo. Get married here, get married there, what difference does it make? We still have to figure out where we'd live."

He took her hands and said slowly and with serious intent, "There's more."

"Go on, then."

"This fellow said that once they were married, he could apply to become an American citizen."

"Why would he do that?"

"Because he wants to come back here and live after they are married."

Eleanor stopped in her tracks. Her cheeks flushed as she took in the full import of his words.

"Giampaolo, are you saying you would consider moving here to live? Marry me and move here?"

"Yes, that's exactly what I am saying."

Overjoyed, she threw her arms around his neck and hugged him fiercely. Then she pulled away, suddenly embarrassed, and just a bit disbelieving.

"Do you really mean that?" she asked, unable to keep the incredulity from her voice.

"Well, I still want to go home." He took her hands in his and looked into her eyes. "Even if it were not required. I want to see my family. I must see my parents and my *nonna,* and see how they have managed. What shape the farm is in. Maybe I could help get things going again. It might take a while. A year or more, even."

She broke into a dazzling smile, her eyes shining, as she searched his face. "Of course," she said simply, but her mind was racing.

"Are you willing to wait that long?" He looked into her eyes and took both her hands in his. "That is what I am asking you now."

"*Sí, sí!* Yes, of course!" she exclaimed joyfully. She hugged him with enthusiasm again, then became aware that they were not alone. She took a step back.

"It's all right," he whispered, clasping her wrists as she withdrew her arms. He turned back to begin to retrace their steps in the garden, then added a note of caution.

"Pay attention to me, Eleanora," he turned to her. "I heard this information third-hand. I still am not sure if this could be a solution for us just yet."

"I understand," she replied, undaunted. "But let's see what we can find out. Do you have to ask the commandant?"

"That would be a good place to start."

Hand in hand, they made progress toward a bench where her mother was seated. Frannie and Mary stood nearby, chatting with Tommaso and Vincenzo. The group seemed to be waiting for them. As they approached, Eleanor spied the surprise package she'd brought along sitting next to her mother, and clamped her hand over her mouth

"Oh, I almost forgot! I brought you something."

Gleefully she bounded toward the group. Donna Sarina looked up in surprise, a slight frown on her face, and lightly admonished her daughter. "We wondered what had become of you."

"*Mamá,* we were only a few steps away, just past that arbor." Then she snapped up the parcel by its twine handles and handed it to Giampaolo with a grin. "Tastykakes!"

"*Ah, sí?*" He looked at her in delight.

"*Sí, tuttu pe ti,* all for you." She laughed. "I remembered that you told me you like them. Take them with you back to camp."

Donna Sarina glanced at her wristwatch. "Yes, it's about time to go for our train." She gathered her things and stood in place.

Eleanor was still holding hands with Giampaolo. Now they shared a warm embrace and kisses on both cheeks, but Giampaolo held her close, paused to kiss her again and squeezed her hand meaningfully.

"*Ti scrivo vitti vitti*, I will write you soon."

"*Nurmali*, of course, so will I."

When they got home from Newark that night, late as it was, Donna Sarina drew a sheet of air mail paper and her fountain pen from the top drawer of the desk to write a letter to her sister.

4 marzo 1945

Carissima Maria Grazia,

After two months, your Christmas greeting finally arrived. It was wonderful to have some news directly from you. I cannot imagine how terrifying it must be to hear the sounds of war so very near you. At least by now the worst has probably passed. We've heard that the Allies are no longer actively fighting in Sicily and most of the troops have left for the mainland. From what the newspapers report, things may be quieter now even in Italy, but the fight still goes on in Germany. When will this terrible war end?

Thank you so much for your information about Giampaolo Stagno's family. We were just visiting him and the Mollicas' nephew today in New Jersey. I am relieved to know that he is from such a good family and a fairly prosperous one at that. With a house in the town of Palazzolo and another in the country at their farm at San Marco, the Stagnos are surely much better off than many in Provincia Siracusa at this point. If they were selling their winter wheat and other crops last year, Signor Stagno must be managing the farm all right with just his eldest son.

From Giampaolo, I've learned more about his family. He has two brothers besides the oldest who works the farm with his father. One is a soldier in the war and the youngest is studying for the priesthood. But he has had no news at all from any of them since he left more than four years ago. I am very glad indeed to learn the information you managed to find out. If the Stagno family has land, they can eat. If they have animals, they can sell or eat what the animals produce, eggs and milk, or butcher them for food. By comparison to many others, it sounds like the Stagnos have managed better than most through these difficult times. So at least Giampaolo will not find himself impoverished, as many others are, when he returns after the war.

There is news on that score. At the new year, Giampaolo asked my Eleanora to marry him. He assumed that she would be willing to go and live in Sicily. I told him that this would be impossible. After all we have been through to establish a good life here, and then losing our beloved brother, I cannot leave, nor do I want to. I am too old to make such drastic changes in my life. But I cannot lose her, too. Eleanora was broken-hearted but now she seems resigned. Although today she seemed very happy when we visited him again in the camp. I don't believe in her heart of hearts that she would want to move to Sicily, even to marry Giampaolo. However, he continues to write and she continues to go to visit him, so I am fearful she still harbors hopes of marrying him.

My dearest sister, especially now that you've reassured me more about his family, I must unburden myself. Please understand that I have no objection to the match. The young man is not the problem; his situation is the problem. I've actually grown rather fond of him. He has always been very kind and respectful to me when he visits or when we visit him. Eleanora seems to have become very fond of him. But sometimes love isn't enough. I just don't see how this story can end, except in heartbreak.

Maria Grazia, I am pouring out my heart to you in this letter because there's really no one here in whom I can confide to this extent. And for now, I will keep these things in my heart and not share them with anyone, especially my daughter, because I worry she may be in for a painful time. Cummari Angelina Mollica is, of course, a wonderful friend, but it's not the same as talking with a sister or a brother. I know that you understand. It helps just to write down my thoughts. At times like this I miss our Carmelo more than ever.

I sent some packages in January. Please let me know in your next letter if they arrived.

Know that you are in my thoughts and prayers every day.

Kisses and hugs from your sister, who loves you and wishes you well always,

Sarina.

Chapter 18

On May 8, 1945, President Harry S. Truman announced "Victory-in-Europe" day, following the surrender of Germany on May 7. Coincidentally, May 8 was also Truman's 61st birthday.

--from the National Archives

May 8, 1945, Jamesport, Pennsylvania
Late one Tuesday afternoon in early May, Eleanor had barely a foot in the door, arriving home from work, when the phone on the desk in the dining room rang. Eleanor ran to answer it. "Hello?"

"Eleanora, sugniu iu, it's me, Giampaolo!" The line crackled a bit, but there was no mistaking the excitement in his voice.

"Giampaolo, ma comu stai? How are you? Is anything wrong?" He had never telephoned her before. Her surprise morphed to worry and then back again.

"Sénti 'a nutizzia? Did your family near the news? *É finita la guèrra!* The war is over!"

She could hear cheering in the background, making it difficult to hear Giampaolo's words.

"Yes, we heard it," she replied, recalling the loud blasts of the factory alarms at two o'clock when the announcement had come over the plant's loudspeakers. "It's wonderful, isn't it?" *"Al fine,* at last! The commandant is letting each prisoner make one phone call, if we want, to someone here in the States. Of course, my treasure, I wanted to call you."

She smiled into the phone. *"Sugniu assài filici,* I am so happy that you called me." Controlling the tremble in her voice, Eleanor hoped she didn't betray the melancholy she had felt on hearing the news. She knew this would mean he would be leaving. Changing the subject, she inquired, "Won't this telephone call cost you a lot of money?"

"Not really. Besides, I get money each week and nothing special to spend it on. So I'm spending it on you!" His voice was ebullient. She could hear another cheer break out in the background as the line crackled again and the volume of ambient noise in the background ramped up.

"What's going on there? It's very loud, I can hardly hear you." She strained into the phone's earpiece.

"Na festa, it's a party!" Giampaolo turned away from the phone to shout to some of his mates.

"Then go and celebrate with your friends. It's so good to hear your voice," she said. "Thank you for calling, Giampaolo," she waited for him to respond.

"Ciao, ciao, mi amuri!" He shouted one last time and then she heard a loud click as the line went dead.

1 giugno 1945

Amore mia,

I write to tell you important news that I just learned today.

There was a meeting in the mess hall for all prisoners, in which the commandant told us that the American government's War Department would begin sending us back to Italy in the fall – most likely in September. Now that the war in Europe is officially over, American troops have already started to return, and the same ships, the Liberty ships, will be taking us back to Italy, to Rome or Naples. This is all we know for now. No dates are firm, but I wanted to let you know what they are telling us as soon as I had any news.

I am rejoicing at this news. I will be able to reunite with my parents and my nonna, and with my brother Salvatore and his wife who have been working the farm in San Marco all of this time. I hope that my brother Peppino will be home from the war, too, or will come home soon. And I hope to be able to see 'Bastiano too, although he may still be studying in Rome. Or perhaps he is ordained by now.

Most of all, I am eager to see how my family managed during the war. When I had no news of them, I feared the worst. As you know, I have missed them very much since being here. I long to see my little hometown of Palazzolo and the farm at San Marco. I hope my family didn't suffer badly during the fighting and Allied occupation. I hope the farm is still intact. I'm almost afraid to imagine what things look like, at home, but still I am eager to see it for myself.

There is another part of me that will be very sad to leave this beautiful, powerful country. I now see many advantages to making a life here. We prisoners have been well treated on the whole, even during this terrible time of war. Almost all of the Americans I have met are wonderful, friendly and generous. No one in Italy can imagine this great country; it has to be seen to be believed. I count myself lucky to have had these two years here.

And of course, if I had never come here, I would never have met you, my treasure. Life sometimes gives us strange twists and turns to travel, but there are often wonderful things down these roads. We meet people who change our lives.

I hope we will still be able to see one another as much as possible before I return to Italy. If "VE Day," as the Americans call it, is any indication, the rules about weekend leave for us prisoners are likely to be more relaxed than before. Eleanora, write to me soon. Now that the weather is warm again, let's make what plans we can.

Yours,

Giampaolo

5 giugno 1945

Dearest Giampaolo,

Thank you for the news about going home to Italy. You must be very excited about it.

This good news for you is sad news for me, because of course it means that soon we will not be able to see each other at all, even on the occasional weekend. I hope you will continue to write to me, once you are home? We will have only our letters by which to communicate. Wonderful as they are, letters are not the same as visits, being able to see one another and talk face to face.

I must also admit to feeling very afraid that when you get home, I will lose touch with you and that will be the end of the beautiful friendship and plans that we have begun here. I worry that you will be so glad to see your family and familiar places that your memories of being here, especially whatever you may remember of me, will fade and seem unimportant. I'm also afraid the idea of coming here to live won't seem as good from a distance, with an ocean between us.

As this is what life has given us, we must shoulder our circumstance and take it as it comes. Know that I love you and still hope very much that we can marry and make a life together here.

Thinking of you often and sending my love,

Eleanora

As she put down her pen and carefully folded the letter before sealing it in its envelope, Eleanor sighed deeply and took stock of her situation. Lately she felt pulled in two directions. On the one hand, she was excited and eager, as she always was – perhaps even more so, now – to see Giampaolo again, for however long his leave from camp or her time off from work would allow. On the other hand, a nagging concern was mounting that this happiness was too good to be true, that the future she hoped for was slipping from her grasp. Perhaps she and Giampaolo were only playing at romance, fueled by the "seize the day" mentality that wartime inspired. A seed of melancholy had taken root in her mind and was growing unabated. Nothing seemed able to prevent it from overtaking her heart.

Chapter 19

As soon as July Fourth began to be celebrated as America's Independence Day, fireworks were part of the plan. John Adams [said that] he hoped the anniversary of independence would be marked for years to come by "guns" and "bonfires" and "illuminations." Because the first July 4 fireworks display happened in the middle of the Revolutionary War, some historians believe they were supposed to be a "morale booster." The celebrations at the time would have also included the firing of cannons and guns, adding to the explosive nature of the festivities.

--*Time* Magazine

July 4, 1945, New York City
Summer was in full flower in southeastern Pennsylvania. The weather grew warmer, and as the June days ticked toward July, Eleanor's doldrums had deepened. For the first time, her anticipation for next visit with Giampaolo was bittersweet. She didn't want to spoil the brief time she had left to spend with him, but she couldn't help but prepare herself for the broken heart she felt was sure to come.

They had arranged to spend the 4th of July New York City. Eleanor and her cousins and the Mollica girls would meet the three Italian soldiers and whichever American chaperones would accompany them for the day. The girls would take the early train in the morning and arrive by midday. The group would take in the sights and see the fireworks over New York Harbor. Prisoners and soldiers would return to camp, and

Eleanor and her companions would spend the night at a hotel in the city. She had secured vacation time from the factory for the day after the holiday as well, so the return home could be leisurely, by the morning train. She dreaded July 5th most of all.

Eleanor wasn't immune to the glamorous lure of New York, even if the extent of her experience was a change of train at Penn Station or a bus transfer at Port Authority. The distraction of playing tourist and seeing the sights would insulate her; if this was to be her final parting with Giampaolo, at least she would always have memories of their Independence Day in New York to salve the grief of separation.

As usual, an excursion by any member of the Luna household had stirred a whirlpool of frenzied activity and excessive planning that quickly dwarfed both common sense and necessity. Eleanor frowned with chagrin as she imagined how much less stressful and more "normal" such a trip would seem to the American women her age, unburdened with the advice of too many family members under foot. Those girls, like the ones she knew from the factory, would take the journey in stride, not over-plan or overpack as she and the whole Luna clan were accustomed to do. For this trip, Eleanor had for once determined to pack only absolute essentials and leave the fussing to her cousins – as if that would reduce the import of this trip to just another visit, and somehow moderate her melancholy that she might be saying goodbye to Giampaolo for good.

She had packed her nightgown and a few other necessities in Suzanne's suitcase; they would take turns carrying the bag until they checked in to their hotel. She had carefully folded and lain out her travel wardrobe on the dresser in her bedroom. She had picked out clothing that would be comfortable and cool, yet as smart and chic as she could manage: a beige linen skirt with a box pleat at the back, and a pretty sleeveless blouse in navy blue – Giampaolo seemed to like her in blue – with a pin-tucked bodice and a matching lace trimmed tie that set off the neckline. A new soft leather handbag, also navy blue, was roomy enough to carry everything she needed – wallet, comb, lipstick -- and a lightweight cotton sweater in case the promised warm-and-sunny weather turned cool. Navy pumps with low heels and a new pair of nylon stockings with a touch of fancy stitchery above the heel (called "clocks," in the trade).

Eleanor cast a second critical glance at her choices of clothing. One couldn't be overdressed, for New York City. She thought of adding a hat – her cherry red straw pillbox would make a smart accessory and in patriotic colors to boot. But then her practical inner voice scolded not to encumber herself with just one more thing to lose or become ruined while traveling. When she pictured it flying off her head in the middle of Times Square and tumbling along the gritty streets, she returned it to the hatbox.

* * *

The train's brakes squealed as they approached the outskirts of New York City. The window left open just a crack admitted an acrid smell of burnt creosote. The windows went dark as they entered the tunnel that would take them, in a few minutes, to a track deep in the belly of Penn Station. Eleanor snapped her purse firmly closed and reached for the bag that had been resting in the overhead rack for the past three hours. This regional train had made agonizingly slow progress from Philadelphia, stopping at every burg and hamlet in the seeming unending stretch of the Garden State until finally approaching the city. The book she'd brought along had remained unopened on her lap for the entire trip. A bout of nerves now gripped her as she checked the seat around her absentmindedly.

Suzanne grasped the handle of the weathered suitcase. "I'll

take the first turn, El," she said with a nod.

Eleanor released the case to the care of her cousin. No argument there.

"Penn Station, New York City, Penn Station!" The conductor's practiced singsong rang through the air as passengers all around them prepared to disembark. The five girls shuffled along toward the end of the car and clambered down the iron steps onto the platform. On terra firma once again, they closed ranks in a semi-circle, an island in the steady stream of passengers flowing around them. Eleanor glanced at her watch, then at Frannie, who from the beginning had relished her the role of chief organizer and itinerary planner.

Frannie consulted her written schedule. "We're meeting them at Lindy's for lunch at 12:30. It's noon now. The restaurant is on Broadway between 49th and 50th Streets, and we're at 7th and 32nd. If we take the 7th Avenue exit, we should be able to hail a taxi pretty easily and get there in plenty of time."

"Is our hotel nearby?" Rosalie asked. "Or maybe we can check these bags here at the station?"

Usually quiet, Mary Mollica chimed in. "Yeah, Fran, we don't want to lug these suitcases all over the city all day long..."

A wiry red-capped porter slowed to a stop. "Help you ladies?"

"Is there a bag check nearby?" Frannie inquired.

"You bet. I can handle that for you." He started piling their suitcases on a rickety-looking dolly larger than he was and hastily scribbled a receipt stub.

"How much?"

"Two bits a bag."

"We'll have to tip him too," Eleanor whispered tersely to Frannie, who turned to her.

"That seems reasonable," she paused, mentally tallying the

price, and whispered back to Eleanor, "Four bags, a quarter each – that's just an extra dollar. We can tip him a dime for each bag."

"For heaven's sake just give him another dollar!" Rosalie chimed in impatiently. "Look at the poor guy." She glanced sympathetically at the skinny fellow in his baggy wrinkled trousers and his too-big jacket with stains over the pockets.

"Too much!" Frannie whispered back imperiously. "Fifty cents is plenty."

Rosalie frowned crossly, but Mary just shook her head and touched her friend's arm lightly, as if to say, let it go. Frannie will do what Frannie will do.

In a trice, the porter handed Frannie the claim check, then opened his palm and gazed askance at the handful of coins she had thrust in his hand. Business concluded, she was already striding away.

Rosalie turned to the porter and surreptitiously thrust a dollar bill into his palm. "Here you go," she whispered, covering her mouth with her hand. "That's for you."

"Thanks, lady!" the porter exclaimed with a smile at the unexpected largesse, and winked at her.

They all followed Frannie as she led them toward the crowded stairs that would bring them up to the street level of the terminal building. The five young women fell into the rhythm of the crowd, all shuffling feet ascending the stairs. Frannie was first to the top, striding confidently through the crowds on the street and thrusting an arm out when she got to the curb.

It was a short ride, just fifteen or so of New York City's short blocks, but to Eleanor it had seemed interminable. The taxi finally pulled up in front of the restaurant, its Lindy's neon sign winking a blue and yellow welcome. Eleanor spied the familiar clutch of Italian young men right away, their khaki uniforms setting them apart. Giampaolo had his back to the street, but when he turned and saw the cab, he moved toward it quickly. Opening the door, he grasped Eleanor's hand and pulled her toward him for an eager embrace.

"*Bon giornu, amuri,*" he whispered. She felt her heart flip as he kissed her on both cheeks. The men enfolded the new arrivals into their circle, shaking hands with hugs and greetings. From a large table at the window, Patsy, Tony, and Rafe waved enthusiastically.

"The Americans went in to get us a table," Tommaso addressed the women in Italian. "Patsy said this place would be busy at lunchtime. It's supposed to be a famous 'New Yawk-style deli,'" he framed the English words carefully, mimicking Patsy Tinelli's terse Brooklyn-ese. They were all laughing as the revolving doors spun and shuttled them inside.

They were barely settled at the table when a waitress trundled over and turned over the thick porcelain coffee cups with a clang onto the saucers set up at each place. "What'll it be?" she asked, pouring the strong black brew unbidden into each cup and readying a pencil to jot down their orders.

Rafe rubbed his hands together. "I've been wanting to try this place for years!"

The waitress rolled her eyes and tapped her pencil impatiently on the table.

The group looked overwhelmed by the dizzying array of options on the enormous cardboard menus in front of them. Patsy took over and addressed the group first. "Pastrami on rye OK with everyone?" He looked around for assent from each in turn. "They'll bring potato salad with it," he added.

Shouting to be heard over the clatter and din, Frannie spoke first. "Fine with me!" She looked at her sister and Eleanor. "It's supposed to be the specialty of the house."

Relieved to have the decision taken out of her hands, Eleanor agreed. "I'll have the same," she nodded, pushing aside the menu, and soon her cousins and Mary joined in. The Italian soldiers quickly followed suit.

Patsy laughed. "You guys look like a bunch of damn Kewpie dolls, all nodding your heads at once!" He bowed his head in an exaggerated imitation. Then he turned to the waitress. "Pastrami and Swiss on rye, with mustard, for everyone. Better yet, on pumpernickel, if you have it," he added as she lifted a finger to count heads. "There are eleven of us," he added. "Three Italians, three Americans and five beautiful broads!"

Tony and Rafe laughed appreciatively, but Giampaolo and his compatriots just looked confused. Eleanor turned to them and explained in Italian. "He used a slang term for women," she paused, then added with a smile, "and he called us beautiful." Now the three Italian soldiers were smiling and nodding. To emphasize the point, Tony framed a shapely figure-8 with his hands, then turned his palms upward in a caressing, cupping motion. The entire group burst into peals of laughter. No translation necessary.

"Eleven Number Two's!" Their waitress had returned in no time, shouting in confirmation and approaching their table with an enormous tray piled high with plates. Two other servers followed her with trays similarly laden. They dispersed the platters around the large table with breakneck efficiency. Each dish sported a massive sandwich crammed with thin rosy slices of pastrami. Completing each platter was an enormous dill pickle and a generous scoop of potato salad dotted with celery seed.

The men fell on their food as if they had never eaten anything so delicious. The women eyed the colossal servings on their plates, then glanced at each other. Eleanor tried cutting each half of her sandwich in half once more, the better to negotiate the mass of meat and cheese between the layers of dark rye bread. Her cousins copied the maneuver with mixed success. Frannie finally shrugged, picked up a fork, removed the top layer of bread and tackled the sandwich fillings less conventionally but in neater fashion.

A short time later, Patsy pushed back from the table and patted his now-full belly. "That was just swell. Don't know why I haven't been back sooner." Only a few crumbs of bread and shreds of pastrami were left on the plate in front of him.

"There's nothing like this back home," Rafe said, his mouth muffled with the last bite of his sandwich.

Tony rubbed his hands together and looked around the table. "OK, lunch at the famous deli. Check. Where to, next?"

The Italians were mute, but everyone who spoke English had an idea and shouted at once.

"The Empire State building!"

"Walk down Broadway"!

"Central Park!"

Frannie, taking charge, said, "We should see the sights here in midtown while we are in the neighborhood. Broadway is practically outside our door," she began unfolding a map from her handbag, "so we may as well start there." Her index finger followed Broadway on the map till she came to something she had circled. "The Empire State building is on Fifth Avenue between 33rd and 34th. That's about a 10-block walk from here."

"I'd love to go to Macy's, too," Suzanne piped up shyly.

"That's back towards Penn Station," Frannie supplied. "We could go there next."

"But we gotta go to Central Park! That's the opposite direction," Patsy countered.

"Maybe we could take the subway uptown and make that our

third stop."

"But leave some time for a walk!" her sister Mary added.

"Of course," Frannie responded. "We should save the Staten Island Ferry ride until after dark – so maybe we can see the fireworks over the Statue of Liberty."

"What are we doing for supper?" Rosalie queried.

"I'm so full from that lunch, I can't imagine being hungry again," Suzanne groaned.

Frannie's sister Mary piped up. "I've always wanted to go to the Russian Tea Room. Could we go there?"

Tony inserted, "I think that's up on 57th. Near Central Park. It would be an easy walk from there."

"You seem to know this area pretty well," Patsy remarked with admiration.

"You're lookin' at a Hell's Kitchen boy!" Tony replied proudly.

"That's great," Frannie said, "then you can help us figure out the subway too – keep us from going the wrong way."

With the itinerary more or less outlined, Tony and Rafe stood up, reached into their pockets and threw down a fistful of bills to cover the check.

Seeing the soldiers' generosity, Mary and Rosalie exclaimed "Thank you!" in unison as they shimmied to the end of the booth.

"That really wasn't necessary, fellas," Frannie remarked, fingering her wallet. "We can pay our own way."

"We know that," Rafe supplied smoothly and pushed her hand away. "Let us do this. We have so little to spend Uncle Sam's money on, it's our pleasure to treat you."

Outside on the sunny street corner, the group separated into twos and threes to negotiate the crowded sidewalks. As they made their way down Broadway, the Italians slowed down, mouths agape and eyes wide as they took in the skyscrapers and bustling traffic.

Giampaolo and Eleanor walked side by side. Edgily, he clung to her elbow, pausing at each corner crosswalk and reaching for her hand before they waded into traffic. Seeing his worried expression, she patted his hand to reassure him.

"*Troppu machine!*" he exclaimed breathlessly. "So many cars!"

"Yes, I know," she replied in English. "*È difficili*, it's difficult to cross a street here."

"*Alluda, amuninni lìsciu lìsciu.*" He glanced furtively right and left at the jumble of cabs and cars and put a tentative foot forward, wrapping her arm more securely in his.

The group made their way across pretty Herald Square, its pink and red geraniums in full bloom in the hot July sunshine. As they turned onto 34th Street, Eleanor glimpsed the towering hulk of the Empire State Building ahead and pointed to it for Giampaolo. She watched as he tilted his head back and his eyes traveled up, up, up... The top of the building could barely be seen. His expression was equal parts astonishment and trepidation.

On Fifth Avenue they stopped across the street from the building's main entrance, the street level wrapped in sleek bands of black onyx, particolored marble and stainless steel. Above the cupola that sheltered the front doors, three columns of gray-green glass with crisscrossing patterns rose like Art-Deco tree trunks, bracketed by concrete columns on either side. The whole effect was of an austere commanding gateway that dared rather than welcomed onlookers to pass underneath. The words "Empire State" were carved across the top of the entrance and painted with gold-leaf, as if there were any doubt about the identity of the edifice.

Frannie and Patsy took advantage of a lull in the traffic to cross the street and the rest followed, pushing their way one at a time through the heavy revolving glass and brass doors. As the lobby's grandeur met their eyes, it was as if they passed into the anteroom of King Midas himself. Everything around them seemed made of gold. A gleaming relief of the building's profile, carved in gold, dominated the wall on one side of the large space, eliciting gaped wonder from the three Italian visitors. Gold tones of marble and metallic décor set off walls, floors, and ceilings. Behind them, a semicircular parapet and the surrounding walls above the revolving doors through which they had entered were set off in a wide band of ribbed gold, looking to Eleanor like an expanse of glistening grosgrain ribbon. On the wall above the doorway, spotlights were trained on three sparkling golden medallions, as large as wagon wheels, embedded in the façade. To one side, more gleaming stainless bands and black panels surrounded the information desk and ticket area. As everyone ogled, suitably overcome by the lustrous flamboyance all around them, Rafe and Tony broke away from the group and negotiated their way across the lobby to make inquiries. Momentarily, Patsy returned and addressed the group, a wide grin on his face.

"Members of the military can ride the elevator to the observation deck for free!" Preening proudly, he fanned out their already-stamped tickets and waved them over his head. "Since you ladies are our guests, you get to ride free too. Courtesy of the U.S. Army!" With a flourish, he led the group across the polished marble floors toward a set of stairs leading up to the express elevators that would take them to the building's legendary observation deck.

Ears popping as they got off the elevator near the building's summit, Eleanor looped her arm in Giampaolo's once more. They moved to the edge of the deck to get a better glimpse of the tower's storied panorama views. The platform's edge was bordered by a substantial cement parapet crowned with thick iron bars arranged crosswise. Above that stretched yet another sturdy barricade of iron bars, their pointed tips curving inward like an ominous procession of so many black scimitars, discouraging would-be daredevils from getting too close.

With bemused wonderment, the Italian soldiers watched Rafe engage one of the coin-operated oversize View-Master binoculars that advertised a bird's-eye prospect. He invited each member of the group to take a peek. Tommaso was the first to step up. He put his eyes to the device and, startled suddenly, he jumped back quickly and cursed softly in Italian. The Americans all laughed, and Rafe helped him adjust the view finder for a better view.

Giampaolo and Eleanor strolled arm in arm around the periphery, stopping frequently to take in the changing vista from each side of the building. From every angle, the city stretched out before them. Tall buildings that towered for many stories or sprawling structures that dominated entire neighborhoods on the streets below looked no bigger than a child's building-blocks in gray steel, beige stone, and russet brick. The streets and avenues themselves fanned out diagonally from the skyscraper's base, and parted the unruly urban scalp of the city at regular intervals. Peering very closely, they could spot minuscule buses and cars like hundreds of beetles crawling their way through a thicket of concrete and glass. The outer horizons glimmered like blue and silver ribbons where the island of Manhattan met surrounding waters – the Hudson to the west, the East River to the east, and, to the south, wider expanses of watery reflection interrupted by the grey streaks of Staten Island and New Jersey.

After everyone had their fill of New York's dizzying cityscape, they made their way toward the elevator for the speedy, stomach-churning trip downward. On the street once again, Giampaolo paused to look up admiringly at the Empire State Building once more. He couldn't seem to grasp the scale of what he'd seen.

Walking again in twos and threes, they retraced their steps to Broadway and back one block to 34th Street. Suzanne gazed excitedly down the block where, above the protective overhang of the main entrance, burnished bronze lettering proclaimed "R. H. Macy & Co.," the home of her favorite department store. She could barely contain her excitement.

They crossed the street in twos and threes and gathered on the corner. Frannie issued Suzanne a stern warning.

"Ok, now, this stop is for you," she shook her finger. "But don't get lost in there!"

"How about we meet back here in forty-five minutes?" Rosalie suggested. "That way, if Macy's isn't everybody's cup of tea, you can do something else for a bit."

"Good idea," Frannie nodded curtly, deciding for the group and settling on a nearby bench with her sister to consult their maps.

Patsy said, "I could use a cup of coffee."

"There's a stand on the street right over there," Rafe pointed to the opposite corner, toward which Tony was already headed. Before budging an inch when his Italian compatriots followed the other men, Giampaolo looked at Eleanor for direction.

"*Vui cumprari 'n caffè?* Should we take a coffee break?"

"*Se tu vui,* if you'd like to," he looked at her uncertainly.

She bit her lower lip, considering, then said, "*Facemu na passeggiata dabanna?* Shall we take a stroll around over there?" She gestured toward the leafy enclosure and beckoning park benches of Greeley Square.

He beamed and led her back the way they had just come.

The pair walked hand in hand until she paused at a vacant wooden seat. She perched on the edge, and he sat beside her. She turned to him and swept an arm in a circle. "*Cchi ci pinsa?* So what do you think of New York?"

He let out a deep breath as he struggled to come up with a descriptor. *"Troppu ranni.* It's so big," he began.

"And…?"

"Troppu scrusciu. Troppu genti," he said simply. "Too much noise. Too many people."

She laughed and reverted to the Sicilian dialect sympathetically. *"Iu sacciu,* I know. It can be overwhelming."

He stroked her hand, getting her attention, and addressed her in a serious tone. "You know, *mi amuri,* now that the war has ended, we will go home soon."

"Do you know when?"

"Not yet. But I've heard it could be any day."

She summoned the courage to say what was foremost on her mind. "Then this could be our last time together."

"Sì."

They sat in silence for a long while. He continued to stroke her hand as if to comfort her.

"Well, then, let's make the most of it!" She swallowed the lump in her throat as tears welled in her eyes, hoping he would not notice.

He sighed resignedly, and rose slowly. "Shall we go back to the others?"

"Not yet." She pulled his arm and he sat once more. "Just a few more minutes."

He wrapped an arm around her and they remained, unmoving. She leaned into him, and he inclined his head toward hers. She wished she could stop the clock and freeze this moment forever.

Soon Patsy Tinelli's jovial tones sounded from behind them. "If it isn't our favorite lovebirds!" he teased.

Eleanor turned in the direction of his voice. The other soldiers were with him, walking towards them.

"I guess it's time to meet the girls." She whispered to Giampaolo in Italian and put on a brave face for the others.

They rose to their feet but kept their hands clasped together. She didn't want to let go, and neither, it seemed, did he.

A couple of hours later, when they emerged from the plush maroon velvet banquettes and sumptuous old-world luxury of the Russian Tea Room, darkness had crept onto the city streets. But the gloom went almost unnoticed in the midst of the brightly lit streets of Manhattan's glittery midtown. Patsy and Rafe speedily commandeered several taxis that sped them southward toward the Battery and the ferry's Whitehall Street terminal. It wasn't until they tumbled out onto the pavement in front of the ferry building that Eleanor noticed how dark it had become.

The bass tones of a boat whistle sent a thrill through her bones. The electric ferry's massive floating frame, overflowing with tourists, residents and day-trippers inched its way toward a wide pier. They watched as the ferry's crew scurried about, throwing lines and deftly wrapping them around the docking stanchions to secure the massive ferry boat in place. Eleanor clung to Giampaolo's arm as they waited behind chain ropes for arriving passengers to disembark first. Being among the lucky few in the front of the line would mean their group would be among the first to board, and on these high-demand nighttime runs on the 4th of July, they would be able to commandeer the best seats outside on the upper deck.

The group of friends eagerly clambered aboard. Giampaolo let Eleanor climb the metal stairs before him, and the ferry's upper deck stretched empty and ready. They rushed to claim spots near the railing.

As the ferry pulled away, the fireworks began over the Hudson.

From their vantage-point, surrounded by their companions, Eleanor and Giampaolo had the best view possible. And the show did not disappoint. Multicolored starbursts exploded in the black night sky. Roman candles swizzled their way toward the water in downward arcs of white light. Like lightening, the sparkling streaks were followed by the thunder of loud cannon booms. Giampaolo's boyish grin let her understand how much he was enjoying the spectacle. Above all, she would never forget how his eyes filled when the ferry got within view of the Statue of Liberty, dramatically backlit by the fireworks in the night sky. As she watched him, she felt a lump rise in her throat, too.

The return trip came to an end too quickly. Eleanor dreaded what came next. The looming Manhattan skyline off the ship's deck signaled that goodbye was approaching. There seemed to be nothing left to say as they moved, hand in hand, behind their friends among the river of passengers shuffling off the ferry. Soon they were ashore. Their companions moved on, leaving the pair to themselves.

Giampaolo turned her toward him.

"*Quannu ci taliamu, amuri?* he asked softly. "When will we see each other again, my love?"

"*Will* we see each other again, Giampaolo?" she echoed his question with different emphasis.

"*Certu!*" he replied with a confidence she didn't share.

"*Ggiá turni a casa, a Sicilia,* you'll be going home soon, back to Sicily," she squeezed his hand as tears rose and the world went blurry. Two big drops fell onto her arm. "I don't know...our situation seems so impossible."

"Will you wait for me?"

"For how long?"

After a pause, he replied somberly.

"I cannot give you a specific time, Eleanora."

"I realize that, but still…"

"You can do me a favor."

"Of course. What is it?"

"Make inquiry at the government office about American citizenship. For me," he said with finality.

"Really?" A thin thread of hope wound around her heart as she searched his eyes for an answer.

"Yes, *gioia mia.* I told you already I would consider coming here to live."

"I guess I still don't believe that will ever happen."

"Whatever happens, we need to know more. I need to have more information."

She dropped her head but grasped both his hands more tightly. Finally she said, "Yes. I can do that much."

They turned and walked arm in arm toward the street.

20 agosto, 1945

Carissima Eleanora,

How are you? I hope this letter finds you well, busy, and happy. I think about you many times each day.

The Americans were rejoicing in the camp the last few days, hearing word that the war in the Pacific is finally over. From one of Patsy Tinelli's buddies, we heard about the all-night celebration in the neighborhood they call "Little Italy," in New York City. Italians in this country were just as glad as Italians who live in Italy to see this war come to an end.

At last we have had word about repatriation. The American officers have told us that they will begin our paperwork next week. The American War Department doesn't seem to know how to do anything without asking us to fill out a form! When that is completed for all the prisoners here in camp, they will begin assigning us to ships and giving us departure dates. I don't know how long that will take or when my departure will be assigned, so I have nothing definite to tell you. I have heard only that the Americans are trying to do a quick turnaround on the ships bringing American soldiers home from Europe to take us back. One of the officers said that there are many more German prisoners to repatriate than Italians. I have not met any Germans since I have been in America, so I suppose they were sent to other camps. No one seems to know who will be repatriated first, or in what order we will go. It's another case of hurrying up and then waiting to hear what will happen.

Several of Patsy Tinelli's friends have returned home. They came by to see him and we all went out to a local bar for a few beers. One of the guys said he thought that the ship they came back on will probably take some of us back to Italy – if not prisoners from our camp, then from another nearby camp in New Jersey.

It is very unsettling, not knowing more than that I could leave at any day. I will be very glad to see my family again, but I will miss America too. That must seem strange to you, since I am in a prison camp. But I have been well treated; all the Italian fellows in this camp feel pretty much the same way. Once we got leave to travel away from the camp, I got to see a little bit of what life is like, for Americans. It seemed happy and comfortable, not at all like the life I was used to, on the farm. I will miss it.

And I will miss you. I miss you every day and think of you with love. Wait for me, my Eleanora. Have patience that we will be together soon.

With an affectionate hug and kisses,

Giampaolo

Monday, 3 September – Labor Day
Carissimo Giampaolo,

I got your letter last week but have been so busy, this is my first chance to respond. I have the day off work today so I have time to write you.

First of all, I have some news – but nothing definite – from my inquiry about American citizenship for Italian nationals who have served as prisoners of war. Now that the war is over, no one in charge seems to know exactly what the rules are, or how they might change. Everything is in motion, it seems. The war has changed everything. I have had several phone conversations and one interview in person with someone at the local courthouse regarding immigration. He told me there is a branch office of the Immigration and Naturalization Service in Philadelphia. There is talk that immigration quotas will be "reviewed" for citizens of Germany, Italy, and Japan who want to move permanently to the United States. No one seems to know yet when, or for how long, or how strict the quotas will be. The best bet still is to be married to someone who is already an American citizen.

I did learn some good news, though. If an American citizen marries a non-American in a foreign country, there is no need to wait until both are in the US. Citizenship procedures for the non-citizen can be applied for immediately. The US citizen would go to the nearest US embassy or consulate to present the marriage license and begin the process. The non-American spouse could emigrate right away, even before citizenship is finalized.

Giampaolo, I have asked for the information that you requested. But I be can't help thinking that all of this is very premature. You don't even know yet when you will return to Italy! You know I am <u>not</u> saying this because I am eager for you to go... Once you are at home again, you don't know what you will find. And once you have been there for a while, you may decide you don't want to leave your home again.

Do send word as soon as you know when you will be leaving. You already feel so far away.

Missing you more every day,

With love,

Eleanora

12 September, 1945

Eleanora mi amore,

I have received my orders for repatriation.

I leave for Italy on the 8th of October. The three of us who came over together – Vincenzo, Tommaso, and I – will all leave together. That's fitting, no? We are told that the ship will take us to Rome or Naples, and once we are on Italian soil, the Italian provisional government will provide transport back to our home cities. Beyond that, only God knows.

I am told that I will not be able to leave the camp between now and my departure. So we will not be able to visit again before I go. I know this will be a big disappointment to you, as it is for me. But please know that, for my part, it doesn't change a thing: I still love you and want you to be my wife. There is still a lot of uncertainty about what I'll find when I get home to Sicily, but that doesn't change the facts or my love for you. I hope you return my affection with confidence that we will see each other again and be together again before long, whether there or here.

I will write you as soon as I get to Palazzolo. You have my parents' address to use when you write to me, but it's best if I investigate first and let you know the best way to reach me.

Sending you kisses and a strong hug from your

Giampaolo

30 September, 1945

Carissimo Giampaolo,

This will probably be my last letter to you at the camp. I would worry if I send it later that it would miss your departure.

I must be honest: I have cried every day, sometimes a little and sometimes a lot. Everything still seems so uncertain about our future. I trust that you love me, but we must be practical about our situation. You don't know what you will find when you return home, nor how you will feel about me when thousands of miles separate us, not just a couple hundred, and when there is no prospect of seeing one another for a long time.

Nothing much will change for me here, in the meanwhile. I go to work each day, do my work around the house on the weekends, and go to Mass on Sunday. It's getting colder now and the days are shorter. I fear it will be a long cold winter ahead.

Know that I think of you many times, each and every day, and send my love to you over the distance that separates us.

Sending you kisses and a strong hug from your

Eleanora

Part II
GOING BACK

Chapter 20

Liberty ships were a class of cargo ship built in the United States during World War II. Though British in concept, the design was adapted by the United States for its simple, low-cost construction. Mass-produced on an unprecedented scale, the Liberty ship came to symbolize U.S. wartime industrial output.

—Wikipedia

Departure: October 1945, New York Harbor
The charred scents of axle grease and hot metal rose from the tracks to Giampaolo's nostrils as he disembarked the train with Vincenzo and Tommaso. The three men squinted in the bright October sun as they shouldered their rucksacks and made for the waiting buses that would take them to the pier, a Liberty Ship, and passage home.

Home. His heart swelled at the thought of seeing his parents and brothers again. And his *nonna*. But as the reunion came into sharper focus, a chill of trepidation coursed through him. For more than four years he had had no word of how his family had fared in the unspeakable hardship of the war in Sicily. He dreaded what he might find. Possibly, the farm at San Marco was too remote to have suffered the ravages of booted feet and heavy tanks. But armies in motion often create new routes through the countryside to get where they are going. He felt himself tense at the thought, and realized these worries were not likely to leave him until he could see for himself.

Giampaolo glanced over his shoulder one last time at the

chain-link fence surrounding the camp. His days as a prisoner of war had come to an end. For two years in one temporary American post after another, and for two years before that in the African desert, he, Tommaso, and Vincenzo had grown accustomed to looking out for each other. In the desert, it had become almost second nature to share their scavenged rations and to keep an eye out for hidden danger. In America, their situation had improved, but even here they had learned to be wary of strangers. As warmly as they had been welcomed among Italian-Americans in their homes and churches, many in this country were all too ready to keep pointing accusing fingers at the enemy.

One thing he would not miss was the procession of vehicles always standing ready to haul them somewhere, to work for a day or a week or to transfer them to a new camp entirely. There always seemed to be a truck waiting for them or a train standing at the track, idling in a cloudy stench of diesel, ready to receive hordes of khaki-clad men. Today was no different.. He and his friends clambered aboard the nearest bus, filing in among hundreds of Italian prisoners with their oval Italy patches still showing on their left sleeves and the round ones on their caps. Throwing his pack on the seat behind him and his jacket on the adjacent one, Giampaolo efficiently snagged places for the three of them.

The short ride from camp to pier took less than twenty minutes, and presently they were shouldering their packs again and climbing off the bus. Awaiting them on the dock was the accustomed phalanx of American military bureaucracy: rows of tables staffed by American soldiers, armed with clipboards and sheets of paper for each prisoner to sign. If the American Army was expert at moving men about, it was equally adept at paperwork. As the prisoners left the bus, two GIs stood by the doors, directing each by the initial of his last name to find the right table.

Although he had grown used to it, Giampaolo still marveled

at how well-planned everything in this country seemed to be. From landing in America till now, he admired the military efficiency, cleanliness, and order of the camps. He recalled the jobs he had performed as a prisoner – working the line at a cannery in Indiana or swabbing the docks in New York. None of these had struck him as very different from duties he might have been assigned as a soldier in the Italian military service at home, with one big exception: everything here seemed organized and purposeful. He had liked it and would miss it, this American devotion to order and precision. What kind of disorder and destruction was he likely to find at home? He tried to tuck away his apprehensions and concentrate simply on the task at hand: signing his repatriation paperwork and getting in line to board the ship.

Giampaolo shuffled into a line of prisoners awaiting the table marked with "S" stenciled on a large piece of cardboard. With thousands of prisoners to process, the lines still moved rapidly. *Chisti 'Mericani*, they can't wait to be rid of us, he thought. His compatriots in line were mostly silent, shifting from foot to foot, fingering in a pocket for a cigarette, striking a match and sharing it with the next prisoner. Puffs of tobacco smoke rose in wispy columns above them and vanished in the warm autumn afternoon.

Waiting his turn, Giampaolo was restless. With a pang, he thought of Eleanor. He recalled wistfully his visits to Jamesport. There, daily life for ordinary Americans seemed well ordered, too, but also full of comfort, ease, and plenty. There was no random chaos, no inefficiency or backward thinking for the sake of tradition like at home. In Sicily, before the war, those things had already begun to chafe at him. The America he'd seen was a country firmly in the modern world, a vast and powerful place that knew how to get things done. Its varied and imposing landscapes, epitomized by the rich farmland he'd glimpsed from the train window and the city blocks he walked more recently in New York, were vital and brimming with promise. The whole country seemed young, energetic, poised on the brink of a bright future. This place was so unlike his homeland, with one foot in ancient tradition and the other struggling to step into a twentieth century now nearly half gone. He thought of Naples with its crowded, cramped streets, where donkey-drawn carts were as much a pedestrian hazard as buses and motorcars rushing helter-skelter in every direction. Not so in America: Even Manhattan's teeming traffic had a brisk order to it that channeled its energy. He'd seen it himself. The United States was a great country, no two ways about it.

Finding himself at the front of the line, Giampaolo gave his last name and took the clipboard handed to him.. His eyes swam at the jumble of incomprehensible English until they lit on a neat line, about the middle of the page, with his name typed below it. The staff GI pointed wordlessly to the line and handed him a pen. Giampaolo carefully inscribed, "Stagno Giampaolo" in the manner he always used on official documents. Below the signature line were more English words and another line which the soldier pointed to, indicating he should sign again. A second soldier took the clipboard from him and brusquely stamped a date at the bottom. It was official: he was on his way home.

Giampaolo looked around for his friends. They were already waiting for him at the gangplank. Vincenzo raised an arm in greeting.

"'Paperwork,' eh?" Tommaso smiled as Giampaolo caught up with them, using one of the few English words he'd mastered during his stay in the States. Vincenzo patted him on the back and let him pass onto the gangplank of the large vessel, one of many in the harbor, that were boarding the prisoners.. At the top of the ramp, Giampaolo stopped and looked back at the pier below. He took in a lungful of air as he watched the long line of prisoners snaking its way onto the ship. A last glimpse, a last breath of America. .

Once aboard, the three men stowed their gear in a cramped bunk-room amidships and climbed back on deck. The ship's deep basso horn sounded as it began to pull away from the pier. Wind whipped at their shirts and they clung to their caps as the vessel made for open water at a fast clip. Suddenly, a space on the horizon cleared and there she was – Lady Liberty, proudly guarding the harbor. Giampaolo remembered his first sight of the statue when he had arrived two years earlier. Her arm never tired of holding her lamp aloft. The points of her haloed crown, the folds of her sleeves, and the hem of her robe brought her outline into stark relief against the bright blue sky. Just beyond was the many-windowed dark brick hulk of Ellis Island with its four towers. Giampaolo imagined that the statue was bidding them goodbye now. The three men stood on deck and watched until the New York skyline faded to nothing more than a smudge of gray on the horizon.

Chapter 21

Between the end of September and middle of October 1945, all of the Letterkenny Italian POWs were repatriated. When they arrived in Italy, they found their country in truly dire straits: countless bridges, roads, and large parts of cities lay in ruins. Economically, many of the ISU [Italian Service Unit] soldiers had to start over from scratch, "roll up their sleeves," and create a new life.

—Introduction to Chapter 9, Conti & Perry, *World War II Italian Prisoners of War in Chambersburg*

October, 1945, Port of Naples
Six days at sea. The trip home seemed improbably short. Their Liberty Ship was blessed with calm waters, weathering only one day of rain the entire week. For a vessel flying the Stars and Stripes, there was no longer any threat of attack from lurking German U-boats. The war was over.

The ship approached the turbulent Mediterranean port of Naples, heaving among countless ships and smaller boats of every imaginable size and condition. Hordes of dirty young men and scrawny children crowded the gangplank as the returning prisoners made their way onto the pier. *"'Mericani! 'Mericani!"* Shouts went up from the crowd as Giampaolo realized they were being mistaken for Yankee soldiers. Some of the prisoners leaned over the people crowding the ship to correct that misimpression: *"Siamo italiani! Italiani, ritornati dagli Stati Uniti!* We are Italians, returning home from the United States!" They didn't seem to hear, or understand: the crush of ragged urchins – the infamous *scugnazzi* feared even by the locals – swarmed in upon them with outstretched hands, hopeful for a windfall of food or cigarettes, or maybe an American chocolate bar. If they didn't beg, they stole. They didn't care from whom they were begging; it mattered only that they did not leave the pier empty-handed.

The children's frenzied desperation saddened Giampaolo. He glanced at his friends and saw the dismay on their faces, too. All of them hugged their packs closely, not anxious to have them plucked from their backs by the surging, scrappy youngsters. After a hundred yards or so of jostling and shoving, the trio finally broke free of the crowds and huddled to take stock.

Some homecoming. The trio made their way to the Verrazano railway station and passage southward. They boarded the first overcrowded train headed for Reggio Calabria. Entering the congested car dank with sweat, the new arrivals' clean-shaven cheeks and crisp khaki apparel drew stares from the scruffy locals with whom they were packed in, shoulder to shoulder. This train would travel the length of Italy's boot to its very toe, where its cars would be decoupled from the locomotive and loaded on a ferry to cross the Strait of Messina. It would make slower progress on the other side, snaking down the eastern coast of the triangular island of Sicily, carrying Giampaolo, Vincenzo, and Tommaso toward the port city of Siracusa.

As the countryside streamed past the train window, Giampaolo peered out at a land he barely recognized, scarred now with the unmistakable ruination of war. In the distance, outlines of bombed out bridges and aqueducts bore grim testimony to recent combat. In the wide-open stretches between cities or clusters of towns, an occasional cement pillbox bunker would appear, its concrete profile stark and alien on the tired landscape, an unruly coil of barbed wire a whimsical, sinister bonnet topping the domed structure. These were clear reminders that armies had fought here.

Occasionally the travelers spied a solitary farmer, his face lined with hunger and resignation, trudging along the dirt path that ran alongside the tracks, an emaciated donkey hauling a cart behind.

In the cities and towns, the wounds of war were still more obvious. Lone buildings or entire blocks altogether were nothing more than skeletons of bare wood and crumbling plaster. They teetered mutely in place, their fresh scars a testament to exploding shells and barrages of ammunition. Gaping holes and exposed interior rooms had been left like so many inanimate carcasses to weather the ravages of torrential rain and torrid summer sun. The children all seemed dirty and ill-clothed, many running barefoot in the dusty streets. Posters and advertising bills celebrating the bygone fascist era bore bullet holes, barely adhering to walls of buildings without windows or doors. The once-inspiring image of Il Duce's wide-legged stance and outstretched arm now dissolved in shredded paper peeling forlornly off crumbling walls. Mounds of debris lay everywhere, forming eerie sculptures banked on nearly every corner.

Sometimes a pile of rubble stood sentinel at a lonely intersection. Perhaps that was all that was left of a home once beloved and lovingly tended, whose mellow light had welcomed home its tired papa at the end of a long day. On another street, a mass of ash and wood formed a sad marker of bygone times. At an intersection of narrow lanes, a cozy, inviting trattoria may have once stood, its tables clothed in linen beckoning to passersby to stop for a *gelato* after their evening turn about the piazza. Everywhere was chalky grey dust. Giampaolo thought the detritus of war had sculpted the modern towns and hamlets of his homeland to resemble the ancient ruins of their proud age-old classical heritage, the footpaths of Carthaginians and Greeks, Romans, Normans, and Saracens. Destruction was everywhere, and everywhere the ciphers of starvation and poverty marked the faces of his countrymen.

Siracusa was the same as Naples and Reggio Calabria, Messina and Catania. No place had been spared the veneer of debris and desolation. As the train slid into the depot at Siracusa, drowsy in the late afternoon heat, Giampaolo embraced his friends and made vague promises to look them up once the dust of home had settled. Then he made his way from the station and out of the city as quickly as he could, setting a rapid pace on foot. On the city's outskirts he finagled a decrepit bicycle from a young boy with two candy bars and a packet of Lucky Strikes. The boy's eyes grew wide at the sight of such American largesse, and Giampaolo felt a momentary pang for him. Mounting the rickety contraption, its tires barely inflated, he managed to make slightly steadier progress than on foot.

Dry scrub and prickly pear cactuses still lined the dusty road to his hometown, Palazzolo, whose contours he finally spied on the horizon. Navigating dusty cobblestones, he glimpsed remains of shelled buildings and avoided smaller side streets blocked by boulders and debris. He turned a corner onto the main *corso,* and miraculously, there stood his home, completely intact. Its green awning fluttered in the breeze like a flag welcoming him home, shading the balcony one story above the street as it always had.

He ditched the bike behind the house and scrambled up the familiar stone stairs, his heart beating wildly. Entering the sitting-room, he found his *nonna* seated in her accustomed chair, fingering her rosary and whispering the prayers softly to herself. He approached quietly, knelt in front of her, and removed his cap.

The look of stunned surprise gave way to a luminous smile that lit his grandmother's wrinkled face and made her eyes shine.

"Giampaolo! *Figghiu miu, figghiu miu!*" Donna Lombardo repeated the filial endearment in her familiar way, her soft dialect music to his ears as she enfolded him in an embrace and rocked him as she used to do when he was a boy.

"*Nonna, sugnu ccá,* I'm here," he muffled the words into the starchy collar of her black dress, and let the tears flow.

"Let me look at you." She held him at arm's length and took careful measure of his face as she patted his cheek. Unrestrained joy shone in her eyes. She pulled him to her again, hugging and rocking him in her arms to assure herself that this was no apparition before her, but truly her grandson returned from the war.

"*Chi c'e da manciàri,* do you want something to eat?"

"*Nun ti scantari, nonna,* don't trouble yourself..." But she was already on her feet, bustling her way around the tiny kitchen. Soon, bread and olives were set on the well-scrubbed wooden table, quickly snatched from beneath clean linen cloths that sheltered a row of bowls in the pantry. Donna Lombardo reached to a sideboard cabinet and uncorked a bottle of wine, finding two small glasses on a shelf and pouring a bit into each before seating herself at the table across from him.

"*Papá e mamá stannu in campagna,* your father and mother are at the farm." She nodded and smiled, stroking the sleeve of his uniform as he stuffed his mouth with bread.

"*Sí, capiscu,* yes, I thought they would be," he murmured between mouthfuls. "*Dumani matina,* I'll go there myself in the morning."

"You are so tanned and strong!" she exclaimed, tilting her head slightly and regarding him coolly. "*Mi pari 'n 'Mericano,* you look like an American!"

Pointing to the oval "Italy" patch sewn on his sleeve, Giampaolo explained that it was in fact an American Army uniform that had been repurposed and issued to him as a prisoner of war. Then the whole tale of the past four years came tumbling out, from the hungry hot torment in Libya and Tunisia, to his capture as a war prisoner, to his journey across the seas. He described the massive new place that was America, the things he saw and did there. While he talked, his grandmother sat with her hands in her lap, looking at him with loving awe. She absorbed only a small portion of his tales of war. Only one thing mattered: her Giampaolo, her favorite grandson, the one with the tender heart, had come home.

In the weeks that followed, Giampaolo settled into a familiar routine on the farm during weekdays and at home in town at week's end. The Stagno family gathered in Palazzolo every Sunday as they always had, for a day of rest and a generous meal, marking the end of one week and the beginning of another. Fresh from his life as a prisoner of war in the New World, he was able to see life in the old one with fresh eyes, absorbing its comfortable rhythms and attending its familiar customs. Giampaolo had missed these things, but he couldn't shake the alien feeling of looking in from outside, as if he were removed from the action of his life and was watching it happen at a distance. An unbidden impatience took root. Perhaps he had outgrown this place that he had always thought of as home.

The war had clearly taken its toll on his father and mother, although they were still in good health. Their faces were more careworn than he remembered, and their hair was thinner and grayer. His father's spine seemed a little more stooped, the lines around his mother's eyes more pronounced. He tried to convince himself, without much success, that possibly these changes marked no more than the passage of time.

All told, the Stagnos had come through the war intact, and even thriving, owing to the self-sufficiency afforded by the land they owned. Its remote inland location, in the midst of rocky terrain and few passable roads, had been just distant enough from the coast to let the war pass them by. Although Palazzolo had not escaped its ravages entirely, the farm in San Marco was remarkably unchanged. Unlike their neighbors who rented acreage or were sharecroppers, the Stagnos were able to continue to work the land they owned, never wanting for food when it had become scarce for others. Don Giuseppe had begun a regular practice of sharing the farm's produce and the meat from the occasional slaughtered pig or lamb. This kindness won the grateful admiration of his cousins and neighbors in the town, and by the war's end, Giampaolo's father was regarded as a man of substance and generosity. For her part, Giampaolo's mother, Donna Concetta, had stoically managed two households, town and country, through the privations of war. She felt a justifiable pride in the grateful respect accorded her husband by the local *paesani* and *contadini*, and she held her head high as she walked down the Corso with him.

Giampaolo's oldest brother Salvatore – Turuzzu as he had always been called – and his wife Margherita now lived at the farm with his parents, and had slowly taken over from the elder couple the daily management of livestock and tending of crops. To Giampaolo, by comparison to the devastation all around them, the farm at San Marco looked well-tended, even prosperous. The tilled fields of red winter wheat and corn looked lush and healthy in the fields downhill from the farmhouse enclosure. The neatly sown rows of grains would be harvested two or three times a year to be milled as flour or used as livestock feed. The stream that meandered through the property was just as fresh and robust as ever, providing irrigation for the crops and fresh drinking water for the family. Fat silvery trout occasionally made their way into the stream from the distant pond that fed it, providing a rare treat at the Stagno dinner table.

As for the farmhouse, it too remained happily untouched by the war: just as before, the squat two-room edifice perched on the farm's highest point was rustic but adequate lodging for a hard-earned night's rest and shelter for the family during the rare rainstorm that moistened the arid plain. Bright green caper plants and hardy rosemary bushes volunteering from cracks in its walls provided tasty herbs for Donna Concetta's kitchen. Livestock, however, was paltry. A skinny old cow still mooed her complaints each day in the one-room barn that adjoined the house. Now only four goats clambered about the farmyard, which was nothing more than a rocky, uneven outcropping enclosed by a rickety wooden fence bordering the farmhouse. The goats shared the farmyard with a handful of scrawny chickens that still produced good eggs, some of which were left to incubate each spring to produce a new generation of chicks. On the first Sunday after Giampaolo's return from the war, his mother had ceremoniously slaughtered one of the chickens and brought it to the house in town for an unusually generous feast later that day.

So the farm, modest as it was, had sustained the Stagnos through the war in far better straits than most of their neighbors. As first son of the family, Turuzzu had always accepted the land as both his birthright and his responsibility, as law and custom dictated, and in the war years he had begun to stake his claim. His wife Margherita, ever mindful that she had married the firstborn of the Stagnos, was of similar inclination and mindset. While Giampaolo was away, she had taken a firm grasp of the farm's household, deferring to her mother-in-law on some routine matters but on others insisting on putting her own stamp on how things were done. On his first morning at the farmhouse, Giampaolo noticed Margherita standing at the old iron stove slowly stirring the pot of milk in the same dented pot his mother kept just for one purpose, making the daily ration of *ricotta* -- the soft cheese that, with a crust of bread and a few olives, still provided sustenance for the Stagno men during long days in the field.

Donna Concetta had always relished making the sweet soft cheese, an almost meditative routine with which she began each morning on the farm. After the cow was milked, she took up her spot at the old stove, rhythmically stirring the rich raw milk until curds started to form. Then she contentedly doled out the still-warm *ricotta* to her husband and sons, watching them devour it with gusto. But now his mother seemed to have ceded even these simple joys to Giampaolo's sister-in-law. She seemed amenable to having the younger woman in charge, but still somehow wistful that the old routines were no longer hers to manage. Margherita was taking her place as the matriarch of the farm, and that was as it should be. But when Giampaolo resumed his old habit of calling his brother by his nickname, he thought he detected the shadow of a frown, barely perceptible, across his sister-in-law's brow.

As the warmth of October gave way to the cool of November at the farm, Giampaolo found himself making comparisons to his memories of life in the United States. He thought of the Luna and Mollica homes, neat row houses each with handkerchief-sized lawns in front and in back, the small kitchen gardens that seemed a mere hobby beside the large rough fields of stubble at San Marco that he now plowed under for a new sowing of grain. The homes in America seemed so substantial and prosperous compared to the two-room farmhouse where again he spent most of his days and nights. Work had seemed more substantial and important, too, in America, even from his vantage point as a prisoner of war. He pictured anew the massive vegetable canning factory in Indiana where he had worked on the assembly line. He called to mind the enormous ships on which he'd worked later, and the capacious harbor and dazzling expanse of New York City itself. He recalled the vast brick factories he had seen in Eleanor's hometown and from trains and buses in the American cities he passed through. What was left was an unforgettable impression of strength, power, and wealth. Summoning these mental pictures stirred in him a restless dissatisfaction he could not dislodge. Here, his family tended a few scrawny goats and one sad old cow, scraped weeds from between rows of planted grain, and did the planting and the irrigation, the reaping and the sowing, unchanging and repeating, one season after another. To Giampaolo, life at home now seemed like an endless cycle of drudgery bereft of the comfort and variety offered by life in America.

In America, even for prisoners of war, there was time to enjoy leisurely pursuits. A small smile played on his face as he remembered the jovial games of bocce in the Mollicas' backyard. In America, everyone worked hard, but they played hard too. He recalled the weekend excursions he had enjoyed, or the cinema at the camp advertising a constant stream of new films. When the workday ended here on the farm, he thought with chagrin, you were too tired to do much besides sleep. But you also didn't have any other choice.

This edgy discontent gnawed at him. Giampaolo found himself imagining what it would be like to live the life he had seen in America. He suspected that he was probably idealizing his memories – things were seldom as good as they seemed. But there was a permanence, a confidence, and an importance about American life that he had observed and absorbed, traits that made his own existence at home now seem trivial, doing his part here on a farm shrunk too small to accommodate his dreams.

Giampaolo thought often of Eleanor. He had written to her only once in the weeks since his return, and he wondered why she had not replied, or whether perhaps she had written to him and her letters had not reached him. So far, the post-war provisional government proved unable to bring normalcy to Italy's crumbled fascist regime. The irregularity of mail deliveries that began as a temporary consequence of the war was now an accepted norm, and the vaunted efficiencies of which Mussolini had boasted – making the trains run on time – were now a distant, short-lived memory.

Chapter 22

All around us is a desert of rock and thistle and dust.

—Mary Taylor Simeti, *On Persephone's Island*

November 1945, San Marco, province of Siracusa, Sicily

One evening, a commotion at the gate that bordered the Stagno farmhouse enclosure drew everyone's attention from the supper that Giampaolo, his parents, his brother, and his sister-in-law were sharing at the well-worn kitchen table. The dogs barked a warning as a stranger approached, alerting the family sheltered inside the farmhouse's thick walls. Suddenly, the barking stopped, followed by soft whimpers and excited yips.

"*Porca miseria!*" A familiar gravelly voice cursed at the animals that impeded the intruder's path at the gate. Giampaolo recognized the voice instantly; his brother Peppino was home. The dogs were the first to recognize him.

The family rushed into the yard. Sure enough, it was Peppino, but the gaunt scarecrow of a man clad in dirty, tattered clothing who stumbled toward the fence looked nothing like the burly brother Giampaolo remembered. A scraggly beard covered cheeks and jowls that had probably not seen a properly sharp razor in some time. Turuzzu shooed away the goats to let him pass through the gate.

Peppino went first to his mother. He hugged her and kissed her on both cheeks, tears of relief and happiness welling in his eyes. Their father enfolded him in a fierce hug and clapped him soundly on the back. Turuzzu stepped up next and hugged him too, and Margherita kissed him gingerly on both cheeks.

Giampaolo hung back, misty-eyed. He and Peppino had gone off to serve in Mussolini's wartime armed forces at the same time, in early 1941, but they had taken separate paths. When Giampaolo had shipped off to the North African front, Peppino's company had been sent north to the Italian mainland, to join other troops preparing to implement a grand Axis design in Europe. While Rommel and his tanks were dispatching Montgomery's British forces, Mussolini's mission farther north was to populate the Italian peninsula with reinforcements against Allied attack, simultaneously subjugating an increasingly uncooperative populace. But the war's best-laid plans encountered a crooked path. Hitler never took into account that the Allies' Operation Torch would outsmart and outflank his Desert Fox, forcing an Axis retreat onto the European mainland. Mussolini never imagined his own people would come to detest him so quickly, making life difficult for his troops in Italy. The trains may have begun to run on time, but Italian soldiers came to be seen as fickle occupiers in their own land – the troops loyal to Il Duce almost as hated in their homeland as the Germans. Peppino was in the midst of this toxic brew.

Finally forsaking the north African continent, the Axis powers were forced to defend the Mediterranean. Giampaolo and Peppino's home island was the first obvious target for the Allied campaign in Italy. It was already occupied by hundreds of thousands of Italian Army forces and soon reinforced from the air by German troops. The invading Allies laid waste to Sicily north and south. They crossed the Strait of Messina, making their way north from the toe onto the calf of the Italian boot. Italy was now an open battleground.

In the ensuing chaos that beset the mainland Italian forces, Peppino's regiment splintered, and he and another soldier found themselves cut off and unable to rejoin their company. As the spring of 1943 turned to summer, Allied incursions continued deep into the Italian countryside and the misfortunes of Peppino and his companion grew more desperate. After a few weeks' time disconnected from their company, not knowing whether they had been given up for dead or documented as absent without leave, they concluded that their only recourse was to hide. So the pair of stragglers resorted to making their way in secret, squirreling away in barns or breaking into abandoned cellars for shelter, stealing what food they could find. On rare occasions, the fugitive soldiers took the potentially fatal risk of begging sustenance from local peasants, needing to hope that they wouldn't be turned over to the authorities.

Cut off from the outside world, Peppino had no way of knowing that the tide of war was turning. Italians were disillusioned by what now seemed like empty promises. Mussolini was deposed in November of 1943 and went into hiding. Not long after, Italy's military formally agreed to collaborate with the Allies. But for the two soldiers still in hiding and many others like them, time held little meaning. Survival became a day-to-day calculus of peril, complicated by the likelihood that they would encounter German troops fleeing the Allies further north into Italy. At the headquarters of the German high command, with Hitler's inner circle becoming evermore isolated, the growing desperation of the German military command meant that German field officers were frequently incommunicado. They often took matters into their own hands, crafting ad hoc wartime rules of engagement out of their own fraught circumstances. Falling into the hands of a local Kommandant could spell death for two Italian soldiers considered to be deserters.

During his clandestine meanderings, not knowing when he would eat next, where or when he could rest, or even if he would survive another day, Peppino taught himself to survive. He and his companion stayed well-hidden until the wee hours of one summer night, when they heard the peal of church bells from the tiny village nearby. After months of hearing only shelling and gunfire or, worse, deadly silence, surely this meant news of a different sort. Only then did Peppino emerge, emaciated and thirsty, the tatters of his filthy uniform fluttering like miserable banners from his shoulders and arms. The two survivors made their way into an isolated hamlet in whose narrow streets a queue of worshippers wound their way in procession toward the village church. The townspeople scarcely took note of the pair's bedraggled appearance – hunger and privation had become commonplace all over Italy – so when he asked one of the residents what had happened, the reply came: "Don't you know? Hitler is dead. The Germans are finally going home. For good. *Grazie a Dio,* thanks be to God."

The war had taken its toll on Peppino in ways beyond the physical. The ever-present demands and constant stress of struggling to survive had so coarsened him that now he was distrustful of everyone. The scars of this psychological injury emerged after he had been home for a few days. By day, he burst forth in bewildering fits of rage without apparent provocation. By night, he slept fitfully, his own screams awakening him when he slept at all. In calmer moments, he retold his wartime survival strategies with bravado, but Giampaolo 's heart ached for his brother. He had been in the throes of the worst that battle-torn Italy had experienced, and he had emerged bodily in one piece but with a damaged soul.

Peppino's experience of war could not have been more different from that of his older brother. After the deprivation in North Africa, which had been bad enough, Giampaolo's days as a prisoner of war had passed with reassuring order and relative calm at the hands of the American armed forces. He and the others in wartime captivity in America had been billeted in comparative comfort on the clean if spartan grounds of various Depression-era campgrounds and military bases that had been pressed into temporary service to house prisoners. Giampaolo now counted himself more fortunate than ever that he was captured when he was and shipped off to the United States. He was glad to be on familiar soil again and accepted with alacrity what he'd found when he returned. His even temper and calm nature accepted the deprivation that the war had imposed on his homeland. Peppino, on the other hand, had well and truly suffered in Italy itself, within sight of the war's damage and destruction. He always had a quick temper and a short supply of patience, traits that were daily in evidence now: this was how he processed the trauma that had befallen him. Peppino wanted life to improve right away now that he was home. He was anxious to claim his due, a predictable if simple life tilling soil that would always provide a meal for the table and an extra lira or two for his pocket.

Unlike his reserved older sibling, Peppino was a born charmer. Before the war had ravaged their lives, he would go for a stroll in the piazza on warm summer evenings, often with one or two pretty girls on his arm. Before he left for the army, Peppino had set his cap for a shy beauty named Francesca Pietri, a distant cousin of the Stagnos, a young woman whose simple ambition was the same as most her age in their town: to marry, to have children, and make her family and her husband the focus of her life. Her dreams, modest as they were, conformed to what she had always known. Like Peppino, Ceccina, as she was called, came from a family of men. Her father and brothers had worked small plots of land as tenant farmers, scratching out a meager living until each brother, one by one, took a wife and staked a claim to additional farmland and ceased to be a drain on the collective family resources. Ceccina's marriage to one of her better-off cousins, the landed Stagnos, would mean a life of comparative ease for her. When Peppino took up courting her once again nearly as soon as he arrived at home, she eagerly accommodated his attentions. A match between them would be good for both.

One day, two letters arrived for Giampaolo from America. Both were from Eleanor. During the war, deliveries from the postal service had become so rare that mail from overseas arriving at the house on the Corso was something of an event. It was a Friday, and everyone in the family except Giampaolo's *nonna* was in the country, at the farm. Donna Lombardo accepted the envelopes from the postman and held them reverentially, like exotic trophies, as she climbed the stairs to the living quarters. With great care she set the missives in the middle of the wooden table, rubbing her fingers over the neat handwriting in black ink. She had two whole days to wonder and stare at the two feather-light blue packets edged in diagonal stripes of red, white, and navy blue. She knew the letters were for her grandson only because the postman had told her their intended recipient, not because she could read the words on the envelope. They landed in her familiar kitchen like alien beings from the unknown.

Giampaolo was the first to arrive at home on Sunday morning, stashing his bicycle noisily beneath the stairs and clambering up to the second story to wash the dust of the road from his face and arms. His *nonna* greeted him with a somber expression and wordlessly handed him the letters.

"*Eleanora!*" A broad smile broke over his face, his joyful expression undisguised by nearly a week's growth of beard. He turned them over, studying the postmarks, and ripped open both letters eagerly.

A look of understanding dawned on his grandmother's face.

"*Nna fimmina 'Mericana, eh?*" She asked him, not really expecting him to answer, for Giampaolo was already engrossed in reading the words on the two thin sheets of paper that fell out of the first envelope.

10 October, 1945

Carissimo Giampaolo,

I thought I would write you a letter that maybe you would find when you arrived home.

"*Mamma mia!*" he exclaimed, taking in the letter's date and looking up. He counted off the weeks on his fingers. "Nearly two months to get this letter!"

He began to read anew.

…when you arrived home. I know how anxious you are to see your family and find out how they fared in the long time since you've seen them last.

Hopefully you found everyone well and your home in good shape. How are things? Write and tell me as soon as you can, because I'm very anxious to know.

Life goes on here pretty much as when you visited last time. Except, just as you are now home in Sicily, many of the American fellows who were serving overseas have returned home from the war. The Mollicas' son Luigi (we call him Louie) is back home, and Cumpari Giuseppe and Cummari Angelina are very content to have him home again. Frannie's husband Joe Vespico is home, too, and they've moved to a small apartment nearby. (You probably always thought of her as one of the Mollica girls, because she had moved home to be with her parents while Joe was away.) It's interesting to hear their stories about the war and the places they've been. But I think there is much that they do not tell us. Joe was in the navy and was shipped to the South Pacific. He saw parts of the world he'd never imagined existed. He also got a chance to spend some weeks in California, on his way out and when he returned. (I've always wanted to go to California!) Louie was in the Army and was part of the D-Day invasion in France, although luckily not among the first to fight there. Casualties were very high, and Cummari Angelina wept when she had no news of him for quite some time, not knowing whether he was alive or dead. All the news we got about D-Day and Normandy was that many had been killed or wounded.

Write me when you get a chance. I miss very much not hearing from you, and I would love to have your news.

Affectionately yours,

Eleanora

Giampaolo impatiently shuffled the sheets of airmail paper until he had the second letter in front of him.

17 October, 1945

Carissimo Giampaolo,

I am writing again in hopes of hearing some news from you. It seems like an eternity since we last exchanged letters.

I don't have much news to report, except for this: Our friend Mary Mollica has a beau. A nice fellow she knew from before the war, named Donny Schmidt, has started to call on her. There's a bit of an uproar in the Mollica household because he's not Italian, but I think that will go away in time – he is such a nice fellow, and he's Catholic. He grew up here in Oxford County and now has a good job at one of the steel mills nearby. (He worked there before the war.) Many of the men returning from the war aren't finding work right away, and that's causing some tensions among families we know. Fortunately, Louie Mollica got a job fairly easily – as soon as the war ended, even before his son got home, Cumpari Mollica had been inquiring among his friends and our neighbors to see what openings there were for veterans. The newspapers are full of stories about how the government is going to set up programs to help the returning soldiers. They can get their schooling paid for, but most of the men we know want to go right to work. Some banks are starting programs to lend veterans money to buy a home or start a business. I suppose things will be in transition for a while here, especially for families with soldiers, but it's not affecting our house directly.

As I told you in my last letter, Giampaolo, I miss hearing from you very much. Even though we exchanged letters and didn't see each other all that much while you were over here, it still seemed as though we had become very close. You seem so far away now, even more so because I have had no news from you. So I must be honest: if now that you have returned home, you no longer want to write to me or keep up our friendship, I would like to know. I will find it very hard to accept, but I do want to know.

Affectionately yours,

Eleanora

"She didn't get my letter!" he exclaimed. He was distraught. "I must write to her again. Right away."

His *nonna* looked at him, powerless in the face of his unwonted frustration.

"*Figghiu miu,*" she began, "She is far away now."

"Of course!" His voice was clipped with impatience. "I know that." He sighed heavily. Then he asked, "Do we have paper in the house?"

She smiled. "*Sí,* yes, I believe you'll find some in Patri Eugenio's desk."

He hustled to the tiny seldom-used room off the kitchen. It was no more than a closet, really. Sebastiano had studied in this space when he was a boy, and now he would retire here to read his breviary. A few books and a Bible lined the single shelf above a simple desk. Giampaolo pulled open the narrow single drawer and found what he needed – sheets of blank paper and a fountain pen. A small bottle of ink sat atop the desk. He began in haste:

2 December, 1945

Mia carissima Eleanora,

Your letters, dated the 10th and 17th of October, arrived just today, together, so I knew that you had not yet received the one that I sent in early November. The postal service, it seems, is recovering from the war just like everything else here, so delivery is extremely slow. I hope this letter, going in the other direction, travels faster.

So I'll repeat most of my news again in this letter, since the other one may be lost in transit. The crossing from New York to Naples was very quick – just six days from port to port – and from Naples I took a train to Sicily. The cities we passed through on the train were badly damaged during the war. Most must have been bombed, because only the remains of buildings are still standing, but there doesn't seem to be any plan in place to rebuild. Fortunately, Palazzolo was mostly spared, because it is farther inland, away from the coastal roads that were overrun during the fighting. I was happy to see that our farm survived untouched, again being far enough away from the coast. My father and my brother Salvatore were able to work the land and tend the animals with hardly any disturbance. My family had enough to eat during the war years but many of our neighbors were without work and unable to feed themselves. My father became a lifeline for many of our paesani, *sharing what we had nearly every single week during the war. As a result, my father and mother have both become like local celebrities. They have the respect of everyone in our town. My brother Salvatore (the one I call Turuzzu) is married now, and he and his wife Margherita live at the farm.*

My younger brother Peppino, who was also in the war, arrived home a few weeks ago. You remember, I told you about him? We left home at the same time but his company was assigned to the mainland. A few weeks in, he got separated from his company and was lost for so long that he would have been convicted as a deserter if he had turned up again. So he moved frequently from one spot to another, hiding out in cellars and barns with occasional help from Italian resistance fighters. Even after Mussolini was deposed, it wasn't safe for him until the German troops finally left. The whole experience has left him a changed man – angry, suspicious, and bitter. I hope he can relax and be more like his old self as time passes, for his sake and for our family. There is some good news for him. He has a zita, Francesca Pietri , or Ceccina, as we call her, and

I expect they will marry soon.

Eleanora, mi amore, I have not given up hope that we might still be together. Please do not give up hope either! I have thought about you frequently, and about your life in America – so different from life here! I can understand why you would not want to give up all of that for a much harder life here, even if you love me. So for now I just ask you to be patient. Continue to write to me and tell me your news, and to know that I love you. Please be confident of that, my love, and we shall overcome whatever obstacles lie in our path.

With my love,

Giampaolo

Half an hour later, he returned to the kitchen, lips set in a firm line, an envelope in hand. He set it on a side table until the morning, when he could take it directly to the town's tiny post office and place it in the postmaster's hands himself.

Noise on the stairway signaled the arrival of the rest of the family from the farm. Voices were raised angrily as his brothers argued about the priority of tasks to ready the farm for the winter months ahead. His mother came in first, her face eerily impassive. She didn't like argument and it was clear there had been a lot of it on the wagon ride home. His father looked openly displeased but said nothing, only giving Giampaolo a knowing look that said, "Don't you start to argue, too, I've already had my fill of your two brothers!" In times past, when the boys were younger, it didn't take many words from his father to quell any dissension between his sons. Now, however, he remained mute. Adding Peppino into the new regimen in which Turuzzu and his wife managed the farm was proving fractious. Turuzzu's new role had begun out of necessity while Giampaolo and Peppino had been away, but as Peppino was quick to remind the family, it did not diminish the two younger sons' birthright claim to a share in the land. Peppino clearly intended to stake that claim promptly, and he didn't seem to care whether Turuzzu agreed with him or not.

Once the family assembled in the sitting room, Donna Lombardo slipped into their midst, and the argumentative mood and harsh tones fell away. Her quiet dignity and gentle demeanor were just what was needed to dispel family tensions. Without uttering a word, she exuded a quiet authority that commanded the respect of her family. Her presence among her grandsons quieted any petty disagreement, even if it now settled into an uneasy silence.

After the family had washed and donned fresh clothes, they descended to the street and walked in double file to the *chiesa matri* at the top of the Corso. The mother church's bells were ringing, summoning parishioners to Sunday Mass. After church, they walked back home in the same silent disposition, climbing the stairs to the welcome aroma of tomato sauce simmering on the stove. Steam rose from another large pot bringing water to the boil for the *maccaruni*. The table was dressed in a gleaming white linen cloth ready for their Sunday repast. Places were set, and the men tumbled into chairs as the women began to serve the meal.

Donna Lombardo's rich tomato sauce had thoroughly softened the tender packages of beef stuffed with a mixture of hard cooked egg, breadcrumbs, parsley and grated Pecorino cheese, rolled up and tied for cooking in the sauce. The older woman nestled generous piles of the soft pasta stirred up in the sauce into each bowl, then passed to Don Giuseppe a small bowl that held an aromatic mound of freshly grated cheese seasoned with black pepper. Meanwhile, Donna Concetta fished the beef rolls from the sauce and placed them on a large plate that would be passed around the table after the pasta was eaten. The two women took their places at the empty seats closest to the stove, and everyone fell on the food hungrily.

Typically at Stagno family dinners, not a lot of conversation happened while there was food to be consumed. No one broke with that tradition today. While the pasta bowls were being cleared, Giampaolo's mother hoisted the meat platter onto the table, and alongside a large fresh salad of lettuces, herbs, tomatoes and slices of onion from the farm. They would eat the salad after the meat. A plate of Donna Concetta's dense, snow-white bread had been cut neatly from a loaf and stacked on another plate; it would make the rounds with the salad. Only the satisfied sounds of chewing and swallowing broke the silence around the table, until everything had been consumed.

While his mother and sister-in-law cleared the table, Giampaolo's father turned to the bowl of fresh fruit set out for easy reach on the sideboard.

"Alluda, miu figghiu, and so, my son," began Don Giuseppe, turning to him as he peeled a pear, "you have told us very little about your time in the United States."

The question lay like another uneaten piece of fruit, inert, on the table. Giampaolo stared wordlessly at his father. The elder man held the question in his expression, raising an eyebrow to his son.

"È 'nn paesi ranni ranni, it's a great big country," Giampaolo began.

His brother Peppino grunted skeptically. *"Bo, ranni sì, ma nun cusì magnificu,* big maybe but not so great."

"Everything is big there," Giampaolo continued, by way of offering evidence. "The farms. The factories. The cities," he gestured with his hands as if to draw skyscrapers in the air. "In New York City, the buildings are so tall, you can't even see the sky between them."

"And the people? How do they live in these big places?" queried his father.

"Case ranne. In big houses. *Tutti simpaticchi,* the Americans I met were all nice," he continued. "Friendly and generous. I

was well-treated."

Peppino punctuated the conversation again with a burst of resentment. "Well, then, you had a better time of it than I did, right here in Italy!"

"Yes, I suppose I did," Giampaolo mused.

"Even as a prisoner, they treated you kindly?" Donna Concetta interjected, her disbelief evident.

"*Sì sì*, oh yes," he reassured them. "The barracks were large and clean, and we each had our own cot with clean sheets and blankets."

"I'll bet the food wasn't so great," Peppino muttered.

Giampaolo laughed. "At first, no, but then they let some of the Italian prisoners run the kitchen a few days each week." A triumphant smile lit up his face. "Then things improved a lot. The food was so much better, even the American officers came to eat in our mess hall."

"'Mess hall'?" Turuzzu looked at his brother quizzically, repeating the English words. "*Cosa? Chi'è?* What is that?"

"It means dining hall. *Sala da cena.*"

Murmurs of understanding rippled around the table.

"*I fimmini 'Mericani?* What about the American women?" his grandmother chimed in with a sly glance.

Giampaolo's cheeks colored, knowing the intent of his grandmother's question, but decided to play innocent. "*Nonna. Fimmini nel campo? Nun c'era. Cchi 'ci pinsa?* Women in the camp? There weren't any. What do you think?"

His abrupt response let the topic fall away. Surmising that was all the detail his son would offer about America at the dinner table, Don Giuseppe rose. Giampaolo was relieved to not be quizzed further, but he noticed a curious glint in his mother's eyes as she looked from her mother's face to her son's still-reddened cheeks. Donna Concetta already sensed there was more to this than his evasive answer revealed.

The men stepped onto the tiny balcony that overlooked the Corso. His father drew his pipe from a shirt pocket and opened a small tin of tobacco. Stuffing the pipe's bowl and setting it alight, he puffed a few times before turning again to face Giampaolo, his back to his other two sons.

"Alluda, duoppo tutto, ti piaci 'a vita 'Mericana? In the end, did you like what you saw of American life?"

"Sí, papá, yes, I did."

His father drew on his pipe pensively. "Enough to return there for good?"

Startled by his father's question, Giampaolo's eyes widened in surprise. Pausing, he schooled his face and responded cautiously.

"Nun sacciu, I don't know."

A few more puffs of tobacco smoke rose into the air. "You know, I tried it myself," his father said, pausing for effect. "Emigrating to another country."

"Yes, I remember, papá, " he responded. "You've told us the story. You went to Argentina."

"Sometimes I regret that I didn't stay longer," Don Giuseppe added softly. "I gave up too easily."

"But you made a good life here, for yourself and for all of us," Giampaolo remonstrated.

"Sì sì, yes, I did," his father replied. "Still, I often wonder what could have been." He paused again, then added casually, "It may be a good choice for you, my son. America. If you liked what you saw there."

Taken by surprise again, Giampaolo stood still, his hands tightening slightly on the balcony's wrought iron railing. Was this his father's way of giving his blessing for him to do what he was already considering? Don Giuseppe's expression was impassive.

Wanting to be honest while not divulging too much, he murmured only, *"Iu ci pinza.* I'll think about it."

Chapter 23

Springtime in Sicily reveals some of the most varied and beautiful landscapes you've ever seen, emerald green from spring rains and dotted with craggy, snow-covered peaks... almond trees in bloom, and fragrant, purple bushes of wild rosemary. And citrus trees, their branches buckling under the weight of more blood oranges, mandarins, lemons and citrons than you could consume in a lifetime.

—from "The Traveler's Lunchbox" blog

Spring 1946, Palazzolo Acreide, Sicily

The almond trees wore their full regalia of delicate white blossoms, sending plumes of soft floral scent wafting into the air. February was a good season for a country wedding, thought Donna Concetta, as she beheld her future daughter-in-law dressed in white lace. Her Peppino was marrying a good woman, she thought, as she lovingly took Ceccina's hands in hers and squeezed. All the better that it was to be a family wedding; distant cousins they may be, but that only reassured her that the young woman went into the match with her eyes wide open. Life on the farm wouldn't be easy, but hard work was nothing new to Francesca Pietri. Her family had toiled on the land, too, so she knew what would be expected of her as a farmer's wife. Ceccina had a sunny disposition and a decided calm about her that Donna Concetta admired: with her gentle ways, she seemed to be able to calm the storms that afflicted Peppino's soul.

Dressed in their finest clothes, the Stagno family made their way to the church. Peppino walked proudly alongside his lovely bride, a small sprig of almond blossoms in his lapel the only accessory that set him apart as the groom. His parents walked solemnly behind the couple, but the sunny smile on Donna Concetta's face evidenced her contentment for her son. Turuzzu and Margherita walked behind them, and Giampaolo brought up the rear of the procession. He was in a new dark blue suit, and he took careful small steps to accommodate the slower gait of his grandmother, her arm tucked into his elbow. Donna Lombardo's tiny figure was resplendent in a new dress of black taffeta that brushed the cobblestones as she walked. On her head she wore a black lace mantilla that set off her cap of snowy white hair and trailed over the tidy bun at the nape of her neck.

As she walked to the church on Giampaolo's arm, Donna Lombardo remembered times long ago. She knew the comforting ritual by heart, and her mind's eye replayed the familiar scenario.

The family's procession along the Corso would be the sign their friends and neighbors waited for, signaling that the nuptial Mass would soon begin. The *paesani*, peering from behind curtained windows, would emerge from their homes and troop behind the wedding procession, following them to church.

Donna Lombardo's youngest grandson, the newly-ordained Patri Eugenio, would be waiting in the sacristy. When he came to the altar, the gold embroidery on his vestments would glisten, backlit by the beams of sunlight descending through the stained glass window behind the altar.

The low rumble of the Latin prayers would echo off the stone walls and vaulted ceiling of the church as the Mass commenced. The young couple would murmur their vows on cue from the priest. From the waistcoat pocket of Giampaolo's new blue suit, two gleaming gold rings would be placed in Patri Eugenio's hand for the blessing. Peppino and Ceccina would take turns slipping rings onto one onto eager fingers, and the young priest would extend his arms over the kneeling couple to issue the wedding benediction.

After Mass the immediate family would eat breakfast together at the Stagno home. Then they would turn out to welcome guests in the narrow courtyard beside their home. Chairs and tables would emerge from every house on the Corso on the arms of the guests approaching for the *al fresco* reception.

Near the main entrance to the Stagno home, a white linen cloth would be thrown over a sturdy pedestal, in anticipation of the enormous platter of *biscotta* and *cunfett,* piled painstakingly in elaborate decorative layers. Donna Lombardo had made many of these confections herself. She would supervise as the cookies were carried ceremoniously from the house by two or three of the womenfolk. And she would beam with pride as a ripple of applause trilled through the wedding guests watching.

Soon her grandson Peppino and his new bride would emerge from the house's cool interior: the groom in his new suit, the almond blossom now wilting in his lapel, his formal discomfiture complete. He would nonetheless smile broadly and turn to accept handshakes and claps on the back from his friends.

Ceccina would emerge shyly from behind him, her white lace veil casting an intricate pattern against her dark hair, her cheeks flushed, a gold cross gleaming at her throat. She would walk alongside her new husband, accepting kisses and embraces from everyone within reach. Soon she would make the rounds of tables and wedding guests, cradling a bowl of glistening Jordan almonds on one arm. She would dispense the colorful candied nuts with a small silver spoon into the waiting palms of neighbors and friends. As she did this, Donna Lombardo would watch the tradition unfold and she would shed a few happy tears.

A ragtag band would materialize from among the *paesani* to play folk tunes in a sad minor key but with an upbeat tempo that would eventually tempt a few hardy souls to assemble a *tarantella*. Donna Lombardo might take a turn at the dance herself. At nightfall, bright candles would appear on the tables to extend the festivities as long as the supply of wine and the guests' stamina held out.

By then the young couple would have retired from the celebration, climbing to their marriage-bed at the top of the stairs in the Stagno household, where everything lay in wait for their first night as a married couple. Donna Lombardo herself would have assisted in the preparations. All would be ready in the third floor bedroom, its newly whitewashed walls lit dimly with a lamp shrouded in a translucent silk scarf, a shiny new crucifix the only ornament hanging over the head of the tall brass bedstead. The mattress would have been carefully festooned by her future mother-in-law and *nonna* that morning, the embroidered snow-white linens and sturdy pillows set off by a silky new bedspread in vibrant colors, its fringe carefully combed and turned back. From their window high above the street, the newlyweds would no doubt hear waning strains of music from the makeshift band and the last inebriated peals of laughter as neighbors bade each other goodnight.

And Donna Lombardo would sleep well that night, knowing that the cycle of love and family and tradition that she held dear would be preserved for another generation.

Chapter 24

Who can really say how decisions are made, how emotions change, how ideas arise? We talk about inspiration; about a bolt of lightning from a clear sky, but perhaps everything is just as simple and just as infinitely complex as the processes that make a particular leaf fall at a particular moment. That point has been reached, that's all. It has to happen, and it does happen.

—John Ajvide Lindqvist, *Harbor*

Summer 1946, Palazzolo and San Marco, Sicily

As the days of summer lengthened, the routine of life on the farm deepened. There was always something to be done: animals to be fed and watered, feed crops to be tended, the kitchen garden to be plucked daily of ripe vegetables or family meals. Giampaolo spent his days doing first one task and then another, a monotonous rhythm that he could perform sight unseen. By night, after the rest of the family had retired, he often sat at the well-scrubbed kitchen table and penned a letter to Eleanor by lamplight, bicycling a couple times a week into the nearby village of San Marco to post them.

On mornings at the farm, he was usually the first one afoot as the sun came blazing over the hill, promising another day of blistering Sicilian heat. Giampaolo's family home in Palazzolo and this country farmhouse in San Marco weren't so far removed from the wilting damp of coastal cities like nearby Siracusa with its sultry tropical humidity, its languid parks and piazzas, its papyrus and palm trees swaying in the humid breeze. Still, this dry rocky patch of farmland was more of an inland desert, cool only in the early morning. Giampaolo relished his quiet moments of solitude in the fresh stillness before the rest of the family stirred.

Once his brothers were awake, the tranquility of sunrise was ruptured by raised voices. Mornings on the farm began with an assessment of the agrarian priorities for the day – was the south field ready for haying? Can the sheep be turned out to a new pasture? Invariably, diversity of opinion would surface over one trivial matter or another. Giampaolo fed the chickens or frisked the ears of the two farm dogs, Romolo and Remo, while his brothers argued over which chore to tackle first. He left the arguments to them, and picked up the slack when they tired of bickering. Many of the same duties had to be handled every day, without fail; arguing about them only wasted time – which his brothers seemed intent on doing anyway.

The new bride and groom had settled into tight quarters in the second of the farmhouse's two large rooms, sharing space with Turuzzu and his wife Margherita. Margherita had made sure to claim the larger of the two double beds crammed into the bedroom, the one positioned to greater advantage between the room's single window and the sooty fireplace that dominated one wall. The larger bed boasted a headboard ornately carved in a shiny dark wood. Its overstuffed mattress sat a good six inches higher than the smaller bed, with its flimsy large cushion and undecorated wooden planks. The larger bedstead's position in the room also afforded better circulation by proximity to the window, where the scant air of summer evenings could cool them, or the warmth of the fire's embers in winter could warm them.

There was a message in the choice. The large bed had been used by Don Giuseppe and Donna Concetta, before the elder Stagnos had moved permanently to the more comfortable quarters of their home in Palazzolo. Margherita made it plain that she and Turuzzu had a right to certain – no, most – of the farmhouse possessions. She found every way possible to assert her claim of primogeniture over her junior in-laws. After all, they were the interlopers. Her husband Salvatore was the firstborn son, and a family's assets, by law and custom, descended to the firstborn and his wife. If her Turuzzu was lord and master, Margherita intended to be mistress of this humble manor in every way possible, and no younger brother with his new wife was going to cheat her out of any part of it.

So as Turuzzu and Peppino began their day in vocal disagreement, Margherita's tactics were more spiteful for their clandestine execution. As she gathered the eggs, she would set aside three of the largest, two for Turuzzu and one for herself, and leave two smaller ones on a plate for Ceccina to cook and share with Peppino. When she made the daily ration of *ricotta*, she would deal out a few measly spoonfuls for her in-laws and hoard the rest for her husband, with the admonishment that they had farm hands to feed, too – this she would claim whether the tenant farmers who sometimes walked over the hill to lend a hand were working that day or not. She would ask Ceccina to draw water from the well – an arduous task that meant walking down a steep hill covered with tough overgrowth that could easily trip her up, carrying two wooden buckets and returning with them, much heavier when full, picking her way laboriously up the steep rocky incline. If too much water was spilled in the process, Margherita would direct Ceccina to return for more, intimating that her sister-in-law wasn't living up to the tasks the household required of her. Giampaolo usually mucked out the barn each morning, but if the three brothers went off to the lower fields before he had a chance to tackle that chore, Margherita's sharp eye noticed and she would ask her sister-in-law to attend to it.

It was at the close of one such contentious day that Giampaolo, exhausted and perspiring, sat by the scant light of the kerosene lamp with a letter that had just arrived from Eleanor.

17 luglio, 1946

Carissimo Giampaolo,

I hope things are well with you and your family.

We are all well, except that it has been very hot here this summer; temperatures have been going up nearly every day for two weeks now. We are all bearing up, but I think it bothers my mother more now than when she was younger. As for me, the weather has made work more uncomfortable than usual. I'm working on the fifth floor of the factory just now, and it gets hotter as you climb. The fans that the bosses installed don't seem to help much unless you stand right in front of them, but I'm always moving around to a different part of the floor.

At least once I'm home from work, there's some relief from the heat. You remember Cumpari Mollica's garden? His son Louie and son-in-law Joe (Frannie's husband) built a nice arbor in the spring – a lattice framework of sturdy wood – and he has trained morning glory vines and even some grape plants to grow all over it. The plants provide a lovely shade all through the day and it's especially pleasant at night. We sit out in the garden, and Cummari Angelina serves us wedges of watermelon with bread. It's a great way to cool off and relax after a long day.

Giampaolo looked up from his reading, and stepped to the open doorway of the farmhouse. Outside the tepid evening air was still, broken only by the steady hum of cicadas. Not a breeze stirred over the uneven rocky outcropping his family called their farmyard. In his mind's eye he saw the Mollica's verdant garden and pictured the arbor Eleanor had described. He could hear laughter as the men played bocce on *Cumpari* Mollica's lush green grass. He could taste the ice-cold beer as it slid down his throat, and the warm light touch of Eleanor's hand in his. His throat grew tight at the memory.

"I could be sitting there right now, instead of suffocating in this God-forsaken place!" He cursed softly to himself, feeling the loss as keenly as he felt the torrid air.

His mind reeled through memories of other times, in no

particular order. Good times, even in the midst of war. The camp's lodgings, spacious and clean. There were always clean uniforms from the camp laundry, and plenty of food in the mess hall, even if it wasn't always to his taste. He and the other Italian prisoners had been treated firmly but fairly by their captors. His American chums, the Italian-American GIs who worked at the camp, usually had time to say hello, to lend him a few quarters for cigarettes, or to arrange outings away from the camp. With a wash of recognition and emotion, he realized: those American men had been showing him a new way of life, and he hadn't recognized it at the time.

The times he had spent with Eleanor were the best. Eating wonderful food at the Lunas' Thanksgiving table. He could still savor the taste of the potatoes and gravy, a delicious difference from the basic sustenance here at home. Later, going to find an evergreen tree at that funny little corner stand in the snow, and dragging it back to the Luna house. The chicken dinners at the church in Newark. The Fourth of July with Eleanor in New York City. The fireworks over the harbor as they'd watched from the Staten Island Ferry. And in the midst of it all, Eleanor's face floated above the memories.

A moment of recognition washed over him. It had all been right in front of him, all along. *Will Eleanora still have me? Did I miss my chance?* He recalled how the envelopes with the American stamps had come in twos and threes when he'd first got home, but lately they'd been dwindling to only one a week, or even longer between letters.

Giampaolo returned to the table. Taking hold of the kerosene lamp, he shone it onto the shelf above the sink, and found the last two sheets of paper and the fountain pen with its tiny bottle of ink. He realized he hadn't even finished reading her latest letter! Nonetheless, he sat down immediately to write. What was the date? August already? He did the mental calculation: it had taken more than two weeks for her letter to reach him.

3 agosto, 1946

Mia carissima Eleanora,

Your last letter, dated 17 July, just came to me. It brought back so many good memories of times in America. I thought of those times and I thought of you.

Eleanora, I hope I am not too late with this letter and with what I want to propose to you, something you have been waiting for me to say.

"Mannaggia!" Giampaolo swore as the pen poked a hole through the insubstantial sheet of paper. The rough kitchen table that was his writing surface was a minefield of knots, gouges and irregularities that made his uneven script even more illegible. He took up the pen once more.

I believe that we should marry. I will come to live in the United States. I will become an American citizen and your husband, too, if you will still have me.

He reread the sentences he had written, wondering if he should stop there and send off the letter. Tomorrow was Sunday. The whole farm entourage would head into town for Sunday Mass and dinner with his parents and his *nonna*. He could leave the letter with a neighbor for posting. It would travel faster from the town than from the village. And he could tell his family about his decision. Then he put the pen to paper again and added a few more lines.

Eleanora, I know it has taken me some time to write these words, but they have always been in my heart. I know now that building a life with you in America is what I am meant to do. I am only sorry that I didn't realize it sooner.

Write and tell me your answer just as soon as you can. Know that I love you, my treasure, and am very eager to hear from you.

With affectionate kisses from your

Giampaolo

The sun was already over the horizon when Giampaolo arose the next morning, as usual the first one awake in the farmhouse. He splashed water on his face from the washing bowl in the kitchen and wiped his cheeks and chin with the rough towel that hung by the wash stand. He dressed quickly, pulling on the coarse serge pants and shirt that did him good service for the farm chores he had to do.

He hadn't slept soundly nor for very long last night; after he had written the letter to Eleanor, his mind had raced, crowded with plans and questions. Still, he felt a new energy course through him as he walked out the door of the farmhouse. The rocky farmyard was awash in the first rays of sunlight slanting from the eastern horizon. The chickens were awakening and starting to scrabble about the hard ground looking for food. The rooster crowed from his perch atop the barn. Giampaolo would be trading these familiar sights and sounds for an entirely different scene – honking cars and careening buses, neighbors' voices over the backyard fence, a radio wafting strains of American jazz through an open window. He would leave this quiet, isolated life on the farm for a bustling one in an American city, a city alive with tall buildings and factories, traffic and crowds. He wouldn't be doing this alone. He would have his Eleanora with him. One step at a time, but together. Every step of the way. A great adventure, really. A new life. A life in America.

Giampaolo walked up the dusty road from the farmhouse to the rusty gates that guarded the entrance to the Stagnos' property. He mounted his bicycle, tethered there since the prior Sunday's trip from town to farm, and began pedaling. Rocky unpaved lanes gave way to narrow switchback roads pocked with ruts that alternately led down sharp inclines and back up the hills on which his home town was perched. He entered the quiet piazza at the lower end of the Corso and made fast work of the town's main street to arrive at the Stagno household, where he knew he would find his *nonna* in the kitchen, making herself a cup of strong coffee to start her day. Hearing his footsteps on the stairs, she turned as he entered the kitchen and reached out for a quick embrace.

"*Bon giurnu, miu figghiu,*" she greeted him in her usual affectionate way with a smile. He hugged her, then stood back and let out a long breath. He knew his decision to leave would be hard on her, but he wanted her to be the first to know. Anticipating her reaction was perhaps what he already regretted most.

"*C'e quàlchi cosa da diciri,* I have something I must tell you," he said, looking her in the eye.

"*Chi 'è,* what is it?"

"I am leaving." He let the words sink in. "I am going to live in America."

The old woman's face drew a blank and she folded her arms over her apron.

"I was expecting this news." She uttered the words dully, softly.

"Don't say anything yet to the rest of the family," Giampaolo implored. "I'll tell everyone at the table when we eat, this afternoon."

His *nonna* nodded grimly, and with a fleeting glance at her impassive face, Giampaolo turned to get washed and dressed for Mass.

Later that morning, walking back together down the hill from church after Sunday Mass, the Stagno family cut a dignified figure in their Sunday best. The scorching midday sun bleached the sky to nearly white. His parents walked arm in arm leading the way, followed by his brothers with their wives. Turuzzu and Peppino had picked up the thread of their latest farmyard disagreement and continued to bicker, Margherita marching in stony silence next to her husband and Ceccina lagging a few steps behind, wearing a frightened expression. The only one walking alone, Giampaolo gained on the small group and passed them to reach the family home first. He was perspiring heavily by the time he ducked into the cool entryway a few steps off the Corso. He clambered up the stairs and was met with the delicious smell of tomato *ragú* simmering on the stove. Even in this heat, his grandmother was bending over a hot stove. She stirred the pot with an enormous wooden paddle, her face dewy from leaning over the bubbling sauce. As usual, a second large pot with boiling water stood farther back on the stove, emitting steam into the torrid air.

"'Bastiano will be with us soon," he told his *nonna,* who glanced up in surprise.

"I didn't know he would be home today!" she exclaimed, pleasure evident in her voice.

"He said the Mass this morning."

She smiled at the news, then turned serious. "I suppose it's best for you that he is here today, too."

"*Sí,* I guess it is."

As the pair of younger women reached the kitchen, they began bustling about to help in the meal preparations. Giampaolo's mother reached the top of the stairs and, with a glance at the already crowded kitchen, she turned wordlessly toward the sitting room and took a seat in one of the two high-back chairs that lined the wall. Don Giuseppe seated himself in the other one.

The brothers' argument had tapered off when they entered the house. Turuzzu and Peppino soon joined their parents in the sitting room, perching together on a long bench that was the room's only other seating. Only the clatter of dishes in the dining room could be heard as Giampaolo faced his assembled family. Margherita broke the silence, entering the room with a silver tray set formally with four small crystal glasses on delicate stems. Each glass held a measure of a dark, almost black liquor: it was Averna, a *digestivo* with a herbaceous citrusy flavor that would lie on the tongue and leave a pleasant bittersweet aftertaste. She handed one to each of the men, knowing her mother-in-law wouldn't take an *aperitivo* and not taking one herself. Giampaolo and his brothers each took a glass and looked to their father to take the first sip. Raising the glass to his lips, Don Giuseppe shot the liquor to the back of his throat and swallowed. His sons did so in turn, and then they all returned their empty glasses to the silver tray that Margherita still held extended.

The murmur of a new male voice sounded in the kitchen, and soon the family's young cleric stepped into the sitting room. Patri Eugenio was dressed in solemn black, with a Roman collar and a black cassock with tiny fabric buttons down the entire front length of the garb. He removed his wide-brimmed shallow black hat and placed it gently on a side table. His new spectacles glinted in the bright light as he faced the window. The young priest hung back a bit, conscious that he was appearing for the first time in priestly garb before his family.

"*Bo!*" Peppino exclaimed teasingly as Eugenio entered the room. "He comes in a priest's dress today!"

Turuzzu smiled too but then grew serious at the stormy look on his father's face.

Most Sicilians would have considered a priest in the family the height of honor, but Don Giuseppe Stagno was not among such people. Don Giuseppe had never wished that for his youngest son, and he couldn't let the grudge he bore die easily. Eugenio's Sunday presence in the Stagno home was a burr in his side, a reminder of the other educated choices that his son could have made. It was an honor to say Mass in his home parish church when he was visiting. and to give his parents the Communion host from his own hands for the first time. But his father steadfastly refused to reconcile himself to his youngest son's choice. The vow of poverty Eugenio had taken meant that any private property in his name would become the property of the order. Don Giuseppe was a proud man, and he did not want to disinherit his son because of his vocation. But he wanted even less to enrich the Roman Catholic Church with any of the modest Stagno legacy. Eugenio's father was bitter about his circumstance, and he showed it without apology whenever the young priest was near.

Soon enough, they were called to the meal. Ecru linen festooned with delicate cutwork covered the table, and on it were set shallow bowls of pasta already dressed with the delicious-smelling sauce that had been cooking all morning. A modest mound of delicately shredded cheese topped each bowl, adding its sharp pungent notes to the flavors that beckoned them to the table. The men sat first while the women continued to move about the periphery, pouring wine, pouring water, setting on the table bowls of fat sausages that had been made on the farm and cooked in the same sauce. They finally took their places, *nonna* the last to sit down. When she was seated, Patri Eugenio intoned a quick grace, punctuating it with a firm "Amen!" Then, forks in hand, the family began eating in contented silence, the only sounds a communal hum of chewing, an occasional greedy slurp, and now and then a clink of fork on stoneware.

After the pasta and meat courses were consumed, Ceccina arose to fetch a large bowl of salad greens, their leaves glistening with olive oil and flecked with dried oregano. Using the same bowls where only a patina of tomato sauce remained, the family helped themselves to a serving of greens, breaking off from the familial loaf pieces of Nonna Lombardo's dense white bread to sop up the remains. Bowls were collected and fruit served. As Margherita slid small plates into place in front of each of them, Giampaolo spoke.

"I have an announcement to make."

Everyone's eyes turned expectantly on the usually quiet brother

"I am going to America to live."

No one spoke. After a tense moment, he continued.

"I met a woman there and have asked her to marry me."

His *nonna* began to weep softly. His mother's eyes, too, filled with tears.

Don Giuseppe was the first to speak.

"So your mind is made up, then?"

"*Sí, papá,*" he replied. "I have been writing to her since I returned, and I have been thinking about taking this step for some time, in fact, even before I returned from the war."

"And what are we to know about this young woman?" his mother managed to ask, staving off her tears for the moment.

"Her name is Eleanora Fazzio. She was born in Siracusa," he continued. "She has family, cousins I think, still living in Florídia."

"So she is Sicilian, too?" his mother queried with a weak smile.

"Oh yes," he replied quickly, to reassure her.

"Well that's something, I suppose." She fell into silence.

"But she is an American citizen now," he added quickly. "And I would become one, too, and go there to live."

His father and brothers began whittling away at the fruit silently, giving everyone a chance to absorb this piece of news.

Giampaolo hazarded a first glance around the table. His nonna continued to sniffle softly into her handkerchief, and the tears in his mother's eyes, too, had spilled over. She wiped at them with her napkin and tried on a brave smile as she looked at her middle son. His father said nothing but Giampaolo thought his expression had turned pensive. As for his brothers, they were for once silent and serious. His sisters-in-law were quiet, too. Margherita was glumly mute, but Ceccina nervously searched Peppino's face for an appropriate way for her to respond.

The table remained wrapped in an uneasy calm for several long minutes. Finally, Giampaolo glanced up and noticed, to his surprise, that his youngest brother Eugenio had a broad smile on his face. The young priest said nothing, just sat there smiling at his older brother with a kind of confidence that communicated itself across the table. With silent assurance, he was bestowing his approval. Giampaolo smiled back in response with a full heart.

He then related to his family how he had met Eleanor, stitching together the threads between his Sicilian compatriot Tommaso Mollica and the Italian American family to whom he was related, who had taken in the prisoners at every turn with kindness and generosity. He told of the parishioners at the Italian Catholic parishes who had entertained them, which returned another quick smile to Patri Eugenio's cheeks, as if gladdened to see the hand of Mother Church in these developments.

Finally, Margherita piped up with the question that was clearly in the forefront of her mind.

"This Eleanora doesn't want to live here with you in Sicily? After all, a woman's place is by her husband's side."

"No, she does not, nor would her mother bless our marriage in that case." Giampaolo looked directly at his sister-in-law. "They have made a life in America. I will, too. It is a good life."

At her look of surprise, he continued.

"Besides, knowing what I know now and having seen what I saw when I was there, I can see the appeal of life in America. I am eager to make it my own," he said with finality. "If she will still have me."

Ceccina smiled shyly, knowing now how she wanted to

respond. Her large dark eyes were shining as she looked at her brother-in-law. "She will be lucky to have you."

Then everyone began talking at once. Giampaolo sat quietly, exchanging another smile with Eugenio as his family peppered him with questions. He would not answer them today. But he would have answers for them all, in good time.

Part III

APART AND TOGETHER

Chapter 25

There's something about letters that modern communication will never be able to duplicate. A letter is the next best thing ·to showing up at someone's door and kissing them on the mouth. Your hands fondle the paper, your saliva seals the envelope, then your letter is carried over their threshold like a newlywed. Everything from penmanship to an ink-smudged fingerprint or a lipstick-kiss reveals character, motivation, intention and desire. It's like tossing an emotional grenade into someone's house; a little arrowhead stuck in your flesh and then broken off. You can't ignore it. During wartime, letters could take weeks or months to arrive so every word had to count; every sentence imbued with meaning and fire. Not one fraction of the page was wasted because they never knew when they would hear from their loved ones again. Now, we correspond in seconds, but we don't put any thought into the language we employ, because communication is disposable. We used to throw pebbles at our lover's window; now we text.

—*The Globe and Mail,* November 10, 2018

A utumn 1946, letters
After nearly a month of waiting, two letters arrived from Eleanor at once. Giampaolo opened them both eagerly, glancing at the dates so he could read them in order.

19 agosto, 1946

Carissimo Giampaolo,

Such joy to receive your letter of August 3rd! It just arrived today, so I am writing back immediately. Mail is still very slow coming from Sicily.

Of course I will marry you! It is not too late. "Where there is love, it is never too late."

There are many practical considerations to decide. When will we marry? And where? If what you learned before your repatriation still stands, I don't think you can return here for us to be married in the United States, so we may have to consider alternatives. But I will find out what the regulations are.

Tomorrow I will also make inquiries about the process for you to become an American citizen. That is the process that will clear the way for you to move here permanently. It may be that we cannot proceed down that path until after we are married. Again, I will find out.

As soon as I have answers, or just more information, for these questions, I will write to you.

Bacione,

Eleanora

...

21 agosto, 1946

Carissimo Giampaolo,

I went to the county courthouse yesterday at my lunch hour to get some more information about citizenship. The Recorder of Deeds office referred me to the regional office of the U.S. Department of State, whom I called yesterday afternoon. The man I spoke to said that the best procedure for us to follow would be to marry in Italy. As a U.S. citizen, all that is required for me is to have a U.S. passport to travel to Italy with the intention of marrying a non-U.S. citizen.

If we marry in Italy, you can apply for U.S. citizenship right away – even before we return to America. There is a wait time of several months before your application would be processed and you would actually become a citizen. If you had an Italian passport, you could enter the U.S. legally but only as a visitor, until your citizenship application is finalized.

So I think the only alternative, Giampaolo, is for us to marry in Sicily.

What do you think of that plan?

I showed my mother your letter and she is very happy that you want to come here to live. She even said it would be good to have a man around the house again. I was surprised, and very happy, that she had nothing but positive things to say about our plans to marry. She was always cordial toward you but I didn't think, until now, that she was really enthusiastic about our seeing one another. It turns out I was wrong – and that makes me very happy.

All of this supposes, Giampaolo, that you will be willing to live in the house where I now live. Now that we are planning to marry, you should be informed of the situation. My mother and I own the house where we live, together. My cousins have always helped pay household expenses. Since we won't have money to buy a house of our own, living here would be the most practical alternative.

Suzanna and Rosalia are very happy for us, too. Rosalia cried and Suzanna said that if we had to be married in Italy, we can still have a wedding reception, or a party of some kind, over here, afterward. That was a very kind thing for her to suggest.

...

8 settembre, 1946

Carissima Eleanora,

I was glad of your letter suggesting that we marry here in Sicily. It will make my parents and my nonna exceedingly happy to meet you before I leave my homeland for good. My brother Patri Eugenio has already offered, with joy and blessings to you, to say the Nuptial Mass at the mother church in Palazzolo, where my family lives.

I know it will require some planning on your part to make a trip here. When can you come?

...

23 settembre, 1946

Carissimo Giampaolo,

I was so happy to hear from you again! Your letters are still taking several weeks to reach me.

I have to tell you that it will take some time for us to save the money for a trip to Italy. My mother wants to accompany me on the trip, so we must save enough for both of us to travel. I can manage to put away something from my paycheck each week, and my mother will do the same. But we have to pay the mortgage on the house each month, and for other household bills, food and expenses. There is not much left to spare after all that is taken care of. My cousins Suzanna and Rosalia have offered to help us pay for the trip, but I cannot ask that of them: they will have a hard enough time keeping the household afloat if mamá and I are away for an extended time. So it will likely take me almost a year to save the money for travel and expenses.

Of course, on the positive side, having to wait a number of months will give us time to make plans not only for the wedding but for your life here in America, for you to become a citizen and find a job.

My mother is writing a letter about our plans to her sister, who lives near Siracusa. I believe that is not too far from Palazzolo? Their name is Palumbo. My Zia Marietta has been a steady correspondent with my mother all these years, and during the war mamá was very worried about her welfare. She and Zio Tonino have had to struggle; he lost his grocery business during the war years but is now trying to rebuild it. They have a big family, too, seven children! Only the oldest two boys were old enough to seek work, during the war. My mother sent packages to my Zia every month for the last several years, hoping the few things we could offer would get through and help them when things were bad. We learned from Zia Marietta's last letter that she got most of the packages but it took months, sometimes, for them to get there. When they arrived, it appeared the boxes had been opened and the envelopes with money that my mother always put inside had been removed. Zia Marietta's letters, like yours, take a long time to get to us. My mother will propose that we come for a visit and stay with her and Zio Tonino while we make plans for the wedding. That will save money we might otherwise need to spend on a hotel or pensione. Mamá seems almost joyful these days at the chance to return again to her hometown and see her sister.

...

A letter from Donna Sarina to her sister.

25 settembre, 1946

Carissima Maria Grazia,

I am writing to let you know that my Eleanora will marry her young man from Palazzolo. They have been writing to one another since he returned home and now he has promised to emigrate to America and live here.

I don't know how he came to this change of heart, but I am very happy for Eleanora that she has found a young man from a good Italian family. I suspect it will be very hard for him to leave his family behind: I remember how difficult it was for me to leave, so many years ago. So I want to make it as easy for them both as possible.

The other part of this news is that, because of the war and American regulations about prisoners of war, Eleanora must come to Italy to be married. This arrangement will be expensive and is not ideal for Eleanora and Giampaolo, but since his family lives so close to you, it means that I will be able to see you again, at last!

My dear sister, I must ask if you can be a part of these plans for us. I don't want to put a strain on your household as I know you have had great difficulties during the war, but I am hopeful that we will be able to stay with you. It will be such a joy to see you again and spend time with your family. As you know, travel to Italy will be very expensive. Eleanora has already begun to save money from each paycheck so that she can pay for the trip. I am doing the same.

But it will help very much to know that we will be able to stay with you for some time before the wedding. Giampaolo has a brother recently ordained to the priesthood, Patri Eugenio Stagno. He has already agreed to say the Nuptial Mass. Other plans can wait until we arrive there.

Please write and let me know if this is possible and other suggestions you have for these important days in the life of my Eleanora.

Sending big kisses and hugs from your sister, who loves her Marietta very much and wishes you well always,

Sarina

...

13 ottobre, 1946

Mia carissima Eleanora,

Greetings from Palazzolo. I hope that my letters are getting through to you now without too much delay. Your last one took nearly three weeks to arrive, but at least I am able to write you back the day after I received it.

Of course I understand that you will need to save money in order to pay for travel to Sicily. So then it seems you will not be able to come next year, but perhaps early the following one? I hope that in a year's time – next autumn – you will be able to make your travel plans and that we may marry the following spring. I will pin my hopes on this unless you let me know otherwise!

Things are slowing down a bit now at the farm. We have harvested the second warm-weather crop and are planting winter wheat. The animals have put on some weight now that we've had more feed to give them each day. Many of our neighbors are still struggling to make ends meet since the war, but we have been fortunate to keep the farm going and even to lease more land to plant, now that Peppino and I are here to lend a hand to the farm chores.

I try not to stay in the farmhouse at San Marco more than absolutely necessary. It is not a happy place, with Peppino and Ceccina living in such close quarters with Turuzzu and Margherita. My elder sister-in-law seems especially to resent having to share the kitchen with Ceccina. Turuzzu says nothing but Peppino explodes routinely now, chafing at being under Turuzzu's direction on farm matters. They don't need me near at hand making matters worse, so I've taken to bunking in the barn when I am there overnight, coming back to the city house most Fridays and not returning to the farm until late Sunday evening or early Monday morning.

The situation at the farm has only made me more sure that I am taking the right steps in my own life – for me it will be an entirely new life, looking for opportunity in America, with you as my wife.

Write to me again soon, amore. *I miss you more each day.*

With affectionate kisses,

Giampaolo

...

1 novembre, 1946

Feast of All Saints

Carissimo Giampaolo,

Your last letter just arrived yesterday – it was the one dated October 13. I am writing you back quickly so that we can have at least one communication each month in both directions.

My Zia Marietta has written to my mother that she will be overjoyed to see us and she welcomes us to stay with her and her family as long as we can, when we come to Sicily. Of course, I barely remember her because I was so small when I left Italy as a little girl. Still, I feel as though I know her from her letters to my mother, and from the stories my uncle used to tell me about his hometown and his family still in Italy. It is hard to believe Zio Carmelo, good soul, has been dead for 17 years now. On this day of All Saints, we remember him especially, as well as my own dear father whom I knew not at all and my little sister who died as a baby. It is many years since my mother made the decision to come to America, one I know must have been very hard for her. Zio Carmelo would have been so happy to get to know you and to realize we are going back to visit soon. I wish that he could be here to see how much our lives have changed and how the world has changed around us, too.

The weather has stayed fairly warm this week, for so late in the fall. It's rainy today but in another month or two there could be snow on the ground. The first snow is always exciting for me, because it sets the tone for Christmas. I hope we have a white Christmas this year.

Rushing now to get this to the mailbox before the next collection time. Be well always, Giampaolo, and know that I love you.

Yours always

Eleanora

...

24 novembre, 1946

Mia carissima Eleanora,

As I write this letter to you, I am remembering a wonderful Thanksgiving weekend we spent together at your home – can it be that it was just two years ago? It feels like I have lived an entire lifetime since then, but I have such fond memories of the delicious dinner we shared, and even our funny little expedition to buy a Christmas tree. Do you remember? Have you celebrated Thanksgiving already? I wish I could be there with you. But in another two years, I am hopeful that we will celebrate the holiday together again, for the second time and for many years to come after that.

My brother Patri Eugenio was at home today for a visit from Rome. My nonna was in her element! She made a special meal of gnocchi for the occasion. He was recently ordained and is full of amazing stories about Rome, the beauty of Vatican City and the kindnesses of the Holy Father toward seminarians studying there. He has had a couple of audiences with the Pope already. He said that after we are married and if we are willing, he will do what he can to arrange an audience and a special blessing from His Holiness. Eugenio said it would be his wedding gift to us.

I know at this time of year your family must be getting ready for Christmas. I remember the marvelous sight of that enormous Christmas tree at Rockefeller Center in New York City, when we went there on a trip sponsored by the church. Even the camp had a Christmas tree in the mess hall. Of course, we don't have that tradition here, but I enjoyed seeing how, in America, you take the best of holiday traditions from many different countries and blend them all together in a uniquely American way. Our Natale here will be the usual routine – fasting on Christmas Eve, then breaking the fast after attending Mass at midnight. We will have a holiday meal on the day itself, but no presents. My mother will have bought us each a beautiful piece of fruit – at this time of year, usually a hardy winter pear – and she will put it in our shoes before she goes to bed on Christmas Eve so that we find it in the morning. My father will roast some chestnuts in a special pan he made for the job, that he takes out only on Christmas morning each year. So much for our traditions!

Write me back as quickly as ever you can – with big kisses and much love from your

Giampaolo

...

13 dicembre, 1946

Feast of Santa Lucia

Carissimo Giampaolo –

Your last letter took only ten days to arrive! I was so glad to hear from you again.

Thanksgiving came late for us this year – November 28 – but I too remembered the wonderful holiday we shared two years ago. I long to share another one with you soon.

Today is the feast-day of Siracusa's patron saint, Saint Lucy. The whole house smells of the cuccía that mamá is cooking today. We honor the saint's day each year in the way we did in Sicily when I was a child. I look forward to it each year, not only because I love the taste of cuccía, the porridge that my mother makes with wheat-berries, but also because I love the tradition that it memorializes. Instead of feeding our cuccía to the poor, as the monks of Siracusa did, mamá prepares a big jar of it for each family household – the Nardellos, the Camastras, even Nick Raffa's mother gets a jar. (She is from Abruzzi, so I guess she doesn't know what it is for.) The Mollicas across the street get some too because Cummari Angelina doesn't make her own.

Soon we will be busy making biscotta and giuggiulena and those funny, very hard cookies Cumpari Mollica loves so much, that he calls ossa di murti. I make several kinds of American cookies, too – chocolate chip cookies, walnut crescents and cutout sugar cookies in Christmas shapes.

...

29 dicembre, 1946

Carissima Eleanora,

I send greetings to you, my love, to your mother and cousins, and to my American friends the Mollicas, for a joyful Natale and a very happy Capo d'Anno. I realize I am writing this to you belatedly, as the holidays will have passed until you read this letter; but I waited until I received yours of the festa di Santa Lucia before replying. Another belated wish to you for a happy compleanno, arriving as it does with the new year. I wish we could be together to celebrate it, but we will be together before long. Of that I am certain.

My parents and my nonna were surprised on Christmas Eve to receive an unexpected visit from one of your Palumbo cousins from Siracusa: Pasquale Palumbo introduced himself as the oldest son *of your aunt and uncle Palumbo and brought us a gift of sweets from the family business. He bicycled all the way here from Florídia. I know what a long trip that was, having done it myself numerous times. I shook hands with him and was very glad to meet him. My mother sent some eggs from the hens on our farm to your aunt and uncle, and we promised to invite them for a meal when the weather is warmer.*

The farm is quiet in these short days of winter, but there are still the animals to tend to and the farmhouse and barn to maintain. I am at home in Palazzolo nearly half of the time just now. At San Marco there are enough hands among my two brothers and their wives to accomplish the farm work. Now that the war is over, many of our neighbors are working to restore their homes which sustained cracks in the walls from the shelling and the tanks rumbling through the town. So I am applying plaster to the walls on the upper floors, restoring some tiles on the roof and repainting inside – doing all of this mostly at the direction of my nonna, who has a very clear idea what she wants!

...

12 gennaio, 1947

Carissimo Giampaolo,

Felice Capo d'Anno! Here it is a new year, and I am hopeful that this will be the year that our wedding plans will finally fall into place.

I went to a travel agent yesterday to research the trip to Sicily. First of all, I wanted to find out how much it will cost, so that I can figure out how to budget for the trip. The agent, who is a friend of Cummari Angelina, told me that to secure a second-class berth on the Saturnia, crossing from New York to Genoa, will require about six months' time before I want to travel. So if I am able to save money for the trip until the fall, I should be able to book passage for next spring! How does April or May of next year sound to you? I know it seems like a long time off, but the time will pass quickly with so much to plan.

It has been very cold here since the new year started. We've had snow several times already. The streets are icy, making my commute to work treacherous. Fortunately I have to walk just across the street for the bus, but I worry about mamá in this weather. Normally we leave for work separately, as soon as we are ready, but lately we have been taking the bus together on snowy mornings so that she can lean on my arm if she feels insecure on the slippery sidewalks.

Write back soon and let me know how things are with you.

La tua affetta

Eleanora

Chapter 26

The bride wearing white is a trend believed to have originated with Queen Victoria, who wore a white lace and silk-satin gown when she married Prince Albert in 1840. The dress outraged English aristocrats as white was traditionally the color of mourning. In the years that followed, it became fashionable for brides to wear white. Royal wedding gowns were typically red at the time.

—from Rebecca Rissman, *Women in Fashion*

February 1947, Jamesport, Pennsylvania
Eleanor sifted through the morning's mail. Nothing from Giampaolo today. This long-distance communication was slow and frustrating; she thought she had prepared herself, but the waiting between letters seemed interminable.

She heard the hum of her mother's sewing machine even before she descended the stairs to the cellar. Donna Sarina was seated in her customary place in one corner of the room, intent on her work, forehead in a slight frown, eyes focused, a pin between her lips. The billows of white satin she was systematically feeding into the maw of the machine obscured most of the sewing-table. She pinched the raw edges of fabric together several inches at a time and raised the needle off the feed dog with practiced pressure on the knee pedal, holding it there while she fixed the fabric carefully under the presser foot. The creases on her forehead relaxed as she eased her toes gently on the treadle until the needle started to bob up and down, slowly at first then with greater speed as she fed the fabric steadily over the needle plate. She stopped to admire the dainty even stitches that emerged on the other side.

"*Chi dici?* What do you say? How's it coming?" Eleanor's eyes were fixed on the glistening pile of white satin that was beginning to take shape as a dress.

Donna Sarina expertly snipped the white threads at the end of the seam she had just produced and pulled the fabric toward her, grasping the shoulder seams and dealing the bodice a brisk shake. Then she leaned back to appraise her work.

"*Beni,* it's going well. Want to see?" Eleanor's mother's eyes twinkled as she held out the wedding dress to her daughter.

Eleanor extended an arm and enfolded the dress carefully over it, lovingly fondling the soft shiny folds.

"*Alluda vidiamu,*" Donna Sarina stood and stepped away from her sewing-table. "Let's see how it looks." She took the dress from her daughter's arm. "Get the sheet!" she exclaimed sternly, pointing to a worn white bedsheet that lay neatly folded on the end of an ironing board set up nearby. Eleanor unfolded the sheet and spread it on the cool green tiles of the cellar floor before unfastening her housedress and stripping down to her slip. With the floor protectively covered, her mother lifted the dress carefully onto the sheet and slowly lowered the hem and edges of the dress to the floor.

Eleanor stepped gingerly into the dress and pulled it up, smoothing the bodice to her torso. She gently slid first one arm and then the other into the long sleeves of white lace. Her mother stood behind her, fastening the long row of white satin buttons down the back of the dress from neckline to waist.

Donna Sarina regarded her daughter shrewdly, evaluating how the gown conformed to her daughter's body. She pinched at the lace sleeves here and there, pressed her palms to flatten the shoulder seams on either side of Eleanor's neck. Frown lines creased her forehead as she assessed the bodice of the dress critically, cinching the fabric at the side seams and at Eleanor's waist. Gesturing for her daughter to step forward so she could extend the broad train of white satin to its full length, Donna Sarina lifted the hems of the dress with a gentle shake and let the fabric float to the floor.

"*Beni, beni*, it fits well," she pronounced after several long moments of silent perusal, circling around the spot where Eleanor stood stock still.

Eleanor gazed at her reflection in the full-length mirror on the cellar wall. "*Mamá, comu beddu stu vestitu!* This dress is so beautiful," she breathed admiringly.

Donna Sarina looked at her daughter's beaming face, then looked away quickly. "Yes, well, it is very nice." The moment passed, and her tone turned businesslike. She cleared her throat. "Rosalia will do the decorative stitching on the bodice." She touched the edge of the bodice where seed pearls and sequins would be sewn by hand to accentuate the pattern of the lace. "Now let's not get wrinkled or dirty." Donna Sarina reached for the buttons at the back of the dress and began unfastening them.

Eleanor continued to take in her reflection as the dress loosened from the undone buttons in back. She sighed, pulling her arms from the lace sleeves. Her mother lowered the bodice and held open the neckline while she carefully stepped out of the cloud of white satin. She quickly put her housedress back on and turned to ascend the stairs, then turned back to her mother once again.

"Need me for anything else?" she asked.

Donna Sarina gestured to a parcel wrapped in brown paper. "That's the tulle for the veil. We'll work on that another day."

Eleanor was already climbing the stairs. "*Sí, mamá,* yes, okay." She paused. "Time for lunch?"

Her mother was enveloped in white satin once more, holding

the wedding dress up to fold it neatly on the sewing-table. "*Sí, sí, spetta dui minuti,* wait two minutes. I'll be right there."

Chapter 27

They none of them threw themselves into the interests of the
rest, but each plowed his or her own furrow. Their thoughts,
their little passions and hopes and desires, all ran along
separate lines. Family life is like this – animated, but collateral.

—Rose Macaulay

March 1947, San Marco, Sicily
Giampaolo wiped the sweat from his neck with a
wrinkled kerchief pulled from his back pocket. He
stood in the middle of the farmyard and gave the persistent
goats milling about him a gentle shove. "Not time to eat yet!"
he rebuked them, shooing them away.

There was always something to do on the farm. This morning
he was repairing a broken fence that since the previous week
had allowed the goats and chickens to roam beyond the
confines of the immediate farmyard. As he moved slats of
wood and wire into place at one edge of the yard, he wondered
what Eleanor would be up to, at this hour on a typical weekday
in mid-March. Probably at work at the factory. A couple of
years from now, what might *he* be doing at this time of day?
It had been bothering him lately, not knowing exactly how he
might occupy his hands when he finally got to America. He did
not want to arrive in his new homeland and be idle. He was
used to being busy. Would he be able to find work? How long
would it take? He resolved to put these questions to Eleanor in
his next letter.

"Giampaolo! Ven accá!" His sister-in-law Margherita's shrill
voice called from the kitchen door of the farmhouse.

Giampaolo wondered why she had to shout so loudly when he was only a few feet away.

"*Sugniu ccá,* I'm here," he responded with a resigned sigh. What now?

"The barn needs mucking out," she announced firmly. "Ceccina didn't manage to do it today."

Giampaolo scowled and shook his head. Margherita never missed a chance to land two blows at once – scold him for a chore still undone and criticize her mild-mannered sister-in-law.

"*Sí, sí,* as soon as I get this fence repaired," he responded, his patience frayed. He picked up a mallet to take out his frustrations on a new wooden stake in place where one of the old ones had rotted and finally fallen away. He repeated the motion three more times, installing new posts at even intervals until the repair met where the old fence was still sturdy. He stretched the wire between the posts, wrapping as he went, and finally fastened it at both ends. Clapping his hands to rid them of dust, he stepped back and surveyed his work, jiggling each new fencepost to make sure it was firmly in place.

Avoiding more testiness from Margherita, Giampaolo headed straight for the barn. It was really no more than an extension of the house, with the same foot-thick stucco walls, a flat roof instead of the house's inclined one but covered with the same clay tiles, and a couple of large windows on two sides to promote cross-ventilation through the interior's close quarters. He paused to sniff the peppery scent of the bright green caper plants that careened from the roof joints down the side of the barn. Soon, his sisters-in-law would harvest the plump buds that emerged from the tightly clustered leaves. His mother would pack them tightly in glass jars, covering them with generous layers of the coarse local salt she would buy at the market. She knew the salt merchant from Avola would have the very best: he would let the briny water evaporate from salt pans he had fashioned himself, until all that was left was the pearly grains of the prized commodity.

Inside the barn, the pungent aroma of fresh cow dung assaulted Giampaolo's nostrils. He reached for a long-handled rake and began to pull together large piles of the stuff to sweep onto a large board and toss in the growing pile just outside the barn. Periodically they would combine the manure with old straw and leftover table-scraps to produce the rich fertilizer that they worked into the soil several times a year, before seeding a new crop. Nothing went to waste on the farm.

The smelly chore completed, Giampaolo immersed his hands and arms up to his elbows in a bucket of clean water kept just outside the barn door for this purpose. He dipped his kerchief in the bucket and sponged his face. With the sun high in the sky, he saw his brothers approaching the house from the lower fields. It was time for the midday meal. Wordlessly, Turuzzu and Peppino performed similar ablutions at the barn bucket before stomping their shoes on the farmhouse threshold. The men filed into the large airy kitchen-salon where the two women were alternately stirring pots of bubbling water and fragrant sauce on the stove and pulling out earthenware bowls in which to serve the pasta.

The bowls clattered on the uneven table as Ceccina set places for the five of them. Margherita was forking the cooked pasta into a large serving bowl and mixing it with the sauce. She transferred the now brimming serving bowl to the center of the table. Next to it Ceccina had set a chunk of *ricotta salata,* a hardened aged version of the sweet product made daily from the farm cow's milk. Uncovered from its tattered paper wrappings, the craggy chunk of cheese made Giampaolo's mouth water. Even before the women had a chance to sit down, he and his brothers began digging into the bowl of pasta, spooning it with the sauce into their bowls, and passing around the cheese with a grater to top off their meal. Soon the women joined them, and the whole household fell silent as everyone devoured the meal.

As soon as Turuzzu put down his fork and wiped his lips with one of the rough linen squares that stood for napkins at the farmhouse, Margherita jumped up to replace the serving bowl of pasta with a large basket of glistening fruit. Turuzzu snagged a couple of the tiny brown Seckel pears that grew on a tree in the farmyard, pared and sliced them expertly into his bowl, and shoved bits of the juicy fruit into his mouth. His brothers followed suit, passing the single paring-knife from one to the other to accomplish the task of ridding the fruit of its rind. The dessert was consumed as wordlessly as the rest of the meal, and soon Peppino and Turuzzu were pulling their chairs away from the table and rising to their feet.

"Won't you take a rest today, *amuri?*" Margherita addressed her husband. He shook his head.

"We're nearly finished plowing the last lower field," he replied. Then, looking at Giampaolo, "I expect the three of us could get it done in another few hours." An impish grin illuminated his face. "That is, if you're done taking orders from my wife.

Giampaolo bristled. *"Spetta dui minuti,* give me two minutes," he responded tersely, dropping his napkin next to his empty bowl. Without another word, Turuzzu shuffled out the door.

7 aprile, 1947

Carissimo Giampaolo,

I am sitting down to write to you on the day after Easter. A belated Buona Pasqua to you and your family! I hope you enjoyed it together.

There is much good news to report.

First of all, last week I called on our neighbor, Mr. Moyer, who lives up the block from us. He is a manager at a plant that manufactures door and window frames. From time to time they have openings for workers who aren't trained carpenters or glass fitters. He promised to let me know if anything becomes available. Of course, you wouldn't actually be starting work for another year, so he would have to fill vacancies in the meanwhile. But he understands that you would like to get right to work when you arrive and he promised to do his best to find something for you.

We have had another conversation with the travel agent about our trip. He is prepared to book us for the ocean crossing by boat next year, probably in May. He recommended not traveling until the weather is warm here, because weather in the North Atlantic will still be quite cold even in late spring. My mother and I would travel from New York to Genoa by boat, then take a train the rest of the way. There is a ship named Italia that is beginning trans-Atlantic crossings on that route next year. The travel agent said that it would serve us best to book passage with a company that is just beginning more trips to Italy. The accommodations will be brand new and the ship will be in top form for the crossing. As for the return trip, we will have to see what he recommends.

Now that we are actually putting travel plans together, everything seems so much more real to me. Even though it is still very far away on the calendar, I know the time will fly and May of next year will be here before I know it....

...

15 maggio, 1947

Feast of the Ascension

Carissima Eleanora,

I hope this letter finds you well and happy. It sounds as though preparations for your trip are going very well. That gives me great joy to know.

At the farm, things are very busy at this time of year. It's been a warm spring, and that means irrigating ripening crops and harvesting them early, if needed. The animals need more attention, too (and more water!) as the weather grows hotter each day.

I am keeping to my schedule of four days in the country, three in the city. Even with the shorter time I am spending on the farm, my brothers seem to have ample energy to accomplish what they've planned. And the extra day in the city gives me time to spend with my nonna, who always seems to have errands for me to do while I am there.

I had a letter recently from Vincenzo Lombardo. You remember him, from my army company? He was with me at the POW camp in New Jersey. He wrote to say that another fellow from our military regiment, from Enna, has married his American sweetheart, too. They were married here in Sicily and have now moved back to America, to her home in New Jersey. I never met the fellow, but we have friends in common – that is how Vincenzo learned this news. So it seems like we are in good company with our plans.

Write when you can, and know that you are always in my thoughts.

With my love,

Giampaolo

Chapter 28

The people who give you their food give you their heart.

—Cesar Chavez

June 1947, Palazzolo, Sicily

The hot midday sunlight on the Corso made the gray cobblestones shimmer. Giampaolo was gazing out into the quiet street below the balcony of the Stagno family home. when the tinkling of a bicycle bell drew his attention. The sound reverberated up and down the empty street as a lone rider came into view at the top of the main street's gentle incline. The scrappy young rider, a dark silhouette approaching down the hill, came into better focus as he pedaled closer. He shed his cap and wiped his brow with his sleeve. In a graceful forward swing of his hips, he dismounted before the house with his hands firmly planted on the handlebars. The visitor looked up, a big grin on his face, and waved his arm in greeting.

"Giampaolo! Nun mi ricanùsci? Don't you recognize me?" The young man shouted up to him and gave him a moment. When he grinned again, a memory clicked into place.

"Ah, sí, sí! Pasquale. Pasquale Palumbo!" Giampaolo's face lit with delight as he recognized Eleanor's cousin from Siracusa. The young man had visited only once, six months earlier, but another glance at his genial face brought back the memory of his arrival as an emissary from Eleanor's nearby family bearing a gift of candies. Giampaolo waved and smiled back. *"Veni da supra!* Come on up!"

Giampaolo ducked away from the balcony window and called

excitedly to his grandmother. "Nonna! We have a visitor!" He dashed down the stairs to greet Pasquale.

The two men shook hands warmly. Pasquale's lean tanned face lit up with a smile, then grew serious. *"Mi scusi u mmiscari,* I am sorry to interrupt you..."

Giampaolo cut him off. "Not at all – *veni, veni ccá,* come inside!"

Giampaolo led the way up the narrow stairs to the first level of the Stagno home. His *nonna* awaited him at the landing, and drew the young messenger into her arms for a warm hug.

"Pasquale! Comu stai? Comu sunnu a famigghia? How are you doing? How is your family?" She too remembered him when he came into full view, and she peppered the young man with questions as she led him into the living quarters, gesturing toward a chair. "You must be tired, coming all this way. And hungry too."

"Pe piacere, nun tiràri," the young visitor addressed Donna Lombardo timidly. "Please don't disturb yourself for my sake. I just came to bring my family's greetings, and this." He rotated his worn cap through his fingers, then pulled a package wrapped in brown paper and tied with string from under his arm. As he thrust it into the old woman's hands, she noticed that the cuffs of his jacket, now too short for his wiry frame, were threadbare and worn. His gaze shifted tentatively from Donna Lombardo to Giampaolo and back again, and then he smiled shyly.

"Ma, chistu, chi 'è? un rigalu? What's this? A gift?" Donna Lombardo exclaimed as she glanced first at the packet in her hands, then at Pasquale. She frowned slightly. "You shouldn't have done this."

"Nenti, it's nothing," he replied bashfully. "Just a small *rigalu* from my parents to you and Giampaolo. For the family."

Giampaolo's *nonna* pulled at the string to unwrap the package. The brown paper fell away to reveal an oblong nest of *marzapane,* almond paste candies exquisitely formed into miniature fruits, wrapped in soft netting and tied with a bit of lace. There were miniature, perfectly shaped oranges, pears, and bananas; apples with tiny green leaves attached; even a slice of watermelon. The old woman's eyes widened with a smile as she examined the exquisite candies more closely..

"Ma chi bedduzzi! How beautiful," she breathed, cradling the tiny fruits in her palms. Then with one wizened hand she gave the young man's thin arm an affectionate squeeze and with the other, as if handling something very fragile, she placed the gift like a prized trophy in the center of a side table. The young man beamed with pride

Recovering herself quickly, Donna Lombardo asked Pasquale, *"Cosa manciàri?* Can I make you something to eat?"

Pasquale's smile faded as he seemed ready to remonstrate, but Giampaolo nudged his shoulder conspiratorially and whispered, *"Megghiu diciri sí, e lássala stari.* you'd better just say yes, and let it go. She won't let you out of here without feeding you!"

The young visitor smiled again and said simply, *"Sí, grazî,* yes, thanks, I would love something to eat."

The old woman beamed at him, then bustled away quickly toward the kitchen.

"We were just about to sit down and have something ourselves, anyway," Giampaolo said to put him at ease.

"Good. I'm glad." Pasquale exhaled with relief, perching himself on one of the straight-back chairs and setting his cap on his knee. "How have you been? "

"Bo," Giampaolo punctuated the monosyllable with a forward nudge of his chin. "Fine. As always. How else?"

"And your parents?"

"They are both in good health, thanks be to God."

A small silence fell between them, then Giampaolo continued.

"My parents are at the farm today, with my brothers and their wives. *Nun è nurmali,* they usually stay here in town."

"And your brothers, how are they?"

"Everyone is healthy and blessed, *grazî Diu,*" he replied. "My brother Peppino is married now. He and Ceccina live at the farm." Giampaolo shrugged and rolled his eyes meaningfully. "So it's easier for me to be in town with *la nonna* for an extra day or two each week. She can use an extra set of hands around here." He gestured with a sweep of his hand. "And your family? *Tutti beni?*"

"*Comu ccá, tutti beni, grazî.* Just like here – everyone is well."

Giampaolo hesitated, something clearly on his mind, then he plunged ahead. "And what do you hear from Eleanora and Donna Sarina?

Pasquale grinned and gave him a sly look.

"Donna Sarina and my mother have been writing letters madly!"

When Giampaolo looked surprised, Pasquale turned up his palms and continued.

"You and Eleanora may be the ones getting married, but those two sisters are planning a grand reunion. *Nna rannu festa!*"

Giampaolo huffed out a relieved chuckle. His *nonna* returned, a glass of water in her hand.

"*Pigghiatílla, figghiu miu,* take some, my son." She proffered the chilled glass, dripping with condensation, to Pasquale. "You must be parched after that long journey!"

Pasquale took the glass gratefully and downed the water in a few gulps. "*Grazî, Donna Lombardo.* Yes, I was thirsty."

The old woman snatched back the glass and turned. "*Ggiá turnu,* I'll be right back."

Giampaolo laughed softly as his grandmother left the room. "Nothing makes her happier than to provide people with something they need. You've made her day!"

Soon Donna Lombardo beckoned the two young men to seat themselves at the kitchen table on which she had spread a broadcloth runner. Three white cotton napkins gave the ordinary kitchen table an air of Sunday best. At each place was set a generous bowl of *gnocchi,* soft pillows of homemade pasta she had made from boiled potatoes mashed and mixed with egg and flour. Over the pasta she spooned the tasty *ragú* that had been simmering slowly since that morning. A delicate cut-glass bowl with a tiny spoon held already-grated cheese to be added to the pasta. On the sideboard sat an oval stoneware platter with steaming chunks of meat and several links of sausage, all of which had been cooked in the tomato sauce.

Pasquale's jaw dropped as he gaped at the mouth-watering display.

"*Chistu è troppu pe mi,* this is too much! You went to a lot of trouble..."

"Didn't Giampaolo tell you, we were about to sit down to eat?" His *nonna* beamed. "We are so happy you arrived in time to share our meal."

Pasquale glanced hungrily from the plate of gnocchi in front of him to the generous platter of meats on the sideboard. It was clear that this culinary bounty was out of the ordinary for him. Giampaolo imagined that it must have been quite a while since the Palumbo family had had a meal generous enough for all to eat their fill. He felt a pang of sympathy as he took in the young man's hollowed cheeks, recognizing what hunger looked like. No matter how brave a portrait Eleanor's Zia Marietta must have painted in her letters to Donna Sarina, the family had clearly suffered hardship over the past several years. Pasquale hesitated, his hand hovering over his fork. Then he closed his eyes, his lips moving silently as he murmured a quiet prayer of thanks.

"Mància! Please eat." Donna Lombardo gestured toward the bowls of pasta. She took her seat, and the two men hungrily scooped up forkfuls of *gnocchi*. She smiled contentedly as she picked up her own fork and began to eat.

3 luglio, 1947

Carissima Eleanora,

I hope this letter finds you healthy and well. It is the height of summer here, very hot in town and in the country too, but we are managing. The heat is a blessing for the crops, if not for the animals.

We had another visit last week from your cousin Pasquale Palumbo. He arrived in Palazzolo at midday and we shared a meal together. Only I and my nonna were here to receive him. He brought greetings from your aunt and uncle, and also a gift of candy. He seemed very well and in good spirits. We sent him home with a basket of peaches from the farm.

As I think I told you, I spend half of my time in the city now and have been making repairs and doing work around the house. Many of the buildings in town sustained cracks and other damage from the shelling during the war. The bombing and fighting weren't very close by, but even miles away the vibrations from the planes and tanks caused a lot of older buildings to crumble. I have made pretty good repairs to our upper staircase and patched a few large cracks in the walls. Now I'm painting everything with fresh coats of whitewash. Nonna is pleased with the results so far; my mother and father haven't yet seen it because they have gone visiting this summer, and are staying for a time with some cousins in Canicattini Bagni.

On the farm, all is as before. Turuzzu and Peppino have been working hard to improve the soil and bring the crops back to the level of production from before the war. And there's another war going on, it seems, between my sisters-in-law. I guess there are just too many adults living at the farm now, and there is very little peace. That is why I am happy to be spending more of my time in Palazzolo these days, keeping my nonna company.

How are the travel plans coming? I am eager to know when you think you can make the trip here so that we can be married. My whole family looks forward to your coming – no one more than me! Among other things, my youngest brother, Patri Eugenio, is especially eager to greet you. While he was a seminarian in Rome, he learned a few phrases in English, and he is eager to practice them again.

Carissima, write soon and tell me your news.

Your affectionate

Giampaolo

Chapter 29

The shortage of fabric also caused the popularity of the two-piece suit known as a Victory or Utility suit. Women could mix and match skirts, blouses, and jackets for a new outfit every day. Even after the war, the suit remained popular due to its comfort and practicality.

—vintagedancer.com

L ate summer 1947, Jamesport, Pennsylvania.

The vaulted interior of the Oxford County Savings Bank was cool and quiet, dark in contrast to the bright August sun outside. Eleanor inhaled a deep breath of cool air as she stepped into the center of the bank's main room. One wall was lined with counters fronted by small metal grates, behind which a dozen tellers stood ready to help customers lined up along the green velvet roping in the center of the spacious lobby. At two large counters of dark green marble on either side, customers endorsed checks, counted cash, and attended to other small tasks before approaching the row of tellers. A glass wall partitioned bank customers from the managers' workspaces – two loan officers and two vice presidents had desks behind the glass, and the grandest, at the center, was the preserve of the bank president. Eleanor knew none of the bank employees personally, although one teller, Betty Hummel, often helped her with her modest weekly deposits.

It was to make one last deposit that she came to the bank today. Eleanor withdrew her bank book from its cardboard sleeve inside her purse, opened it and reviewed the neat rows of figures. She and her mother had opened this account as a sort of wedding travel fund. Their departure date had now been set: Sunday, May 9, 1948. It was no longer a pipe dream but a red circle on next year's calendar.

Today's deposit was a bit larger than usual since it included part of her vacation pay along with her usual weekly sum. Soon they would need to withdraw the funds to purchase their passage on the ocean liner *SS Saturnia.* The travel agent had counseled for a late spring departure next year, but now Eleanor wished they could have gone sooner. She tapped her foot impatiently as she waited in line. She hoped Betty would be free when her turn came up.

When the man in the seersucker suit hefted his briefcase and sidled away from the window bearing the sign, "Miss Hummel," Eleanor stepped briskly to the counter to take his place. "Hi, Betty, how are you?"

"Well, hello, Eleanor. I'm just fine." The teller greeted her brightly with a grin of recognition. "What can I do for you today?"

Eleanor slid the savings account passbook underneath the grate. "I'm making a deposit, please." She reached into her handbag for a small manila envelope and drew out the bills.

"I'll be happy to help you with that." The teller opened to the page with the last entry, counted the cash Eleanor had handed to her, and noted the amount and the date in neat ciphers on the next line in the passbook. Eleanor watched her closely, then closed the clasp of her purse with a firm snap.

"Could I ask you a question?"

"Sure can." The teller looked at her expectantly.

"I'm going to make a withdrawal from this account, probably next week. Can you tell me how much is in there with interest, including today's deposit?" Eleanor had already totaled the figures at home but she wanted to be sure her sum agreed with the bank's. No nasty surprises needed at the last moment.

"You bet," Betty replied brightly. "I'll be right back."

The teller stepped away to a counter where an adding machine stood at the ready, and began entering numbers, following each with a firm tap of the sums entry key. The machine fed out a tape as she proceeded, and when she had entered all the figures from the two pages in the passbook, she hit the entry key a final time and neatly tore off the tape of figures. She took the tally to one side and pulled a large ledger off a shelf. Flipping the pages open, she turned them one at a time until she located the information she was looking for in the middle of a tall column of figures. With her index finger she traced the column and compared each sum to the paper tally in her hand. After jotting a few figures at the bottom of the tape, she closed the ledger with a satisfied nod and replaced it on the shelf.

"Here you go." Betty handed her the tape and pointed to the sum at the bottom. "I've added at the bottom the interest you've earned since you opened the account. That sum is up to date as of today."

Glancing down at the paper, Eleanor nodded and took the receipt in hand. "Thank you very much, Betty."

"Any time."

Eleanor moved to one of the counters where she could review the tape more carefully. A wave of relief washed over her as she reviewed the column of figures. The total matched the one she'd calculated at home, and the interest added up to about what she'd expected. It was always smart to double-check. She carefully folded the strip of paper several times and slipped it into her purse.

As she returned to the heat of the August afternoon, Eleanor could no longer hide her elation. She released the jubilant smile she'd been holding inside and did a little jig right there on the steamy sidewalk. There was finally enough money in the account for her wedding trip to Sicily. With joy in her steps, she moved to the next errand.

Eleanor's next stop was Schaeffer's Dry Goods store. Now that her mother had put the finishing touches to the wedding dress, Eleanor wanted to plan the rest of her travel wardrobe: several dresses for everyday wear that would be cool and would pack well, and a smart travel suit to wear when she and Giampaolo left for their honeymoon. Honeymoon! Her heart leapt at the word.

Eleanor knew she was spoiled by her mother's skill as a seamstress. There was almost nothing Donna Sarina couldn't do with a needle and thread, even more so with the help of her trusty Singer. Just because the Luna girls were poor didn't mean they had to settle for looking that way. Her mother made all of their clothing, and she worked at lightning speed, a skill well practiced from piecework in the factory. Eleanor's friends would sometimes ask if her mother had the time to shorten a dress or alter a seam to make their store-bought clothes fit better. Donna Sarina would oblige if she had the time, often leveling a few *sotto voce* criticisms as she worked about the cheap feel of the material or the poor quality of the stitching on the ready-to-wear garments.

Eleanor had been planning this expedition for some time. A few weeks ago she had found Butterick patterns for a dress and a suit. She had also found three lightweight fabrics for the dresses, two cottons and a linen: the same pattern would produce several dresses that could be embellished in various ways with different types of trim – a contrasting sash for one, a smart set of buttons on another – so the result would be three frocks very distinct in appearance. If these turned out well, she thought with some satisfaction, she might even entice her mother to make a fourth dress.

Today she was on a mission for fabric. Eleanor accomplished the short walk from the bank and arrived at the dry goods merchant's door with a broad smile on her face. The shop's wide picture windows boasted a riot of color. Folds of shiny taffetas and silks were arrayed to best advantage, some draped luxuriously over headless models or sewn into garments gaily suspended from hangers. Bolts of bright calicos stood side by side, tempting the would-be quilter. She gave a passing glance at the displays as she pushed the door open and stepped inside.

The saleswomen in this store knew all the Luna girls on sight. They came in so frequently and made purchases so regularly that they were among the shop's best customers. That was one reason her mother insisted that they patronize this establishment and no other, and also because the proprietor lived on Muhlenberg Street in their old neighborhood. He wasn't Italian, nor was he even Catholic, but he was a decent man who had long ago passed muster with Donna Sarina. And that, Eleanor knew, was a high bar indeed.

She made her way through the familiar racks to the bolts of cotton gabardine. Knowing precisely what she was looking for, she promptly selected two – one a soft pearl gray and another a crisp navy blue. Setting the two bolts on the large wooden cutting-table, she took the pattern from her purse to consult the yardage chart more precisely.

One of the salesgirls gave her a pleasant smile. "May I help you?"

Eleanor smiled back. "Yes. I'm making a suit. I think I want the gray, but I wonder what you thought about mixing and matching with this navy blue?"

"You mean using the darker color for the skirt?"

"Well, yes...I'd make the entire suit in the one color but though it might be good to have an extra skirt."

"Hmmm, let's see," the salesgirl stepped back to the shelf from which she'd selected the bolts she had in hand. "How about this?"

She brought forward a bolt of a pale houndstooth check, in the same gray hue and a contrasting shade of brown. She laid the fabric next to the ones Eleanor had chosen.

"Oh yes, that's very nice," Eleanor's eyes flashed approval.

"You could make the entire suit out of the gray gabardine, and then make another skirt in the check."

"And I could wear the jacket with both…"

"That's the idea," the salesgirl looked at her sagely and winked.

Usually Eleanor would weigh her options for a while and linger over them. But today, she was decisive. "I'll take them." Confident in her choices, she set aside the bolt of navy blue and fingered the fabrics to ascertain whether they were lightweight enough for hot weather.

"How about notions?" The salesgirl fanned out three packages of zippers and held them against the gray fabric.

"No, thanks," Eleanor declined firmly.

One of the secret benefits of having an entire family working in the garment industry was a ready supply of everything they else needed beyond the fabric. Every so often, she and her cousins brought home boxes of "seconds," spools of thread, buttons, and zippers no longer needed for the newer styles – extra items that the factory would have discarded otherwise.

In fact, the Luna basement was a veritable treasure trove of all the finishing touches a professional dressmaker needed. There was almost always something among the miscellany – a zipper of just the right length or thread in just the right color – so there was never any need to spend money on those extras. For other items, she could freely choose from the round metal tins stacked neatly on the basement shelf next to her mother's sewing table. One tin was filled with snaps, another with hook-and-eye sets, yet another with tiny pearl buttons. The Lunas had accumulated such a large supply of extras that an old armoire had been pressed into service, its drawers brimming with these and many other items of the sewing trade. A large hat-box stored dozens of spools of thread in myriad colors. An empty shoe box held hundreds of buttons of all kinds and colors – horn and wood, fabric-covered and plastic, mother-of-pearl and rhinestone. Sometimes it was a scavenger hunt sifting through that box to find a complete set of matching buttons for a new blouse or dress. But that was part of the fun. And there were other sewing supplies and notions, too, waiting to be pressed into use for her latest project: bias and binding tape for hems; yards of silky lightweight lining fabric; strips of lace in various widths and designs, neatly rolled and sorted by color; sets of ornate French-braid "frog" closures that were unneeded at the factory and had found a home in the Lunas' basement.

The salesgirl rang up her purchases, wrapped them carefully in brown paper and neatly tied the package with twine. Eleanor beamed a smile of thanks, took the package from the clerk and palmed the change she offered, then flipped her hand in farewell.

Chapter 30

More will be asked of a man to whom more has been entrusted.
– Luke 12:48

Autumn 1947, Palazzolo and Florídia
"Almost there, Renzu," Giampaolo spoke quietly to the donkey, gently urging him on for the last few steps on the cobblestones to the house before he dismounted from the cart. The trek home from the farm had been a long one for the Stagnos' trusty pack animal. When the family had acquired the burro from a neighboring farmer, Donna Concetta had remarked that it would befit an animal whose job it was to carry food to have as his namesake St. Lawrence, patron saint of cooks. Giampaolo and his brothers promptly foreshortened their mother's choice, Lurenzu, to "Renzu."

Not that the burro hadn't traversed miles pulling heavy loads before, to markets in the hill towns around San Marco. But this was different. The roads from the Stagno farm to the family home in the town were hilly and dusty, switching back and forth to lessen the incline for exactly such loads as the donkey pulled today. And this cart was intended for only a few miles' travel. Giampaolo clucked to the donkey until he budged the cart the few last feet into the alleyway that separated the Stagno home from their nearest neighbor. Renzu would have to sleep under the stairway tonight. No barn shelter here. Giampaolo would feed and water him and let him take his well-earned night's rest before completing their journey toward Siracusa in the morning.

The wagon had been packed that September morning with

brimming baskets of freshly picked fruits and vegetables at their peak of ripeness. His sister-in-law Ceccina had carefully wrapped and then covered the produce in cotton cloth, to lessen bruising en route. Although the crops hadn't completely returned to their lush pre-war status because it had been a dry summer, Giampaolo congratulated himself that the produce was looking pretty good this year. He was certain the tomatoes would make the most flavorsome *sarsa* and the *virdura* would compose the freshest salad the Palumbos had eaten in quite a while. He lifted the basket from the donkey's back but left everything packed under its protective cover and set it to one side.

As he wearily climbed the stairs to the kitchen, Giampaolo heard his *nonna* calling to him. "*Beni,* you're here finally. You must be starving."

Giampaolo yawned and stretched. "I must take care of Renzu before I do anything else." Stuffing a couple of carrots and an apple into his pockets from the baskets on the kitchen sideboard, he headed toward the threshold to give the donkey a good brushing and put some soft grass in the old manger and water in the bucket under the stairs. "He did well on that long journey, so I must reward him. *Ggiá turno,* I'll be right back."

Donna Lombardo turned back toward the kitchen. A heavy cast-iron pot of hearty soup sat at the back of the stove where it would keep warm for a long time without the need to burn more wood. She ladled a generous portion into a bowl, then reached for a loaf of bread to carve a piece for her grandson. She smiled as she set out the simple supper. Even as a boy he had always put care for the animals first.

Giampaolo clambered up the stairs again and took a seat at the table. He pulled the bowl of soup toward himself and began wolfing it down while his *nonna* looked on.

"*Vui frutta,* would you like some fruit, too?"

"*No, grazî, Nonna,*" Giampaolo pushed away the now empty

bowl and stood up, stretching his sore arms over his head. He ached all over, from heaving cargo in the morning and from the twenty kilometer trek on foot from San Marco. The trip to Floridia the next day would leave him still more sore, but it would be worth it to put smiles on the faces of his future in-laws.

Giampaolo arose the next morning just as dawn broke over the hills. Donna Lombardo was padding about the kitchen, still in her nightclothes. She was just placing the tiny coffee-pot over the burner to make their morning *espresso.*

"Vui caffè latte stamattina, would you prefer coffee with milk this morning?"

"Sí, nonna," he murmured gratefully, one foot on the top step. "But I need to see to Renzu first." He descended the stairs to find Renzu waiting patiently for him. He patted the donkey's haunches and spoke softly to him and picked up the pitchfork leaning against the stairs. As he forked a good shovelful of fresh grass into the manger, the animal nosed him on the hip to reach the food.

"Bo, pacenza, piccoleddu! Have some patience, little guy," Giampaolo swatted the burro softly about the ears, then chuckled as the donkey buried his nose hungrily in the fresh feed.

Ascending the stairs once more, Giampaolo found a glass of coffee with milk on the table awaiting him, and alongside it one of the delicate *biscotta* for which his *nonna* was justly famous. Giampaolo smiled and sat down to make quick work of his breakfast. As he did so, Donna Lombardo nudged a brown paper package tied with twine across the table.

"I made a few extra. With all those mouths to feed, the Palumbo family can enjoy these." Giampaolo could tell she had wrapped a goodly number of the *biscotta* in the sturdy packet, lining the layers as she often did with soft cloth to keep the cookies from crumbling before the gift was unwrapped.

"*Grazî, nonna,*" he gave her a quick peck on each cheek as he rose. "I'll get going now."

He led the donkey into the alley-way and hitched him to the laden wagon.

"*Nn po' chiu luntanu oggi,* a little farther to go today, Renzu, before we take another rest."

He urged the animal forward into the street and tested the wagon's tethering. Glancing over his shoulder, there was his *nonna* on the balcony above, waving her hand in farewell.

Approaching Siracusa, traffic clogged the roadways – bicycles mostly, but other carts like his and a few motorcars and dilapidated trucks. He didn't need to enter the city itself, but could circumvent it toward the suburb of Florídia. He stopped to ask directions from a fellow traveler.

"That way," an elderly man, toothless in a soiled cap and worn clothes, pointed down a road less crowded than the one he was on. Giampaolo clucked softly to the donkey as they turned toward their destination.

"*Aruvamo presto,* we'll be there soon, Renzu." His en route conversations with the pack animal made the time pass more quickly. The dusty trail made for a bumpy ride, flat but rutted with potholes and rocks jutting up here and there. He noticed a bicycle approaching from down the road. As he came closer, the cyclist took off his cap and waved wildly.

"O, Giampaolo! *Si tu?* Is that you?" The bike sped directly towards him and skidded to a stop. He hopped down from the cart as he recognized Pasquale Palumbo's broad smile. "What are you doing here in Florídia?"

"Coming to find you!" Giampaolo clapped the lean young man on the shoulder.

Pasquale took in the laden cart and asked, "Are you headed for the market?"

"No, no – tutti pe te, pe 'a famigghia, this is for you and your family." Giampaolo grinned, then sobered. "The crop at San Marco has been good this season," he explained. "My father sends a few gifts to your family."

In truth, the Stagnos had never wanted for food throughout the wartime years. The Palumbos had not been so lucky, and had many more mouths to feed. At least they would have a few good meals from the farm's early harvest. Giampaolo suspected that Eleanor's Zia Marietta knew very well how to stretch a little food to feed a lot of hungry mouths, and would make the most of this bounty.

"Can you show me the way?" Giampaolo asked.

"Certu!" Pasquale turned his bicycle back the way he had come.

Together, bicycle, donkey and wagon made their way down the bumpy road, the two men chatting and laughing. Soon they approached a small square structure with a meter-high stucco border surrounding it. A few scrawny chickens gamboled about in front of the house, scratching the ground. Sensing the donkey's approach, they clucked noisily and skittered together on the far side of the yard. Pasquale leaped over the barrier and called to his parents.

"Pasqualeddu! Chi suces'?? What's happening?" His mother's voice sounded a note of alarm as she came into the yard, wiping her reddened dripping hands on the stained apron hanging from her waist.

The woman who stood in the doorway bore a striking resemblance to Eleanor's mother, but Donna Maria Grazia Palumbo was smaller, her hair grayer and her face more careworn than her sister's. A pair of thick black eyeglasses masked her face. Her clothes were simple work garments, nothing like the nicely fashioned clothes Eleanor's mother always wore. This woman was thin and her complexion pale, not plump and rosy and healthy as Donna Sarina always appeared. Giampaolo could see how the years had been kinder to her older sister in America. The differences between the two sisters, living disparate lives separated by war and an ocean and twenty-five years, were painfully apparent.

Pasquale led his startled mother to the edge of the yard where she could see for herself the cart laden with baskets of fresh fruits and vegetables. It also held two large terracotta jugs, one filled with olive oil and the other with wine, and three large sacks of grain and flour.

From the seat beside him, Giampaolo snagged the brown paper parcel his *nonna* had entrusted to him that morning, and presented it to Donna Marietta, taking off his cap and introducing himself. *"Pe 'a famigghia,"* he said finally, gesturing toward the cart.

She took it all in, surprise giving way to comprehension. Behind the thick glasses, her eyes grew glassy and spilled over with tears, tracking down her careworn cheeks. Without speaking a word, she reached for Giampaolo, threw her arms around his neck and hugged him forcefully. He was surprised at the sinew of those seemingly frail arms, and he let himself be rocked back and forth in her embrace.

She finally broke free, dabbing her wet cheeks with a corner of her apron and smiling brightly. Then she turned to Pasquelino with a scolding frown.

"Where are your manners, *miu figghiu*? Get a glass of water and help Giampaolo with the donkey! Quickly! *Lestu lestu!"* She gestured toward the doorway, then looked at Giampaolo with a small smile he recognized immediately. It was one he'd seen on Donna Sarina's face. "Won't you come inside and take a rest?"

Tying the donkey's reins to a bush that leaned over the enclosure, he followed Donna Marietta and her son inside, chickens scattering at their feet.

The square doorway opened onto a single large room with a table and a half-dozen chairs crowded around it. The room itself was spotless: unadorned whitewashed walls punctuated by windows on two sides that looked onto the yard and on a third side by a wide doorway to another room. A massive all-purpose shelf made of rustic wood held all manner of kitchen items -- crockery, baskets, pans and pots, cooking utensils. Everything stood neatly in its place, ready for action at the antiquated stove nearby.

A thin young woman with a familiar resemblance tended a large pot of something simmering. The same aquiline nose and strong chin, the same dark brown eyes and abundant lashes that Giampaolo recognized and admired in Eleanor— all were present here in a fragile beauty that made him think the girl's mother must once have been beautiful like this. She stirred forcefully, then looked up, registering surprise at seeing him, and smiled before returning to the pot. In the doorway, a little girl stood barefoot in a thin knee-length cotton dress. Her light brown hair was braided, and little loose tendrils escaped to frame her face. She had large dark eyes like her older sister, and she hung back shyly, half hidden by the rough wooden door that stood ajar.

Donna Marietta pulled a chair away from the table and set it in the middle of the room. She patted the fraying cane seat and urged Giampaolo to sit, the guest of honor. A bit embarrassed, he stepped into the room and took the place she offered.

As she moved another chair toward him to seat herself, Donna Marietta mentioned that her husband and her other sons were not at home but would likely turn up soon for the afternoon meal. She inclined her head toward the stove where her eldest daughter stood, implicitly inviting him to stay and share their meal. Giampaolo recognized the expected common courtesy from one household to another under normal circumstances. But the times were not normal. Since the war, polite invitations to share perilously scarce food would give anyone pause. He suspected that whatever was in the pot would be all the family would eat that day, and for courtesy's sake Donna Marietta would stretch it to make do. But he had already seen enough, elsewhere since he returned and now in this simple home, to comprehend that the Palumbo family were still strapped for daily necessities. He recalled Pasquale's visit to Palazzolo, how hungrily he had consumed his *nonna's* pasta. The struggle this family had endured throughout the war and even now were acute. Yet Donna Marietta was too proud to let go of the habit of sharing food with guests, even strangers. The family would have less to go around, but she wouldn't dream of sending him away hungry.

The produce and other provisions he had brought would be put to good use, of that Giampaolo was certain. In fact, Donna Marietta would waste nothing—not even a crumb of his *nonna's biscotta*—with so many mouths to feed. But their circumstances doubled his resolve to steal away and be on the road again as quickly and politely as possible. He would arrive at home after dark, exhausted and hungry himself, but he was not about to take food out of the mouths of those little girls with the big dark eyes. Drinking a glass of water, Giampaolo sat politely for just a few minutes longer. Then he rose, explaining that he needed to unload the cart and begin the trip home.

Donna Marietta's eyes were round with wonder at the nutritious abundance Giampaolo and Pasquale unloaded from the wagon, stacking the baskets and containers just inside the kitchen door. Giampaolo turned to Donna Marietta to make his farewells. Resisting her repeated remonstration to stay and eat, he turned determinedly toward Pasquale, shook hands and then looked at his fiancée's aunt. Snagging a couple of small pears from the top of one basket, he quipped lightly, "*Chistu basta pe mi,* this will be enough for me."

He set his cap on his head and departed.

Plodding homeward with an empty cart behind him, Giampaolo was grateful to be alone with his thoughts. His father's instincts had been correct in sending him on this mission. Like so many neighbors in their town, the Palumbo family had clearly suffered great privation during the war. It had been perhaps worse for them as city dwellers, not living near farms that could provide food. When the roads were crowded with tanks and trucks and soldiers, a simple journey from one village to another was practically impossible without risking lives.

On his visit to Palazzolo, Pasquale had mentioned that his father had been unable to maintain his business during wartime. The family had been left with no steady means of support. Even with all the Palumbo sons scouring Siracusa daily, the jobs they found were unstable and the pay meager. It seemed the war had been unkinder still to those who lived in or near cities, like the Palumbos.

Little work and low wages weren't the only scourges of war. Hunger had beset Giampaolo's homeland just as surely as it had afflicted him as a soldier in North Africa. Deprivation had become a daily visitor at the Palumbo table. There was not enough to feed four growing sons, the sylph-like adolescent daughter, and the two little girls he'd glimpsed in the household. Eleanor's Zia Marietta had soldiered on, admirably making do with almost nothing. It was no wonder she was so grateful for her sister's almost-monthly packages from America. Although the household items, notions, and fabrics Donna Sarina sent didn't literally put food on the table, the things she supplied had certainly helped with other everyday needs.

Giampaolo thought again about the kitchen he'd just left and the oldest Palumbo daughter stirring a pot of, what was it? Watery soup, a thin *minestra* with a few dried-out vegetables scrounged from the bottom of a vegetable cart? An insubstantial broth with a few grains of rice or *pastina*? That would scarcely satisfy the tummy of one of those little girls, let alone feed a family. As his own empty stomach grumbled, Giampaolo thought of the tasty pasta he ate nearly every day, always with a rich tomato sauce; of the plentiful supply of meats and vegetables at home and at the farm; of how his family had wanted for very little during the war and now afterward. Of how his father had surmised the likely state of affairs at the Palumbo household, and generously packed up the donkey cart without comment, simply bidding his son to take this food where it would be needed and used. Giampaolo remembered chewing on needles of rosemary and eating unripe prickly pears in the desert when the Italian army was perpetually undersupplied. He shuddered and steeled himself to never again let the fate of being hungry befall him or his loved ones.

The patient donkey quickly lapped up the homeward miles between Siracusa and Palazzolo, relieved of his heavy burden and trotting on now-familiar roads. Before he knew it, Giampaolo was turning onto the Corso, peering down the hill in the dusky sunlight toward the familiar outlines of his family's home.

Chapter 31

My mother used to tell me that when push comes to shove, you always know who to turn to. That being a family isn't a social construct but an instinct.

–Jodi Picoult

F ebruary 1948, Jamesport, Pennsylvania
In her stocking feet on the cool cellar tiles where her mother had spread the old bedsheet, Eleanor stood in her wedding dress. She fingered the delicate white lace that formed the overblouse of the bodice. Turning for a side view in the full-length mirror, mindful not to tread on the folds of rich satin that surrounded her, she allowed a small smile to break over her lips.

Donna Sarina reached around her daughter to the sewing-table, where clouds of white tulle lay ready for fitting and fashioning into a long veil that would match the train of the dress in length. At one end the airy netting was gathered around a piece of wire covered in white satin ribbon, onto which her cousin Rosalie would sew tiny white fabric flowers that would form a headband. As her mother placed the veil lightly on Eleanor's hair, streamers of the satin ribbon fell in long cascades on either side of her face. Her mother had hoped to convince her that these would set off the veil elegantly, but to Eleanor they seemed old-fashioned, superfluous. It reminded her of the veil in an old wedding picture taken years ago of a cousin nearly her mother's age. She frowned as her mother set the wire headband lightly like a circlet crown on her hair and stepped back to evaluate the effect.

"Mamá," she began, fingering the strands of satin. "This ribbon. You know I don't like it. *Nun mi piaci cusí."*

Her mother said nothing, reaching up to fiddle with the stiff satin band. Eleanor batted her mother's hands away lightly, took the circlet in hand and stretched it lke a headband across her hair. *"Megghiu accusí,* it's better like this. I want to wear it this way. But then the ribbons hang down too far." She pouted, letting her words sink in while her mother walked around her, taking in the effect of the veil from all sides.

"Va beni, okay," Donna Sarina nodded with a resigned air.

Eleanor fiddled again with the headband, firming it against her hair. "How does it look from the back?" She had visions of a smooth lace mantilla like she had seen in the Sears catalog, or a chic handful of flowers on the crown of her head, as was the current fashion – not a crown like a First Communicant or, worse, a fitted cap of lace like something her cousin Annie Camastra would have worn fifteen years ago. Even a broad-brimmed hat of lace and silk like bridesmaids wore would have been preferable.

Her mother gathered the tulle in one hand and opened it, letting it spread down the length of the dress. Her fingers searched for the edged hem of the diaphanous fabric, and pinching it carefully, she lifted the whole and shook it softly so that the tulle unfolded over the train.

"Beddissima!" her mother intoned softly, looking at the whole of the veil and taking Eleanor by surprise. Donna Sarina was not a woman given to easy compliments, much less superlatives. She caught her mother's face lit momentarily by a peaceful smile that disappeared just as quickly.

Evaluating the effect now with the eyes of a seamstress, she pursed her lips and got back to business. But when her mother took the veil in hand, Eleanor thought she glimpsed a mist of tears in her eyes. She touched her hand lightly.

"Grazzi, Mamá, beni acussí, it'll be nice like this," she whispered, her heart full.

* * * * *

The Luna house was on the verge of uproar.

A large furniture truck pulled up to the curb, parking precisely in front of the house, and the driver cut the engine. He and another burly fellow dismounted from the cab and clapped their hands together to warm them in the brisk January air. Donning thick work gloves, they secured the truck's door latch and set in place a metal ramp behind it, ready to unload their delivery.

The furniture delivery on this cold January day would outfit a bedroom for Eleanor and Giampaolo. Existing furniture would be shifted and repurposed, in the thrifty Luna way, and later filled in with new pieces only when necessary. Deliveries of brand-new things were rare enough that when it happened, it caused quite a stir.

Suzanne held aside the living room drapes, peeking out the window. She cupped a hand to her mouth and called out in a loud voice, turning her head toward the staircase so she could be heard upstairs. "They're here!"

From where she stood at the living room's picture window, scuffling and banging could be heard right above her on the second floor, in the large bedroom at the front of the house.

Upstairs, Eleanor had a similar view of the truck from one of the bedroom's two windows that overlooked the street. The front porch roof jutted out just below the windows, partially obscuring her view of the deliverymen readying the truck for their delivery. The room in which she stood was now mostly empty of furniture, making it appear larger than it was.

"Maybe they can help move this thing upstairs for me." Rosalie, grunting and perspiring freely, stood in the doorway with both hands grasping the edge of a small but sturdy table she was struggling to budge through the door. It was the last piece to leave. The two Luna sisters had shared this second-floor bedroom until a week ago, when all of their furniture – beds, armoires, dressing tables, chests of drawers – had been moved up a level to the third floor.

The entire third floor of the Luna home had stood empty until this turn of events -- but as usual, never empty for long. Two large rooms of about equal size occupied most of the uppermost floor. One had a good-sized closet, the other had an attic crawl space for storage. A sunny smaller room at the back of the house looked out to a square rooftop deck with a view of the back alley that ran behind the Luna home. It boasted a pretty bird's-eye view of all the neighborhood gardens. This room also had a sink in it, so it had been converted to a kitchen, from time to time, as needs dictated.

On and off over the years, the top story of the Luna house had served the family well as a separate apartment: it was a temporary landing pad for whatever portion of the extended family needed it. Most recently it had been the newlywed apartment for the youngest Luna girl, Veronica, and her husband Nick Raffa, who had vacated it just weeks before for a small home of their own. Before that, the extra space had been an expedient refuge for a string of young families – first for the Camastras, and then for Angelo and Doris Luna – until each successive branch of the Luna family tree could take root elsewhere.

Eleanor smiled, remembering her young nieces and nephew trooping down the stairs for help with tying their shoes and buttoning their clothes before going to school. During the time the Camastras lived in that third-floor apartment, their youngsters had become the heart and soul of the household. The younger Luna girls doted shamelessly on the Camastra children – three girls and young Sammy – spoiling them every chance they got. It was never too much trouble for the delighted young aunties to take loving charge of Annie and Buddy's brood.

Rosalie would fashion clothes for the little girls' dolls using leftover fabric from Donna Sarina's sewing projects. She would set the dollies in a row on the stairs, where the girls would scream in delight on seeing their dollies' new duds. Suzanne kept a supply of candies and bubble gum in her apron. It was a game they played: the children resisted their aunt's bear-hug attempts with dismissive pecks on her cheek even as they burrowed eager fingers into her pockets for the hidden treats. Eleanor would while away her time with the children reading to them. She'd sit amid her diminutive audience on the deep-cushioned sofa, and open the large picture-books she borrowed from the public library, making sure each child got a good view of the colorful illustrations before she turned the page.

To keep the children amused on rainy afternoons, the three aunties sometimes helped the youngsters stage musical entertainments in the family living room. They would string empty cigar boxes with rubber bands to fashion makeshift guitars for the children to "play." The little ones obligingly warbled off-tune from their improvised "stage" on the landing, a few steps up and in full view of the living room. From cast-off clothing they let the children play "dress up" or fashioned costumes for theatrical renditions. When the Camastras moved away, the house seemed dreadfully cold, empty, and quiet without the babble of so many little voices and the shuffling of so many little feet. For Eleanor and her cousins, memories of those times were always happy.

As the fortunes of the extended Luna clan ebbed and flowed, the house became a bedrock of security in times of trouble, an island of safety in the storm. As a by-product of its third-floor being pressed into service in the way that it had, everyone thought of the house as their home. In good times and bad, its seasonal rhythms had become the very heartbeat of the whole family, from holiday gatherings at Christmas and Easter to impromptu picnics on hot summer nights.

Inevitably, home meant food – traditional flavors and dishes, always made in quantities sufficient for whomever lived there or visited. Donna Sarina had acquired the thrifty habit of annually canning and preserving food, long before it became a recommended belt-tightening tactic during the war years. Stretching the food budget to feed many mouths came as second nature to the Lunas.. Each autumn brought the annual round of canning whole tomatoes and peaches, cooking vats of quince and apple jellies, and preparing large batches of tomato sauce. These provisions brought the taste of summer to their table through the cold winter months. Jars of these staples found their way into the Camastras' cold cellar and onto the storage shelf above Connie Nardello's massive stove.

And there was the sharing of celebratory food around holidays and seasons of the year. In December, Donna Sarina would assemble tins of her Christmas cookies, delicate swirls of dough decorated with multicolored nonpareils suspended in a layer of thin white icing. Come springtime, the largesse shifted to square pans of Easter *torta di ricotta* studded through with bits of citron and chocolate chips. Every household got a *torta* to share. On warm summer days, Donna Sarina would mix massive vats of homemade yeast dough for pizza and *schacciata*, and some went home to each family in dispersion, just as if they were all sitting at the table together.

In every aspect of life, if there was one thing the Luna family knew how to do well, it was share. And share they had: food, clothing, even beds. Having bunked together for as long as they could remember, the two unmarried Luna girls, now in their thirties, were finally about to inherit bedrooms of their own. Unused to having so much individual space to themselves, Rosalie and Suzanne felt as though they were moving into a third-floor lap of luxury. With her nieces moving upstairs, Donna Sarina reconfigured the house's second-floor plan yet again, too. She had moved into a smaller bedroom at the back of the house to free up the larger one in front for the newlyweds.

The front door stood open to the wintry blast as the two furniture deliverymen hefted the first piece, a mahogany chest of drawers carefully wrapped in protective blue quilting, onto the porch. They paused momentarily to strategize how best to fit it through the front door frame. As the men measured the doorway, the Luna girls took up their posts. It had all been orchestrated ahead of the truck's arrival. Suzanne stood sentry by the inner door that led from the tiny vestibule into the living room, holding it open as wide as she could, fearful that a corner of the furniture would clip the door's fragile stained glass. Eleanor had come down and now stood opposite Suzanne, ready to give the two men access to the stairway. Rosalie positioned herself on the stairway landing, ready to ascend ahead of the deliverymen and lead them down the hallway to where the furniture should be situated. Eleanor would follow them upstairs and direct any necessary repositioning.

Naturally, everyone in the family had an opinion about the ideal arrangement of the new furniture, but Eleanor was determined that her choices would prevail in the bedroom that would serve her and her new husband. Besides the chest of drawers, there were two nightstands, a four-poster bed frame with a box spring and mattress, and an ample mirrored dressing table waiting in the truck for offloading.

Grunting and sweating despite the wintry temperature, the delivery men slowly eased the new piece of furniture through the double doorway and set it to rest in the middle of the living room.

"Maybe you should set up the bed first..." Eleanor began,

already second-guessing their strategy.

"Lady," began the bigger of the two men, who was also the truck's driver. He looked her square in the eye, "we had to get this piece off the truck first to *reach* the damn bedframe." He pulled a large wrinkled kerchief from his back pocket and mopped his brow. His sidekick waited mutely, content to let his partner do the arguing with the customer.

Eleanor fell silent. Realizing he'd probably sounded harsh, the truck driver began to apologize. "Sorry, lady, it's just that we've got another delivery today, after this one." The hour was already nearing noon.

The two men left the chest where it stood and returned to the truck for the bed frame, shipped in pieces that they would have to assemble upstairs in the bedroom.

Eleanor's fears were assuaged as the men made quick work of conveying the bed frame's various long parts into the bedroom without incident, and then set about assembling the frame, readying it for the mattress and box spring. Those pieces ascended the stairs next, before the men turned to the chest once more. They conveyed it expertly to the stairway landing, then one scaled the stairs nimbly backwards while the other leaned the furniture toward him before elevating it carefully up the steps, a few risers at a time.

Eleanor and her cousins marveled at how well the two men worked together. They brought each successive piece of bedroom furniture into the house and up the stairway, tilting and raising each piece and then angling it to fit around the tight bend where the top of the stairs reached the narrow second-floor hallway. They conveyed everything to the bedroom and fit each item snugly in place. After the bed and bureau were situated, it didn't seem as though there weren't many options for placing the other pieces. But Eleanor had anticipated that and kept doggedly directing them until everything was in place just as she had pictured. When they were finished, the driver stepped back to admire the arrangement of the shiny new furniture.

"Whoo-ee! Looks nice, but I gotta tell you, young lady, I didn't think all this furniture would fit."

Eleanor smiled proudly, pleased that her careful measurements at the furniture store had paid off. Suzanne handed her cousin her pocketbook, and Eleanor withdrew two crisp bills. "Thanks." She proffered the money to the men. "You did a great job." The men nodded their thanks, descended the stairs one last time, and left the house. The truck's engine started up with a rumble and the vehicle pulled slowly away from the curb.

Both of her cousins were still hanging about. Rosalie surveyed the furniture with a critical eye. "Well, it's very nice, but it'll show the dust right away, being so dark."

Eleanor was unperturbed by her cousin's critical comment. "I just love mahogany. I've always wanted mahogany furniture." She fondled the graceful curves of a bedpost lovingly and glanced about the room with a contented air.

Donna Sarina appeared at the doorway. Her blank expression left Eleanor wondering what was on her mother's mind.

"*Ti piaci, Mamá?* Do you like it?"

"*Sí, certu,* of course I do," she responded after a few moments looking around the room at all the new furnishings. Then, from behind her back, Donna Sarina brought forward the familiar dark-blue cardboard cylinder of salt, quickly poured some into her palm, and threw the salt crystals on the bare mattress. As she did so, her lips moved in a silent incantation. Then, without speaking a word to the three young women still staring at her, she turned and left the room.

Rosalie smirked. "Well, I guess you're saved from evil spirits now!"

Suzanne smiled more indulgently. "Well, you know Zia and

her superstitions..."

Eleanor frowned. "I don't think she even puts much stock by all of that claptrap," she muttered impatiently. "But she wouldn't think of not going through the motions."

"Aren't you going to get a dustpan and brush that salt off your new mattress?" Rosalie inquired.

"No," Eleanor said slowly, not wanting to admit her unwillingness to buck superstition. "I'll just leave it be, for now."

Chapter 32

The Italian liner *Saturnia*, hastily reconditioned in Genoa after serving throughout the war as an American hospital ship, docked here yesterday on her first post-war voyage, carrying 1,560 passengers, the largest number to come from the Mediterranean since 1940.

–New York *Times*, February 6, 1947

May 1948, departing Jamesport

Eleanor checked her pocketbook one last time for everything she might need for the first leg of the long trip. The train ride to New York would be easy enough. She had done that numerous times when Giampaolo had been billeted in the camp, during the war. It was the rest of their journey that had her stomach in knots.

The new trunk and two large suitcases, closed and locked, stood in the middle of the living room, ready for loading into Nick Raffa's car.

She tried to recall what she had packed and where. Organizing for a stay of several months in Sicily had seemed daunting at first. But Eleanor was a list-maker, and over the past months she had made lists of her lists. Now minutes away from leaving the house, she was second-guessing her careful organization. But it was too late for regrets. She prayed that everything they needed for the journey was in those suitcases, because once they were aboard ship, the trunk would be stowed for the duration of the transatlantic voyage.

Their travel agent advised her to secure a porter when they got to Penn Station in New York. For a dollar tip, the red cap would load all of their luggage on a cart and transport it to the taxi stand outside. From there, it would be a short ride to the seaport where their ship, the *Saturnia,* would be taking on passengers for the five-day crossing to Gibraltar. The next day they would reach their destination, the port of Naples.

Eleanor felt the tension in her neck as she bent to check the locks on the trunk and suitcases. She had already checked them three times, once last night and twice this morning, before Nick had dragged them downstairs for her and her mother.

Donna Sarina seemed content and serene – unusual, Eleanor thought, for someone who did not enjoy travel and was easily seasick. Her mind drifted back to the last time they were on a ship together. Her mother's nausea and dehydration had been so acute that she was consigned to the ship's infirmary for most of the voyage. A stab of the terror she'd felt as a five-year-old hit Eleanor now, as she recalled watching her mother being carried from their steerage cabin by the ship's medical orderlies. She shook her head, shaking herself free of those unsettling memories. She had no capacity for that today.

"Tuttu beni, Mamá? Is everything ok?" Eleanor turned her attention toward her mother, to take her mind off her own nervous energy.

"Sí sí, figghia mia, yes, my girl," her mother replied calmly.

At that moment, Nick came in through the front door, an impish grin on his face, and rubbed his hands together. "Okay, the trunk of my car is ready for loading. Are the world travelers ready to go?" He and Eleanor's cousin Veronica, whom he called Ronnie – and now everyone else did, too – were still near newlyweds themselves, married not two years ago. Nick was so proud of his new Ford sedan that he sought the smallest excuse to show it off, and that generously included serving as chauffeur to his in-laws. Ronnie beamed at him from the staircase.

Nick went to his bride and pecked her on the cheek. "I'll take Zia and Eleanor. You follow in Louie's car. He's out there waiting for you."

A veritable caravan of well-wishers was gathering to see them off at the train station. Nick's car would lead the way with the travelers and their luggage, followed by Louie Mollica and Frannie's husband Joe Vespico, in cars of their own: Joe would take his wife, Suzanne, and Rosalie; Louie would bring up the rear with Ronnie, his sister Mary, and Mary's new husband, Donny Schmitt.

Mary Mollica had been a "war bride" like so many others. During the war years, marrying your sweetheart often seemed perfunctory, aided by special discounts for nuptial items like wedding veils, and lenient bosses giving time off to their female employees to squeeze in a quick "honeymoon" before their new husbands reported to military posts near or far. Now that the war was over, it seemed that nearly everyone they knew was either newly married or engaged to be. Many returning veterans and their sweethearts felt an urgency to return their disrupted lives to "normal" as quickly as possible. They all wanted similar things, anyway – a home and hearth, a loving spouse, and eventually a family. So it was no surprise that Donny and Mary had courted and become engaged with what seemed like breakneck speed. Eleanor had been a bridesmaid at their wedding here in Jamesport, so she had a very recent example, down to the last minuscule detail, of what she would forsake by being married in Italy.

Donna Sarina had said her farewells to *Cumpari* Mollica and *Cummari* Angelina the night before, when the neighbor family hosted a send-off party for them. There had been plenty of toasts, as Nick and Louie kept topping off everyone's glasses of ginger ale with generous glugs of *Cumpari* Mollica's homemade wine. Eleanor kept diluting hers with more soda but it didn't seem to matter. All the young men in the family seemed determined to make the most of the occasion. Any excuse for a party: that was another new consequence of the war's end.

"Siamu pronti, Mamá?" Eleanor knew her mother had been ready to leave for the past half-hour. It was far too early for the train, but they could wait on the platform. Besides, it would take some extra time to unload their bulky luggage and for the whole farewell contingent to arrive and gather at the station.

For the fifth time that morning, Eleanor folded her lightweight traveling coat neatly and slung it over her arm. She secured the handles of her pocketbook on top, checked that the purse's latch was well closed, and started for the door. Nick and Louie Mollica had transferred the trunk from the living room to the front porch and were shifting it down the stairs to the curb, where the trunk of Nick's car stood open. Eleanor went onto the front porch, too, and waited for her mother and cousins to emerge. Rosalie was trying to carry one of the suitcases onto the porch.

"What do you have in this thing?" she huffed as she set it down heavily. "Feels like bowling balls."

Louie rushed to take it from her. "Don't you be trying to bring that down here yourself! It's too heavy." He pried her fingers from the handle, lifted the heavy case effortlessly, and shambled down the steps toward the car.

Rosalie stared after him disbelievingly. "He made that look so easy."

"Never mind that, Ro. Let's get in the car," Suzanne hurried her sister toward the curb where Joe's car stood waiting for them. Ronnie followed her sisters and waited by Louie's Chrysler, the third in the curbside caravan.

Frannie and Mary crossed the street and climbed into the waiting cars. Mary's husband Donny claimed the shotgun spot in front next to his brother-in-law. On the porch, the two elder Mollicas stood arm in arm, and lifted their hands in farewell.

The three-car entourage had no problem staying together for

the short two-mile journey to the train station. Soon they were rounding the corner to the depot's main entrance. Nick hopped out and opened the door for Eleanor.

"You and your mom go inside and get everything squared away. We'll take care of the luggage."

The other two cars had pulled up close behind, and her cousins and friends spilled onto the pavement. Louie and Joe parked nearby while Nick began pulling the bags from the trunk of the Ford.

Inside, the depot was cool and dark. Squinting to help her eyes adjust to the dim interior, Eleanor consulted the schedule posted on the wall outside the ticket office to verify the departure time of the New York train. All was in order. Tucking their traveling papers back into her pocketbook, she promptly returned to the gathered family and friends, forming a large semicircle in the middle of the cavernous waiting room. She knew there would be no sending off anyone early, to make this a less boisterous and teary goodbye than it promised to be. Everyone wanted to stay until the bitter end, to play their parts in the melodrama as the train pulled away, white hankies waving and happy tears falling.

Besides being more nervous than for any other farewell in her life, Eleanor was melancholy and sentimental this time. Saying goodbye would mark a singular change in her life: she was moving onto unknown territory, as a traveler, yes, but also as a bride and prospective in-law of a large Sicilian clan of whom she had met only one member – Giampaolo, her groom. Her breath caught in her throat, and a jolt of panic seized her. Even after the years of writing letters, the months of planning, the weeks of anticipation, this whole venture struck her, all of a sudden, as an enormous risk. Why had she upended her comfortable if unexciting life for all of this? She smiled nervously and fingered the clasp on her pocketbook. Then she noticed, as if she were looking in a mirror, the same nervousness, the same vague sense of dread written there on her mother's face. The Luna family didn't register change easily.

The train's arrival was announced with a muffled echo from a loud speaker overhead – the only words Eleanor could make out clearly were "New York," but that was enough to propel her toward the boarding gate. Tickets grasped firmly in one hand, she reached for her mother's arm and urged her gently toward the train. The pair of travelers left the moving and loading of their baggage to the men in the party: they seemed to have it well in hand already, as she watched Nick and Louie disappear through the large platform doors with their suitcases and trunk in tow.

Eleanor and Donna Sarina led the parade of well-wishers onto the platform and stopped halfway down the length of the train, near the doors of one of the middle cars. The conductors were just now sliding open those doors and a line of passengers was forming at each one, eager to begin boarding.

The time had come to say goodbye.

Eleanor first hugged Suzanne who was standing next to her, and gave her an audible kiss on the cheek. Then she turned to Rosalie and grabbed her cousin's shoulders firmly as she swallowed the lump in her throat. Rosalie's eyes were already brimming over.

"You are happy for me, aren'tcha, Ro?" She whispered into her cousin's ear, hoping to stanch the flow of tears rising in her own eyes.

"Of course!" Rosalie choked out the words and wiped her eyes. Ronnie followed suit, silently and hurriedly hugging her cousin and aunt but not trusting herself to utter a word.

Frannie, recognizing that the scene was rapidly devolving into an Italian-American vale of tears, took charge of the situation. "You need to get on that train," she declared with ringing authority and only the smallest catch in her voice, as she hugged Eleanor firmly and then moved out of the way for her sister Mary to do the same.

Eleanor stepped on the lowest rung of the three wrought iron steps that led to the passenger car's door. The conductor slid a strong arm under hers and grasped her elbow firmly as she ascended. She turned to watch her mother bestow a quick hug and a word of thanks to each of the men in turn. Then Donna Sarina turned one last time to her nieces.

"*Diu sabbinirìca, figghie mie,* God bless you, my girls – you know what to do while we are away." With that, she stepped briskly up the three steps and stood beside her daughter at the train door.

"The porter has loaded the luggage," Nick shouted to them as they turned to enter the car. "Ask the conductor to help you when you get to New York!"

The train's shrill whistle sounded a long loud trill, so the travelers heard nothing more from their family on the platform. The conductor pointed to their seats, and Eleanor slid to the window for a last glimpse of familiar faces. Her family and friends stood in a tight knot, clinging to each other, waving and smiling through their tears as the train lurched forward. Eleanor watched their faces recede and silhouettes fade as the train left the familiar platform behind.

From almost the minute the train left the station, Eleanor dozed on and off. She hadn't slept much the previous night, so when the commotion of boarding and getting settled was behind her, it was easy to nod off in her comfortable velvet seat. Hours must have sped by, because when she opened her eyes they were almost at their destination. Soon, darkness enveloped them and the train's whistle reverberated in a hollow echo as they entered the underground passage for Penn Station. Lights and steel columns of the underground platform gradually came into view, and the train's brakes squealed as it decelerated, signaling their approaching stop.

Eleanor was reaching into the overhead bin for her jacket when a familiar profile popped into view outside their window. Patsy Tinelli walked slowly by their window and peered inside. Spying him outside, she rapped on the glass and, seeing her, his handsome face broke into a wide smile.

"Eleanor!"

"What are you doing here?"

Her heart skipped a beat at the unexpected surprise of seeing the American GI who had befriended Giampaolo in the POW camp. In a moment, a second surprise: his sidekick, Tony Ferraro, appeared next to him, grinned, and lifted a palm to his forehead, performing a military salute by way of greeting.

Delighted, she waved and smiled back. It seemed strange to see them out of uniform. The last time she'd seen the two American soldiers was on the Independence Day trip to New York City three years before. So much had happened since then.

""*Mamá! Talè!* Look who's here!"

Her mother turned toward the window and clasped her hands over her heart in delighted surprise. Eleanor turned to the window again and slid it open. She pointed toward one end of the passenger car where travelers were beginning to get off the train.

"We'll come out that way," she enunciated carefully to make her voice heard over the din of the railway platform. Patsy made the "OK" gesture with thumb and forefinger and the pair headed toward the doorway of their car.

Eleanor had barely stood up and turned around when the two men appeared at the end of their train car, clambering past departing passengers like salmon swimming upstream to get to where Eleanor and her mother were gathering their things.

Donna Sarina clasped each man in turn in a warm hug before Eleanor took her turn.

"How did you know we were coming?"

"Frannie Mollica wrote her cousin Vincenzo, who has been corresponding with Tony," Patsy explained. "He said you and Giampaolo were getting hitched!" Both men beamed at her.

"A kiss for the bride!" Tony took both her hands in his and pecked her lips.

"My turn," Patsy shouldered his friend to one side and leaned in for a kiss of his own. Eleanor drew back, her cheeks aflame, and glanced at her mother. Donna Sarina was taking in the proceedings with an indulgent smile.

"So," Tony looked around, "Where's your luggage?"

"We need to see the conductor and get a porter," Eleanor responded.

"No need for the porter, with two strapping veterans here to help!" Patsy exclaimed. Elaborating, he offered, "We'll see you safely to the ship."

"Yeah," Tony added with a grin. "Did you forget so soon? We know our way around the Big Apple."

"That would be just *wonderful.*" A wave of relief flooded over her, crowding out the joyous surprise at seeing the two men again, and she felt her eyes mist. Eleanor realized just how tense she had become, worrying about navigating their transfer from train to ship. The *Saturnia* was in the harbor at this very hour, preparing to take on its passengers for the transatlantic departure later that day.

Months ago, Eleanor and her mother had forked over the (for them) unimaginable sum of more than five hundred dollars for tourist-class berths they would share on the well-known Italian vessel that had recently resumed its passenger service across the Atlantic. The travel agent had advised them every step of the way and negotiated all the logistics ahead of time, but there was still a lot to manage during the journey. Like most large ocean-going vessels, during the war the *Saturnia* and her twin ship the *SS Vulcania* had been pressed into military use for troop transport and, for a short time, as hospital ships. Newly cleaned, repainted, and refitted for commercial passengers, both steamships were plying peacetime harbors now, ferrying a growing trade of tourists and travelers to foreign and domestic destinations. This voyage would originate in New York, with a port of call in Gibraltar before continuing to Genoa and Naples. Eleanor and her mother had bought round-trip tickets but, at the suggestion of their travel agent, they had left their return voyage reservations open. They would select the date for their trip home with a third traveler – Giampaolo, Eleanor's new husband.

Eleanor glanced about the train seats they had occupied, satisfied that nothing was left behind before following the men and her mother onto the platform. Tony was piling their suitcases on top of their travel trunk as Patsy forked over a tip for the conductor. Tony had cleverly commandeered a porter's dolly, which made it much easier to negotiate the bustling waiting room one level up from the tracks. The foursome moved efficiently through the crowded station to the taxi stand outside, where other passengers were hailing cabs. Relieved and grateful, she realized how difficult these maneuvers would have been without the help of Giampaolo's two American buddies.

Tony wheeled the conveyance past the taxi stand and trundled another half-block down 33rd Street. Knowing his pal would move quickly, Patsy paused every few steps to wait for the two women as they struggled to keep up with his long strides.

"Where is he going?" Breathless, Eleanor pointed at Tony and turned to Patsy for an explanation.

"Don't you fret, we got this covered," Patsy exclaimed triumphantly. Stepping confidently into the street and inserting two fingers into his mouth, he emitted a shrill whistle loud enough to stop traffic.

And stop traffic it did. A shiny yellow taxi screeched across two lanes of traffic and stopped at the curb nearby, where Tony waited with the luggage.

"See?" Patsy turned back to the two women with a shrug of his shoulders and a smug grin on his face. "Got it covered."

The driver opened the trunk of his cab and helped Tony load the steamer trunk first. The other suitcases were soon wedged in tightly next to it, and the cabbie joined his customers at the curb. "Where to?" He looked at Patsy and Tony.

"Port Authority," Patsy replied, and then added, "Know that big beautiful ship that pulled into Pier 90 yesterday?"

"What, the *Saturnia*?" The driver removed his cap to scratch his head.

"Yep, that's the one," Tony chimed in. "These two lovely ladies are on it tonight, leaving for *Italy!*"

The driver breathed an impressed whistle between his teeth as he waved with his cap, then slammed it back on his head. "Yes, sir, on the double!"

Tony clapped the cabbie on the back and climbed into the front seat next to him.

"Ladies first," Patsy exclaimed with an elaborate flourish of his hand as he held the taxi's back door open. "Once you're in, I'll take the jump seat," he said, pointing to the small pop-up seat that could be unfolded from the floor of the cab.

The taxi made its way toward the pier, whizzing past buses and cars and many other taxis.

"We'll be there in no time," Tony tossed the comment over his shoulder from his vantage point in the front seat. "He says the traffic is light today." Looking at the scrum of cars and cabs outside the window, Eleanor wondered if Tony was taking in the same view.

"Yeah," the cabbie agreed, "at least it's Sunday. Nothin' like rush hour!"

Patsy made small talk with her mother all the way to the harbor, but Eleanor didn't notice what he said. The logistics ahead preoccupied her – boarding the massive ship, locating their stateroom, settling in for the journey. Disbelief had set in: were they actually on their way to Italy, where she would be married? She had thought the day would never come. To quell her nerves, Eleanor unclasped her pocketbook and reached inside to finger the bulky envelope that contained their tickets and passports.

The taxi drew alongside the pier. From the window, she could see only a large black wall with metal and ropes hanging everywhere off its sides. But once she stood on the sidewalk, Eleanor gazed up and realized that the black wall was actually the enormous hull of the *Saturnia*. Hard to believe this monstrosity could float, let alone steam its way across the ocean. Just making their way around this floating city would take some effort. Realizing she had been holding her breath since she stepped out of the cab, she forced herself to exhale.

Four gangplanks, each several stories high, had been set at steep angles to the starboard side to receive passengers into portals for different classes of passenger service. Although the massive ship itself seemed impassive on its secure moorings, smaller vessels – tugboats and Port Authority service boats – bobbed about in the harbor. From the depths of memory came that sensation of being afloat – lapping waves shifting gently around her and the sand underfoot pulling away while she stood waist-deep in the ocean on an Atlantic City beach.

Patsy's voice drew her from her musings. "I'll need your tickets to get your luggage safely aboard," he said. Tony had set about finding a member of the ship's crew for instructions on stowing the trunk.

Eleanor reached into her pocketbook and drew the documents from the envelope. "Here you go. We'll come with you. We'll have to show our passports."

Tony was concentrating intently on the instructions he was being given by a crew member. He turned when he saw them approaching.

"This guy can check your documents and stow your gear," he told them, "but he needs to know which pieces to take to your stateroom and which to stow for the voyage."

Eleanor pointed to the trunk. "That's the only item that can be stored. The two suitcases should go to our room."

The crew member greeted them and tipped his hat. *"Buona sera, signore,"* he addressed the women politely. Surprised to hear him speaking Italian, Eleanor had a flash of realization. Since the *Saturnia's* line was Italian-owned and -based, they would be hearing Italian spoken throughout the journey. Many of the ship's crew also spoke English, including the captain.

With the luggage remanded to the care of the crewman, Patsy turned to Eleanor and her mother. "I guess this is where we shove off," he said, eyeing Tony at his side. Tony returned their travel documents and pointed to a sign some twenty yards away, showing passengers where to board. "That crew fella says you should go over there," Tony instructed. "They'll take your documents and check your passports, and then you can get on board."

Eleanor felt a lump in her throat as her eyes misted over again.

Patsy enfolded her in a hug as Tony did the same for Donna Sarina. *"Buon viaggio,"* he whispered. "Tell Giampaolo that I said he is one lucky guy."

Tony reached over to give her a quick hug while Patsy said

goodbye to her mother. The two men stepped back and waved. It was time to go.

Eleanor took her mother's arm and, with one last wave to the men, urged her toward the large sign that read "Third Class." They stepped forward to take their places in line.

Chapter 33

When you're traveling, you are what you are right there and then. People don't have your past to hold against you. No yesterdays on the road.

–William Least Heat Moon

May 1948, en route to Sicily

After five days in open water and two ports of call at Gibraltar and Genoa, the SS *Saturnia* docked at Naples. The minute Eleanor and her mother stepped off the gangplank, they were swamped by a suffocating wave of porters shouting and crowding them. To a man all dirty and shabbily dressed, these hired hands clambered insistently to be chosen by the well-dressed passengers arriving with bags in hand, Donna Sarina pointed at one she deemed the least objectionable of the lot. He immediately whipped a soiled cap from his pocket and put it on his head before reaching for their heavy suitcases. Speaking in clear, commanding Italian, Donna Sarina demanded portage to the central train station.

Realizing the lone middle-aged porter had more than he could manage, a couple of scrawny young accomplices spotted an opportunity and scampered forward, settling their hands possessively on the trunk's bulky handles. They looked like grungy little scarecrows in their bare feet and tattered clothes. But their dark eyes shone and they smiled brightly at Eleanor as they stepped forward to help, and hoisted the heavy trunk between them with surprising ease.

Just when she feared they would never set eyes on their luggage again, Donna Sarina leaned over to the porter and explained in a stern, no-nonsense tone that she was paying only him for the service. The porter nodded his understanding and eyed the two youngsters with irritation. Although he couldn't handle all their baggage himself, the porter knew he would have to pay these two from whatever the signora gave him. He steered the two women as best he could toward the open doors of a rattletrap taxi whose driver also seemed to be his partner in the improvised dockside enterprise. They climbed in the back seat, Eleanor wary and nervous, her mother serene and unusually self-possessed. The porter clambered into the front seat next to the driver, and the scruffy youngsters hopped on the running board for the short ride to the depot.

Having deposited the women and their luggage safely at the station, the porter and his crew slunk away, the two older men arguing and the younger ones eagerly counting the coins that had been tossed their way.

Inside the depot, Donna Sarina seemed to be in her element. While Eleanor waited with the luggage, she circumnavigated the waiting-room, eventually approaching a ticket window to buy passage to Sicily. Her transaction complete, she studied the signs posted at other service windows until she found a telegraph office. She walked over to the desk and took a blank form, writing a wire message to her sister and paying the operator to send it. Then they proceeded to the platform where their baggage awaited them, to board the ferry train for Sicily.

Steam rose from the rails as they walked onto the platform, evaporating to reveal a sleek passenger train. The overnight train service to the south had just been restored recently, its cars refurbished and its rails repaired from wartime damage. The trip to the ferry would take thirteen hours. At Reggio Calabria, the entire train would be loaded directly onto the ferry: the tracks on land were switched to a track bridge that allowed the train to pass right into the cavernous belly of the ship. An hour later, when the ferry docked at Messina, the process would be repeated in reverse. A few hours later they would finally arrive at their destination of Siracusa.

Eleanor glanced at her watch. The train wouldn't depart for another hour, so she found an empty bench to one side of the tracks where she could keep an eye on their luggage until it was time to board.

The air was hot and still as the train shifted slightly. Or was it the boat?

Eleanor felt as though she'd been perspiring for days. She and her mother were still tucked into the same berth in the double sleeper wagon they had boarded in Naples, as the ferry now started its journey from the port of Villa San Giovanni in Reggio Calabria across the Strait of Messina. The train stood braked onto the tracks inside the ship's hold, so the bright sunshine outside didn't filter down to the train car where they slept. The sound of voices outside their window awakened her, so she arose and wrapped herself in her traveling coat and stole quietly out of their compartment. She needed air.

She strolled off the train and climbed the stairs into the warm daylight spilling onto the ferry's upper deck. During the daytime service, passengers often left the train cars the moment the ferry pulled away from port for the bustling café bar at one end of the boat, where beverages and snacks could be bought for a few lire. The short trip across the strait was just enough time to down a quick dose of morning caffeine. From her perch at the top of the stairs, it was evident that the establishment was doing a brisk business already, doling out steaming cups of *espresso* and *biscotta* to passengers standing three-deep at the counter.

Eleanor shielded her tired eyes from the bright sun, then rubbed them sleepily. It was still early morning – barely six-thirty – but the ship's crew bustled about, intent on their chores, politely skirting their way around passengers who milled about the deck

The ferry approached landfall, the jumble of rugged blue-gray mountains that formed Sicily's northeastern coast etched itself against the blue sky. As she leaned on the ship's railing, the lines of ecru and beige on the horizon slowly materialized into a distinct urban landscape, the buildings and churches of the port city of Messina.

Eleanor returned downstairs to the ship's hold and their compartment in the train. Her mother had folded the linens and thin blanket she had used during the night and was sitting up, buttoning her dress and fastening the belt cinched at her waist.

"*Chi tempu fa oggi?* What's the weather like today?" she queried her daughter.

"*Fa cauddu ancora.* Hot again, of course, and sunny. There's not a cloud in the sky," she added, the thought cheering her that even the sun was greeting her arrival in Sicily. "*Vui un caffè?* Would you like some coffee?"

"*C'è tempu,* there's time. Maybe in a little while," Donna Sarina replied. "We still have another two hours until we reach Siracusa."

The train had traveled about half an hour into the Sicilian landscape when Eleanor noticed them. The salt pans stretched as far as the eye could see, an eerie landscape of rectangles of shallow boggy acreage, their low barriers of packed earth defining the borders. Here and there, a creaky windmill reached into the air, its arms rotating lazily in the heat. Not a soul stirred on the wide watery expanse. The solitary air of the place gave Eleanor the odd sensation that she had arrived not in Sicily but in some other country entirely. Every so often, between the stretches of evaporating ocean water, chalky white hills of sparkling salt lay piled up haphazardly, testament to the salt harvest. The ancient commodity, basic to so many aspects of life for millennia, had been raked here from its watery bath to dry in the morning sun. There it would remain until it was packed in large sacks and loaded onto carts, trucks, and trains for transport all over Europe.

"What time is it?" she asked her mother idly. The steward had come by earlier and brought them each cups of *espresso* that had taken the edge off her drowsiness, but Eleanor still longed for a large cup of American-style coffee with milk.

Sensing her daughter's question was less about the hour on the clock and more about how much time was left in their journey, Donna Sarina said, *"Figghia mia, n'altra ura e mezz',* we still have another hour and a half."

Eleanor smoothed her blouse and tucked it more firmly into the waistband of her skirt. What will he see when he looks at me again?

Donna Sarina read her daughter's thoughts. *"Mi pari bedda.* You look beautiful." She smiled and reached out with uncharacteristic tenderness, caressing her daughter's cheek softly.

The last hour of the journey seemed the longest in Eleanor's life. The train's brakes finally squealed and the outlines of the station at Siracusa came into view. A row of sturdy but intricately carved lampposts met the underside of the roof like outstretched branches of a tree, serving as supports for the platform's overhang. The dark green filigree trim of the depot's steep roofline was a fine lace edging against the warm yellow walls of the building. The place's tidy simplicity warmed Eleanor's heart but did little to ease her jitters.

Clots of people stood on the platform waiting to greet relatives and friends. One young man stood apart, cap in hand. Donna Sarina immediately recognized the outlines of the grown man's face from the boy in the pictures her sister had sent her.

"Pasqualeddu!" Donna Sarina cried out the open window as their carriage slid past the young man. Hearing his name, he looked up. His aunt was beaming, waving a handkerchief out the window to flag Pasquale Palumbo's attention.

The train rolled to a stop and Pasquale awaited them at the door. In an impatient rush of clasped hands, Donna Sarina enfolded the young man into a long embrace, hugging him as if she would never let go. Eleanor's unease evaporated when her cousin wrapped his arms around her neck and sighed her name: *"Eleanora!"* The young man released her and hugged her mother warmly once more.

"Tu si troppu màuru, figghiu miu!" Donna Sarina exclaimed. "But you are so thin!"

Pasquale brushed off his aunt's concern by holding up his arm and flexing his bicep.

"Mai sulu màuru, zia, ma màuru e fortu! Not skinny, auntie, but lean and strong!"

"Bo, a bisugnu di chidda forza," his aunt quipped, gesturing toward their luggage. "You're going to need that strength now."

Pasquale ran to one side of the building and returned with a decrepit-looking wheelbarrow. He pulled it abreast of the trunk, tipped the conveyance sideways and then tipped the heavy trunk on its short side and into the wheelbarrow with surprising ease. He turned and grinned at the two women.

"Màuru, sí, ma fortu però!" he intoned, flexing his bicep again.

Donna Sarina laughed heartily. Eleanor couldn't recall the last time she heard her mother laugh so freely and without restraint. The sheer joy in her heart was plain on her beaming face.

The trio made their way to the other side of the train station slowly, each of the women carrying a suitcase and Pasquale sauntering beside them with the trunk in tow. He stopped when he got to a substantial-looking cart to which a donkey was tethered. A bench seat was fastened to the front of the cart, from which a set of reins dangled.

Eleanor regarded the contraption with dismay. Her cousin sensed her discomfort.

"Mi dispiace..." he began to apologize. "I am sorry but we have no automobile."

Donna Sarina took control of the awkward moment by taking his hand firmly in hers.

"Aiùtami, figghui miu," she said, undaunted, gesturing toward the back of the cart. "Help me up, my boy."

Pasquale grinned and helped install his aunt in the back of the cart, on some soft blankets left for the purpose. Eleanor's jaw dropped, astonished to find her dignified mother seated in the back of a donkey cart. She couldn't decide whether that was the bigger surprise of the day, or the nimble way Donna Sarina had stepped up and into the rustic wagon, as if she did it every day.

After her cousin efficiently transferred the trunk into the cart behind where her mother was seated, there was still plenty of room for the two large suitcases. He upended the wheelbarrow over the whole lot and turned to her.

"Alluda, Eleanora," he said with a grin as he leaped up on the bench seat and stretched his hand out to pull her up. Pasquale's sinewy arm balanced her with bracing strength as she stepped unsteadily onto the footrest. Grasping her arm firmly, he pulled her into the seat beside him. Flustered but pleased to have made it in one go, Eleanor yanked on her skirt and settled herself on the bench. Her cousin took hold of the reins, clucked to the donkey, and they were off.

Her sister's overcrowded, noisy house was a homecoming of sorts for Donna Sarina. Although she had never seen the Palumbos' home, the neighborhood was familiar: she and her husband had lived in a modest structure nearby, next to a greengrocer's shop near the main *piazza*. Her intimate familiarity with the town returned in a flash. She knew its sounds and smells as those of home, for she had grown up there. She recognized many faces, neighbors or family friends, older now with wrinkled skin and fewer teeth, but with the same neighborly smiles and greetings she recalled as a young girl, then as a wife and mother.

Sadness overlay this homecoming for Donna Sarina as well. Leaving her homeland in 1920 had been prompted by tragedy and grief, losing her young husband suddenly while he was away in the army. Italy was not at war in those days, so Gaetano Fazzio had not died a hero's death in battle – a loss that Donna Sarina could perhaps have understood as justified. No, her musical young husband was a member of a military band, and he had contracted pneumonia while on tour. What a senseless waste. It made losing him all the more bitter for her to swallow. She had not had time to properly grieve him when less than a year later her baby died, an infant daughter whom Gaetano had never met, born when Sarina was already a widow. She lived in a somnambulant state of shock and grief; being deprived of half her young family so swiftly could not be assuaged, not by her faith nor any larger power. Eventually she had sternly hardened her resolve to make something positive out of so much pain and misery. She needed change in her life. And there was a new world beckoning across the sea.

So it was that Donna Sarina Fazzio, grief-stricken and only twenty-eight years old, had traveled to America with her little daughter to make a new life there. In the intervening years a familiar emigré legend had grown up around her here, like the well-tended vines in her sister's garden. As recounted by family and neighbors in Sicily, Donna Sarina had emerged as a woman of substance from the young widow who sailed away with only a few lire in her pocket. She had taken her five-year-old Eleanor by the hand and uprooted their lives for the dream of something better. She had arrived in a strange land without benefit of language. But she had made her way. Practically from the very start, she earned a living plying her skill as a seamstress. She raised her widowed brother's children as if they were her own. She moved into the house he owned and organized his household. She buried that same brother, taken from his family too soon. After he died, she sold the house and bought another. She helped a younger generation of the family get started, offering them bed and board when they could not afford it, pulling them through successive waves of the Great Depression, war, and the myriad hardships of trying to survive as newcomers in a country that didn't always welcome them with open arms.

If for her mother this homecoming was a bittersweet mix of memory and renewal, for Eleanor, once arms had been clasped and tears shed, it was all about reuniting with Giampaolo. On the ride from the train station, Pasquale regaled them with the story of his visit to Palazzolo, meeting Donna Lombardo and sharing a meal at the Stagno table. In a voice thick with emotion, he told of Giampaolo's harvest-time generosity, sharing the relative bounty of the Stagno farm with his family. Eleanor swallowed the lump in her throat. Giampaolo's letters had mentioned only that he and Pasquale had met. She staved off tears now, learning how he had embraced her extended family in the kindest, most practical way.

Giampaolo came the next day, bicycling from Palazzolo to see her. They kissed and embraced modestly in full view of her aunt's substantial family. There seemed no time nor place for the pair to greet each other and talk privately, as Eleanor would have liked. After a meal at her aunt's crowded table, she and Giampaolo had taken a leisurely evening *passeggiata* arm in arm around the town's rustic square. But they were scarcely on their own. Her young cousins trooped after them, completely enamored of the wartime romance of their glamorous American cousin, the couple's benign but unwitting chaperones on the twilight stroll. Giampaolo climbed onto his bicycle and left early that night (too soon, Eleanor lamented), promising to return the next day when he would bring her and Donna Sarina to meet his parents.

Donna Lombardo leaned over the balustrade of the balcony that opened onto the Corso. She would often pull up a chair and sit discreetly hidden by the lace panel that framed the doorway, observing the scene below, content to see but not be seen by passersby on the street.

But not today. Today, she was eager to see this American bride that Giampaolo was bringing home.

Uncharacteristically, he had announced his decision to marry and emigrate to America confidently but unequivocally. His parents had accepted it without question or comment. This was what the modern world had come to. Donna Lombardo found it unsettling for the normal order to be upended to precipitously. There would not be time nor need for rounds of visits as the couple's families met, chaperoned the courtship and ultimately approved the match. In the usual course of things, bride and groom would have grown up together. The families would have been neighbors, sometimes for generations – *contadini* and *paisani,* even *cugini,* in the same small towns all their lives. As youngsters still, the boys would have begun helping on the family farm or loaned out to landowners for similar work. The girls would have learned from a tender age the tasks and responsibilities of being farm wives and mothers. The couple would have been baptized in the same parish church and attended the same local school. The local priest would bless their marriage and baptize their children in turn.

Donna Lombardo felt an undercurrent of dread as she waited for her grandson and his American bride. She would never admit that she played favorites among her grandsons.

Still, Giampaolo's kind heart and natural reserve had always endeared him to her more than the other boys, boisterous as they all were. She also doted on her youngest grandson, the newly ordained Patri Eugenio, because he was a puzzle to her, with his studious, serious air and quiet ways. So, happy as she was that he had found a woman to marry, it was a mixed blessing because she would lose her Giampaolo to a different world.

At the far end of the Corso, she spied the rounded roof of the local bus that had plied its way among a cluster of the smaller towns in the interior of the province to arrive here in Palazzolo. It pulled into its customary stop, its metal roof glinting in the late morning sun. She couldn't see the doors open to disgorge passengers on the other side of the bus, but she knew her grandson would be among them.

Presently, with a grinding of gears and a belch of black smoke, the bus pulled away. Donna Lombardo discerned three figures walking down the cobblestone street toward the Stagno home: the familiar figure of her grandson, tempering his usual impatient stride now with two women beside him, one on each arm. He looked handsome and fit in a collared white cotton shirt and pressed trousers of brown serge. His shirt had short sleeves and was open at the neck against the summer heat. Both women were well-dressed too, in their Sunday best. As they drew nearer, she absorbed more detail of their clothing: the younger woman wore a cap-sleeved shirtwaist in a pattern of soft pastel, the older, a tailored green dress with a belt of the same color. The older woman wore a straw hat that sat on the crown just forward of the neat steel-gray bun at the nape of her neck. The younger woman was hatless, her cheeks a rosy tint as she talked animatedly to Giampaolo, who leaned toward her and grinned affably. Her hand was tucked in the crook of his right arm, and he held it close to his body. He wore the mother's arm formally on his left side, turning toward her occasionally to guide her steps, making sure she didn't slip on the slick worn cobblestones.

As they approached the house, Giampaolo spotted her on the balcony and flipped his hand in greeting. His *nonna* took a step back from the railing, suddenly shy as the two women glanced up and noticed her. She waved back, a small smile on her face, and turned in toward the house.

As she heard her grandson's voice murmuring and his bride's excited tones in reply, Donna Lombardo glanced self-consciously down at her own black dress. It was a sturdy cotton frock with tucks at the bodice. She had added a belt to dress it up a bit today, sure she would feel self-conscious next to her guests. She swallowed hard as her grandson ascended the stairs with Eleanor and her mother following.

Giampaolo drew the two women into the sitting room, which his grandmother had brightened this morning with touches she had crocheted, lacy doilies on the tables and antimacassars on the chairs. A vase of brilliant red gladioli adorned the side table. The high-backed chairs covered in heavy gold velvet stood along one wall like soldiers on parade, ready to salute their guests.

Donna Lombardo stood silently, waiting for a cue from Giampaolo.

"*Chista è a mia nonna, Donna Filomena Lombardo.*" Her grandson took his grandmother's arm and smiled shyly.

"*Nonna,*" he began, a bit stiffly, "*chista è Eleanora,* this is Eleanora." He paused while his grandmother placed both of her wrinkled hands in Eleanor's. She smiled and pecked the young woman on both cheeks. Eleanor returned her smile and squeezed his *nonna's* hands.

"*...e su matri, Donna Rosaria Fazzio,*" he continued formally, stepping back to let the two women regard each other fully.

Eleanor's mother broke in, "*Pi piaceri, sula Sarina,* please just call me Sarina," she corrected him as she grasped the older woman's shoulders and touched her cheeks with her own, side to side.

"*Piaceri,*" his *nonna* murmured softly and gestured toward the chairs. "*Pi favori assiettàti dduóco,* won't you please sit down over there?"

After taking her seat, Eleanor grasped Giampaolo's hand and pulled him toward the chair next to her.

Donna Lombardo scurried to her tiny kitchen where she had left a small silver tray set out with a set of small glasses etched in a delicate pattern, a matching decanter set in the middle. Returning, she placed the tray on the table.

"*Pi piaceri, pígghiassi quàlchi da biviri?* Please, will you have something to drink?" Their hostess poured out small amounts of *amaru,* a bitter aperitif, from the decanter. Giampaolo handed the glasses around and they each took careful sips.

Donna Sarina began a conversation in Sicilian dialect, and his *nonna* relaxed in her perch on the chair next to his bride. She chatted familiarly about their travels, the ship's crossing to Naples, then the long train ride to Siracusa. Eleanor marveled at the effortless way her mother put Giampaolo's *nonna* at ease. It was a side to her mother she had not seen. Donna Sarina related experiences the older woman could only imagine, in a cordial way that put them both on a comfortable footing. Giampaolo heard the friendly respect in Donna Sarina's tone, imparting a recognition of their age difference, something he knew his *nonna* would notice and appreciate. Now and then Eleanor punctuated her mother's banter with a detail or an exclamation, all the while holding Giampaolo's hand and giving it an occasional squeeze. Her grandson sat, attentive and smiling, giving his Eleanora an occasional loving glance.

Donna Lombardo finally relaxed enough to insert some comments and a few quips that drew a smile to Donna Sarina's lips. The two older women were soon chatting like old friends, Giampaolo's *nonna* gently probing Eleanor's mother for details of life in America and for memories of her young married life. For her part, Donna Sarina supplied the familiar narrative of their emigration to America and the close-knit family of nieces, nephews, cousins and their spouses. She sketched just enough detail to intimate the outlines of a life that awaited her grandson in America. The way Donna Sarina told it, the world to which Giampaolo was going no longer seemed so far away and foreign, and his *nonna* could appreciate why he might be drawn to it. The war had changed so much. It would be devastating to say goodbye to him, perhaps for good, but at least now she dimly understood why he had chosen to go, and that he would be happy in his choice.

Giampaolo grew restless and turned to his grandmother. *"Cosa da manciàri?"* he queried. "Is there something to eat?" When they had arrived, he had been surprised to find no table set, no pot boiling on the stove.

"Manciàmo da Pietri stassira, we are going to the Pietris' for dinner today," she supplied. "Your parents are waiting for us there." The Pietris were his brother Peppino's in-laws, Ceccina's parents. Donna Angela Pietri was known throughout the town for the quality of her pasta and the richness of her *sarsa.*

Giampaolo's eye's lit up. *"Magnificu!"* he exclaimed and leapt to his feet.

"Ascuta, Eleanora, listen, my dear," Donna Lombardo leaned over and tapped the younger woman's knee, whispering conspiratorially. *"A prima amuri di chistu carusu sempri é manciàri.* Eating has always been that boy's first love."

Chapter 34

We are weaned from our timidity

In the flush of love's light

We dare be brave

And suddenly we see

that love costs all we are

and will ever be.

Yet it is only love

which sets us free.

–Maya Angelou, *Touched by An Angel*

July, 1948, a wedding in Sicily

Bleached coarse linen cloths covered every surface of the beds and dressers on the topmost floor of the Stagno home. The covered furniture would have suggested a house that wasn't lived in – if every inch of the fabric's surface hadn't been covered with *biscotta*. Cookies of every imaginable shape and sort lay carefully placed, warm from the oven, on the linen to cool thoroughly before being arranged onto platters in decorative layers, with *cunfetti* – Jordan almonds and little sugar-coated hard candies, twists of cinnamon and other spices, all in pastel colors – that would be tucked into crannies and crevices among the cookies.

There were tender Italian butter cookies curled into "S" shapes and decorated with glossy white icing and multicolored nonpareil sprinkles. There were sable-colored *mustacioli* in chocolate, and lighter ones shot through with almonds, pistachios, and currants. Still other *biscotta* were flavored with anisette and cognac. There were lemon cookies shaped into figure-eights and topped with a sprinkling of lemon zest. Delicate wreath cookies were flavored with anise and wine. There were *cucciddati,* small snail-shaped folds filled with figs and almonds. Golden mounds of orange-flavored dough hid walnut-sized nuggets of figs and hazelnuts. Golden piles of losenge-shaped *biscotta a mennula* were heaped in one corner. In another, pyramids of *crispeddi,* delicate orbs of batter fried to a tempting bronze, awaited a filigree of honey as the crowning touch. There were light-as-air *pizzele,* and *pignulati* – circlets of vanilla cookie studded with toasted pine-nuts. Strips of fried dough were tied in love-knots and sprinkled with confectioner's sugar.

And there were other delicacies that saw the light of day only at holiday time or on very special occasions. Trays of *giuggiulena,* diamond-shaped, golden-brown bites of crunchy sesame brittle, were arranged on smaller plates, as were *ossa di murti,* dead man's bones – small white irregularly shaped lumps of meringue baked slowly until they were very hard. Rows and rows of dainty golden shells for *cannoli* – lady's curls – sat waiting to be filled with ricotta and decorated with chopped citron.

These delicacies were the handiwork of Giampaolo's *nonna,* Donna Lombardo, with the expert help of Ceccina's mother, Donna Angela Pietri, and a phalanx of other women in preparation for tomorrow's nuptials. For these baked wonders, only the finest ingredients had been procured, often from some distance and at some expense, as postwar shortages still prevailed. Fortunately, with a little searching, many of the delicious raw ingredients were available in Sicily itself. The best pistacchios from Bronte, in the Etna foothills, were brought in, and almond paste was procured from Erice, the medieval hill town near Palermo whose *marzipani* was sought after all over Italy. But many of the best things were nearer to hand, from the Stagno family farm. The flour had been milled from wheat they had harvested. Wild honey had been collected from San Marco's own beehives. Almonds and lemons and oranges were picked from the Stagnos' trees. Turuzzu's wife Margarita had made the ricotta for the *cannoli* filling from the milk of cows that Giampaolo himself tended.

The cookies were the crowning touch, the special surprise, the *pièce de resistance*. They were gifts that a Sicilian bride traditionally bestowed on her wedding guests. The caliber of the cookies that newlyweds offered to friends and family spoke volumes about the pair, and as far as Donna Filomena Lombardo was concerned, there would be only the best for her favorite grandson and his bride.

When she reached the top level of the Stagno home and saw the abundance of delicate baked jewels spread out before her, Eleanor's eyes widened and her mouth watered. She looked around her, trying to take in the quantity and variety of tasty things. Her mind reeled, knowing how much work it took to make a batch of just one or two of these delicacies.

Climbing the stairs right behind her, Donna Sarina reached the top step. When she took in the same view that had stunned her daughter, she smiled and crossed her hands over her heart, full and grateful that Giampaolo's family had gone to so much effort for the wedding party, to make them feel welcome and to impart respect to their wedding guests.

As the two women were still recovering from this glorious surprise, Donna Lombardo stepped in from the recesses of a back room. Donna Sarina enfolded the petite old woman in a warm embrace that spoke her thanks more eloquently than any words could. Eleanor waited her turn and did the same, kissing Giampaolo's *nonna* on both cheeks.

It was early July, usually one of the hottest months in Sicily. This July day did not disappoint.

Eleanor rose early and bathed quickly on her wedding day, before the rest of the household was afoot, in the tiny bathroom down a narrow hallway from where her mother still slept in the tall double bed they shared in her aunt's overcrowded house. Some of Eleanor's cousins had been parceled out to neighbors during their visit, so that Donna Sarina and her daughter could have the larger of the tiny home's two bedrooms to themselves.

Eleanor hadn't been able to sleep the night before, or pretty much since she'd arrived in Sicily, for the nervous stomach that had plagued her reunion with Giampaolo. She was nervous, yes, but underneath she harbored not the slightest doubt that she was meant to marry Giampaolo Stagno. Beads of perspiration already stood on her lip, and a sheen of sweat covered her arms. She'd have to swipe a cool cloth all over herself again before she put on her wedding dress.

Slipping back into the bedroom quietly to allow her mother to sleep, she unlatched the massive doors of dark wood on the oversize armoire that dominated the bedroom. The soft rustle of satin and tulle played a tune in her heart as the doors opened and the hem of her wedding dress, hanging on a hook to one side, cascaded onto the floor. Eleanor wiggled her bare feet on the tiles still cool from the night air. She peered closely at the bodice, admiring once more the hundreds of diminutive stitches on the sequins edging its sweetheart neckline. She ran her fingers lightly over the fine lace overblouse, and stretched her hands over the voluminous folds of the skirt. The train lay in neat folds at the bottom of the wardrobe, and Eleanor took pains not to disturb it. Gently she coaxed the dress back into the armoire and reached next to it for a handful of tulle. Her veil was beautiful, long and diaphanous and gauzy, as carefully gathered and sewn by hand at the crown as were the details of the dress. She let the gossamer fabric slide over her hand, admiring the way the veil had been carefully folded upon itself to keep from wrinkling. She reached up to where the headpiece hung on the hanger and examined it in turn – clusters of tiny ivory flowers of silk and seed pearls artfully set off the gathers of the tulle where it was fastened to a headband of bone wrapped in satin ribbon. She sighed, then put a hand to her hair, imagining the veil there and worrying a bit about how her cousin would tuck her springy dark curls in place so that the veil would remain firmly in place. Lucietta had told her confidently that she would help with this important detail. Glancing with envy at her cousin's lovely, well-coifed red-gold mane, Eleanor knew that she would be in capable hands.

Her cousin Lucietta Palumbo was her maid of honor. Her lovely peach-colored silk dress hung in the armoire next to Eleanor's. She knew the dress would set off Lucietta's rosy coloring and shiny hair perfectly. In an astute gesture of outreach to his new in-laws, Giampaolo had invited Lucietta's brother Pasquale to be the best man instead of asking that favor of either of his married brothers. Deeply touched, her cousin had shaken Giampaolo's hand vigorously and thanked him in a voice thick with emotion.

Eleanor's mother stirred, turning to face her daughter from where she lay in bed. *"Come va stamattina?* How is everything this morning?"* She smiled and propped an arm behind her as she sat up.

"Assira non dommìa bonu, last night I didn't sleep too well," the bride smiled ruefully and looked out the window. *"Matri, chi cauddu oggi!* It's so hot today." Not a single leaf stirred on the lemon tree outside.

Her mother scooted to the edge of the bed and pulled her nightgown down to cover her bare legs. *"N'mporta,* it doesn't matter. *Tuttu si beni oggi! Iu sacciu.* Everything will go perfectly today. I just know it."

Some thirty miles away, Giampaolo stood gazing out the window of the balcony of the Stagno home at the still-quiet Corso below. He was restless but not nervous, anxious but confident. He felt a sense of urgency about the day, wishing the wedding festivities were behind them and he had leapfrogged to getting on with his new life with Eleanor, in America.

His father's voice echoing from the next room drew him from his reverie.

"*Giampaolo! Ven acá,* come here, son."

He murmured an assent over his shoulder, but he was reluctant to turn away from his post at the window.

Giuseppe Stagno stood to one side of the large banquette that held dishes and other serving pieces. Giampaolo noticed that his *nonna,* a constant presence in the kitchen, was nowhere about. Dressed in a good cotton shirt and his Sunday dress breeches, his father looked uncharacteristically formal and pensive. By remaining silent, he gave the older man the lead to say what was on his mind.

"*Figghiu miu,*" Giuseppe began by addressing his son in an unusually tender way. "My son, there is much I need to say, and much that I do not need to tell you."

He nodded, staying silent as his father continued. "*Oggi accuminci na vita nova,* today you will begin a new life with the beautiful Eleanora."

Giampaolo let a small smile light his face. "*É veru,* it's true, papà." He resisted the urge to say more, wondering what was really on his father's mind.

"You know I am proud of you, my son. You have seen more of the world than I ever have, or ever dreamed possible. This is a good thing, and it is a reason for a father to be proud."

"*Sì, papá,*" he responded, "Yes, papá, I know. I have been to places far away from here that I never imagined seeing in my lifetime. Some of it was bad but a lot was very good. And sometimes it seems like it was all just a dream."

"Except for Eleanora," was his father's reply. "She will make a new kind of life possible for you. She is your dream come true, and your home will be with her now." Giuseppe said these last words softly, with a catch in his voice.

"But now I must be firm with you. Once you go in the direction you are headed, *mai turnari,* there is no turning back." He paused to let the words sink in. Giampaolo knew what an effort it had cost his father to say this. His father was telling him not to come home.

"*Sì, papá,*" he repeated quietly. "*Capisco beni,* I understand very well."

Don Giuseppe turned then, looking away from his son, and added gruffly, "*Tu si omo,* you are a grown man, for many years now, so I know I don't need to offer any lessons on how to be with a woman."

Embarrassed at the turn of the conversation, Giampaolo blushed and shifted nervously from one foot to the other. Not knowing how to respond, he waited silently for his father to continue.

"It also goes without saying that you must always try to be kind to her." He chuckled softly to himself, and tapped the side of his head with an index finger. "That's not always easy, when a woman gets an idea in her mind."

Relieved and prompted by his father's jocular tone, Giampaolo stole a glance at him and lifted a corner of his mouth in a crooked grin.

Eye to eye, Don Giuseppe gave his son a final loving look and said nothing more. Then he turned abruptly and left the room.

Staring after his retreating figure, Giampaolo had the sense that there was more his father wanted to say, and wished the moment hadn't passed so quickly. The dreams Don Giuseppe spoke of were not only Giampaolo's dreams but those of the father for his son, those of an erstwhile emigrant for the excitement of finding a home elsewhere. Years earlier and before the responsibilities of children of his own, Giampaolo's father had emigrated to Argentina for a brief time before returning home, disappointed and disheartened. Perhaps he still harbored regrets about his own failed adventure. Perhaps his father would live vicariously through his experience, in some ways, from now on. For a brief moment the burden of that responsibility weighed on him, and then he let it pass. So much about the future was unimaginable that he could only move along through the coming days, weeks, and months, and see what time and a new home would lay at his feet.

Eleanor beheld her image in the oval-framed full-length mirror that her aunt had borrowed from a neighbor. A resplendent bride gazed back at her, in the lovely dress that seemed somehow transformed today. Perhaps she had never worn it as she *felt* today, filled with a confident hope for what lay ahead. The scent of orange blossoms drifted to her from the headpiece of her veil. Zia Marietta had insisted that a bride must wear some fresh flowers on her wedding day, for good luck. Her aunt had taken the veil in hand and interwoven the fragrant white blooms into the silk-flower creation so that a seamless thing of beauty now crowned her dark hair. She had threaded two blossoms on sturdy stems around her gold loop earrings, so even Eleanor's wedding jewelry was enhanced with fresh flowers. A cross of delicate gold filigree hung on a chain around Eleanor's neck, floating over the lace overblouse and resting above the circle of sequins.

As Eleanor turned one way and another for a side view of her veil, Donna Sarina bustled about, pinching the sleeve seams and smoothing the lace bodice. She fluffed the voluminous tulle veil so that it covered the train in a soft white cloud that would billow as Eleanor walked. Lucietta rustled behind her in her silk bridesmaid's dress the color of ripe peaches. Although Donna Sarina had to alter her niece's dress, taking in waist and side seams and shortening the hem, now it fit her perfectly. Lucietta blushed at her reflection in the mirror, next to the bride.

Zia Marietta chose this moment to bustle into the room. Her thick glasses cast a shadow over her eyes and face, but Eleanor could see the glisten of tears as her aunt took her in from head to toe.

"Beddissima! How beautiful she looks!" she murmured to her sister as, standing side by side, they both gazed at Eleanor's reflection in the mirror. Both women's eyes clouded.

Eleanor took her mother's arm by way of comforting her.

"Mamá, nun chianciri oggi, no crying today," she chided her gently, then exclaimed, *"Oggi, sula bona furtuna e allegrìa.* Today, there's room only for good fortune and happiness."

Her aunt drew a large white handkerchief from the pocket of her dress. *"Figghia mia, chiste sugnu làcrimi filici*, these are happy tears," she whispered as she wiped her eyes.

Lucietta gathered the bride's train carefully on her arm as they went down the narrow stairs to the front door. As the bridal party made their way to the church, neighbors came out to smile, gaze and wave.

The small band reached the church door and paused before going in. Eleanor turned to look behind her and found that a small parade of neighbors and friends of the Palumbo family had formed behind her and awaited their chance to pass into the church.

"Tu si abbanniata, Eleanora! You're a celebrity," Lucietta whispered as they entered the church and moved to one side of the large vestibule. The neighbors followed them into the church and passed by, smiling and nodding as they continued into the nave for Mass. Donna Sarina and her sister were already inside, at the front of the wide aisle formed by unmatched chairs and rickety kneelers facing the altar.

Lucietta carefully placed a fragrant bundle of white lilies and orange blossoms in Eleanor's arms.

As the church bell began to peal, her cousin Pasquale entered the vestibule from a side door, looking handsome in a new navy blue suit with a tiny orange blossom boutonniere in his lapel. With a big grin, he proffered an arm to his cousin. *"Bedda, beddissima!"* he breathed in her direction.

Eleanor blushed and smiled back, as Lucietta side-stepped around the cloud of tulle to precede her cousin toward the altar. The church bells sounded a melodious accompaniment as the trio started down the aisle. Eleanor looked up as she approached the altar. Giampaolo stood there, handsome in his navy blue suit, a nervous smile on his face as he caught her eye. *There is my future,* she thought, as she stepped forward to join him at the altar rail.

Chapter 35

Rome was a poem pressed into service as a city.

– Anatole Broyard

Mid-July 1948, a honeymoon in Rome
After their wedding breakfast, it was still early enough to begin their journey northward, so Giampaolo and Eleanor boarded the afternoon train. From Siracusa they would stay on the train all the way to Rome, traveling most of a day to get there. It would be the first time both would see the city, although Giampaolo had passed through as a soldier, getting only briefest glimpses from the windows of a troop train.

So Giampaolo and Eleanor spent their first night as a married couple holding hands and sitting upright, alternately nodding off on the hard benches of the train as it lurched northward. In the morning, they and the other passengers in their compartment were awakened by the tinkling of a little bell in the corridor outside. A man in a white chef's coat was passing through the train selling coffee and hard rolls. It was a meager breakfast. They both devoured the small hard rolls hungrily, and let the strong espresso work its magic to refresh their sleep-deprived bodies. The train hurtled its way northward through towns and countryside that still bore scars of war. The newlyweds gazed absently at the landscape, frequently closing their eyes to nap. Before they knew it, the conductor called from one end of their carriage: *"Roma! Stazione Termini, Roma!"*

It was a relief to the newlyweds that Patri Eugenio had agreed to meet them and help them navigate the city. He had eagerly insisted on putting them up and showing them the capital city he had grown to love during his time as a seminarian. Although the war had delayed and then curtailed the time he spent studying in Rome, he had used every minute of free time to indulge his boundless curiosity and his appetite for history, absorbing Rome's beauty both ancient and new: grand piazzas and glittering fountains, abundant churches and dazzling works of art.

Giampaolo was pleasantly surprised by the changes he had noticed in his younger brother. He still wanted to call him 'Bastiano, as they did when he was a boy. Even then he had been serious and studious, but as a priest he had an air of worldliness about him that seemed to suit him as well as his black cassock and Roman collar. There was much in the Eternal City to distract and amuse even the most dedicated seminarian. Sebastiano had feasted on the rich culture and deep history of the ancient city. He read voluminously about the Roman world he now embraced, classical and ecclesiastical, ancient and modern. Giampaolo was impressed by the man his brother had become. The young curate Patri Eugenio seemed comfortably Roman now.

Descending from the train weary and stiff, the couple made their way to the middle of the cavernous waiting-room in the gleaming new depot. In the bright mid-morning sunshine that spilled in through its arcade of skylights, the Termini station was humming with activity. They set down their suitcases and looked around.

"'Paolo! Eleanora!"

Eugenio was dashing toward them, cassock flying behind, one hand on his head to keep his broad-brimmed hat from flying off.

"*Mi dispiace, sugnu lentu!* I am so sorry I am late," he rushed up, breathless and grinning with delight, to find his brother and sister-in-law in the crowded salon.

"Nn mpurtanti, arruviamo nuàutri 'n dui minuti. Don't worry," Giampaolo reassured him, clapping him soundly on the back. "We just arrived."

"Binvinuti a Roma!" he cried with a flourish. "Welcome to Rome. *E tanti auguri,* congratulations, you are married now!" He took both of Eleanor's hands in his and kissed her on both cheeks, then wrapped his brother in a bear hug and kissed him too. "I want to hear all about the wedding. And I want to make sure you see all of *Roma.* It is one of the most beautiful places on earth! Come on, let's get you settled." Although he was slender and wiry, Eugenio hoisted their suitcases effortlessly, setting off at a quick pace through a set of large glass doors that opened onto a large piazza.

Eugenio's excitement about Rome was infectious. Tired as she was, Eleanor felt suddenly energized and eager to experience everything. Giampaolo took her hand as they hustled after his brother, threading their way through the maze of parked cars crammed haphazardly into every available inch of space in front of the massive depot.

Catching up with the young priest and pausing for a breath, Giampaolo and Eleanor found Eugenio cramming their bags into the trunk of a decrepit-looking Fiat. He slammed the trunk hood down with finality and grinned at his brother.

"Does this thing actually run?" Giampaolo looked askance at the vehicle, taking in its dents and scratches. He peered in the open window at the car's single passenger bench next to the steering column, the torn upholstery frothing with stuffing in several places.

"Sí, certu!" Turning serious for a moment, he reassured his brother. "But don't worry," he continued with another grin, "if it stops you can always get out and push."

Not sure whether he was kidding, Giampaolo nonetheless helped Eleanor climb into the car and scooted next to her, folding his legs up until his knees crowded his shoulders. He looked so comical that Eleanor swallowed hard to suppress a laugh.

"Giampaolo, nun ti metti cusí, don't sit like that – you can't be very comfortable," she remarked. Her new husband just rolled his eyes and then fidgeted a bit on the seat to accommodate himself better to the cramped quarters. Eleanor crossed her arms in front of her and wiggled in the seat to give her new husband more room.

"N' mporta," Eugenio breezily waved a hand at them from the front seat, where he was already grinding the gearshift noisily back and forth. Giampaolo looked at her, lifting his brows dubiously. "Never mind," he continued, "it's a short trip. We aren't going far." With that, he launched the vehicle into the chaotic stream of Roman traffic, alternately lurching forward and pumping the brakes, eliciting shouts and honking of horns from the drivers all around him.

Eugenio had been ordained just as the war was ending, and after his ordination he remained in Rome. His first assignment was as a junior curate in one of Rome's most historic churches, Santa Maria in Montesanto. It was one of the famous "twin churches" of the Piazza del Popolo, and the piazza was a tourist destination in its own right.

Despite Eugenio's promise of a short trip, it seemed like the little car spent quite a long time in close traffic with car horns bleating insistently on all sides. He ignored the unruly din, pointing to his right and left, and all the while keeping up a running commentary for his captive back-seat audience about the famous landmarks they passed. To Eleanor's relief, Eugenio finally turned into an elegant green space and they were immediately enveloped in hushed serenity. It was as though they had been dropped into a verdant bit of heaven, far away from the din of Roman streets. Eugenio told them this park was called the Pincio, and he traversed it quickly (too quickly, Eleanor thought), picking up the narrow road with deep switchbacks that eventually led to a large cobbled oval. As they descended, Eugenio explained that the Pincio had the best view of the Piazza del Popolo, and indeed, the elegant square soon lay before them in all its cobblestone glory.

The piazza's boundaries were outlined by graceful semicircular walls that embraced it on two generous sides. Around the open part of the perimeter, a series of squat stone cylinders defined the square as a pedestrian space, separating it from the bustling streets that surrounded it. An Egyptian obelisk, its ancient hieroglyphs still very distinct, punctuated the center of the enclosure and formed the focal point for a teeming fountain. Stately carved lions at the base of the obelisk spat water into the shimmering pool.

To one side across the square the honeymooners could see the dramatic Porta Flaminia that marked one of the entrances to the ancient city. A trio of archways displayed the heraldic symbols of Popes and patrons. Then as now, people passed by these gates on their way into the very heart of Rome.

There were three's everywhere in the piazza: three arches in the gateway; three churches on the piazza. As they motored over the cobblestones toward one of the churches, Santa Maria in Montesanto, Eugenio pointed out the three thoroughfares that defined the Tridente – the three-tined pitchfork pattern of streets that led away from this open-air "place of the people" and lent its name to the neighborhood just beyond. Giuseppe Vasi had etched his "grand views" of the Eternal City two centuries before from just this vantage point. The Tridente's focal point, the Piazza del Popolo, was a somewhat more prosaic public space than its grander relatives elsewhere in the city. The welcoming Piazza Navona, dubbed "the drawing room of Europe"; Michelangelo's spectacular

Campidoglio with its stunning black-and-white geometry, crowning the Capitoline; the resplendent Piazza San Pietro, eye-popping vestibule to the Vatican – all of these outshone the unpretentious square in front of them. But the Piazza del Popolo was true to its name: it was popular, as evidenced by the many people traversing it. Many seemed to be hastening to destinations beyond the square, but others paused at the fountain, regarded the churches or sat at one of the caffés on its periphery.

Eugenio pulled the car to a stop, and his passengers climbed out in front of Montesanto, his new parish church.

"You may not believe it, but this church has a historical connection to Sicily," he began as he pushed open the smaller of two wooden doors fitted into the church's original massive entrance. The three walked into hushed darkness, a welcome respite from the bright sunlight and chaotic noise of the piazza outside. Above their heads stretched an enormous domed ceiling with a matching smaller dome over the main altar. The building's distinctive oval shape was revealed in the sweep of these graceful arches overhead.

"I called it a church, but actually it's a *basilica*," Eugenio paused, putting emphasis on the word.

Eleanor had read a guidebook on Rome while on the Atlantic crossing, and for a long time she had known about indulgences promised for the faithful who made the pilgrimage to Rome's four major basilicas. "Is this one of the four---?" she began.

The young priest smiled indulgently. "No, no, Eleanora." He continued. "It's a *minor* basilica. But that's still an honor bestowed by the Pope on very few churches. It's a sign of exceptional favor and privilege."

"I see," she murmured politely, not really grasping the distinction that seemed so clear in Eugenio's keen mind.

The priest continued in hushed tones as they walked through

the apse toward the main altar. "The church was built with seven altars for the Carmelites who served this parish to say Mass. That tradition goes back to the early sixteen-hundreds, and that's where the connection to Sicily comes in."

He related the story of how the Carmelite order had metamorphosed from desert mendicants in the Holy Land in the fifteenth century to city-dwellers in Sicily two hundred years later. The monks had requested a mitigation of their religious rules to better suit their new urban lifestyle. The Pope agreed to let the order reform itself, and so it established a new community in a village called Monte Santo, in the outskirts of Messina. That same Carmelite group came to Rome about twenty years later, hoping to form a community there. "The Pope gave them this church as their headquarters even before construction was finished," he continued. "So they called it Santa Maria in Montesanto after their original home in Sicily."

Now remember, I said the church was still unfinished. Apparently all it takes is an ambitious bunch of Carmelites to finish the job. Nothing like a Papal mandate to make things happen!" he remarked with a smirk. "They even got Bernini involved, and he redesigned the church to fit the narrowest part of the piazza."

When Giampaolo and Eleanor looked confused, he explained.

"Gian Lorenzo Bernini was probably the premier architect and sculptor of his time. The mid-sixteen-hundreds." Then he added, mostly for Eleanor's benefit, "Some say he was to sculpture what Shakespeare was to drama." He was speaking animatedly now. "You've seen pictures of the Vatican? That massive square, the *Piazza San Pietro*, with all the columns? That's Bernini's design, too." He paused for a breath. "When we go to the Vatican tomorrow, you'll see the piazza and you can judge for yourself. Bernini also designed an amazing structure over the main altar inside St. Peter's Basilica di San

Pietro. It's called the *Baldacchino,* and it sits over the main altar as an elaborately carved canopy. Many call it Bernini's masterpiece. For me, though," the young priest's eyes turned dreamy, "there's nothing like his sculpture. *Apollo and Daphne* is my favorite." A wistful smile crossed his lips, and then he continued.

"It was Bernini who changed the shape of this church from round to oval." Patri Eugenio pointed upward to the ceiling above them and continued, as keenly familiar with the details of its design as if he had been there at the time. "He did it mainly for space considerations, but it was something of a scandal at the time because its twin church, just across the way on the piazza – it's called *Santa Maria dei Miracoli* – had a circular plan, and the two churches were supposed to match." He shrugged in resignation. "But at least the Carmelites got their church finished. The other one took another five years to complete."

The young priest walked around the church, pointing out two additional altars that Bernini's improved design had added to the interior. He glanced at his visitors and realized they had been putting up a brave front to mask the exhaustion now plain on their faces. He took Eleanor's hand.

"Ma, scusami, Eleonora, nun si stancha? I'm so sorry, Eleanor, you must be tired. Tomorrow there will be time enough for all of this, and more. Rome has been standing here for thousands of years!"

Eugenio led them to the refectory in the adjacent building that served as the priests' residence. They were met by Donatella, the plump, genial Roman housewife who functioned as cook, housekeeper and one-woman welcoming committee for parishioners, penitents and others who knocked on the priests' door. As it was midday, she had prepared a meal for the visitors, beginning with a delectable *salumi* of prosciutto and salami, with cheese, fruit and bread that lay awaiting them on the table. Eleanor's mouth watered.

Donatella explained that the spread was at Padre Eugenio's explicit instructions. *"È normale mangiare la pasta al pranzo,"* she began apologetically in clear Roman tones. "Normally I'd make *pasta,* perhaps *con un po' di salsiccia e contorni* for the midday meal, you know. Sausage and some *verdure,* green vegetables. But the good father, your brother, thought"—she glanced at Giampaolo doubtfully—"that you'd be more tired than hungry, and a light meal would sit better in your stomach if you followed it with an afternoon nap." She shrugged with a sideways glance at the priest, as if their very fates hung in the balance if there was no afternoon *pasta* on the table.

After they ate, Eugenio withdrew his breviary from his pocket and excused himself for afternoon prayers. With a nod and a smile, Donatella showed them upstairs and opened the door to a bedroom that had been prepared for their stay in Rome. It would save the newlyweds the cost and effort of finding a hotel, not to mention the trouble of navigating their way in the unfamiliar city. Eleanor fell onto the comfortable bed and was asleep before her eyes had closed.

She awoke what seemed like minutes later with Giampaolo gently jostling her shoulder. "Eleanora," he whispered her name softly in one ear. *"Eleanora. Mi amore, sugnu i sei.* It's six o'clock, my love." She rubbed her eyes and glanced toward the single window set high on the wall near the ceiling. There was still daylight but it was a mellow gold now, bathing their room in soft light and shadow.

After refreshing themselves, the couple stepped into the narrow curving hallway and descended a long curved staircase to the entrance hall. Eugenio greeted them with a glad smile. *"Ah, bono, ccá ci sunnu viàutri. Sintiti cchiu megghiu ùora?* Here we are. Feeling better now?"

Gesturing toward the door, he led them into the street. "First, food for the mind and heart, then food for the stomach." He waggled his eyebrows at Giampaolo, whose love of a good meal was legendary in the Stagno family.

The young priest led them across the piazza to an unassuming church with a set of narrow steps in front. "Inside this space," he gestured toward the door at the top of the stairs, "are examples of the mastery of Roman art. You'd never know it from the outside." They ascended with him and stepped inside.

Eleanor's breath caught as she looked around her in wonder. Here was the Rome she had hoped to see. Her eyes misted as she let the beauty all around wash over her.

The interior of the church was dim except for the far end, where the main altar was ablaze with light and color. Eleanor drank in the riot of elaborate carving, painting, and sculpture that appeared wherever she looked. Massive columns lined the main aisle, reaching their arms toward the vaulted ceiling where they met airy marble arches. Everywhere was ornamentation: the tops of the arches, the supporting vaults overhead, every inch of the walls and even the floors.

"Oh my!" She breathed the words almost as a prayer. Eugenio smiled knowingly.

"*Iu sacciu,* I know," he whispered softly to her in dialect. "I felt the same way, the first time I came here. We Italians have a word for it: *Stendhalismo.* It means being so overwhelmed by artistic beauty that you feel dizzy."

Eleanor clung to Giampaolo's arm as they strolled slowly up the main aisle and Eugenio began to tell them about the church.

"Raphael was commissioned to design a tomb inside this church. Unfortunately, he died before he completed the work. But Bramante designed the apse," he gestured upward, "and Bernini had a hand in it, as well. That's three spectacular artists right there, *uno, due, tre,* in this one little church." He flicked his fingers as he counted. "It's like that, all over Rome!" His enthusiasm for his subject shone in his eyes.

When it seemed like the newlyweds had got their bearings, the young priest led them toward a small chapel at the back of the church. Positioned over the chapel's altar was a beautiful fresco of the Virgin Mary's assumption into heaven, its vivid blues, golds, and rose tones immediately captivating Eleanor. The painting felt familiar, a scene not unlike those on some of the prayer cards in her missal at home. She looked at it in wonder, as if the saints had come to life before her.

Her brother-in-law told the story of the chapel before them, that had first been imagined as a tomb for the Cardinal of Venice. The cardinal knew that this church was favored by the Pope, and he wanted to curry favor with him.

"Oddly enough," Eugenio continued, "Pope Sixtus isn't really remembered for this church, but for a much grander work he commissioned for the Vatican apartments. Sixtus, Sistine: the Sistine Chapel bears his name." Eleanor's eyes widened as she made the connection.

Eugenio continued the story of the little chapel in front of them. "A hundred years later, a different pope made this church his favorite. And once again, a powerful cleric wanted to gain the Pope's favor. His name was Tiberio Cerasi. So he commissioned this chapel which was named after him: the Cerasi Chapel." He paused. "Popes and politics. The two forces behind some of the world's great art."

Eleanor was as fascinated by how much her brother-in-law knew. She touched the priest's arm lightly. "How did you come to know so much?"

Eugenio smiled. "Eleanora, being a bride, you'll understand. When you fall in love, you want to learn everything about the object of your affection. It's simple. I fell in love with Rome."

Eleanor blushed and glanced sidewise at Giampaolo, who returned a tender smile.

Turning back to his story, Eugenio explained how Cerasi had chosen an artist to decorate his chapel "It was common for wealthy patrons at the time to deliberately pit two artists against each other as a sort of *Combattimento,* or competition. This way, it was thought, you'd get the best work out of each man."

"Rather than choose just one artist, Cerasi chose two. One did the beautiful altarpiece of the Virgin Mary in front of us. But the other, Carravaggio, is the one whose work everyone comes here to see."

Having chosen the artists, Cerasi then chose the subjects for the paintings. After all," he paused and nodded knowingly, "these paintings were *'n ranni grazî,* a sort of big 'thank you' from patron to the Pope, you might say, for his patronage," Eugenio continued. "He chose the Blessed Virgin as the subject for the main altarpiece, and two saints, Peter and Paul, for the side paintings. And here's where it gets interesting – and there is another connection to Sicily – to Siracusa, in fact." He said this last in conspiratorial overtones, and then paused, looking directly at Eleanor.

Eleanor was rapt, listening to the priest's story.

"Which is...?" Eleanor asked. She waited expectantly for the rest of the tale. With an enigmatic smile, Eugenio let the tantalizing detail drop, and turned back toward the chapel.

"Carracci painted the Assumption altarpiece in the middle," he pointed to the familiar looking painting Eleanor had just admired. "Now, Carracci was a popular fellow. *N carusu abbaniatu.* He received lavish commissions from prominent patrons. He lived well and cultivated the rich and famous. In short, he was, as the English say, 'a man about town,'" Eugenio winked at his new sister-in-law, using the English words, and paused for emphasis.

"Caravaggio, on the other hand, was *not* socially acceptable. *N carusu bruttu.* In fact, he was a widely known 'bad boy' of his time." A look of mischief crossed the young priest's face. "Caravaggio was always broke, constantly drunk, often thrown out of the towns where he lived. The *carabinieri* knew him by name. He was also fiercely independent in his style of painting – so much so that his work was criticized and even reviled during his lifetime." Eugenio pointed to the paintings on either side of the altar. "Caravaggio painted these."

Eleanor gazed first at one and then the other. They were beautiful, too, but had an undercurrent of violence that stood them in clear dichotomy with the angelic scene above the altar.

Eugenio and his guests stepped into the altar-space, as close as they could get to the paintings. "Look at the painting in the center." He pointed to Carracci's work. "This was the style idealized and sought after in Rome in 1600. Beautiful, bright colors. A heavenly, uplifting scene. Everything in order and everything inside the frame.

"Now look at the Caravaggio paintings." He indicated the side altarpieces. "They're both painted in extremes of dark and light. The subjects spill off the canvas – no neat borders and well-organized scenes. Both paintings are scenes of violence." Eleanor nodded; that was exactly what she'd felt when she first looked at them. "On one side, St. Paul has been thrown off his horse when he hears the voice of Christ. It's the moment of his conversion, from Saul the Roman tax-collector, to Paul the Christian preacher to the Gentiles." Eleanor studied the canvas closely, relating it to the pious stories she'd heard as a girl. The saint lay on the ground, bathed in light, his arms outstretched upward, while a groom stands to one side holding his horse's reins.

"In the other painting, St. Peter is being nailed to the cross on which he would die." Eleanor turned her attention to the other side and studied the canvas. She shuddered as her eyes lit on the nails already piercing the saint's hands and feet. "You remember the story? St. Peter asked to be crucified upside down because he felt himself not worthy to die in the same position as Jesus. This painting shows that moment."

Eugenio paused to let them look more closely at the paintings, then continued. "Caravaggio used to recruit people from the street to model for him. Look at the face of Peter." He pointed. "This is no well-fed nobleman, but probably a guy the artist dragged in from the street." He pivoted to the other painting. "The same goes for the horse's attendant. Dirty clothes and dirty feet!" He turned again, waving at the men nailing Peter to the cross. "Using common people as models for paintings to be hung at an altar! This was unheard of in Caravaggio's time. He was revolutionary, but not in a good way. No, he was hated and ostracized, not only for how he chose to live but for what he produced as an artist and how he practiced his art."

The young priest paused and studied the paintings himself. Giampaolo and Eleanor were spellbound and speechless. "This is why I love Caravaggio's work so much. *Nuàutri tutti sugnu umani.* All of us humans are flawed and frail. In painting our humanity, he shows us the brilliance of God's love."

Realizing he was sermonizing, Eugenio tried to lighten the mood. He pointed at the *Crucifixion of St. Peter.*

"The guy had a sense of humor, too. See the bright brown britches of the fellow bending over just here?" He pointed to the foregrounded figure. "Now look over here." He pointed to the *Conversion of St. Paul.*" See the highlighting on the horse's rump?" He smiled. "Some think Caravaggio might have been making a comment about the Pope and the Church of his time. Also –" Eugenio chuckled knowingly, "Caravaggio points the horse's rump toward Carracci's painting!"

Giampaolo laughed heartily, but Eleanor looked shocked until she caught a gleam in Eugenio's eye.

"Patri Eugenio!" she exclaimed.

"Well, the two artists *were* rivals..." Eugenio let the suggestion speak for itself.

"Hey, you forgot to tell us," Giampaolo broke in. "What's the connection between Caravaggio and Siracusa?"

Eugenio smiled mysteriously. "Did you know there's a Caravaggio masterpiece in Siracusa?"

The pair shook their heads.

"Apparently on one of his many misadventures, Caravaggio had been thrown in jail on the island of Malta. When he managed to escape, he fled to Sicily, to Siracusa, where a Roman friend helped him secure a commission to paint the altarpiece *Burial of St. Lucy*. It hangs in the church that bears her name, *Santa Lucia al Sepolchro*." he concluded his tale. "The perfect subject for an altarpiece of that church."

"*Ah, sì, iu ricanùsciu chista!*" his brother exclaimed. "I know that church! It's in the Borgata district."

"*Alluda,*" Eugenio waved his hands, suddenly impatient with the subject. "*Basta cu chisti 'belle arti' ccani* Enough 'fine art' for now." He grinned and offered his crooked elbow in Eleanor's direction. "*Manciàmo?* Shall we eat something?"

"*Matri, chi fame aiu!*" Giampaolo rubbed his abdomen. "I'm starving!" Suddenly, Eleanor realized she was famished too.

Eugenio laughed and flipped his thumb toward his brother. "*Chistu ccá.* This one here. He knows only one answer to that question."

As they made their way to the church door, Eugenio told them that he had made friends with the owners of a little *osteria* just on the other side of the piazza. "*Nu postu rumanu veru,* it's an authentically Roman kind of place," he elaborated. "Owned by a lovely family. Until recently it was a butcher shop. In fact, they call the place '*Dal Pollarolo*.'" Then he supplied the dialect words. "*U Puddaru.*"

That drew a guffaw from Giampaolo. "So we're going to eat in a chicken-coop?" He shook his head in disbelief. "*Chisti Rumani.* These Romans. I guess there will be straw on the floor.'"

Eugenio turned to Eleanor. "*N'ngrisi, si dici,* 'At the Chicken Coop'?" She laughed with delight at her brother-in-law's carefully enunciated English.

They crossed the square and walked a short way on the Via di Ripetta. The three were greeted warmly in the tiny eatery as the proprietor extended his hand to the priest, who ordered liters of water and wine. When the restaurant owner had scooted through a curtain of beads into the kitchen, Giampaolo leaned forward to his brother and whispered urgently,"You're not going to try one of Angelo's tricks, are you?" Eugenio closed his eyes and shrugged, noncommittal.

Giampaolo turned to Eleanor and explained. "My brother Patri Angelo cultivates all the restaurant owners in town, and he's so popular – and often alone – so he usually gets his meals free. Then he returns to the places that make the best food, usually with a pack of friends." Giampaolo grinned knowingly. "When the meal arrives, he puts on this pious look and says a blessing on the meal, praising the food *and* the owner. This usually gets them *all* a free meal. The guy has no shame."

Patri Eugenio had secured a special wedding gift for the new bride and groom: a private audience with Pope Pius XII. He had told them that it was customary for the Pope to bestow a special blessing on newlyweds who made their way to Rome. Custom notwithstanding and Vatican regulations being famously complicated and bureaucratic, Eleanor was certain her new brother-in-law must have gone to great pains to arrange it.

Candidly, she was rather overwhelmed by the prospect of coming face to face with the Pontiff. Consulting with her pastor at home had done little to ease her nerves. Even the

391

dress code for a Papal audience was strict and specific: a woman's arms and head must be covered; dresses must have a modest below-the-knee hemline; clothing should be a dark color, preferably black. Eleanor had brought with her mainly lightweight frocks, sleeveless shifts, and blouses in light colors. But she had neatly packed away her dark gray traveling suit after arriving in Sicily for this express purpose. It was made of a summer-weight cotton fabric and so it would be cool in the heat of high summer in Rome.

The night before their Papal audience, she carefully draped the jacket over the back of a chair and arranged the skirt on the seat. Underneath the jacket, the plain neckline of the sleeveless blouse she'd chosen would set off the gold cross and chain that she'd worn since her wedding day.

Eleanor's nerves were tightly strung as they set off early for Vatican City the next day. As the taxi bore them across the Tiber. She glanced furtively at Giampaolo. He was peering out the window as the Castel Sant'Angelo loomed into view. But he turned toward her when she put a tentative hand in his, and he squeezed it reassuringly.

At Patri Eugenio's instruction, the cab had deposited them alongside an imposing ancient wall a hundred feet high clearly meant to discourage idle wanderers from going further. They walked quickly through an unassuming entry way into the hushed opulence of an enormous anteroom already full of people. Eleanor realized with relief that she needn't have worried. They would hardly be alone. Dozens of couples were assembled there already, all nervous newlyweds like themselves, all there to obtain the Pope's nuptial blessing. Eugenio and others who had chaperoned the couples into the anteroom were led away toward a wide staircase where they could observe the proceedings from an enormous gallery overhead.

The next minutes passed in a blur of color, noise, and motion.

A squadron of Swiss guards, four abreast, filed past the assemblage with military precision, their boots clacking on the stone floor. Resplendent in gold and blue stripes, jaunty red ostrich feathers bobbing from their silver helmets, they marched the length of the room, ceremoniously shouldering their halberds as they reached a wall of heavy scarlet drapes. The curtain parted, and there was Pope Pius, luminous in pure white robes, seated on a gilt red velvet chair. The papal throne's platform was well above eye level, to enhance the spectacle. The room erupted into raucous applause at the sight of the pontiff, and his guards took up protective positions strategically surrounding the dais.

Prompted by pontifical aides, the couples formed a double line facing the pontiff. Eleanor vaguely remembered being jostled into place, Giampaolo holding her arm firmly and whispering reassuringly every now and then, as much to quell his own nerves as to comfort her. She watched wide-eyed as each couple was given a brief moment at the Pope's feet. When their turn came, she and Giampaolo mimicked what the others had done, kneeling on plush velvet cushions placed before him. Pope Pius touched the tops of their heads in blessing and then lowered his hand so they could take turns kissing his ring before they rose and moved off to one side.

When the last couple had had their moment of blessing with the Pope, the newlyweds were ushered into an elaborate chapel adjacent to the reception hall. Even though the guidebooks described it as a chapel, the vaulted space seemed more like a cathedral to Eleanor. Not an inch was spared a touch of vibrant color. She gazed about the frescoed walls, arches and ceilings as Giampaolo found them a place to stand and watch the rest of the pageantry unfold.

The Pope descended from his chair and climbed onto a portable chaise on which he was hoisted into the air, onto the shoulders of twelve men in scarlet uniforms. On the back of the moving throne, Eleanor could make out the papal coat of arms emblazoned in gold. The Papal procession made its way in a wide circle around the chapel, the Pope extending his right hand in blessing to the faithful while a choir filled the chamber with ethereal music.

When the procession reached a sumptuously decorated altar, the Pope was handed down from the chaise onto the altar platform where he turned to face them. A cheer went up as he raised his arms in recognition. Eleanor strained to hear over the noise, her gaze fixed on the Pope's figure before them, a detached and otherworldly expression on his face. The faithful all dropped to their knees as the pontiff extended his hand toward them. As he intoned the familiar Latin words, Eleanor signed herself with the cross, and next to her Giampaolo did the same. Then as the choir continued with a Gregorian chant, the Pope was spirited away from the jubilant crowd.

The audience had taken less than an hour, but it felt like a moment out of time.

Eleanor was still dabbing her eyes when Eugenio met up with the couple outside. She squinted and blinked furiously, trying to adjust her vision from the interior darkness to the blazing Roman sun.

"Eleanora, vui biviri 'n caffé?" he inquired of her genially. "Shall we have some coffee?"

Eleanor's first thought was how sweetly solicitous Patri Eugenio was to them both, going out of his way to think of their every comfort and concern. And also how the simple act of having coffee would allow them some restful minutes to absorb the Papal grandeur of the morning.

It was just what they needed. Walking a short distance into the winding backstreets of Vatican City, the newlyweds and their host found a modest café bar with tables and chairs set out on the street. Seating themselves, Eugenio ordered coffee from the proprietor who promptly appeared at their table. He nodded respectfully, eyeing the priest's Roman collar, and stole away, returning in a few minutes with three cups of espresso. Eleanor inhaled deeply before taking a deep draught of the viscous black liquid.

A short while later, refreshed and energized, they retraced their steps along a narrow cobblestone pavement. Eugenio hailed a cab and the trio squeezed themselves into the back seat. As the taxi set off across the Tiber once more, the young priest resumed his enthusiastic monologue. The Eternal City was breathtaking, the bustling energy all around them undiminished by the sultry summer heat. At the priest's direction, the driver pulled to the curb at the Piazza Venezia, and they set out again on foot.

Eleanor learned that morning how dangerous it was to be a pedestrian in Rome. Simply crossing the street was perilous, an incongruity of pre-war Rome limping its way into the twentieth century. Carts and wagons of all sizes and conditions, their horses or donkeys blinkered against the chaos and noise, snaked their way along the boulevards. Bicycles whizzed by, cyclists anxious to be on their way, paying no mind to pedestrians, other vehicles or each other. Vying for space with the bicycles and wagons on the worn cobblestones were masses of speeding automobiles careening around corners and ancient lumbering buses belching sooty gray smoke in their wake.

But Patri Eugenio was intrepid, stepping lightly off the curb with a confidence at which Eleanor and Giampaolo could only marvel. His priestly garb seemed vested with some magical power to stop the Roman drivers in their tracks. And stop they inevitably did. Surely he had an angel on his shoulder.

Providing opportunity for appreciation beyond the teeming traffic, the busy Via del Corso gave way to tiny quiet piazzas tucked behind the warm yellow sandstone buildings. Everywhere in Rome, ancient ruins rose like jagged hulks, cheek by jowl with the architectural splendors of Bramante and Bernini, Leonardo and Michelangelo. Fountains sprouted plumes of water that splashed and trickled over stone sculptures of creatures real and imagined—gods, humans, and beasts. On wide squares and in narrow byways, cloth-covered tables spilled out onto the sidewalks from grand *ristorantes* and small *caffés*, their doors and windows agape and their awnings stretched wide to create a benevolent shade against the summer sun.

With an earnest young priest as their self-appointed tour guide, the couple's itinerary was plentiful with churches and pious reasons to visit them. Eleanor had learned about the pilgrimage to the four great basilicas, and her new brother-in-law did not disappoint. During the parade of sunny days that followed, the cool cavernous interiors of the sacred places they visited gave respite from the heat; the serene quiet cloisters they entered were Edenic retreats. Ancient stone benches provided a moment's repose, in which the sightseers rested aching feet and relaxed tired limbs.

Eugenio's love of Rome was contagious. He adored its glory and its grit, and he wanted to show these sides of his adopted city to Giampaolo and Eleanor. So he seasoned their sightseeing hours with the time-honored Italian art of *dolce far niente*. One morning's trek began at the open-air market in the Campo de' Fiori, stopping at a favorite bakery to partake of delectable *biscotta,* almond-paste cookies that they gobbled down with their morning *caffè*. After they had eaten their fill of biscuits, with a sidewise remark about wanting to stay in Donatella's good graces, the young priest proffered a few coins at the *forno* and they walked away with fragrant loaves of bread still warm from the oven tucked under their arms for the rectory's repast later in the day.

On another day, they climbed the endless steps leading up from the Piazza Venezia to the Campidoglio, pausing breathless at the top only to have their breath taken away again at the sight of Michelangelo's spectacular square and its equally spectacular views of Rome's hills. Eugenio thoughtfully planned an evening *passeggiata* in Trastevere, backing onto its crooked narrow streets from the Tiber's banks and winding past his favorite haunt for an evening *gelato*.

And then night would fall. Although to Eleanor it felt vaguely sacrilegious that their *letto matrimoniale* was in, of all places, a monastery, these nights in Rome were a first chance for marital intimacy, to kiss and embrace in private, to caress and draw loving maps of each other's bodies, to join in the coupling, now blessed by the Church, that would grow easier and more natural with time. *Is this what all the fuss is about?* Eleanor thought on their first night together, not yet understanding Giampaolo's urgencies or able to respond to the rhythm of his lovemaking. She didn't comprehend the quick thrusts that caused stabs of pain on her part but apparent relief, on his. So she lay in acquiescence, and afterward she found refuge enfolded in his arms. She loved the tender, possessed feeling of his tanned forearm across her midriff as his breathing evened out and he slipped into slumber. As she listened to her new husband's soft snores next to her, she closed her eyes and succumbed to the fatigue that lay heavy in her limbs. Exhausted at the end of each day, sleep easily overtook her, but her memory of those nights and the mornings that followed would be of a perpetual contented weariness that followed into each new day. Even the bright sun that spilled over their high window sill each morning couldn't completely erase the drowsy stupor of those honeymoon days.

What Eleanor found even stranger: to be, and to be seen as, part of a couple. Everywhere they went, people smiled and looked at them solicitously, as something special. And they *were* newlyweds, after all. She sometimes wondered if the word was emblazoned across her forehead. But in a city that attends at every turn to the art of love, people always took appreciative stock of lovers. She and Giampaolo walked arm in arm on the street, taking strolls in the dusky summer light of Rome. They held hands as they entered one of the myriad basilicas on Patri Eugenio's itinerary. Giampaolo tucked her arm affectionately under his as they paused at a magazine kiosk near the Trevi fountain where Eleanor casually scanned the headlines of the English-language newspapers on display.

She was used to being with people – indeed she liked being in company, and had grown used to it long ago, an only child in the improbable circumstance of growing up in a big family. But this was different. The unconscious fellowship of always having cousins nearby, family members whom she scarcely remembered being without, was one thing. Being with a grown man to whom she was now related but who was still in many ways a stranger, was something else entirely. Being part of a couple was going to take some getting used to. Eleanor had waited so long for this, for a life mate who would share her hopes and dreams as well as her sorrows and troubles. In the flush of newlywed love, she didn't let her mind run to the difficulties they might face together; she knew they would come. She just gave herself over to being in one of the world's most romantic places with the man she loved, the man to whom she now belonged.

Part IV

COMING HOME

Chapter 36

"At first you maybe start to like some person on the basis of, you know, features of the person. The way they look, or the way they act, or if they're smart, or some combination or something. So in the beginning it's I guess what you call features of the person that make you feel certain ways about the person. ... But then if you get to where you, you know, love a person, everything sort of reverses. It's not that you love the person because of certain things about the person anymore; it's that you love the things about the person because you love the person. It kind of radiates out, instead of in. At least that's the way ... That's the way it seems to me."

– From *The Broom of the System*, by David Foster Wallace

J amesport Eagle, Sunday, September 26, 1948
Eleanor Fazzio and Giampaolo Stagno
Special to the *Eagle*.

Eleanor Fazzio, 34, of Kensington Street, Jamesport, was wed in Italy July 3 to Giampaolo Stagno, 35, of Palazzolo Acreide, Province of Siracusa, Sicily.

The wedding took place in Florídia, Sicily, where the bride was born.

Mrs. Stagno is employed by Jamesport Knitting Mills, Jamesport. She is the daughter of Rosaria (Luna) Fazzio and the late Gaetano Fazzio. A naturalized American citizen, the bride emigrated to Oxford County with her mother in 1920. She is a member of Holy Family Parish.

The groom is the son of Giuseppe and Concetta Stagno, also

of Palazzolo. An Italian citizen who was a member of that country's armed forces during the war, Mr. Stagno was serving in the North Africa campaign when he was taken prisoner of war. He was in the U.S. from May, 1943 until October 1945; he met his future wife during that time.

The couple will make their home in Jamesport.

January, 1949, Jamesport, Pennsylvania

The Luna household was ablaze with light, warmth against the wintry cold outside. What heat the incandescent light didn't provide, the crowd of revelers jammed into the first-floor rooms – living room, dining room, kitchen – abundantly supplied.

The occasion was an American wedding reception, of sorts, for Eleanor and Giampaolo Stagno. Family, friends and neighbors had gathered to welcome the newlyweds, many of them eager to get their first glimpse of this Italian soldier Eleanor had married.

It was also an American welcome for Giampaolo, who had only just arrived in his new homeland.

The most distressing moment of her wedding trip to Italy had been when Eleanor realized that Giampaolo wouldn't be able to accompany her home on the Atlantic crossing. Although she and her mother had left open the return leg of their itinerary for precisely this reason, their tickets – and the favorable price they'd paid – would expire if they didn't book passage before October. So Eleanor reluctantly agreed to return home in the fall and leave her new husband behind until he could make his own arrangements to travel.

After their week-long *intermezzo* in Rome, at Eugenio's urging the couple had taken the train to Florence for a few days and then to Venice, before turning back toward Sicily. Those sojourns had been far too short for Eleanor to recall much except a few singular impressions of each city. In Florence, the taxi from the Santa Maria Novella train station had taken too many tight turns on narrow corners through the city's stoic gray buildings. As they screeched around one last corner, the walls suddenly parted and Eleanor's heart stopped as the Duomo's magnificence materialized before them, all graceful white arches, black-and-white stripes of marble, and red roof tiles. Of Venice she would remember their sweet little hotel room, its tall windows thrown open to the humidity of the lagoons, and falling asleep curled in Giampaolo's slumberous embrace to the soothing sounds of water slapping on the canal bridges and footsteps on the cobblestones.

Returning from their honeymoon, Giampaolo's family had made room for the newlyweds in one of the upstairs rooms of the city house in Palazzolo. In Floridia, the Palumbo household had righted itself to an everyday normal pace after the nuptial upheaval had dissipated, and Donna Sarina and Donna Marietta mustered every minute of time they could spend together.

So, for the last several weeks of their stay, Eleanor found herself at a remove from her aunt's more familiar household. And it had made her unaccountably homesick.

To distract his new wife from her melancholy, Giampaolo took Eleanor to San Marco to spend time at the family's farmhouse. Together they went for short strolls on the property, as he pointed out his favorite childhood haunts: the almond trees he'd climbed to harvest the bitter green nuts; the brook where he'd caught trout with his bare hands; the farmhouse itself, its thick walls cool shadowy protection against the blazing late-summer sun. In the cramped farmhouse, Eleanor observed firsthand the tensions between her two sisters-in-law, the elder Margarita, now pregnant with her first child, making no effort to cloak her disdain for the younger, shy Ceccina. Even if she had been inclined to stay in Sicily, she could scarcely imagine herself and Giampaolo as an unwanted third party in the overcrowded household. Without need of any explicit explanation, she understood that the unhappy situation at San Marco had probably hastened and firmed his resolve to make a home in America.

Eleanor and her mother left Sicily in late September, after long tearful goodbyes with Zia Marietta's family and more formal farewells at the Stagno household. Only Giampaolo's *nonna* had embraced "her Eleanora," as she had come to call her, within the diminutive circle of her arms, and she wept openly as they descended the stairs. Giampaolo accompanied them by train to Naples where they embarked for the Atlantic crossing. The couple parted on the pier, beneath the long shadows of the ocean vessel looming over them. When the moment came to say goodbye, Eleanor couldn't hold back her tears, try as she might to muffle her sobs on Giampaolo's shoulder. He simply enfolded her in his arms and patted her back as she cried, murmuring soothing syllables and chuckling to lighten the mood. But nothing would comfort her, and when she finally tore herself away, she saw tracks of tears glistening on his cheeks.

But now the painful separation was behind them. Giampaolo was here, truly for good now, shyly smiling amidst the boisterous merriment of Eleanor's family. Of course there was food – the dining-room table was laden with familiar treats both savory and sweet. Smack in the middle of the plates and platters towered a four-tiered wedding cake bedecked with elaborate curls of white frosting and delicate sugar flowers. On top sat a tiny statuette of a bride and groom standing beneath a heart-shaped arch of satin ribbon and silk flowers.

Glasses clinked as Nick Raffa called the guests to attention. Until he did, Eleanor hadn't noticed his wife, her cousin Ronnie, circulating among the guests carrying trays of glasses with sweet Prosecco already poured.

"A toast to the newlyweds!" he shouted above the din, and

waited for quiet. Conversation slowed to a hushed murmur and then stopped entirely, as everyone turned to where Nick stood next to Giampaolo and Eleanor.

"A little birdie told me," he snickered with glee, "that there was a long toast at the wedding dinner for these two kids, and it had something to do with red wine and white wine. Something about the Old World and the New World." He paused for effect. "I don't think I'm up to that," he paused as everyone laughed, "but I can certainly wish health and happiness and long life to Eleanor and Jumpowlo!" He lifted his glass as shouts of *"Salute!"* and *"Cent' ann'!"* engulfed the room.

"Let's have a kiss!" someone shouted from the back of the room, so Eleanor turned and shyly gave her new husband a modest peck on the lips.

"No, we want a real kiss!" came a cry from elsewhere in the room. Giampaolo caught on immediately, and he turned Eleanor into a thorough embrace and, bending her backward, planted a long kiss on her mouth. When he lifted her up, her cheeks were pink and her eyes dazed in surprise.

An approving roar went up as everyone applauded. Suzanne materialized at Eleanor's elbow with a long kitchen knife festooned with a big bow of white satin ribbon.

"Time to cut the cake!" she cried, thrusting the knife handle into her cousin's hand. Eleanor leaned over and made for the first layer of icing, when Suzanne stopped her. "Wait a second!" She grabbed Giampaolo's hand and placed it over her cousin's. "Now, go ahead and cut!" Everyone around the table laughed as the pair made a first pass with the knife. More applause followed, and then Suzanne and Rosalie drew the wedding cake toward them and moved it to a side table where dessert plates and forks awaited.

With the last of the wedding cake eaten and the last of the Prosecco sipped, family members and friends bundled in winter coats and hats and filed onto the icy sidewalk. People kissed Eleanor goodbye and gave Giampaolo companionable pats on the back.

In a few weeks the Luna home had settled into a comfortable tempo. Giampaolo had a temporary job as part of the receiving crew on the shipping dock at the factory where she worked. It was backbreaking work, heaving heavy boxes of fabric off the delivery trucks or loading cartons of finished garments for outbound delivery. For his part, he was glad to be going off every day and working at something. Their neighbor was trying to secure him a better job for more pay at the millwork company where he was the supervisor, but nothing had materialized yet.

Giampaolo took his new life in stride. He was earning money regularly for the first time, and the weekly paychecks that he got here in America were something of a revelation. Having worked on the family farm all his life, there was no formal exchange of money for work. Earning one's keep on a farm was an tacit barter of labor for food and shelter that had existed for centuries. As a prisoner of war he had received monetary compensation for his work, and that had come initially in the form of scrip or coupons that were good for purchasing items at the camp's base exchange. Only toward the end of his American imprisonment had he received a meager weekly pay of a few dollars in currency. So it was a strange new experience, this weekly errand to a bank to exchange an official-looking piece of paper with his signature for more money than he'd ever had in his pocket in his life.

At first the formality of the bank's enormous waiting room with cashiers' windows lining all sides made Giampaolo uneasy. It felt too similar to the impersonal government offices he had come to know in Sicily, before and after his military service. Nothing much that was good had ever come out of those places, only long waits and disappointment. But he soon came to find this new American ritual strangely energizing. It didn't take long for him to appreciate the habit of weekly gratification for his hard work

Giampaolo thought of this exchange as the average American's most tangible symbol of "the American way." You worked hard and you got paid for it. You got two days off each week to rest up. The idea of a day off on Saturday as well as Sunday surprised him at first, but in his new home it was a well established practice. For Giampaolo, it was another example of the comfort and luxury that epitomized American life, something Americans took for granted. It was certainly a welcome change from life on the farm, where there was always work to do no matter what season it was, where the animals needed care and the land needed tending on "weekends," just as much as Monday through Friday. Where more hard work was the only expectation, and where no one paid you for what you did.

Just before Giampaolo had arrived, Eleanor had installed a new easy chair in the living room with her new husband in mind. All the married guys she knew had their own special spot for relaxing at home, so she took it as a kind of rite of passage. Eleanor told him to "break it in," an English expression he didn't understand. She explained that new furniture was often stiff and needed softening with use; in other homes, new furniture was reserved for guests, but she secretly hoped he'd make this one his own. Giampaolo took to the assignment with gusto: it was easy to look forward to this comfortable spot each evening after supper, positioned at an advantageous angle to the radio if he was inclined to listen. Before long, it had become Giampaolo's chair. Eleanor had never been so pleased.

As for the radio, Giampaolo indulged his in-laws in their fascination with this newfangled technology even if he didn't share it. Rosalie was mad for the swing-band music of Benny Goodman and the dulcet strains of the Andrews Sisters—and anything sung by a *paesano* named Sinatra. He didn't pretend to share the same affection for this American music – at least not yet. He was a bit more curious on spring evenings when Suzanne tuned in to a baseball game. He would cock an ear toward the radio set but would eventually give up. None of it made sense, and the announcers all talked so *fast*. Eleanor's cousin Angelo, a real devotee of the sport, had tried a few times to explain the intricacies of the game. Angelo probably knew too much about baseball to break it down into very basic terms. Unlike the rough and tumble pick-up rounds of simple kickball that Giampaolo had played as a boy on Sunday afternoons in the Corso, there wasn't anything simple about this American baseball. It was an unintelligible confusion of arrogant shouts from someone called an "ump," a rapid-fire soliloquy from an announcer, and a lot of hurry-up-and-wait for an occasional crack of the bat and roar of the crowd. All of it in a language he was only slowly coming to comprehend.

Still, there was much that was familiar to him about his new home. Not least were his new wife's efforts to make him feel welcome through the most basic medium: food. She would query him about his favorite foods, and the next day one of them would appear in his lunchbox or on the supper table. Eleanor had taken to heart the advice of Giampaolo's *nonna:* he embodied proof of the adage that the way to a man's heart was through his stomach. His mother's dense white loaves with hard crust had been a staple all his life, so there was always plenty of bread on the table. This American bread was different, though; it was very soft, with a tender crust, so it took more of it to satisfy him, and he would easily put away five or six slices of an Italian-style loaf at supper each night. The ricotta was different here, too – the soft sweet cheese that he loved so much at home had a different texture here, not nearly so creamy as what his mother made each day on the farm, with cow's milk still warm from the udder. Here it was firmer and almost gelatinous from refrigeration. But if Eleanor creamed it with a little milk and seasoned it with salt and pepper, it still made a fine sauce for a bowl of just-drained hot pasta. To Giampaolo, it was a taste of home.

There were many other purely American culinary staples that Giampaolo had no problem embracing from the start. He looked forward so much to the miniature fruit pies that Eleanor put in his lunch box – that sometimes he would not wait until noon, devouring one at his mid-morning coffee break. And he had no trouble savoring the Sunday roast chicken and the Thursday night steak that made regular appearances on the Luna table. The soup broths were just as tasty as his *nonna's*, and the fresh fruits and vegetables that were available year-round were of even better quality than what he was used to in Sicily.

In a house full of women used to doing much on their own, Giampaolo easily found ways of being useful. He took to accompanying Donna Sarina and Suzanne on the weekly outings to Connie and John Nardello's grocery store across town. They would go there on Fridays after work for meat, milk, sugar and flour, canned goods, soap, and detergent. He liked exchanging pleasantries in Italian with John, whose English was heavily accented like his own. On Saturday mornings he would take his mother-in-law and cousin to the farmer's market downtown for fresh produce and bread. There he marveled at the aromatic German-style pastries – long twists of cinnamon scented dough topped with a vanilla glaze and the substantial bear claw buns generously studded with pecans. These would make their appearance alongside the coffee percolator, china cups, and saucers on Sunday mornings after they returned from Mass.

Once at home with their weekly haul of groceries, Giampaolo always helped carry the heavy paper sacks from the trunk of Suzanne's car to the kitchen table. He would bring to the basement any items that needed to be stored in the cold cellar. Hefty net sacks of potatoes still studded with dirt and bags of small yellow onions shedding their papery skin would go into large flat baskets on a makeshift table made of an old pine plank supported by sawhorses. Canned goods and dry goods like flour and sugar were stored in tidy aisles in a large narrow cabinet, alongside Donna Sarina's jewel-toned jars of quince and apple jelly and rows of quart jars of peach and pear halves, tomatoes and tomato sauce.

Giampaolo also took upon himself the task of hand-grating the wedges of hard Italian cheese that were a staple ingredient of so many of Donna Sarina's recipes, from soup and pasta to meatballs, cutlets, and savory casseroles. He would come upstairs from the cold cellar to find that his mother-in-law had set out a clean dishcloth and the box grater with the wooden handle at one end of the kitchen table. He would unwrap the jagged hunk of Romano or Parmesan from its waxy paper stained with grease spots, its familiar piquant aroma immediately filling the kitchen. He would then scrape a wide edge of the cheese against the grater with even strokes, the product forming a snowy pyramid on the wax paper. Then he would carefully spoon mounds of the fluffy grated cheese into a quart mason jar, finally tilting the paper into the jar's mouth so that not a crumb was wasted. After devouring the last morsel of cheese that was too small to grate, Giampaolo would stow the jar on the top shelf of the refrigerator, where it would be retrieved for sundry uses, not least the midweek pasta supper.

One day a letter addressed to Giampaolo arrived in the afternoon post. It was on featherweight airmail paper, franked with Italian stamps and written in the familiar hand of his youngest brother in blue ink. Patri Eugenio had now left Rome, having been given a parochial assignment as curate to a parish in Siracusa. Eleanor noticed the letter first, and with a strange sense of foreboding she handed it to her husband. Giampaolo ripped open the envelope and read it carefully.

My dear Giampaolo,

God has called our beloved nonna, Filomena Lombardo, into His arms. She died peacefully in her sleep last night—

Giampaolo glanced at the date at the top of the letter. March 19: it was already April. She had been dead for three weeks, and only now was he learning of it. Tears sprang to his eyes as he continued reading:

...and I remembered the repose of her soul at each of the Sunday Masses today. It was on the feast of Saint Joseph, so I am certain that the blessed saint personally guided her gentle soul upward as a special favor on the day when we remember the Blessed Savior's protector here on earth. You should be comforted by the fact that she did not suffer, good soul that she was, moving from this life into her eternal reward with no travail or illness. She died in her sleep, a restful and simple end to a long and loving life.

The tears spilled over as he finished reading the letter and handed it wordlessly to Eleanor, leaving the rest unread. She sat on the living room couch and read from the beginning, while he sank to her side, covered his face with his hands, and sobbed openly.

For days after the letter arrived, Giampaolo moved through his daily routines stoically, with no joy in his voice and no spring in his step. Eleanor expressed her concern in spontaneous hugs and loving looks, but she didn't know how to comfort him. When she tried getting him to talk, his eyes would fill and he would walk away, silent. Donna Sarina had hugged him warmly when she'd heard the news but she, too, was stymied as to how to help him through the often long haul of grieving that follows the death of a loved one. Rosalie and Suzanne cast sad glances his way, and murmured their sympathies to their cousin, beseeching her in cautious whispers to tell them if there was anything they could do for him.

After a couple of weeks, Giampaolo seemed to brighten somewhat – at least, Eleanor noticed, tears didn't seem to spring to his eyes every time she looked at him. Maybe now was the time, she thought, to raise an idea that might soothe his grief. One evening after supper, she sat on the sofa and patted the cushion next to her, gesturing him to join her. It was an unaccustomed move, so he acquiesced and took a seat.

"Giampaolo," she began in a tentative soft voice, addressing him in Italian as she had become used to doing, "*vui turnari a Palazzolo pe un po'*? Would you like to return to Palazzolo for a while?"

He looked up, surprised at the suggestion; then his glance fell to his hands folded in his lap. He said nothing for several moments, and she feared he hadn't heard her.

When he looked up, she saw hope glimmering in his eyes.

For Eleanor, the next few weeks were a blur as she prepared to say goodbye—again—to Giampaolo. Of the four weeks that the trip would take, half of it would be in transit, on the ocean crossing. Even though she knew he wouldn't be gone long, a month still seemed like a long time. As newlyweds, they'd been apart almost as much as they'd been together. She didn't dare to voice her worst fear: that he would not want to return.

When he left his family in Palazzolo in January, Giampaolo had told himself – he had really believed – that the goodbyes he said then would be forever. From that trip and from what he learned from Eleanor about her journey the previous year, he knew it was an expensive proposition, one they could scarcely afford. Eleanor brushed those objections aside, saying they would find a way to pay for his ticket if he wanted to go.

Somewhere deep in her soul, Eleanor understood that the loss of his grandmother had shaken her husband deeply. Waves of homesickness had displaced his habitually calm disposition: she knew – one never really forgot – what being homesick felt like. Now this had happened, just when he was finding his footing on new soil, trying to forge a new identity in his adopted homeland. No matter how much his wife and her family tried to make him feel at home, being in America –

becoming an American – was a difficult journey. Eleanor piled up her hopes that a return to the familial roots he missed – especially now, in this defeating moment of grief – would enable him wholeheartedly to put down new ones here when he returned. Maybe he could release any lingering regrets he harbored. Maybe the trip would free him to return to her with an open heart.

The rainy May morning of Giampaolo's departure matched Eleanor's mood. Had it been just a year ago almost to the day when she and her mother had left for the same destination on so much happier terms? Eleanor decided to travel with him as far as New York and see him board the ship. It would cross the Atlantic on much the same route that she and her mother had followed the year before.

Dressed in his still-new travel clothes, Giampaolo embraced Donna Sarina, Suzanne, and Rosalie when the taxi pulled up to the curb in front of the Luna home. He gripped his small suitcase, and they turned to leave. As he and Eleanor descended the steps, he looked up and spied their Mollica neighbors across the street – *Cumpari* Mollica, Angelina, Frannie and Mary and their husbands – arrayed on the porch. The elder lady waved a handkerchief in farewell, a sight Giampaolo found poignantly touching. He raised his hand and saluted her in return while the taxi driver loaded his bag into the trunk. Then he and Eleanor dodged the raindrops and climbed into the cab.

On the train, as green farmland and pine trees whizzed by, Eleanor was alone with memories of the trips she'd made to the church hall in Newark. Each of those trips had been filled with thoughts of the man who sat next to her now. He was a stranger then but was a stranger no more. Those trips had been punctuated by goodbyes, as would this one. But how different it felt. She grasped his hand and held on as the rural landscape gave way to gritty streets, crowded rows of houses and shops. Finally the lower Manhattan cityscape came into view briefly before the train was swallowed by the darkness of the Penn Station tunnel.

From the station they made their way by taxi again to the Port Authority piers and the ocean liner that would take Giampaolo back to his homeland.

As they stood together at the bottom of the passenger gangplank, the deep timbre of the ship's whistle signaled the time to say goodbye. She buried her face in his broad shoulder and clung to him, not wanting to let go. He returned the sentiment, enfolding her in his arms for a long embrace. They stood together like that, unmoving, until the ship sounded its basso voice a second time. He stepped out of her arms and stooped to pick up his suitcase, then turned toward the gangplank, reaching into a breast pocket for his travel documents. She placed a palm on his shoulder and let her hand slide down his back as a final sendoff. When he got to the top of the metal passageway and stepped onto the ship's deck, he was swallowed up momentarily by other passengers crowding on deck and waving goodbye to families and friends on shore. He emerged farther down the ship's deck, and Eleanor cried out, "Giampaolo!" waving frantically to get his attention once more. When he spotted her, he smiled and waved, then tapped two fingers to his lips and blew her a kiss. Eleanor couldn't stifle the sob that climbed into her throat as she continued to watch and wave to him.

Soon all the lines and chain-work that held the ship to the pier had been drawn up and the vessel started to move, slowly, away from the dock. Giampaolo stayed in his spot on the deck, waving to her, until the ocean liner's shoreside staff started hastening crowd away from the piers. Reluctantly Eleanor stepped away, swabbed her eyes and cheeks, and turned to make her way back home.

Chapter 37

No man ever steps in the same river twice, for it's not the same river and he's not the same man.

–Heraclitus

May 1949, Siracusa, Sicily
Palm fronds waved in greeting on the steamy station platform as the train huffed to a stop at Siracusa. Giampaolo rubbed his eyes. Almost there. At last. Outside his window, he spotted a young priest, the wide brim of his black hat casting his face in shadow. He was scanning the passengers disembarking from the train. Giampaolo tapped on the window to get his attention.

"Eugenio!" he called out loudly through the glass. Hearing his name, the priest motioned toward the end of the train to indicate a meeting point.

Giampaolo soon found himself enveloped in black serge as Patri Eugenio hugged him and patted his back. The happiness in the greeting evaporated as the brothers mutely acknowledged the reason for his visit. Eugenio looked his brother straight in the eye, his own moist with unshed tears. Not a word was spoken.

Giampaolo gave his brother a watery smile as they began walking toward a shiny black car parked nearby. The director-general of his brother's religious order had sent the car.

"*Cum' è?*" Giampaolo broke the silence. "How is it here? *Chiu assai a matri*, especially our mother?"

Patri Eugenio raised his shoulders in a resigned shrug, a

simple gesture spoke volumes, telling Giampaolo everything he needed to know.

The car's tires rumbled over the ancient cobblestones of the Corso. Nothing had changed in the short time Giampaolo had been gone, except for the curiosity on the faces of his *paesani* and neighbors at the unaccustomed sight of the large new motor car. At Ronco Rossini where the Stagno house stood, the sedan glided to a stop, and Patri Eugenio offered a profusion of thanks to the driver, one of his parishioners.

Suitcase in hand, Giampaolo scaled the narrow steps two at a time to find his mother waiting at the top of the staircase. He went into her outstretched arms and let go a volley of tears. Looking up, he saw his father watching, patiently awaiting his turn to embrace his son.

When Giampaolo finally stepped back from their teary greeting, he beheld his mother fully and realized that she looked careworn, her hair grayer and her face more lined than even six months before. It struck him then how much she resembled her mother. How had he never noticed that before? His father's shoulders, too, seemed more stooped, the suit coat he'd donned for the occasion a bit more threadbare than Giampaolo remembered.

Giampaolo was wrenched by the visit he paid to his *nonna*'s new gravesite later that day. Afterward, he needed the refuge of the Stagnos' kitchen table, its encompassing circle surrounded by familiar faces and laden with familiar food. It seemed strange and empty not to find his *nonna* bustling about the room, urging him for seconds, refilling plates and removing empty ones. Their good neighbor Donna Pietri, Ceccina's mother, had stepped in to fill the void. Soon after they had eaten, a steady stream of neighbors ascended the stairs into the Stagnos' parlor, paying respects once more to the reunited family. Their greetings of sympathy were overlaid with curiosity to see the expatriate son and assess how he seemed to be faring in his new American life.

Arriving as he did on a day other than Sunday, Giampaolo knew that not even his arrival from thousands of miles distant would pull his brothers away from their toils on the family farm. He could go to them on his bicycle, still stored below the stairs, or he could wait until they returned on Sunday, as was their habit, for Mass and the afternoon meal.

Early the next morning, he pulled out the bicycle now gathering dust under the stairs and set off for San Marco.

The countryside he had traversed all his life welcomed him with its familiarity, but seemed somehow drier and more barren compared to the lush green of the pocket-sized lawn he tended now in his American backyard. The cactus plants that lined the dusty roads were sprouting little knobs of fruit that, he knew, would turn pink and then red as the hot days of summer progressed. As the morning sun climbed the sky, he reached for a cloth to wipe his brow. He found the red bandana that Eleanor had washed, ironed, and folded in the workaday trousers he had donned for the ride to the farm. He smiled and lifted the square of cloth to his nose, its fresh scent of detergent and sunshine taking him back to the basement of his new home. He could see Donna Sarina, stooped over the large metal tub of the washing-machine, her face red from the steam rising off the hot soapy water as she engaged the appliance's wringer and fed the sopping load through it, one piece at a time. He had at first been fascinated with this modern American invention that made the drudgery of doing laundry for a large family so much easier. He smiled again as he tried to imagine what his mother would do if she observed it in action.

In the Lunas' basement next to the washing-machine stood two sturdy wooden ironing boards with linen covers. Eleanor would press the wrinkles from his shirts and hang each one neatly on hangers that would make their way into their bedroom closet. All he did each morning was reach inside for a freshly washed set of clothing to wear to work. Eleanor's cousins would do the same for the family tablecloths and linens as well as their own well-maintained dresses, skirts, and blouses. Every woman in his new life left the house each morning in clothes that were neat and well-pressed – it was no wonder, he thought, that Americans were always perceived to be rich, as they were invariably so well dressed.

There were no such conveniences, mechanical or otherwise, in the house in Palazzolo, much less at the farm in San Marco. The farmhouse didn't even have running water or electricity. But then, he supposed, there was no need for shirts or trousers without wrinkles when all you were doing was feeding sheep and chickens, mucking out stalls, or harvesting winter wheat.

Reaching the rusty iron gate that opened onto the rocky path leading to their farmhouse, he unknotted the rope that stood in for a latch. He thought of the sturdy gate of black wrought iron that guarded the back yard in Jamesport, how it swung open with an easy nudge, then closed shut in a tight clasp of springs.

As he made his way toward the farmhouse, the wheels of his bicycle squeaked a welcome to the perpetually parched rural turf that had been home for most of his life. His sister-in-law Ceccina stood in the doorway of the farmhouse and shaded her eyes against the sun's glare. Her mouth dropped open in disbelief when she saw the figure approaching across the rocky farmyard.

"Giampaolo!" she exclaimed. "*Si tu?* Is that really you?" She ran to greet him, then called out for the others. Soon he was surrounded by his brothers and their wives as they stood in the middle of the farmyard while the chickens preened and pecked, clucking busily at their feet.

The accustomed barnyard sights and pungent smells

bombarded his senses and drew him back to an earlier time. He looked around wistfully now with new eyes, mentally aligning the images of these spare surroundings with those of his new home in America. The sturdy whitewashed walls of the small farmhouse, soot-stained where the chimney poured out smoke from the cooking stove within, seemed confining now. The wire fence he had spent many an hour mending, crooked in nearly every place it stood and bent badly where the goats leapt over it, appeared the rusty relic of another age. Even the familiar caper plants careening from the roofline cracks, their leaves a vivid green against the terra cotta roof tiles, seemed quaint and somehow foreign.

Not long ago, this farmhouse and the family home in town had circumscribed the contours of his life. This was all he had known. The war had changed all that. Going to America had changed all that, so that now this place felt more like a distant memory than home.

All too soon, it was time to say goodbye, once again, to his home and his family. He mused that his days seemed filled with goodbyes lately. Giampaolo had grieved his beloved *nonna* in the proscribed rituals, but it had done nothing to erase the stubborn uncanny sense that she could not be gone forever. He had spent evenings letting his mother reminisce about her mother, as if talking about her in the past tense would drive home the reality of her death. No, he could not fathom that. He could not shake the feeling that the next time he turned around, there she would be, a sunny presence in the kitchen and at the table. Eugenio had spoken of her spirit living on in this place, but his words were cold comfort. He knew, now that the time of his departure was upon him, that it would be hardest to bid farewell to the house where he would always picture her.

He had patiently answered his father's many questions about "how things were in America." He had watched as admiration bloomed in the straightforward stares and sidewise glances of neighbors and friends who had known him all his life but now looked at him differently. After all, he hadn't been gone but a few months. But there had been a shift in how others, his family, his former neighbors, perceived him. He also bore the taunts of a few envious *paesani* who challenged him to explain how life in America was better than right here, *at home.*

At the farm, he had observed his brothers' hard toil, the endless chores of farm work which he knew as well as the time-carved calluses of his own hands. He had heard his sisters-in-law bicker, Margarita's sarcastic taunts bordering on cruelty toward Ceccina, and Ceccina responding in turn, in her quiet passive-aggressive way. The farmhouse was not the tranquil place of his childhood recollections. There, the family peace seemed to have ruptured irreparably. That new reality saddened him, much as he reasoned it probably was inevitable. His brothers and their wives were living together in such close quarters and manacled to the unending grind of the farm. Their fate would have been his, too.

In the brief time they spent together over the past days, Giampaolo had tapped into an unspoken kinship with his father. Don Giuseppe had observed his middle son's melancholy resignation and his restive quiet. So it didn't surprise him when his father sought him out, the day before he was to leave. They stood together on the balcony overlooking the Corso. With a contemplative expression, Don Giuseppe raised his eyes to the roofs of the neighboring houses, as if seeing some far-off horizon. To his son, he murmured softly,

"Put this place behind you, *miu figghiu.* Your life is there now."

When Giampaolo looked up, his father's eyes were glassy.

Nothing communicated better the finality of his leaving than the somber expressions on Turuzzu's and Peppino's faces as he said goodbye. There was a familiar sense of emptiness in his brothers' rough embraces, their mouths set in a straight line to fend off open weeping. As rural *contadini*, hadn't they witnessed a similar ritual so often before, as neighbors left for America or sons went off to war? But then, it had been someone else's heartache.

So he would say his goodbyes again, this time with a purpose and permanence that had been missing a few months ago. This time, he wasn't wistful about the many "last times" that he had chalked up mentally that had characterized and overshadowed his first departure. This time, even as he left this place he knew so well, Giampaolo knew that he was truly going home.

* * *

The day he was to arrive in New York, Giampaolo awoke early and strode to the ship's deck. Even as a third-class passenger, his modest accommodations on board felt luxurious compared to the way he had traveled into this harbor seven years before, a frightened and half-starved prisoner of war, or when he sailed out three years later for his repatriation. The port of New York was a faint gray line sketched on the western horizon. Other passengers were soon milling about the deck, too. The ship's staff was forthcoming in response to queries about docking in New York: At what time would they arrive? How long would the docking process take? Once they had landed, where could they retrieve belongings that had been in storage during the crossing?

The answers to all these questions interested Giampaolo, but none more than the one he had been asking himself since he embarked: will I be able to see the Statue of Liberty? The memory was indelible. He could recall with clarity the muted green shadow that grew into the strong outlines of the beloved monument as the captive soldiers' ship approached. They had looked in wonder at the statue's serious face, her expression serene and aloof, seeming to take in without seeing the vessels of all sizes and shapes that passed before her. The folds of her gown remained unruffled as the watchful guardian angel of the harbor looked on, a calm strength in her pose. This was the memory Giampaolo kept locked in his heart, one he had shared with his fellow prisoners as they approached New York in 1943, and then again as they steamed away in 1946.

More pensive than hungry, Giampaolo had descended to the dining room in search of a last breakfast meal, as much to pass the time as to put something into his unsettled stomach. He was just finishing the last forkful of ham and eggs when he heard the shouts go up, and he knew immediately they were approaching the harbor. Hastily he took one last sip of his large cup of American coffee, slid out of his chair and quickly climbed the stairs to find himself a good spot on the upper deck.

As he gripped the railing and lifted his eyes, there she was: Lady Liberty, lifting her arm in welcome beside the golden door of New York harbor. Just beyond her shoulders but barely visible next to the crowded piers of the shipping channel, four onion domes topped with spikes towered over the hulking red brick edifice on Ellis Island. Giampaolo kept his eyes fixed on the statue until he could no longer make out her face.

As the vessel approached the piers steadily and slowly, an orderly commotion ensued, a fever of nonstop activity by officers and crew to ready the decks of the behemoth ship for its dockage. Giampaolo's eyes scanned the throngs of greeters on the pier for a familiar face. They seemed miniature from the height of the deck where he stood, gradually growing as several tugboats sidled the ship closer to the protection of the dock.

His hand gripped his suitcase as he continued to peruse the crowd on shore. Finally, he spotted her: there was his Eleanor, a cherry red pillbox hat on her head, waving indiscriminately and turning her head this way and that as she tried to find him among the crowd of passengers awaiting to disembark.

He shuffled into the line three-deep of disembarking travelers, awaiting his turn on the gangplank but keeping a keen eye all the while on her red hat. He knew the moment she recognized him when a beaming smile lit her face. She held her hat in place with one hand and raised a white handkerchief in the other, waving pointedly at him and grinning happily.

Giampaolo had come home.

ABOUT THE AUTHOR

Marianne Rutter

A first-generation Sicilian-American, Marianne Rutter was born in Reading, Pennsylvania, into a large extended Italian family. She attended parochial schools in Berks County and was the first in her immediate family to graduate from high school. She earned a bachelor's degree in English from Bryn Mawr College and moved to Boston, where she and her late husband raised two children and where she worked in publishing for forty years, retiring in 2017.

Marianne is an avid traveler and an accomplished home cook. She shares family photos and recipes of dishes described in the book on her website.

HOME ELSEWHERE is her first novel.

Join HOME ELSEWHERE's reader community, read the author's blog, get travel suggestions on Sicily, browse home recipes featured in the book, and check our calendar of events at: https://mariannerutter.com

Glossary of Sicilian Dialect

In *Home Elsewhere*, when using Sicilian or Italian language, I place the English meaning side by side wherever possible. In the event I have failed to convey meaning in this way, or for dialect words used more than once in the book, I have included this glossary. The Sicilian dialect or Italian words or phrases appear in italics, and immediately following, the closest English translation (word or phrase) to its meaning in context.

A

A musca disgraziata, vattine! -- Shoo, fly!

A prima amori di chistu carusu sempri é manciàri -- Eating was always that boy's first love

Abbiamo mezz' ora -- We have a half hour

abunnanza -- plenty

accatari -- to buy

acini di pepe -- pepper seeds; name of a fine pasta used in soup

agosto -- August

Aiùtami, figghiu miu -- Help me, my boy

Alluda -- then

Alluda, amuninni lìsciu lìsciu -- Then let's walk very slowly

Alluda, duoppo tutu, ti piacisti la vita 'Mericana? -- So, in the end, you liked life in America?

amuninni, amuninn' -- Let's go

amuri -- sweetheart

andiamo -- Let's go

aprile -- April

Aruvamo presto -- We'll be there soon

àrvulu -- tree

Ascuta, Eleanora -- Listen, Eleanor

assài -- so, very

assetta ccá -- Sit here
Assira non dommìa bonu -- I didn't sleep well last night
áutru -- other, another

B

Badagghiu -- sandwich
basta -- enough
Basta cu chisti 'belle arti' ccani --
Enough of the 'fine arts' now
'Bastiano -- Sebastiano (nickname)
bedda, beddu -- beautiful, lovely
beddissima, beddisssimi -- most beautiful, loveliest
Beni, tuttu beni -- Very well; everything's fine
Binario numero tre -- Platform (track) number three
Binvinutu -- Welcome
birra -- beer
biscottu, viscotta -- cookie, cookies; biscuit, biscuits
bisugnu aiutari -- do you need help
Bo, a bisugnu di chidda forza --
Well, you'll need that strength
Bo, pacenza, sceccureddu --
Hey, have patience, little donkey
Bo, ranni sì, ma nun cusí magnificu --
Well, big, maybe, but not so great
bon giornu -- good morning, good day
bona sira -- good evening, good night
bubbidda -- little doll

C

caccagnu -- heel
caffè -- coffee; a place to purchase coffee (caffè bar)
calcio -- soccer
Caminamu 'n po'? -- Shall we take a walk?
cannoli -- "lady's curls," a pastry filled with ricotta
carusu abbaniatu -- famous guy
carusu bruttu -- bad boy

capisciu -- I see, I understand
capisciu beni -- I understand very well
carni -- meat
cauddu -- heat, hot
ccá, ccane -- here
Ccá ci siamu -- Here we are
Ccá ci sunniu viáutri -- Here you are
Cchi ci pinsa? -- What do you think?
C'è carni dentro -- There's meat in it
C'è prublema? -- Is there a problem?
C'è quàlchi cosa da diciri -- I have something to tell you
C'è tempu -- There's [enough] time
certu -- certainly, of course
chi bedda frutta! -- what beautiful fruit!
Chi dici? -- What do you say?
Chi è? -- What is it?
Chi fai dumani? -- What are you doing tomorrow?
Chi pensi tu? -- What do you think?
Chi succes'? -- What's happening?
Chi tempu fa oggi? -- What's the weather like today?
chidda, chiddu -- that one
chiesa matri --
the "mother church," the town's main church
chista, chistu -- this one
Chista è a mia nonna -- This is my grandmother
chiste sugnu làcrimi filici -- these are happy tears
chisti 'Mericani -- these Americans (pejorative)
chisti Romani -- these Romans (pejorative)
Chistu basta pe me -- This is enough for me
chistu ccá -- this one here
Chistu è troppu pe mi -- This is too much for me
chiu -- more
chiu assai a matri -- especially our mother
ciao -- hello, goodbye
cipuddi -- onions
com' é? -- what is it?

comu beddu stu vestitu -- this dress is so beautiful
Comu ccá, tutti beni, grazî --
Just like here, everyone is well, thank you
comu si, comu su -- how are things?
comu stai? -- how are you?
Comu sunnu a famigghia? -- How's the family?
con un po' di salsiccia e contorn --
with a bit of sausage and vegetables
contadini -- peasant farmers
cosa da diciri -- something to say
cosa da fari in casa --
[I have] things to do around the house
cosa da manciàri -- something to eat
Cosa pinsari? -- What do you think?
Cosa sbagghiada? -- Is something wrong?
crispeddi -- fried dough
Cuccía -- wheat porridge made for St. Lucy's feast
cui, cchui -- who
Cui canusciu? -- Who knows?
Cum' è? -- How is everything?
Cummari --
godmother; affectionate term for older woman
Cumpari -- godfather; affectionate term for older man
cumprari -- to buy
confetti -- confections, hard candies

D
Dabanna -- down there, over there
Damílamía! -- Give it to me!
daveru -- truly, really
daveru bono -- really good, great
ddá, dduóco -- there
dentru -- inside
dicembre -- December
difficili -- difficult
Dimmi -- Tell me

Diu sabbinirìca, figghie mie -- God bless you, my girls
Diu, chi cauddu! -- God, it's so hot!
dolce far niente -- sweet nothings
Donna -- woman; a title of respect for an older woman
dorci, dolci -- sweet; dessert
duluri -- pain, hurt
duoppu tuttu -- in the end, after a
dumani -- tomorrow
dumani mattina -- tomorrow morning

E

e a sua matri -- and her mother
È bono che tu si ccá -- It's good that you are here
È difficili -- It's difficult
É finita la guèrra -- The war is over
E le fimmine 'Mericane? -- And the American woman?
È 'n paesi ranni ranni -- It's an enormous country
È normale mangiare la pasta al pranzo -- It's usual to have pasta at the midday meal
É veru -- It's true
Ecco -- Look here

F

Fa beni | fa beni cusí? -- Everything is fine; [question] is it okay like this?
Fa cauddu ancora -- It's still hot
Facemu na passeggiata dabanna? -- Shall we take a walk down there?
Fazzu iu   -- I'll do it; [question] shall I do it?
febbraio -- February
festa -- party, celebration; holiday
feste degli santi   -- religious feast days
ficupali, ficu' d'indi, ficurini -- prickly pear plant (*ficus d'India*) and its fruit
figghia mia, figghie mie -- my daughter (sing.), my daughters (pl.)

figghiu -- son
filici -- happy
fimmine -- women
fimmine nel campo? -- women in the (POW) camp?
Forsi ci signu 'Taliani qui? -- Maybe there are Italians here?
forno -- oven; bakery
frittata -- omelet

G
gaddu (see also *iaddina, jaddina*) -- chicken
gelato -- ice cream
gennaio -- January
genti -- people
Ggiá turnu -- I'll be right back
giá, ggiá -- now, right away
Ggiá turni a casa, a Sicilia -- Soon you'll go home, to Sicily
gioia mia -- joy of mine
giuggiulena – Sicilian sesame almond brickle candy
giugno -- June
giusto -- exactly, right
granni (also *ranni*) -- big, large
grazî | grazî Diu -- Thanks | Thank God
guèrra -- war

I
iaddina (see also *gaddu, jaddina*) -- chicken
intermezzo -- intermission; holiday or honeymoon
iu ci pinza -- I'll think about it
iu nun sacciu -- I don't know
iu ricanùsciu chista -- I recognize this one
iu sacciu -- I know
iu viniu -- I'm coming

J
jaddina (see also *gaddu, iaddina*) -- chicken

L

Lestu lestu -- Quick, quick!

letto matrimoniale -- marriage bed, double bed

Lèviti dduoco -- Scram | get out of there

Lèviti 'i ccà -- Scoot | get out of here

lisciu -- slowly

luglio -- July

M

Ma -- but

Ma com'é? -- What? | What on earth?

Ma comu stai? -- But how are you?

Ma picchí no? -- But why not?

Ma, scusami, Eleanora, nun si stancha? -- But I apologize, Eleanora, aren't you tired?

maccarune, maccheroni -- pasta or macaroni; smooth short tubular pasta

maggio -- May (the month)

Mai màuru, zia, ma màuru e fortu -- Not skinny, auntie, but lean and strong

Mamá! Talè! -- Mother! Look!

mància, mànciari -- eat, to eat

Manciàmo -- Let's eat

Manciàmo da Pietri stassira -- We are eating at the Pietri's house tonight

Mannaggia! -- Damn it!

marzo -- March (the month)

Matri -- Mother; (expletive) Mother of God

Matri, chi cauddu -- Mother of God, it's so hot

Matri, chi fame aiu -- Mother of God, I'm so hungry

Màuru, sí, ma fortu però -- Skinny, yes, but strong too

Megghiu accusí -- [It's] better like this

Megghiu biviri l'acqua -- Better to just drink water

Megghiu diciri sí, e lássala stare -- Better to say yes, and let it go

'Mericana, 'Mericano -- American (f.)

'Mericano -- American (m.); [pejorative] damn Yanks

mettiri nell'acqua -- put it in water
mezz'ora -- half hour
mi amuri -- my love; sweetheart
Mi dispiace, sugniu lentu -- I'm sorry I'm late
Mi dispiace / Mi dispiace molto -- I'm sorry | I'm very sorry
mi pari bedda -- you look beautiful to me
Mi pari 'n 'Mericano -- you look like an American
Mi scusi u mmiscari -- Forgive the interruption
milinciana -- eggplant
minestra, minestredda --
soup of vegetables in meat broth
musca -- fly

N

n'altra ura e mezz' -- another hour and a half
Natali -- Christmas
Nenti -- nothing
N carusu abbaniatu -- a famous guy, a big shot
N carusu bruttu -- a bad boy
N mporta -- It's not important, it doesn't matter
N'ngrisi, si dici -- In English, you say
Nn mpurtanti, arruviamo nuàutri 'n dui minuti --
It doesn't matter, we just got here two minutes ago
Nn po' cchiu luntanu oggi -- A little bit farther today
'Nna donna 'Mericana | nna fimina 'Mericana --
an American woman
Nna ranni festa -- a great big party
nonna -- grandmother
Nonna, sugniu ccá -- Grandmother, I'm here
novembre -- November
Nu postu rumanu veru -- an authentic Roman place
nuàutri tutti sugniu umani -- we all are human
nun chianciri oggi -- don't cry today
nun cusí pegghiu -- not so bad, not much worse
Nun è nurmali -- It's not usual
nun mi piaci cusí -- I don't like it like this

Nun mi ricanùsci? -- Don't you recognize me?
Nun sacciu -- I don't know
Nun ti metti cusí -- Don't sit like that
Nun ti scantari -- Don't worry, don't be afraid
Nurmali -- [It's] usual, of course
nutizzia -- news
nzemi -- together

O

Oggi accuminci na vita nova -- Today a new life begins
Oggi, sula bona furtuna e allegrìa --
Today there is only good luck and happiness
ossa di murti --
"dead man's bones," a hard egg white candy
ottobre -- October

P

paesani, paesane --
neighbors; townspeople of one's home town
Papá e mamá stannu in campagna --
Your father and mother are at the farm
Pasqualeddu! Chi succes'? --
Little Pasquale! What's goin' on?
passeggiata -- stroll, walk; popular evening pastime
pastina -- finely cut pasta used in soups
pe me -- for me
Pe piaceri, nun tiràri -- Please don't fuss
Pi favori assiettàti dduóco -- Please, sit down over there
Pi piaceri, pígghiassi quàlchi da biviri? --
Please, would you have something to drink?
Peppino -- Joe (diminutive form)
Pi favuri, manciámu, tuttu! -- Please, everyone, let's eat!
pi piaceri -- Please / it's my pleasure
picchí | picchí no -- why | why not
Pigghiatílla, figghiu miu -- Take some, my son
pignulata -- pine nut cookies

pizzelle -- crisp waffle cookies
poi -- then; in that case
pregu -- please
primu -- before; or, a meal's first course
pronto -- ready
prosciutto 'bollito' -- boiled ham
prublema -- problem
Puro iu -- So will I; me too
Purtiamo -- Let's carry it

Q

Quannu ci taliamu, amuri? --
When will we meet again, my love?
Quinni -- Then; in that case

R

ranni -- big, large
ranni grazî -- a big thank you

S

sala da cena -- dining hall
sali -- salt; salty
sarsa -- (tomato) sauce
schacciata --
double crusted pie of pizza dough made with spinach and
potatoes
scrusciu -- noise
Scusami -- Excuse me
se tu vui -- If you want
Sénti 'a nutizzia? -- Did you hear the news?
settembre -- September
si tu? -- is it [really] you?
Sí, capisciu -- Yes, I understand | I see
Sí, certu! -- Yes, of course!
Siamo a casa -- We're home
Siamo arrivati -- We've arrived
Sicundu -- second; or, a meal's second course

Sintiti cchiu megghiu ùora? --
Do you both feel better now?
sivu -- suet; meat fat
spetta dui minuti -- wait two minutes
Sta 'ttento -- Be careful; pay attention
Stendhalismo --

"Wow" effect, being overpowered by beauty, coined by 19th-century French writer Stendhal
stimburadu --
melting; smothered [as in a cooking technique]
stunat' -- fool
succosa -- juicy
sugniu, sugniu iu -- I am; it is I
Sugniu assài filici -- I am so happy
sugniu ccà -- I'm here
sugniu I sei -- it's six o'clock
sugniu prontu pe te --
I am ready to help, I'm at your service
sula Sarina -- only Sarina; just call me Sarina

T
Talé -- Look here; also, take these
Taliamu -- Let's take it
Tante machine -- So many cars
Tarantella --
Italian folk dance (also means a female spider)
tastari -- to taste, to try
Te' ccà -- Here you go
ti fazzo duluri -- I hurt you; did I hurt you?
Ti piaci? -- Do you like it?
Ti scrivo vitti vitti -- I'll write you very soon
Ti vulio ben' assai -- I like you a lot
torta -- pie or cake
tri dorci -- three desserts
treno -- train
troppu genti -- too many people

troppu ranni -- too big

troppu machine -- too many cars

troppu scrusciu -- too much noise

Tu si abbaniata -- You're a celebrity

Tu si omu -- You're a man

Tu si troppu màuru, figghiu miu --
You're so skinny, my boy

turnari -- return

Turuzzu -- Salvatore [diminutive nickname]

Tutti beddu e giustu oggi! --
Everything is beautiful and as it should be today

tutti simpaticchi -- all very nice

tuttu -- all

tuttu beni --
Everything's fine | [question] is everything okay?

tuttu pe te -- all for you

U

U puddaru -- The Chicken-Coop {restaurant in Rome)

uguali -- the same; equal

Unn' é mamá? -- Where's your mother?

unni giurnu -- one day, one of these days

un rigalu? -- a gift?

V

Va beni -- Okay; all is well; it's going well

vagnátu -- juicy

Ven accá -- Come here

Veni da supra -- Come on up!

Veni, veni -- Come on, come on

virduri -- salad greens; vegetables (generic)

viscotta a mennula -- almond paste cookies

vitti vitti -- very fast

vrodu -- broth; soup stock

vui -- would you like

Vui accatari n' àrvulu? -- Do you want to buy a tree?

Vui assitari ccá?   -- Would you like to sit here?

Vui biviri 'n caffé? | Vui cumprari 'n caffé? --
Would you like a cup of coffee?

Vui caffè latte stamattina? --
Would you like coffee with milk this morning?

Vui frutta? -- Do you want some fruit?

Vui tastari 'n badagghiu? --
Would you like to try a sandwich?

Vui turnari a Palazzolo pe un po'? --
Would you like to go back to Palazzolo for a while?

Z

Zita -- fiancée, girlfriend

Author's Note

My dad and I were driving to Hartford, Connecticut, in November of 1977 when I first heard his prisoner-of-war story. He told me the whole saga, soup to nuts, without interruption and barely pausing for breath. He had his older daughter to himself for a five-hour drive, a rare occurrence in our nuclear mostly-female family where my father seldom got a word in edgewise. I was never sure if he chose that moment to tell me his wartime memories because of an urgency for one of his children to know the story, or if the telling of it was meant to ward away potential driver fatigue (I was behind the wheel). Unfortunately, I never wrote down a note while the tale was fresh in my mind, not realizing its import at the time. In the ensuing years, the few details I remembered clearly became amplified and distorted, even as the story probably gathered its own aimless momentum the way a snowball grows while tumbling downhill.

When I sat down to write this book, I was challenged with sorting fact from legend. I wanted to reconcile the outlines of my father's story within the larger contours of World War II's campaign in North Africa and the experience of Italian POWs who ended up in the U.S. in its aftermath. In focusing on the latter, I discovered a frustrating paucity of written information. (I've mentioned these in the acknowledgements.) I chose to make this a fictional account partly because I couldn't verify my plot with the kind of accuracy that a personal history or a true memoir would demand. As a novice writer, I also wanted the freedom to create characters that were neither quite out of whole cloth nor two-dimensional stand-ins for the real people I'd known and loved. I came also to realize that these stories–the stories of nearly half a million Axis prisoners, 51,000 of them Italians, who spent a good portion of World War II in the United States –

had not been told. And I had one such story right in my hands.

I have made every effort to "get the history right" in the book. I gave my characters personal histories not unlike those of my father and mother, but not precisely the same. For example, not knowing exactly where or how my father was captured or when he was shipped out to the U.S., I made his personal story follow the plot line of most of the Italian POWs similarly situated. My characters hail from Sicilian places where my family lived, and they came to American places where my family emigrated.

I devoted a lot of time researching the details of daily life in the mid-1940s American home front because they were important to a historically *plausible* story. Dates on the plot's timeline parallel historical events very closely. I verified the locations and aspects of places and things, details of wardrobe and situation, as much as possible to fit the tenor of the times, although inevitably my own memory colored the telling somewhat. I wanted to be as accurate about details of what people wore and how they went about their lives as I was in ascribing how their personal roles intersected with the larger drama that was unfolding on the world stage.

By May of 1943, nearly a quarter-million German and Italian soldiers had been taken captive after Rommel's Panzers and supporting Italian troops capitulated in North Africa. (By the war's end, Italian POWs worldwide would number more than a million.) Many of these captives were imprisoned initially under the aegis of Free French forces none too eager to babysit their former enemies. Soldiers were crammed into freight cars like cattle and released into primitive, near subhuman conditions in desert camps and holding pens like the one at Bizerte, where the band of three Sicilians we meet at the beginning of the book were held. (The POWs recall the trauma of that imprisonment later in the story.) German and Italian prisoners of war were relocated in large numbers to the United

States and remote parts of the British empire (Australia and Canada) because the European war was being waged in their home countries. It would have been a logistical nightmare for the Allies both to wage war on the European front and to attempt to shelter POWs in safe conditions there.

The sorting and transporting of this massive influx of prisoners of war was a knotty logistical problem for the Allies – chiefly the British and Americans. Casablanca, Morocco, and Oran, Algeria, had been the two major landing points for U.S. troops in February of that year. Oran subsequently became the embarkation point for captured Italians bound for imprisonment in the U.S., among them Giampaolo Stagno, the protagonist of my story. In my father's telling, he was given a choice whether to go to a camp in Britain or the U.S. True as this detail may have been, I chose to depict it differently in chapter 2 as a bit of luck based on rumor when Giampaolo and his buddies crowd into the line of prisoners that seemed to be waiting for the ships bound for America.

Once in the United States, German and Italian prisoners were interned separately in venues with military-style barracks and amenities. Some camps were on sites with familiar American military names, like Fort Dix in New Jersey and Fort Ord in California. Many others had been constructed as post-Depression Civilian Conservation Corps work projects in remote areas, hastily refitted for wartime purposes. And they were all over the place: data from the U.S. War Department shows that some 280 POW camps were scattered among 44 of the lower 48 states and Hawaii.

Most of the Italian prisoners came off transport ships in New York but were shipped by train for processing at Camp Atterbury near Kokomo, Indiana, a progression undergone by the characters in the book. Most prisoners were promptly given work assignments to shore up a sorely depleted American labor force. Some were assigned to local farms to pick crops, while others worked in non-military industry. My father packed sauerkraut at a canning factory in Indiana, a detail I give to my protagonist in the book. Although their journey as POWs started in the middle of the country, most Italian prisoners were eventually assigned to camps elsewhere in the U.S. Giampaolo and his compatriots are sent to a camp in New Jersey.

After the Axis catastrophe in North Africa, the Italian National Fascist Party lost confidence in their leader, Benito Mussolini. In July, 1943, just as our story's POWs are being resettled in camps in the U.S., Mussolini was removed from power by the Italian king, Victor Emmanuel II. Two months later, Italy signed an armistice effectively making the nation "co-belligerents" with the Allied powers for the remainder of the war. The armistice fundamentally changed the relationship between captors and captives, yet the Geneva Convention did not say anything about what to do about prisoners of war if a country changes sides in the middle of a war.

Ambivalent as it was, Italy's change of status from enemy to something less than an ally had a direct and mostly beneficial effect on rank-and-file Italian POWs held here. The American government's solution to this ambivalence was to establish entities called Italian Service Units at the Italian POW camps. Italian prisoners could enroll in an ISU by agreeing to cooperate with the U.S. government in its wartime efforts, in effect joining Italy in becoming co-combatants in the Allied war effort.

The overwhelming majority of Italian prisoners chose this route. Toward the end of chapter 2, we learn how the three Sicilian POWs in the story debate the pros and cons of joining an Italian Service Unit. Some captured Italian officers did not make the same choice as the band of three enlisted men in the story, choosing to retain their prisoner status rather than sign an agreement they felt would betray their country. These

POWs were often relocated to more remote camps, to make dangerous or traitorous behavior that much harder.

Because of their unique status as ISU members, Italian prisoners could now be assigned to non-combat war work and, in payment for it, were given a small amount of cash as well as the military scrip they were already receiving. In his letters to Eleanor, Giampaolo describes being bused to work on the New York docks and in chapter 6 he mentions the princely sum of $8 cash per month he was receiving. With enrollment in the ISU came other privileges and freedoms as well, like weekend leave and sponsored outings.

Giampaolo and others like him who were assigned to camps on the eastern seaboard were fortunate to be near cities like New York, Philadelphia, Boston, and Baltimore, with large populations of Italian Americans. These cities had well-established Italian Catholic parishes in their neighborhoods, whose curates shared the prisoners' heritage and spoke their language. Social scientists have written about the role that local ethnic churches played not only as centers of worship but as social hubs of ethnic communities. It was in such a community that the book's female protagonist, Eleanor Fazzio, grew up. It was such an Italian Catholic parish in Newark, New Jersey, that hosted Italian prisoners of war like Giampaolo Stagno and his mates. And it is there that Giampaolo meets Eleanor.

Italian immigrants in America were overwhelmingly from the *Mezzogiorno* – the south of Italy and the islands of Sicily and Sardinia. For turn-of-the-century Italian immigrants in particular, *campanilismo* was a familiar ethos with deep cultural roots. Their world in the Old Country extended only as far as the parish church bell (*campana,* in Italian) could be heard. Once in the New World, Italian Americans narrowed their actions and movements to small social circles with their parish church as the center. The Fazzio, Luna, and Mollica families depicted in the book lived in just such fashion.

It's well documented that Italian Catholic parishes in America during World War II came to the aid of Italian POWs housed in nearby camps. In some communities, too, Italian-American civic groups actually co-managed logistics and supply of the prisoner camps, and helped informally to bridge the language barrier. This was a characteristic of the Italian POW experience that doesn't seem to have had a parallel for German POWs. It's unclear exactly how this outreach on both sides of the war effort began, but most likely it started with the prisoners themselves. Even before they were organized into Italian Service Units, POWs could write letters home, but also to relatives and friends in the U.S. Giampaolo's friend Tommaso Mollica writes to his uncle and aunt to let them know he is in America.

On the home front, Italian-American families like the Mollicas no doubt worried about the fate of their own sons serving in American uniforms–some half-million Italian Americans enlisted in the U.S. armed forces after Pearl Harbor, among them the Mollicas' two sons. But many Italian Americans still had strong ties to their homeland, too, and they welcomed any chance for news about how relatives in Italy were faring during the war. The Luna family matriarch, Donna Sarina, exhibited this attachment and shared these worries about her sister in Sicily, to whom she wrote and sent packages frequently. After all, the war in Italy was being prosecuted in precisely those parts of Italy – Sicily and the south – from which most Italian-American immigrants hailed, so it was most often their villages that were under attack. Italian Americans naturally saw these Italian prisoners as a primary source of information on their families and former hometowns.

I give these motivations to the characters in the book. When the Mollicas learn that their nephew is a POW in the U.S., they are eager to connect with him. From their first meeting with the young women at the church supper, despite some hurdles with language, the Sicilian soldiers establish commonalities and connections with them. And the affection is returned: Tommaso and his friends are promptly invited to visit the Mollicas when they are able to obtain a weekend pass and American GI's to chaperone them.

It's no accident that the Catholic church is the fulcrum for this activity on behalf of Italian prisoners and Italian Americans living here. It was a familiar and trusted social infrastructure for immigrants, and its rituals and customs bridged language differences. Throughout the war, the Vatican maintained a much-criticized formal silence on the plight of Jews and others detained (and worse) in concentration camps on the European continent. Pope Pius XII's public reticence to wade into the politics of the war, even in the face of atrocities perpetrated against Catholics, was legendary. Not so, on this side of the Atlantic: with the approbation of U.S. military authorities, Catholic prelates visited the POW camps and celebrated the liturgy for prisoners. In some locations, Italian POWs asked permission, and got it, to build chapels on the grounds of their camps so that local priests could say Mass and hear confessions.

Although prisoner treatment and camp conditions for Axis prisoners in the U.S. were much better than elsewhere in the world, the situation wasn't always rosy. Hostility and distrust were often in evidence among everyday Americans who encountered POWs among the general population. In a café in the Newark train station on Thanksgiving morning, Giampaolo and his fellow POWs encounter this prejudice firsthand in chapter 11, when the waitress scolds Rafe Pirone, the American soldier accompanying them, for consorting with "the enemy."

Italian-American members of the U.S. armed forces were

often selected for auxiliary roles working with the POWs, such as translating and chaperoning, especially if they had some facility with the language, like Rafe Pirone. Prisoners were always chaperoned by approved military personnel on excursions away from the camps, and it is thus we encounter two other Italian American GIs, Patsy Tinelli and Tony Ferraro in chapter 6. I invented Rafe, Patsy, and Tony for the story to remain true to events as they would have transpired. Later, I learned anecdotally of American soldiers, fathers, grandparents, and relatives of friends who served as guards, attorneys, and translators for Italian POWs.

All is relatively serene for Eleanor and her family and friends in Jamesport, Pa., but Rafe Pirone's family experience was modeled on the more than half-million Italian Americans who were subjected to some form of restrictions because of their enemy alien status. Rafe recounts that his parents in California were caught up in new government regulations intended to "quarantine" Italian Americans–less drastic and widespread than the outright imprisonment of Japanese Americans, but nonetheless devastating to the affected families.

Italians like Rafe's father and mother, whose citizenship and loyalties were suspect because they were part of the Italian community, were forced to move and live under strict curfews that effectively tore the social fabric of the tight-knit immigrant community and imposed poverty on many. Several hundred Italians were interned in camps, and others were subjected to unfounded searches of their homes and seizure of their property. Although such trials didn't beset the Lunas and the Mollicas, the visit of a young Italian-American soldier, born in Italy like Eleanor was, brings the plight of their immigrant countrymen elsewhere in America into sharp focus and exposes readers to these unfortunate episodes for perhaps the first time.

Nowhere is the POW story more poignant than for Italian soldiers who met and fell in love with American women. Although fraternizing was allowed and romances were inevitable, marriage was strictly forbidden between American citizens and enemy combatants, both German and Italian prisoners, while they were on American soil. Abetted by the social opportunities provided by Italian Catholic parish communities, it's not surprising that Italian POWs had more freedom to forge lasting friendships and even romantic relationships than did their German POW counterparts. Couples like Giampaolo and Eleanor likely never knew the countermanding regulations until the subject of marriage came up, as it does for them. And then it was almost certainly a cause for heartbreak.

Provisions of the Geneva convention held that prisoners of war must be released and repatriated to their countries of citizenship promptly after hostilities cease. Giampaolo gets news of his impending repatriation back to Italy in late August, 1945, but the wheels had been turning for some time before that. POW members of the Italian Service Units were prioritized for repatriation, so the three Sicilians in our story, who were billeted near the New York Port of Embarkation, get fairly prompt passage back to Italy.

When POW repatriation began in earnest in 1945, prisoners like Giampaolo had no idea what conditions they would find upon their return. Coupled with the ban on POWs marrying American citizens, this circumstance injected uncertainty into the calculations of Italians like Giampaolo who were torn between a desire to return to a war-ravaged homeland and the appeal of making a new home elsewhere.

Giampaolo is forthright with Eleanor about his need to discover what had happened to his family during his absence. Heightening dramatic tension in the story, he leaves with no firm commitment to marry Eleanor. Eleanor is unwilling to return to Sicily to live, and in any case her mother is opposed to the marriage on those grounds. This is one of the gaps in my parents' story where fictional invention aided the plot line. Other couples in this situation may have worked through the logistics, become engaged or exacted a promise of some kind from each other, before being separated. Perhaps my parents did, too, but they never told me. It was probably the case in other POW romances that the Italian POW and his American sweetheart parted with an understanding about their future, but some likely did not.

Leaving that question to be resolved in the story puts the onus on Giampaolo to make up his mind from afar about marrying Eleanor emigrating to America. Giampaolo's indecision afforded me the chance to paint a picture of some of Eleanor's Sicilian relatives, and for Eleanor's mother to reconcile herself to her daughter's long-distance relationship. That reconciliation seems to come with finality when Donna Sarina's sister in Sicily has nothing but positive reports about the Stagno family – too delicious a true detail from my own family legend to omit from the story.

Eleanor's preoccupation, aired in her letters to Giampaolo after the war, about securing him a job even before he has arrived in the U.S. may seem like placing the cart before the horse. But it was a real concern for newcomers to America wishing to assimilate as seamlessly as possible into American life. Applying for citizenship and achieving it was often a long process. Many immigrants reasoned that if one could be seen to be a productive member of the community in the meanwhile, so much the better. After the war there was increased leniency for spouses of American citizens to emigrate, and post-war legislation like the War Brides Act of 1945 (the name says it all) was a specific response to pressure by returning American GIs to reunite with their foreign-born wives. Another piece of legislation, the Alien Fiancées and

Fiancés Act of 1946, extended the privileges of the earlier law and eased restrictions specifically for Filipino and Asian Indian prospective spouses. The most straightforward way for any other foreign-born national to become a citizen after World War II was pretty much the same as it is today: marry an American citizen, file for citizenship, get in line if restrictive quotas apply, and wait.

Part IV of the book hinges less on what was happening on the world stage than on the personal lives of the characters. But here, too, I strove for as much accuracy as possible to complete a plausible picture of post-war life.

Acknowledgements

There are many family members and friends who deserve my thanks, without whose encouragement and assistance this book would not have been possible. Any omissions from this list are utterly unintentional, and also go with heartfelt gratitude for assistance, ideas, references or encouragement to others not mentioned here.

I would like to acknowledge the following people:

Teri Coyne, my writing coach, who got me started and gave me goals to reach, redirected me with practical and candid advice, and never doubted that I'd publish this book;

David Dietz, my friend and a true editor's editor, for his work through two drafts of the manuscript and beyond, whose skill, advice and humor made this book so much better than it was;

My children, Lucia Rutter and Malcolm Rutter, for their encouragement that meant so much; for taking time out of their busy lives to read, suggest and help me improve upon the first and subsequent drafts of the manuscript, for cheering me on at every turn, and for useful historical facts and tidbits from my son (the history major!);

My sister-in-law Sally Rutter, for reading the first draft, for caring about my characters so much, and for telling me she loved my writing – something every writer, fledgling or experienced, needs and loves to hear;

Helen Bryant, throughout my writing journey and much of my life a great listener, tireless cheerleader, even better friend;

Mike Wheeler, my eminent friend and fellow writer, who in this project's early days shared his father's memories of the

POW camp at Fort Knox and gave me several suggestions of books to read for background;

Patty Urso James, cousin and family genealogist, who shared transcripts of her uncle's memories as background for my sketches of the Mollica family;

Claire Mauro Campbell, for commiserating with a fellow writer when we hit speed bumps or celebrated advances. and for her childhood recollections of Our Lady of Mount Carmel church in Newark;

Terri Kuhlmann, for reading the first draft and for sharing her father's experience as an American soldier with Italian POWs; also Laura Ranney and Joan Sedita, for invaluable feedback on the first draft;

Joe Del Guidice, for loaning me his father's two-volume *History of the Thirtieth Infantry Regiment, World War II,* edited by Donald G. Taggert, and Barbara Thoreson, who gave me her only copy of Massimo Sani's *Prigionieri*;

The Gang of Five (you know who you are), for letting me turn our lunch group into an early Zoom reading/Q&A session;

Members of the Hatter's Point book club (Nan Becker, Leslie Childs, Carole Cowie, Mary Kenealy and Rita Mullis), who let me read an early chapter, told me they loved what they heard, and gave me oodles of practical advice to boot;

My neighbor Agnes Manning, for introducing me to her friend, fellow author Colleen Tierney, who offered great advice on self-publishing;

Another neighbor, Dave Meleedy, for his courteous interest, who never failed to ask me, "How's the book coming?"

And Sister Miriam Scully, IHM, my teacher in AP English in my senior year of high school, who always encouraged me to write, who read several early chapters and who, since my high school days, has been asking me, "When are you going to write the great American novel?"

In Italy, thanks go to:

My late cousin Anna Gallo, for sharing family recipes that I in turn adapted and shared on my website;

Caravaggio scholar Lauren Golden for reading some pages from the Rome chapter and correcting my errors;

Professor Flavio G. Conti and his Stateside co-author Alan R. Perry, for publishing two books on which I relied for background and quoted in epigraphs, and especially to Professor Conti for sharing information about my father's POW experience;

Chef Michael Sampson of The Sicilian Pantry in Palermo, for imparting his comprehensive understanding of Sicilian culinary tradition in such clear and memorable detail; and for painstakingly tracking down details of a prized family recipe, complete with commentary on Sicilian dialect;

Chef Guido Santi of Convivio Rome, for his online classes teaching me and others simple techniques to make me a better home cook of classic Roman recipes, and for patiently answering my questions about regional culinary differences; and to his wife Sally Ransom, for her unfailing kindness and prompt communication.

The following works were sources used in writing this book:

Flavio, Conti G., and Perry, Alan R. *World War II Italian Prisoners of War in Chambersburg.* Charleston, SC: Arcadia Publishing, 2017.

Flavio, Conti G., and Perry, Alan R. *Italian Prisoners of War in*

Pennsylvania: Allied Prisoners on the Home Front, 1944-1945. Teaneck, NJ: Fairleigh Dickinson University Press, 2019.

Sani, Massimo. *Prigionieri: I Soldati Italiani nei Campi di Concentramento, 1940-1947.* Turin, Italy: ERI (Edizioni RAI), 1987.